S.L. FRANCISCO

The Kraden Job
Games with Dangerous People Book 1

Copyright © 2022 by S.L. Francisco

All rights reserved. No part of this publication may be reproduced, stored or transmitted in any form or by any means, electronic, mechanical, photocopying, recording, scanning, or otherwise without written permission from the publisher. It is illegal to copy this book, post it to a website, or distribute it by any other means without permission.

This novel is entirely a work of fiction. The names, characters and incidents portrayed in it are the work of the author's imagination. Any resemblance to actual persons, living or dead, events or localities is entirely coincidental.

S.L. Francisco asserts the moral right to be identified as the author of this work.

First edition

ISBN: 9798815231931

*This book was professionally typeset on Reedsy.
Find out more at reedsy.com*

To Renée, who asked me to write of pirates

Contents

Chapter One	1
Chapter Two	15
Chapter Three	43
Chapter Four	61
Chapter Five	75
Chapter Six	93
Chapter Seven	127
Chapter Eight	144
Chapter Nine	166
Chapter Ten	193
Chapter Eleven	219
Chapter Twelve	230
Chapter Thirteen	249
Chapter Fourteen	262
Chapter Fifteen	272
Chapter Sixteen	291
Chapter Seventeen	306
Chapter Eighteen	312
Acknowledgments	318
About the Author	320

Chapter One

"I'm not going to ask you again. What was your crew after?" the woman demanded, leaning over her prey, as the group of mercenaries around her chuckled. They stood in a semicircle around Airen, who was bound to a chair; dark blonde hair falling in front of her face. The female mercenary growled in frustration, and moments later the sharp sound of flesh on flesh filled the room as she backhanded Airen. The woman rubbed at her knuckles, as though the blow was equally painful for her. "Do you have any idea how much danger you're in right now?" she snarled the question into Airen's face.

Airen spat out a mouthful of blood, causing the woman to jump back to avoid the spray, cursing. "I'm starting to have some sort of idea," Airen stated.

"Why you -" the woman started, rage contorting her face. She pulled a knife from her belt advancing forward but a hand grabbed her wrist before she could complete the fatal swing.

The Kraden Job

Airen winced. She wished she hadn't. There was a scuffle among the mercenaries, as they debated the appropriate level of violence when dealing with pirates, when a figure came into the doorway.

"Enough!" A voice rang through the room with authority. The shoving of the mercenaries stopped as the intruder came further into the room. Airen tensed in the chair. That voice was painfully familiar. Harsher perhaps than she remembered but regrettably unforgettable. The mercenaries melted towards the sides of the circular room as the man strode forward, the echo of his footsteps rising up against the stone walls. Airen hung her head slowly, discreetly tilting her face towards the ground. A small pool of blood shimmered in the candlelight. She focused on it, trying to ignore the boots that came into focus.

The room was filled with a tense silence as he took in the scene before him. Airen had on the simple clothes of a woman at sea: a loose, dirtied dark tunic tucked into dark trousers. Heavy and strong leather boots, with a thick belt around her hips, currently empty of any weapons. There was a collection of knives and a sword piled on a nearby table, thrown haphazardly on top of a gray weather-worn jacket. Airen was bound tight into the chair, each booted shin tied to a chair leg and her wrists bound to each armrest with strong rope.

He crouched down in front of her but she averted her eyes to hide them from him. Blue eyes searched her face, making note of the grit and blood smeared across it. He made a move to touch her chin and asses the damage. She flinched at the action.

"Get out," he said low, his voice holding a sharp edge. No

Chapter One

one moved. He looked over his shoulder. Airen took the opportunity to catch a quick glance at him in his blue coat, the hint of glittering pins half-hidden by a black cloak. His scruff had grown out. "Get out!" he repeated.

There was a noisy shuffling as the group of mercenaries scrambled to comply with his demand. The man in the cloak dragged a chair in front of Airen. His stance was less rigid than she remembered. He swept off his cloak, folding it over the back of the chair neatly before sitting down. He then took off his leather gloves in a slow, deliberate, and practiced motion.

Airen cursed a thousand suns in her head. She'd made over twenty plans for this endeavor; he hadn't been in any of them. She studied a pebble on the stone floor, licked blood off the front of her teeth, swallowed it, and came to a decision.

"You have a bad habit for trouble," he said, never taking his eyes off her face.

Airen straightened in the chair, as much as the binds allowed, rolling her shoulders slightly, but keeping her face angled towards the ground, eyelids lowered. "It's a talent."

"I'd say." He didn't seem happy to see her either. "Those are some dangerous people out there. I'd hate to think of what they might do with you alone."

She snorted. "They've already started. Not that it matters to you." Airen thought she saw him flinch. "Though I'm curious, since when did you keep company with mercenaries anyways, Commander Jenkins?"

The Commander's eyes were hard as ice, but she heard the creaking of leather as he tightened his hand into a fist around his gloves. "I suggest you start being cooperative before I, too, lose my patience."

The Kraden Job

She couldn't help but laugh at that, throwing her head back and regretting the decision immediately when pain shot down her spine and through her ribs. She smirked at him, blood slithering down her chin. "You going to hit me, Commander?"

Commander Jenkins tensed in his chair, frustration rolling off him in almost palpable waves. "I'm in no mood to indulge in your jests. Just tell me what I want to know. Now!"

Airen shrugged. The rope cut into her wrists, which were becoming increasingly raw. The anger in his voice was new, and not something she wanted to test at the moment.

"Fine," she said. "Where do you want me to start?"

"Tell me about Allison Kraden."

She nodded, the motion sinking her gaze lower until only her boots were in focus. She rolled her ankle experimentally and felt the rope tug at her boot where it secured them to the chair. She smiled.

"Why am I not surprised?" Airen muttered. She fidgeted uncomfortably as he watched her, waiting for an assent to the request. Allie wouldn't like to be talked about, Airen knew that much, but the situation was somewhat limiting. There were versions to the tale, as with any pirate story. She debated on the various tales in her mind while Commander Jenkins sat there, for all his talk, waiting patiently for an answer. His posture was rigid, and he was working the leather gloves in his hands, twisting them in tight circles. It came to her then, that this time, she felt like telling the truth.

"Alright," she said finally, "but I'm telling it my way."

"Understood," he said, his voice steady but the twisting of the gloves stopped and he sunk down into the chair.

Airen took a deep breath and began. "What you have to understand about Allison Kraden is that she didn't have any

Chapter One

grand plans at the beginning. She thought I was a bit out of my mind, actually. So, to understand the famed Allison Kraden of today, you have to go back to the day we met. The first of many days in which we were sentenced to die."

~~~~X~~~~

We were somewhere around the Beratide Isles, my old crew and me. My first crew, you could say. I was eleven at the time. Think they kept me on because of how useful my father had been to them before he died. Did odd jobs mostly, but at eleven, I didn't have much interest in the running of the ship. My interest lay more in books of legends and in sleight of hand. I often made mistakes while on board; the biggest one was when I was supposed to be up in the crow's nest.

My father had taught me to read and I was deep in the adventures of Alexander Crawford, instead of watching the sea. It was a lazy day. A luxury day. We'd just come off a fantastic haul. One of those small trade ships, packed to the decks with rum. I'll never forget it. That's when I had my very first sip. Thought it was awful to be honest. Thought I'd never get an appreciation for the stuff. Ah well. My point being, there was near no one on the deck. The crew were mostly drinking and playing cards below. It was supposed to be smooth sailing. I near got the boat sunk on a reef. Seems that was the last straw for those who were still keen to keep me on, for some old debt to my dad.

They'd done me proper. I woke up neck deep in sand, staring out on a foreign coast. An island I'd never been on before. And all that I could see was the white, hot sand spread out to meet a never-ending crystal blue sea. I'll never forget the sound of that water lapping against the shore. A noise I had once found comforting, but with my arms strung to a post and the morning sun beating down on me, all I felt was panic. Honestly, I was just glad that they didn't keelhaul me.

You know what the worst part about a shore-death is? Watching the water. You know the tide is what's going to kill you. No matter how thirsty or hungry you get, what kills you is the tide. Drowning in four inches of water. It's terrifying.

By the time I heard feet shuffling behind me, my throat was burning from thirst, my eyes squinted from the blinding glare of the day. At first I thought it was my imagination. That whole hallucination bit. And who could blame me. I'd been on the beach for hours; the only sounds were of the seagulls high above, and the waves, inching ever closer in their steady strokes. But these noises grew louder and more distinct. There were male voices. And laughter. When they drew closer still, the sounds of dragging and muffled screams.

"Lookie here," one of them was saying. "Looks like this spot's being used. Think we should find a new one, Captain?"

"No, I think this will do just fine. Dig here." The sound of a shovel hitting the ground came from my right. "That way she'll get a perfect view."

I tried to crane my neck and see them. No such luck. The world lapsed into relative silence then. Just the sound of ocean and the noise of the shovel. I was trying to think of a way to talk my way onto their crew, though it seemed like a long shot.

A man stood in front of me. The sun was blinding, making him a silhouette. I focused in on his sword, a silver handled beauty. Meant for one hand. A small emerald in the hilt.

Chapter One

These were clearly hard working professionals.

"Hey there, laddie. Anger the big boys, did you? You're a scruffy little lad, aren't you? Plenty of filth on you."

I jerked away as a boot shoved against the side of my face and sneered at him. I'd been mistaken for a boy. Again.

"Oi," another voice called, "I think I got it dug enough. Let's get the girlie in there."

The man went back to the group. He kicked a bit of dirt in my face when he passed by. There was a noise of dragging and some high-pitched, unintelligible noises; gags can be like that. At least she seemed like a fighter. There was a thud, followed by a groan. A fresh peel of laughter from the men. The sound of the shovel shifting the dirt pile back.

"Oh, don't look so upset, honey," the last word was given special attention. "It's just business. Look, there's even a little friend to keep you company."

"Yah," said another. "Perhaps you'll hit it off. He looks about your age. Nice little match you got here. Course you'll have to watch him die." A bout of laughter ripped through the men as I seethed. At that moment there were more pressing matters than the fact that I was being mistaken for a boy, but that didn't make it any less annoying.

"We're done, Captain."

"Well done, boys. Enjoy your stay on the island, fair lady." I always imagine he swept off his hat at that. I don't even know if he was wearing a hat, but it seemed like something my Dad would have done. He wasn't exactly a friendly man, strictly speaking.

There was laughter as they walked away. They'd taken off her gag, something I was not thrilled with at the time.

"Don't you leave me here! How dare you! You know who I

am! Come back here right now!" She was screaming at them in a pitch that soon became unrecognizable as speech. She kept at it for a while. Gave me a headache. I almost wanted to kill her myself.

"Shut up!" I yelled finally. "I'm busy trying to die over here. Silence would be nice." The voice behind me stopped. "Thank you," I called back.

Maybe an hour went by. Or maybe it was only minutes. Time is strange when you're caged. I imagine that she was sulking, pouting, and brooding in equal parts. That fits some of her early years. Back before she knew the world. Or herself. Can't say that I blame her now, knowing what I know. But back then, I had less patience. I didn't have a very clear head on my shoulders. After a while I heard her shifting around a bit and grunting.

"What," I couldn't help but ask, "are you doing?"

"Getting comfortable."

"We're buried to our necks in sand, arms bound to planks, and you're trying to get comfortable? You can't be serious!"

"Well, you want silence when you die, and I want to be comfortable. So, exxcuuuse me. Besides, my arms aren't bound," she snapped.

I thought about this for a moment. "But they...you're buried to your neck though, right?"

"Yes."

"But your hands are free?"

"Yes."

"And you're trying to get comfortable?"

"Yes!"

I ran my tongue over the edge of my teeth, a habit I picked up from the skipper on my dad's crew. He did it whenever he

Chapter One

got a good hand at cards. I tended to do it in agitation.

"Then what," I started calmly, "are you doing? If your hands are free, why aren't you trying to get us out of here?"

There was silence. I twitched, digging at the sand between my fingers. It moved a bit, but not enough to matter.

"Would that even work?" came the doubtful response.

"Well, I think it's worth a fucking shot!" The waves were coming in faster now. I could see the sand grow darker as it got wet not ten feet in front of me. "Unless of course, you want to give up and have a shore-death."

I've never been sure how she managed it, but she got out. For me, the water had begun to get frighteningly close. I could smell the salt. One big wave had come in and I felt the warm, smooth heat of water against my throat. Panic rose higher and higher. Suddenly, a figure blocked me from the sun. I squinted up.

It was true what the other pirates had said, she looked around my age, with light brown hair falling around her shoulders. She smiled in triumph. Her dirty and ratty dress hanging ill-fitting on her.

"I did it," she beamed at me. The water came in and lapped against her heels. She didn't seem to notice.

"That's great! Now, if you could help..." I trailed off.

"Oh, right." She fell on the sand around me, scooping up handfuls and flinging them aside. The tips of her fingers were burnt dry by the heat of the sand. She dug against the rising tide. Water came at a rush and smashed into my face. I coughed as it went back out, the salt burned my throat. She let out a small shriek and dug faster. I remember fidgeting in my boots, trying to make a hole where they were, pushing upwards. It wasn't very helpful.

She dug and dug. More and more frantic as the tide came in. Fear will do wonders. Somehow she had the strength, grunting and sweating, to drag me out of the hole. Plank and all. We panted as she collapsed on the sand next to me. The waves rushed in and soaked our clothes where we lay, but it didn't matter anymore. I was free, more or less. My arms ached from being tied up.

"There's a knife in my boot," I said between ragged breaths, kicking one foot up in the air.

"What?" she asked in a muted and dazed voice.

"You're gonna have to cut me off." I nodded at the ropes on my wrists.

"Oh, right," she said after a moment. She pulled off my boot, sand slithered out into the water that was now creeping up to my waist as I lay there. She hacked at the ropes. If I had been more together, I probably would have noticed the pattern of her dress. Or the fact that there even was a pattern on her dress. Or even noticed the nice fabric the dress was made out of. I might have noticed the absolute panic in her face. Signs that she wasn't used to seeing this sort of thing. But at the time, I was just happy to escape the immediate face of death and relieved that the captain had left my knife. It had been my father's. Maybe the captain figured since my father hadn't died with it, someone should.

"Careful," I said, when her shaking hands slipped and almost nicked me. I rolled over when she got one of my hands free and took the knife from her. She grumbled a protest but let me take the blade, her hands were shaking as she gathered up her dress's layered skirts and danced out of the water. I cursed under my breath when I sliced into my hand a little. When I was free, I stumbled up and scampered out of the water.

Chapter One

I had never been so happy to be on the dry sand before. I could feel the panic leave me. I could hear the water swooshing down into the hole where I used to be. I'm not proud of it, but I vomited. I felt a hand rubbing my back as I dry heaved.

"You okay?" she asked.

"Yeah," I said, getting to my feet, equal parts embarrassed and annoyed. I tried to dust myself off, but my raggedy clothes were mostly covered in mud. "Thanks," I said, not looking in her eyes. I looked down both sides of the shore, vaguely aware of her chattering. I stuck the knife back in my boot and walked off towards the north.

"Hey," she said, running after me. "Where are you going?"

"Not sure yet," I said, which was true. "Hoping to find some people. There has to be a town somewhere on this island."

"Oh right, that makes sense," she said, shuffling after me. "My name's Allison, but you can call me Allie. All my friends do."

"I'm not your friend," I said on reflex. She stopped walking. I kept going, feeling maybe a little bit guilty. But only a little. I had other problems on my mind. First, finding food. Then shelter. Wondering if I could find the captain and get him to take me back, or if I could teach him a lesson.

"Hey, I think we should be friends though. Just stick together for a little while. I mean, we are in the same situation."

I stopped to give her a look over. She was wearing a pretty, but dirty dress. Gorgeous hair, hazel eyes. Quick glance to soft hands. I couldn't imagine the two of us having anything in common. She had a fierce look of determination on her face.

"Look, Allison. I'm going that way. I'm not sure I'll find

The Kraden Job

anything that way, so why don't you go the other way and see if there's people over there?"

"But what'll I do if there isn't?"

"Not my problem," I said, walking off again.

"But you have to take me with you! I don't know what else to do!"

"I'm sure you'll figure it out."

"You owe me! I saved your life. You *have* to take me with you!" she shrieked after me. I froze. She'd pulled the life debt card. Calling in a life debt was a nice move on her part. Though I think she did it unintentionally at the time. Pirates tend to take these things rather seriously. Someone saves your life, you owe them. The most dishonorable thing would be to leave them to die themselves, not that leaving her on the beach would have been a death sentence, but it certainly wouldn't have ended well. I sighed, there was no real way around it.

"Well are you coming or not?" I threw over my shoulder.

"Oh yeah," she scampered to me, gathering up her skirt. I rolled my eyes and began to move on.

"Hurry up Allison."

"Call me Allie," she said, catching me up. "So, what's your name?"

"Airen."

She grabbed onto my arm, leaning in towards me. A big smile on her face. "That's a nice name."

~~~~X~~~~

Airen laughed. "You know, she didn't realize that I was a girl for another five days. I can't really blame her. It was a common problem when I was younger. Androgyny was

Chapter One

a curse of mine. But being a young lad had its advantages, so I didn't bother to tell her otherwise. I had no idea who Allison Kraden was at the time, or who her father was. I didn't find out her last name for years, but that's a different story altogether and, well, you know how I got on with the rest of the Kradens."

"I'd like to the rest of that tale from your side one day," Commander Jenkins said. He dragged his chair in a circle to get closer to her.

She smirked. "I'm not sure I'm willing to tell you that one."

"I think you owe me more than one story," he said in a serious voice.

"I don't think that I owe you anything," she ground out, shifting her eyes along the floor. Airen winced at the sound of the chair smashing against the floor as he surged to his feet.

"You don't think you owe me anything?" The anger radiated off of him, and she cringed. "Let me tell you something. The only thing that's keeping those thugs from ripping into you right now is me. So I'd think twice before testing me. You know, they're only keeping you alive because they think you have answers for them."

"And for sport, I don't doubt. I have lots of answers. Not likely to share them with just anyone," she said in a calm voice, though her heart was pounding in her chest at his outburst. "You should know that by now."

A hand grabbed the bottom of her jaw roughly, forcing her to look at him. Their eyes met. He was seething until the light caught her eyes. He cursed and jerked his hand back as if he'd been stung. Airen shook the hair out of her face and looked at him properly for the first time since he entered the room. He turned his back on her, his shoulders were hunched, a move

The Kraden Job

he made when trying to calm down.

"You've got the Sheen done," he said low and cold.

Airen's yellow eyes shimmered with the flickering candles, cutting brightly into the darkness of the room. "What did you expect? I'm a pirate."

"I don't even know you anymore," he said in a voice so quiet she wasn't sure she was meant to hear it. Commander Jenkins glared off towards the wall. The flickering candle throwing him in relief against the open door. Airen's eyes slid over him and then to the table that held her daggers, sword, and coat.

"What makes you think you ever did?"

"A foolish mistake," he said. "One I won't make again."

He slammed the door on his way out, the draft causing the candles closest to the door to go out. Three were left alight, one so close to the wick, it would be out in minutes. She felt the panic start to rise again as the shadows crept further in. The darkness would fall soon. The Sheen in her eyes would help her see, but she didn't know how many more times she could handle the silence in the darkness. When they left her alone after their questioning and she was left to wonder if it was day or night. When they might come back. If they would feed her. In the black, all alone, there was no way to stop her mind from wondering where things had gone wrong. Nothing to do but look at the door or count stones in the wall. She'd was able to see the outline of her coat and weapons, sitting agonizingly out of reach.

Airen jerked her right arm, testing the strength of the rope. It was tighter than she thought it was. This might be a problem. Airen wiggled her fingers against the wood of the chair, a sliver splintered and dug into her finger. She shook her head and took a deep breath. It was going to be a long night.

Chapter Two

"They've been arguing all morning about starving you until you talk."

Airen looked up to see Commander Jenkins leaning in the doorway. Today, he'd shed his cloak and coat, choosing to wear a simple shirt tucked into his trousers. There was still a sword strapped around his hip, a dagger balancing on the other side. His leisure was forced, but still, the illusion of calm was enough to put Airen on edge. Her fingers ticked on the wood of the armrest. Knocking out a beat.

"They'll be waiting a long time," she said, in a voice stronger than she felt.

"I figured," he said, pushing himself off the door frame. "They clearly don't know enough of your history. You're resilient. How long were you in Ersten Prison?"

She eyed him with annoyance. He seemed more in control today. More calm. Of course, he hadn't slept in a chair. "Three months."

The Kraden Job

"How'd you like your stay there?" he asked, advancing into the room.

Airen glared at him. "None of us liked it very much."

"That's right, you were incarcerated with most of your crew, weren't you?"

He seemed rather well informed. More informed than she would have liked. "Is there a point to your questions, Commander?"

"There is. My employer would like to know a lot more about your relationship with Allison and how she got to be the way she is now. He's very curious as to where she went wrong."

Airen couldn't help but laugh, which she regretted as a sharp pain blossomed in her chest. "I bet he is. I highly doubt he's interested in my story. Which makes me wonder: why aren't you tracking down Allie for this enjoyable interrogation?"

Commander Jenkins shook his head. "I *have* been tracking her. That's how I arrived here in the first place. Your crew is rather difficult to track. But they didn't catch Allison here. They caught you. A feat that I'm not quite sure how they managed, if half the stories they say about you are true."

There was an implied question in there, but Airen chose to ignore it, simply replying, "I got clumsy."

"I heard you took a nasty tumble off the fortress wall."

"I said, I got clumsy."

"I heard you were pushed," he said. Fixing her with an almost amused stare.

"I got clumsy with who I trusted."

Commander Jenkins shook his head, striking a match. Airen watched him apprehensively, but he only lit a candle on the table. He fixed some nearby candles and set to putting

Chapter Two

light back in the room. Past the candles, she could see her supplies, oh, how badly she wanted them. He picked up her dagger, feeling the weight of it in his hand. It was silver, engravings running up the side. It was a fine blade. Hard won in blood, and it had served her well. The Commander touching it rattled her more than he would know. He ran his finger along the runes.

"Tell me more about the beginning years?"

She forced a laugh. Fear rising steady in her throat. "You threatening me with my own blade?"

He gave her a cold look. "No. I'm offering you something else. Besides, I'm not sure you rightly own this blade. It's a bit rich for an outlaw, isn't it?" He put the dagger back on the table nevertheless. Picked up a jug she hadn't noticed him carry in. "Water," he stated simply, swooshing it back and forth. Reflexively, she licked her lips. He pulled out the cork and took a swig. Then held it out towards her. Even if she leaned in, it wouldn't be close enough to even smell it. Her throat suddenly felt rougher than it had minutes before.

"Deal," she said. Allie would criticize her for giving in so quickly. But it was just too tempting.

He smiled at her, as if he'd just managed to pet an incredibly disobedient cat. She glared at him as he came closer, pressing the lip of the jug to her mouth. A small feeling of victory sprouted in her when she noticed that, despite his calm demeanor, he was avoiding eye contact. He let her get three good mouthfuls before pulling the jug away. She tried not to whine when the cool liquid disappeared, dripping down her chin. It tasted a bit odd, but she wasn't about to complain. The mercenaries had kept her locked up in this hole without water for two days.

The Kraden Job

"You can have more after you tell me what happened next."

She licked her lips. "Can't I just have a smidgen more?"

Commander Jenkins gave her an indulgent look, bringing the jug once again to her lips. Yet he refused to tip it. Merely holding it there. She could feel the water on the lip of the jug but couldn't quite taste it. She glared at him. He smiled and swung the water away from her.

"So, you *have* come to torture me today?"

"Not quite. You get more water when you answer questions."

She groaned and rolled her neck, letting it crack. She could feel his eyes on her. She cracked her chest, her bust rising with the motion, noting that, while he looked away quickly, his eyes were still drawn to the motion. "How long have they kept me here?"

"You've been here a week."

Whistling low, Airen looked around the room. She guessed about six days with the rate of the candles burning down, a day off wasn't bad. "Hmm. I lose track of time in a place like this. In Ersten there was at least a window and I could count the setting and rising suns. You don't realize how much you'll miss the sun 'til you can't see it."

He let the jug rest on the floor. A glimmer of guilt running over his face.

"Have you brought me some food?" Airen asked.

"Clarissa forbade it. She said they'd given you enough bread and apples that you'll be fine for a few more days, albeit uncomfortable. She even went as far as to pull a blade on me when I suggested bringing you more. I found it in my best interest not to protest."

"Typical," she grunted, attempting to whip her hair out of

Chapter Two

her face. Unsuccessful, she blew at it.

"She would love to have your head. Maybe even more so than my employer. Why does she hate you so much?"

"I stole her map."

Commander Jenkins looked at her seriously for a moment before bursting into laughter. "She's carrying a grudge over a map?"

"It was a very nice map."

"Where did it go?"

"It was meant to lead one to a lovely little island with, the rumors say, five full chests of gold and jewels."

"And were there five chests of jewels and gold?" he asked, leaning towards her, scrutinizing her eyes.

Airen smiled. "No idea. The ink ran when I got into water. The map was destroyed. Don't think she's quite forgiven me for that."

"I doubt she believes you."

"I suppose I'm not exactly the most trustworthy."

"No, you certainly aren't."

Fidgety, Airen licked her teeth clean, a slight taste of blood lingering. He met her eyes and tensed. Once upon a time, he'd looked at her so differently. But now suspicion and anger was reflected in his gaze.

"You have yet to ask me a very important question. Or have you not even asked it of yourself?" Airen asked, giving him a scrutinizing look over.

"What do you mean?" Commander Jenkins voice was wary.

"Have you not wondered what they've been asking me about? Don't you even wonder what they're doing in this little part of the world in the first place?"

"I don't need such answers," he said, yet the side of his jaw gave a noticeable nervous tick.

"Ah, you're turning the other way for their little law breaking."

"They are not pirates."

"No. You're right," she said sarcastically, "They're mercenaries. Criminals for hire rather than one's who choose their own path. That's so much better."

"Are you going to get back to the story or not?" He made to stand up. "I could simply leave." She eyed the water jug by his feet, wondering if he'd knock it over when he left.

"Fine," Airen said, "but I warn you, this next bit is a tad boring. We happened across a cottage with a fisherman and his wife. They lived a ways out of the city, partially to get better fish, and partially because Frank didn't much trust city folk. He brought the fish into the city every second day to sell, but besides that, they really kept to themselves. Their son had struck out on his own three years before, and their daughter had recently gotten married. They were a family recently without children in the home. Any empty space they longed to fill.

"Needless to say, Susan liked the idea of having kids around and her husband enjoyed the idea of free labor. So, we found a place to stay for a time. I did things their son would have done, helped with the fishing and fixed the nets and traps. I had a knack for it Frank couldn't place. I was hardly going to tell him I'd learned it on a pirate ship. They actually didn't question us too much about where we came from. Not that I can fault them for that. Years later, I learned that those were trying times. Everyone was struggling to make it by, and they probably thought we had either run away or been sent from home.

Chapter Two

"For her part, Allie learned mostly from Susan, baking and cooking, something that would quickly became a love of hers. And then, every other day, we would help Frank bring fish to the market. It was several months in, right about the time we'd really settled into a routine that things begin to get interesting…

~~~~X~~~~

As cities go, it was a smaller one. A city that, after selling our wares in town three times a week for four months, I'd already explored all the back alleys and knew them well. The deal was that we got seven pennies for every day we spent helping Frank at the market place. And another three, if we took our own crate and sold it before he had finished. Allie and I liked to do this best, mostly because playing the role of poor little children gave us an edge. I liked the trickery. Allie loved the acting. She came up with detailed backgrounds on our imaginary parents. The woes at home, a sick baby more often than not.

Women were especially likely to buy from the poor little boy and girl that were hungry and just trying to get rid of their fish. The wonderful thing about people with money is that if you don't have any, they tend to look right over you. There were several people that we would go to every market day and, without fail, they wouldn't recognize us and buy our fish. In addition to getting extra pennies for finishing before Frank, we also got free time to wander around the city. Those were my favorite days. They were some of the most peaceful days of my life. Though at the time, I didn't appreciate them but felt rather bored by the routine.

The Kraden Job

Allie was blooming there. She was discovering a passion for cooking and, much to her surprise, enjoyed working with her hands. She'd actually developed calluses. At first, the idea horrified her, but within a fortnight she was proud of their development, constantly showing them to us around the house. I think, in a way, she wanted to live there forever. Just continue with Frank and Susan until we were old enough to find someone to marry and have our own domestic lives. It was the sort of romantically hopeful notion she'd hold onto at the time.

Frank and Susan assumed I was a boy as well, which played mostly to my conveniences, so I saw no reason to contradict them, but of course it made me aware of the fact that we, well at least I, could not stay their permanently. Though I was determined never to turn into a proper lady, with all the finery, I realized that at some point I was going to develop a feminine figure. The notion kept me up at night. How would they treat me when they found out? What would happen to me when I was discovered? What path would be left for me?

At the same time, I still longed to be on the sea. Practically being born a pirate means that one never wants to stop. I missed the ocean, the constant moving from place to place, the adventures, the thefts, the jewels, and the men, whose gruff rudeness was all I knew of childhood. I was tempted to reject a place of stability to go off adventuring.

One day, I was alone in the marketplace. I had finished selling off my share of fish and I remembered what it was like when the crew would send me off into the town to pick pockets. Often, while they were busy with their part of a plan, I would be sent to get a small amount of money. Something to help to keep them in rum. Off I would go, to pick the pockets

Chapter Two

of the wealthy. I had gotten quite good at it.

And so, when I found alone in that in the middle of the city, with plenty of money jingling around in purses, my hand began to itch. I wanted it, I wanted to delve back into their pockets and come out with the glitter of coin. It wasn't that I wasn't grateful for all the things that Frank and Susan had given me. I was, but I also wanted to have a life that they couldn't give me. A life that I took on my own terms. The rich people jousted me in their great dresses and clothes; they'd jerk their cloaks away from me, as if my poorness would rub off on them. As if the filth would get on their person if our clothes touched.

Across the market, I saw a young man, his silken clothes swirling around his body. The rich colors still bright, proof that they had recently been purchased. The laziness in his gaze suggested that he had a lot of spare time and didn't know what to do with it all. His hair was perfectly combed, and he had the audacity to wear a sword to a market. Not that he looked like he could use one much, but it was certainly a display of prosperity. Oh, how badly I wanted to steal from that man.

I took a deep breath, ruffled my hair up a bit. In my mind, it made me harder to recognize. Childish fancy, no doubt. I slipped through the crowd. Snuck around. Weaving in and out of the busy area, moving closer and closer to this young nobleman. I could feel the sweat jumping from my forehead to my palms. I hadn't been thieving in a while. I snuck along and felt my heart beating faster. Almost there, I was almost there. And then I fell.

I tripped on a cat. I was splayed out on the ground then. Covered in the filth of the street. I had scraped the base of my hands. They stung, the blood slithering down my arm. I felt the urge to cry, but resisted. It was probably one of the most humiliating experiences of my young life that no one noticed.

I slunk back to the cottage by the shore. I tried to sneak by the kitchen, but was a bit less than successful. Susan was outside, probably plucking flowers or something. Allie was pulling bread out of the small oven. She had adopted simple, faded brown dress since we'd arrived, which was now under a threadbare apron, and was partial to humming to herself as she baked. I froze in my sneaking. I glanced over to our shared room. I could make a run for it but I doubted I'd make it unnoticed. I rubbed my arm self-consciously.

"Hey," I said quietly.

"What happened?" she asked, shock and fear coming all over her face. No doubt thinking I'd been bullied rather than fallen prey to my own clumsiness. She rushed towards me, all concern.

"Oh. I tripped. Got myself a little scraped up."

Allie grabbed hold of my arm, forehead frowned in worry. "Want me to bandage those up? They look a little dirty. I didn't think that you were clumsy." She pulled me towards our shared room, pushing me to sit on the bed. She went to the kitchen and came back with some cloth and water. "So, you want to tell me about it?" she asked, dabbing at my wounds.

"Ha. Not exactly," I said, glaring at the wall. Allie gave me a look. It annoyed me that Allie was good at seeing through me. She could always figure out when I was trying to hide something from her. "Look, I really did just fall down. The ground out there at market, well, it's all cobblestones and dirt."

"Fine," she said in a snit. "Don't tell me. But don't expect me to be gentle then."

Chapter Two

I hissed, as she rubbed the dirt out of my wounds, rather than gently washing it out. I glared at her in silent indignation. I kept my secrets, at least for the time being.

One would think that injury and the evidence that I clearly had forgotten how to do thieving properly would stop me from pursuing it any further. But, of course, I'm not exactly normal. Once you get the thieving twitch, it's hard to calm it down; in fact, the only way I know to calm it, is to satisfy it. A lifelong pursuit of mine.

So, instead of giving up, I decided I needed to go back to basics. It was clear to me that I had spent too much time idle. I started with little things, things at home, my own things. I would try to slip my daily allowance off my bed instead of picking it up. I'd try to sneak my roll off the table and eat it, before anyone noticed I took it. Magic tricks of the disappearing coin. Frank found it a frivolous waste of time. Susan thought it was endearing. Allie found it suspicious.

I started to sneak out to town when I could escape my duties at home. The seasons were beginning to change, making catching fish harder. A time of year, Frank said, to tighten our belts, and let the ladies eat their fair share, whilst he and I shared a more modest one. I didn't mind much. It gave me time to sneak away. I took different routes to town. Slinking around the city, I delved further into my discovery of the curve of the alleys, the little windows into shops that previously went unnoticed. It was like a game, a wonderful, and thrilling game. Once when I was feeling particularly brave, I stole a flower from a stand for Susan, I had almost got home, when I realized they would all wonder where I had gotten such a beautiful thing. It was far too expensive for me to buy. So, I stuffed it in a bush by the side of the road.

The Kraden Job

I'd started to horde my money. Usually Allie and I would go into town and buy ourselves a little something; a sweet treat, but no longer. I procured myself a little coin purse and stowed what little money I had. Allie watched me warily, but I was too distracted to notice.

Every week at market I watched for him, the man with the silken shirts that never looked worn and his smug, disinterested face. His day was coming, I could feel it. The thing is, if you rob someone like that, you have to be absolutely sure you're going to get away with it. He was the kind of man who might smack you around for getting filth on him; to think of what he would do if he caught me wrist deep in his purse was frightening. But I was young, foolish, and determined. Not necessarily in that order.

So I practiced. My greatest accomplishment of that year was getting a book. I'd learned to read on the ship at a young age, mostly because my father figured if I couldn't be a proper pirate, at least I could try to forge documents. But books were not common for someone in my position. I wandered into one of the dozens of bookshops downtown. A store that was always busy around noon. I chose it because I'd seen Allie looking inside the window, often at one book in particular with a gold and red cover.

I didn't actually read the title of it. I didn't care. I just wanted to get it for her. The storekeeper didn't even seem to see me as I snuck off with it. Allie was less than amused however, when I presented it to her.

"Where did you get this?"

"From a book store."

"The one downtown?" she asked, eyeing the book with distrusting eyes. I held it out towards her, but she made no

Chapter Two

move to take it.

"There are many stores downtown," I said, trying to be casual about it, "Go on, take it. It isn't going to bite."

"You stole it, didn't you?" Allie accused, glaring down at the offending article.

"Maybe," I said dismissively.

"Airen!" she slammed shut the door to our bedroom, before turning on me, her face bright with anger. "How could you *steal* it? What would Susan and Frank think? What if you got arrested?"

"I'm not going to get arrested. No one saw me."

She seemed to think about this for a minute before choosing another mode of attack. "Why did you steal it?"

"Because you wanted it. I mean, you like it, don't you? And, I'm a pirate. That's what I do. I steal things. I thought you'd like it." My voice went from anxious, to angry, to the tune of dejection.

She eyed the book, puzzled and conflicted. "It isn't that I don't like it. It's very nice to have a book, I just meant… People tend to pay for things." She took the book from me, running her fingers over the edges.

"Pirates don't."

"But we aren't pirates."

I crossed my arms. Striking what I deemed to be a fearsome pose. "I'm a pirate. Why else would they put me on shore death?"

Allie looked confused for a moment, then realization stuck in her eyes. "Oh." She turned the book over in her hands. "I didn't know. I thought you were there for the same reason as me; ransom not paid. Is that why you're trying to go away?"

"I… what? I'm not…" I trailed off under her scrutiny.

The Kraden Job

"Oh, please, Airen. You've been gathering your pocket money. Don't think I haven't noticed. And you keep looking at the sailors that come into town. It's like you are waiting for something."

I tried not to meet her eyes, instead looking around our modest room. It had all the minor comforts we could hope for. We each had our own bed and one nice blanket. There was even a little table that we could share to put our small amount of personal items. There was a little chest by the foot of my bed. It held my two changes of clothes, and Allie's four dresses. It seemed strange to want for more.

"You're planning on leaving, aren't you?" she asked, her voice sad. She hugged the book to her body. I rolled my eyes and tried to tidy up my half of the room, but she grabbed the blanket from me and threw it to the ground. "You promised you wouldn't leave me."

"Come on-"

"You *promised!*"

I threw up my hands in exasperation. "You probably wouldn't like where I'm going anyways."

There were tears in her eyes. "But how can you tell? I don't even know where you're going."

"*I* don't know where I'm going. It's a pirate ship," I hissed out, keeping an eye on the door. "And one doesn't choose where they go; they just get on the ship and go where the captain says. It'd be awful boring for you. There isn't much for you to do on a pirate ship. You'd never know where we're going. And there would be a lot of stealing of things. Which, clearly, you don't like."

"That isn't fair. I've been on a pirate ship too! You don't know what I did there," she accused.

Chapter Two

I raised an eyebrow, doubting she did much more on that ship than sit in the brig and cry. "Can you pick pockets?"

"Well no - "

"Can you sneak with the stealth of a cat?"

"No, but - "

"Have you stolen things before?"

"No, but - "

"Can you kill people?"

"What? No. Never!"

"Then, exactly, what do you think you would do on a pirate ship?"

"I ... but... you just... that isn't fair," Allie whined.

"Pirates aren't fair," I said, feeling the pleasant hum of victory for a brief moment.

"I could cook!" she said, jumping up in excitement.

"What?" I asked, completely perplexed.

"Yes. I could do that. I could cook for them. Someone needs to take care of the kitchen and the food is awful on those ships! Surely, even pirates like some decent meals."

I gaped at her. "I don't think pirates think that much about food."

"Everyone thinks about food," she said dismissively, waving a hand at me. "So, what do you think? Me, being the cook of the pirate ship! Isn't it grand?" she smiled at me. Clearly under the impression she'd won the argument. "We'd be a team. An unstoppable team."

I thought about it. It didn't seem like the best idea there ever was. It could end badly. It would be hard to talk my own way onto a ship, let alone talk on two people. One of whom would not be useful for getting money.

"I don't know...." I started, noncommittally.

The Kraden Job

"You promised you wouldn't leave me," she said again. The tears had begun to trickle down her cheeks. "I don't want to be left behind. Please, don't leave me here. I'd rather wander around than be left here alone."

Allie sat down on the bed and dissolved into tears. Raking sobs shaking through her. I stared at her blankly for a moment. Growing up on a ship there weren't many occurrences of people crying. I wasn't quite sure how to handle it. I remember when I was seven, I fell down on the deck and scraped my knee. It was a bloody mess. It hurt so much I started weeping. I received several swift hits from the first mate and a long lecture from my father. 'Pirates,' he said, 'Pirates don't cry.' Somehow I felt that this was not advice to tell Allie, another sign to me that she really didn't belong where I wanted to go. I walked over to the side of the bed. Patted her awkwardly on the back. I wondered if that was the right thing to do. It only seemed to make the sobbing louder.

"It's okay," I said in what I hoped was a soothing tone. "I won't leave you. You can come too."

"Do you promise?" she snuffled. Wiping her nose with her sleeve.

"I promise," I murmured, rubbing her back.

Her eyes were red and puffy when she looked at me. "Will you make a blood oath?"

I cursed under my breath. Of course she knew what that was. "I don't know," I said slowly. "I mean, that stuff is kind of dangerous. I remember my dad telling me stories that if you broke a blood oath you'd drop dead."

"That's stupid. And impossible," Allie rolled her eyes, the effect ruined slightly by her rubbing her running nose on a sleeve. "No one can just drop dead from words."

Chapter Two

"The magic is pretty powerful, they say."

Allie looked at me like I'd gone crazy. "Magic isn't real, Airen. Don't be so silly."

"If it's silly then why do you care if I do it in the first place?" I argued.

"Because it's a promise. A forever promise. You told me that pirates take it serious."

"Well yeah. Lots of pirates still believe in magic. I mean, not that there are wizards and stuff about any more just… you know… little things. Just because we don't see magic everyday doesn't mean magic isn't there. They say there are remnants laying around."

"Who are they?"

"I don't know, Allie," I said exasperated. "Pirates and thieves and folk. I don't want to go messing with magic."

"That's ridiculous." Allie pouted. She'd stopped crying but the tears were still slithering down her face, hanging onto her jaw.

I sighed. Though most people take a blood oath as a joke, pirates still hold them as serious bonds. The slight promise of magic to make it a contract for the rest of our days. There are a lot of stories amongst pirates that travel over ships and are told in the relative isolation of the sea. It's easier to believe such things when all you can see around you for days is a vast nothingness. Being out on the sea for weeks at a time, there's something in the wind at night.

Most folk have dismissed magic, since no one has seen a feat of magic in a few hundred years, but pirates, we hold onto it. At least the smart ones of us do. It runs in our history. Tales of blood oaths that have destroyed empires and stories of deadly consequences for more than one good crew. They say there

The Kraden Job

is honor amongst thieves. But pirates don't need to simply hold to honor, we have blood oaths. Bonds that will never be broken. As a kid, I didn't understand the whole history of blood magic, but it still wasn't something I wanted to take too lightly. At the same time, Allie's easy dismissal of it made me feel somewhat foolish to holding onto what seemed akin to a ghost story.

"Fine," I said.

"Really?"

"Really. But you have to take it serious too. This will be the first thing you do as a pirate, and pirates don't joke about blood oaths. You got that?"

"Yeah. Okay. I got it. Promise," she said, mopping the tears from her face. "I'll get my knife."

And so we swore, cutting small lines across our left palms and mixing our blood in that little cottage, to never desert each other. I didn't think that it would make such a great change as it did. Suddenly, Allie wasn't spending her pocket money either, but preferred to keep track of it. She asked Susan for an old ratty cloth she was going to throw away and began to make us each a knapsack. She became more alert and observant of the traders that would come into town, poking at my arm occasionally and asking: "Is that a pirate? Couldn't we ask that one?" It was strange, but welcome. Now that she knew she was coming with me, she was almost as anxious as I was to find a ship to go off on.

We only needed to wait another two months before an opportunity presented itself. It was on a day that I had wandered off into town by myself. I'd decided to swing by the port. For no real reason other than if I couldn't be on a ship, I would much desire to look at them.

Chapter Two

It was a cold and foggy morning. Frank had decided that catching fish would be pointless on a day like that. We would simply lose our nets in the sea. And so he gave me the day off. Allie was busy learning the finer points of muffin making, and I had a lot of time on my hands. The ships stood majestically in the water. Gorgeous and wonderful. That was when I noticed one that was not quite like the others. The paint on the name was too new. This may sound silly to you if you don't understand ships very well, but it was a trick pirates used to use when going into a new port for trade. Sometimes pirates didn't have the luxury of going in guns blazing; sometimes they needed a more subtle approach. And on such occasions, they would often paint over the name of their ship and name it something innocuous like the *Eleanor*, which was the name of this particular one at that moment.

I wove my way through the crowd, never letting my eyes wander from the ship. There was something about it. Something that called to me. I could see gruff men throwing around their cargo on board, the harsh commands, the shifting, suspicious eyes as they adjusted their clothes. Pirates. There wasn't any doubt in my mind that these were pirates. Finally, I had found some. I then did something that was incredibly dangerous and foolish. Though I didn't even think about it at the time, I tailed them.

A group of three pirates had left the ship, getting a slap on the back from a man who seemed likely to be the captain. I slunk into town after them. They continuously looked at a piece of paper they held. A map presumably. The trick to tailing people is not to think about them, but be aware of your surroundings. Any good pirate would notice me if I just walked several feet behind them all the way through the

The Kraden Job

city, so that wasn't an option. But I had the edge. I knew the city. They would head down a street and I would wander down one that I knew would intersect in a few blocks. That way, they wouldn't come to recognize me. They clearly had more pressing things on their minds. They stopped near an alleyway. Coming together to have a heated conversation.

"He said it was this shop right down there," one said.

"I'm not saying that isn't true. I'm just saying, did you notice it as we walked by?" the one holding the map questioned, looking around with some confusion.

"What about it? It's got all the shinnies in the window. We know what they got in their vaults upstairs."

"They also have three royal guards on the outside and I could've sworn, I saw one inside the window. We don't know how many of them they have."

"You saying you're questioning captain's orders?" the third, and tallest, man asked.

"I ain't questioning anything. I'm just saying. I don't think this is gonna go as smooth as he was hoping for. Royal guards! Do we really know what's in that safe?" the one with the map bit back.

The tallest man gave him a stern look. "The captain knows exactly what's in that safe. Now come on. We got a job to do, so let's do it, shall we?"

There was a substantial amount of grumbling at this. I watched them from my vantage point on a little tower built into the wall. I was too high to be reached by anyone on the ground. I smiled down at them. This was my moment. A make it or break it deal. If I couldn't convince them to let me into this job, then there would be no way that I could talk them into taking me and Allie onto the crew.

Chapter Two

"Let's just go in full force through the front. Cause a bit of a commotion in the market place. I dunno how, create some kind of terror or something. Then we'll run into the front and take out those guards," the one with the map said, pulling a blade from underneath his long coat.

I tugged at my shirt, making it look more presentable. I was nervous, that was for sure. I took a few deep breaths. Cracked my neck, cleared my throat.

"It won't work," I called down to them. Their heads snapped up. The one on the right had a knife out faster than I had thought possible. I held up my hands quickly, to show that I was there for talking. It also showed them that I was unarmed. "Whoa, whoa. No need for that."

"Come down here, little runt, and I'll show you what you get for eavesdropping on people like us," one man growled out, making a violent gesture towards me.

"I rather think I like it up here, thank you very much. By people like you, you mean pirates." It wasn't a question.

The man with the dagger out tensed. He eyed me. I must have looked rather strong from my vantage point, not in the typical strength kind of way. But being so high up and looking down on them, I looked much more the thief than I ever was at that stage in my life.

"Who're you?" the tallest man asked slowly. He clearly was the brains of this particular venture. He had an interest in getting things done. He wasn't a brute strength man, but a strategy man.

"No one really," I said, trying to maintain a casual air. My heart was racing, and I could feel the adrenaline begging my body into action. I allowed myself a small fidget. "I couldn't help but overhear you, and I was simply wondering, if I could

The Kraden Job

offer some assistance."

"What kind of assistance? The kind that gets you a big share of the cut?" one of the other men growled at me.

I waved my hand ambiguously. "I'm not that interested in what you're trying to steal. Besides, there isn't anything you can offer me. I want to talk to your captain."

Two of them laughed. "Oh ho ho. Is that all, little one? A meeting with the captain, is it?"

"Well, just so happens, we're with the captain right now," said the one holding the dagger, as he nodded towards the tallest of the three men. "So, what you be wanting with him?"

"Don't be stupid," I said. "He's not your captain. Your captain wouldn't go on such a trivial mission as scouting in town. He's back on the boat."

The tall man smiled in a testing way. "We can do it just as well by ourselves."

"If you want it to be messy, sure. Have good luck getting out of here! There are more soldiers about than just the few your seeing in town. I've seen 'em out by the taverns. Sure, you can get in fine, but I don't think the captain would be happy if you made a blood bath of a mess on the way out."

The tall one gave me an interested look, waving off the other two. They grumbled, but relaxed themselves, stowing their weapons. "You know a way in?"

"I know a way in."

"You won't tell me, will you?"

I shook my head. He smiled then. An honest and happy smile. "Alright," he said. "I'll get you a meeting with our captain. You'll have to come with me."

"I'd prefer to meet you on the boat."

He nodded his head. "Come in two hours. It's the—"

Chapter Two

"Eleanor. I know." I slunk back up the wall. A little trick I had learned several weeks earlier. This was one of my favorite hang outs, so I knew how to quickly get up the wall, without being noticed. From down below it would look as though I had evaporated up into the wall. It was a nice little move.

I stumbled over the rooftops in a bit of a haze. This was it. They had given me a shot. As soon as I was back on the ground, I sprinted back to the cottage. I banged in through the door. Susan gave me a reprimanding look, but I grabbed hold of Allie's arm and tugged her into the room.

"What are you doing?" she asked.

I was panting and flailed my arms about me. "Things!" I gasped out, "You have to gather all our things."

"I don't understand."

I grabbed a hold of her shoulders. "I met some pirates in town. I think I might be able to talk them into taking us on board, but we have to be ready to go in an instant, so you have to gather our things. Make our packs ready. I need to borrow your knife, where is it?"

"Over here," she said, in the voice of someone who clearly hadn't processed the exact situation yet. "You mean, they're going to take us soon?"

"Well, I don't know," I said, ripping open the trunk and grabbing out my black shirt. I changed into it quickly. "They are doing a job in town and if I can help them, I may be able to talk them into letting us on. But I don't know details yet. It's better to be prepared than not. Get things ready will you? So when I come for you, we'll be ready to go."

She smiled then slammed into me with a hug. "I can't believe it. We're going to go adventuring."

"Alright," I said. "Thanks, but you have to let me go. I need to get to their ship and talk to the captain."

"Oh, alright. But don't forget the knife."

"Thanks," I said, before I was yet again on my way.

I was panting again by the time I reached the docks. It'd been a few hours and I had to make my appearance soon. But I kept away from the ship for a bit; first, to make sure I was not being led into a trap, but also, partially, to slow my breathing down. I had to seem in control of myself when I got onto the ship. They needed to think that I knew what I was doing and running onto the ship a panting mess wouldn't make the right first impression. And so I waited for a few minutes, got my breath back, and searched the docks for the tall man. I crept up behind him but, from the way that he tilted his head, I could tell that he knew I was there. He was an incredibly sneaky one. My mind raced with all the things that I might be able to learn from him.

"Ah, the little street rat," he said, looking at me. He waved me toward the boat. I did a mock bow. He smiled and I followed him on board. We walked past the majority of the crew, some of whom regarded me with a bit of curiosity, and some that glared. We moved past them all, down a set of stairs, to the captain's quarters.

The captain was sitting in his chair before the window when I entered. He squared me up with an intense look. It made me feel tense and uncomfortable. He had the air of power about him; I didn't doubt he was the captain. The ease of the man behind me made me realize something slightly terrifying. I had been mouthing off to the first mate.

The captain held me fixed with a stern gaze. "So, you're the little boy from town that was pestering my men?"

"Yes, sir."

Chapter Two

"I've often had people killed for impeding my plans," he said, fixing me with an even stare. I gulped. But he only smiled more at me and stood up from his desk. "So, you know we're pirates, even though we took pains to conceal that fact. Would you care to share how you came about such knowledge?"

I fidgeted. I hadn't expected to make answers for myself. I'd simply hoped to talk about the job, but being demanding wouldn't have been in my best interest. "I just knew. I used to be on a ship not too long ago."

"Really?" he asked, actual interest showing in his eyes. "Do tell me more. And why aren't you on that crew now?"

"Well, my father died. Guess they didn't want a young one hanging about decks. Though I'm useful. I know how to keep a ship and pick pockets. I'm a good thief and a sneak."

The captain scrutinized me and I became aware of just how still the man standing behind me was. You learn fast and young on a pirate ship that the lack of movement can be more dangerous than a man drawing a sword for an attack. The captain smiled at my discomfort. "So, you think you can help us in our little endeavor then?"

"I know I can," I declared, brimming with a false confidence.

"And how is that?"

I cleared my throat. "Well, sir, some of your men seemed to want to storm the shop. I don't rightly know what they're after in there, but what I can tell you is that storming that shop isn't really the best idea."

"And why is that?"

"It's guarded pretty heavily. The owner seems paranoid. He has several different types of guards, including royal ones. Most of them stay on the outside, guarding the front and the back entrances. But I've seen there are more who lurk inside.

The Kraden Job

If you kill one of them, than twenty more will rush upon you. It will be a bloodbath. No matter how good your men are, it would end messy and you'd draw notice to yourself. Not to mention that a wealthy man, whose known to hold a grudge, would be able to put forces into tracking you down. Not that you couldn't handle it, it just seems to me, that it'd make your life a lot less convenient, Sir."

"Those are good reasons, child. Now," the captain nodded approvingly, "tell me how you plan to help me."

I smiled. Here was where I could scheme to get myself on the ship. "I want to strike a bargain first before I help you."

"Smart lad," the captain said with a laugh, looking over my head to address the first mate. "Wants his end of the bargain discussed first. What is it that you'd be wanting?"

I took a deep breath. This was it. "I want your word that I'll be able to join your crew. If I do well, that is."

The captain scrutinized me. "Can you fight?"

I fidgeted. "A little. I've been taught the basic moves, though it's been a bit since I used them," I said, rubbing the back of my neck.

The captain nodded to the men standing behind me. I heard the noise of a blade being drawn from its stealth. I tensed. There was a warning ringing deep in my mind. No good could come of someone pulling out a blade in a closed room. The man circled to stand in front of me. He held a blade that was between a dagger and a sword. For him, it looked smallish but for someone like me, it was more than half the length of my arm.

It was pointed towards me, blade first. I rapidly began to think of words to beg forgiveness for whatever offense I had committed, when the man tilted the blade. Holding it

Chapter Two

perpendicular to the ground, he had a very lose grip on the hilt between us. He motioned for me to take it. I looked up at him with a question in my eyes, and then looked to the captain, who simply stared.

I hesitated before taking the knife. The first mate smirked. As soon as I had a decent grip on the weapon, I needed to use both hands to hold it. It was heaver than it looked. I got in a fighters stance as he drew one of his other blades.

"A demonstration," the captain said. "A gentle one," he added giving a look to his first mate.

"Of course," the man said, adjusting the grip on his own blade.

Suddenly, he shot out his arm. Our blades clanged as they met. The force of his blow nearly knocking it out of my hand. I took a step back. We carried on for only a few minutes, but it felt a lot longer. My arms weren't strong enough to contend with such blows for long. We paced around the small room quickly. Doing a quick game of backwards and forewords.

"Enough," the captain's voice rang out. I was sweating and gasping for air. The first mate looked mildly amused, but had no signs of exertion. "You aren't awful. There's some promise. And you say you're a bit of a thief?"

"Yes, sir. They used to have me pick pockets, mostly for drinking money, but I've never been caught."

"You could be of some use to us then, perhaps," he said turning towards the window.

"There's more."

"More?" the captain questioned.

I plowed on ahead, ignoring the annoyed look of the first mate. "My sister wishes to come with me. She was also cast out from the old ship when our father died."

The Kraden Job

"What use is a girl on a ship?" the first mate asked, as if the notion was ridiculous.

I swallowed down my own resentment. "She's a very good cook, sir," I said, addressing the captain, since ultimately he was the one who needed to be convinced. "She's good with her letters and could forge documents for you. She's smart and I don't think I could be parted from her."

"And what if I don't grant you this request?"

"I guess, I'll just wish you luck and get out of town for a bit," I said with a shrug, well aware I was playing a very dangerous game. I was banking on him being either amused or impressed by my tenacity. If he wasn't, then I might not make it off the boat.

The captain smiled at me. "You got guts, kid. I'll take on you and your sister *if,* and only if, you prove useful. I don't have quarters for the two of you, but I could use a better cook. I'm tired of eating gruel. You'll keep quarter in the kitchen and be responsible for keeping it in proper upkeep."

"Yes, sir," I said, with a big grin slammed over my face. I couldn't help it. It was all I wanted.

"Now," he said, going back to his chair. He indicated for me to take the one across from him. "Tell me about this way in."

Chapter Three

Airen looked up at the ceiling in the cell. Slowly, she licked her lips, as though she was coming out of a daze, the path of memories taking a long time to retreat from. She looked at him again. Commander Jenkins was leaning forward in his chair, held to the story, curious to see how it would unfold.

"I think I could do with some more of that water. Unless you want me to stop. My throat is getting a bit dry."

"What?" he asked, blinking several times. "Oh, yes, of course."

He let her drink her fill this time. She savored the water. Airen resisted the urge to drink it all, knowing, that if she did, she would only get sick. "Thanks."

Commander Jenkins didn't move away from her when she stopped drinking. Instead, he studied her face, too close for comfort. She tried not to look at him as he scrutinized her. He cursed softly under his breath before pulling a handkerchief out of his pocket. He wet it and brought it to her forehead. She

The Kraden Job

winced as he wiped at the dried blood there. He gently washed it off. His eyes narrowed when he reached the three jagged scars above her left eyebrow. The cloth was surprisingly gentle as he unearthed that trail of scars downward into her cheekbone.

"You know, you shouldn't do that," Airen said, her voice quiet in the small room.

"Why not?" he asked, eyes intent on his work.

"They'll be asking you a lot of questions if they come in to find you cleaning me up. They might even string you up yourself."

"Whatever they may be, they know who pays them, and if that means I tell them to not enter this room, then they'll keep out of this room," he sighed, then muttered, "though, honestly, you shouldn't have this sort of effect on me."

Airen smiled mockingly. "Commander Jenkins, kneeling on the ground nursing a pirate's wounds. I'm not sure anyone would believe that to be honest, so I suppose you'll be safe from occupying a chair next to me for the night."

"Quiet, or I might not be so gentle," he said, but she saw a half smile creep up on his face. She bit the inside of her cheek to keep from retorting. "So, why'd you get it done?"

"Hm?"

"The sheen." His fingers were a bit rougher as he said it.

"Oh. That," she looked towards the door. "It seemed like a good idea at the time. It's practical for my work."

"It labels you as a thief, though."

Airen smiled bitterly. That was part of it sure, but in many ways the man was still naive to those he hunted. "Well, yes. I am a pirate."

"Now you are, but there's no reversing it for when you..."

Chapter Three

"What? For when I what?" she snapped, giving him a glare. Annoyance flared through her at his ignorant comment. Of course, it wasn't his fault he didn't know what the sheen meant, what it truly implied, not that many knew. He faded under her yellow-eyed glare.

"Nevermind," he said, going back to his chair. He was looking at the floor. He tossed the dirtied and bloodied handkerchief on the table, avoiding her eyes. She could see the briefest hint of a blush creeping up his neck. "So, what did you tell them about the building?"

Airen kept her eyes steady on him, making him more uncomfortable. He shifted in his seat. She watched him squirm for a bit before she spoke. "I told them about the window in the alleyway. In that time, the old city buildings didn't have a basement, rather they had two floors. The top floor often held the safe and valuables, and for that reason had no exterior windows, at least not clearly visible ones. There was a very small window up on the top of the second floor that one could access from the alley. It was hard to get to, and incredibly small."

"So in other words, they needed your help because you might be the only one small enough to fit?"

She smiled. "Exactly."

~~~~~X~~~~~

We planned it for that night. I would have liked more time to prepare, but their forged papers only let them stay in port for two days. They had hoped to be gone by that evening. The plan was to pull the haul, run for the boat, and then be off into the water. It made my life a bit more complicated.

The Kraden Job

First, I had to run back to the cottage and let Allie know. We told Susan and Frank that we were going out for a bit, that there was a show of street performers downtown we wanted to see. Susan didn't care much for street performers and Frank never went into town unless he had to.

Allie had shoved our bags out the window, so we snuck around the house to retrieve them before we scampered off down the road. She was more than a tinge nervous when I introduced her to the captain, but she took well to the lie of being my sister. It was a useful thing, that. Meant that the crew would understand if I was protective of her, and also you didn't mess with the crew's family. Not while they were alive anyways.

The captain was very courteous to her. I think, she may have been a bit smitten with him. She had told me the other ship had been full of foul smelling pirates who swore constantly and were gruff. This crew was something quite different. That captain, Captain Hernz, liked to call himself a subtle pirate. He was into disguises, the art of never been seen, and theft. He was a more a maim and leave, than a killing sort of man. They got on well in no time.

The first mate, Jared, took me aside and introduced me to the small group that would be going on the venture. The men I had seen him with earlier in the alley, were not there. Two others had been chosen from the crew, Mike and Jason. Apparently, they were known more for brute force than subtlety. This sort of stealth job required different types of minds. Jared would be there to make sure things went well, or salvage the job if things began to go poorly. Mike and Jason were also coming with us. They would help transport the haul.

Chapter Three

"Try not to worry too much, kid," Jared told me, as we went back towards the main part of the city. "I'll be with you the whole time. You get the goods to me and you're one of us. Hopefully, the guards will be none the wiser. Now, let's get ourselves up on that rooftop of yours."

I couldn't help but smile as we made our way out into the chilly night. Excitement, fear and adrenaline all mixed into one. I had never played such an important role in a job before. This was my first big heist and I couldn't wait.

It was amazing to see how busy the city was during the night. Even though the only light we had was from the moon, there were plenty of people out in the streets. Mostly men off to brothels, and the painted ladies on street corners. Some whistled at Jared but he paid them no mind. I'm not sure if ladies were really quite his thing. When he's on a job nothing will distract him. He moved through the town with a confident smile and ease. Mike smiled at the women. He even grabbed a lady in red for a moment before kissing her. He laughed as Jared grabbed hold of his shoulder and pulled him away.

"Not now," Jared hissed. Mike protested slightly.

"There won't be time later," he said, keeping a hand firmly on the prostitute's arm.

"Then at the next port," Jared said giving Mike a harder tug back onto the street.

"Fine," Mike grumbled, releasing the woman who pouted after them. She called after us, but I didn't pay attention to what she was saying. I hadn't been in many cities after nightfall. My father had always said the city at night was no place for a child. I found that he'd been right. The cities more temperamental lot came out in the night. I stayed close to

The Kraden Job

Jared as he wove through the crowd. He kept a close watch on me, at times tugging on my arm.

"Which roof?" he asked in a whisper. I nodded towards the east side of town. He smiled. "You'll do well, kid. If you can pull this off the whole crew will accept you."

There was an abandoned building three stores over from the one they wanted to rob, which was near the end of the street. Few people ventured that far down the street this time of night, so there was little chance of being seen. I showed them the back way. It was a bit easier to scale than other parts of the buildings. I climbed up it, expecting to be alone for the rest of the journey. I was quite surprised to find Jared coming up onto the rooftops behind me. He smiled at me in the moonlight.

"Come on, Airen. Let's get to that window."

~~~~~X~~~~~

"There's isn't much to tell after that point really. I found my little window, broke it in, sacked the room, handed the bags to him and we went on our way."

Commander Jenkins looked at her with the most displeased of faces. "You're cutting corners."

"Am I?" she asked with an amused tone. She cocked her head to the side, as if she was listening for something that wasn't there.

"What are you trying to hide? I think you can tell me now. After all, it happened a long time ago, and it isn't like you're going anywhere."

"Fine. I'll tell it to you the long way. I'm not hiding anything, if anything I wasn't exactly sure what the things were we took.

Chapter Three

Most of the valuables upstairs were gems, jewels, and gold. But there was also a box that the Captain Hernz wanted. Jared had been very specific in mentioning the box. It was full of documents; to this day, I am unsure of their true nature."

~~~~~X~~~~~

The little window shone in the night, the glass shimmering in the full moon. That was the doorway to my success. It was an awkward height down the wall in the alley. Jared looked down on it and whistled. The space it offered was too small for anyone but a child, and at eleven, I did seem to be a very small boy. The buildings were a good distance apart.

"How do you plan to get over there?" he asked me.

I felt the joy and exhilaration of the adventure creeping up my spine. "Jump!"

He looked at the space between the two buildings, then at me. He chuckled. "You're going to be quite an asset. If you don't get yourself killed first."

I had often taken a nasty tumble down the walls, when I attempted to make this particular jump previously. I prayed silently that it would not happen this time. I got a short running start before throwing myself across the alleyway. The building stung and scraped my hands as I slammed into it, grabbing hold of the roof and digging in. I still needed to work on my landings.

"You know how to work that hatch?" Jared called out lowly.

I looked back at him. In the darkness, I could only see the silhouette of his body. I shook my head. I clung to the wall and climbed over to the window. I hung on the wall precariously before I took a deep breath. I pulled back my

The Kraden Job

arm and slammed it into the window.

It didn't shatter. I winced and bit back tears. I slammed my elbow into it again and again. It cracked, but at a high cost. My elbow was already beginning to bleed. I took one last deep breath and shattered the window. Knocking out the little bits of glass in the window frame before I slithered through it. When I landed in the dark room my limbs were shaking, from hanging onto the building and from the pain of the cuts. I allowed tears to creep down my cheeks as I took out a small candle and lit it.

I gave the signal. Three spurts from the candle and soon I found a hook thrown through the window. I attached it to the floor, tugged on the rope, seeing that it was strong and firm. I looked at the sacks that were along the line, each had a small rope tied to it so that Jared could pull them back. I began my work quickly.

Grabbing anything shiny and stuffing it into the bags. The box was harder to find. Honestly, I stuffed three boxes into the bags, not sure which one was right I chose to take them all. Jared said I would know the box when I saw it, and I feared to come back with the wrong one. But in the end, I found the box they were looking for. It was more ornamented than the others, with gold inlay into the sides and a hefty lock keeping it closed. It joined the others in the bags. I watched the sacks being tugged over the alleyway in the moonlight and it was the most exciting moment of my young life.

Jared threw a cloak over me as we made our way back through the city, as casually as we had strode in, an attempt to hide the blood that was flowing freely down my left arm. Mike and Jason carried the sacks, but they did not seem out of place in the evening of city life. Jared carried the one with

Chapter Three

the boxes. He had one arm protectively over my shoulder.

"You did well," he said, before we got on the boat. "Very well indeed."

"Thank you, sir," I said on reflex. I was biting down on the inside of my cheeks. The pain shooting up my arm had not lessened and my dark shirt was becoming saturated with blood. Allie would have to look at it as soon as I got back on board.

"May I ask you just one small thing?" Jared asked.

"Of course." Panic was rising in me. Had I done something wrong? Were they going to change their minds?

"I was just wondering why you chose to bring your sister on a pirate ship. Surely you know, it is no place for a girl. 'Specially not a sweet and pretty one."

I smiled at him. "There was no help for it. We made a blood oath that I'd never leave her."

Jared gave me a look and shook his head. "A blood oath! Don't you believe in the consequences of breaking such a thing?"

"Oh, I believe in it, sir. Allie doesn't though."

"Brave or foolish, I cannot tell," Jared said. Though if he was talking about me or Allison I didn't know.

I gave him a large smile. "Me either."

Jared laughed. "You'll either be a great pirate or die a fool. Only time will tell."

~~~~~X~~~~~

"And that was that," Commander Jenkins said marveling, "That was how it all began."

"Yes," Airen smiled at him. "That was how it all began. Did

you expect it to be more exciting?"

"No, actually, I thought it might have been harder."

"Captain Hernz was a great man. He was a caring sort of pirate. You don't find his sort so much anymore, especially not among pirates. He was kind and gracious to us, always. I think he saw the usefulness of having a member of the crew that could creep into small places. A person who could always be talked into the most fearsome jobs. After all, all they would need to do is threaten my 'sister', and I would do anything for them."

Airen smiled at him, with a twinge of bitterness. He didn't return the smile. He had a look of mild disgust on his face, but if it was for her or Captain Hernz, she couldn't tell. "How about a little bit more water?" she asked, simply to get the look off his face.

Jenkins picked up the jug, swishing it around. "There is only a little bit left."

"I'll have it, if I may."

He took a swig first before tipping the rest of it into her mouth. She licked her lips, his eyes followed the motion. He wiped the stray drops away from her chin, smearing the dirt that had collected there.

"So, what are the mercenaries here for?" he asked, looking away and wiping his hand on his pant leg.

"Why, for the most profitable of ventures of course," Airen said. He regarded her with confusion. "Theft, Commander Jenkins. Pure old good fashioned theft."

"Simple as that, you say." He laughed a mocking laugh. It echoed in the room. "We're several days from civilized land. There is nothing out here to steal."

"Of course there is. There have been rumors of a heist like

Chapter Three

this for months. After all, word spreads when mercenaries say they are going to rob a stronghold."

"A-a what? They're going after a stronghold?" Jenkins scoffed.

There were three strongholds placed around the kingdom. Years ago a paranoid king had created fortresses to hide away anything of too great value to keep in the central palace. They were all placed in remote locations, notoriously difficult to travel to, home to a small force of guards who were generally stationed to a stronghold after committing a crime that was deemed to vicious for the man to remain in the regular military forces. To attempt to breach a stronghold was suicide, to steal from it was to gain the wrath of the royalty.

Airen smiled. "Did you not know there was one close by? It's about two days sail from here. They say one fifth of the king's wealth is in there. He should have known better, placing so much in one place seems like a challenge."

Laughter rippled out of his throat as he threw back his head. She smiled indulgently at him, watching the wax of the candles slither down to the table out of the corner of her eye. It was almost time.

"The mercenaries mean to rob the king? And they think they'll get away with that? I knew that they were a proud and stupid lot, but not that stupid. It's a suicide mission. Even if they managed to land a boat on the island there is half a company of soldiers posted at this stronghold. They'd be slaughtered before they made it through the gates."

"You quite misunderstand. It is the perfect place to rob, for the king shall say naught of it. Admitting that it could even be robbed would make him appear weak. Also it is said that the King has certain documents there. Some you may

The Kraden Job

have heard of. Surely you've heard the rumors that there are some documents that attest to the legitimacy of his children, himself as ruler, and include his will. Which, I am told, would be quite scandalous to reveal before his death."

Commander Jenkins froze processing this information for a moment. "They mean to blackmail the king? That's treason."

"Hmmm. Yes. Yes, it is," she said, letting the irony sink in that Commander Jenkins was doing business with treasonous mercenaries. "Quite frankly, I don't think they'd have the stones to go through with it."

"How do you know all this?"

"Oh, come now. You've never been daft. Why do you think my crew is here? These idiots make the perfect scapegoats."

"Was," Commander Jenkins said. "Your crew was here. They left you."

Airen looked at him. She smirked, fixing him with the full force of her bright yellow eyes. He swallowed hard. She started to speak. Stopped herself. Fought down a wide grin. "You don't quite seem to grasp the situation yet, Commander Jenkins. So, allow me to make this quite clear. A pirate does not back out of a blood oath. Allie would never leave me for dead. Just as I couldn't leave her. She's a real pirate now."

He sputtered. His face morphed from disbelief to panic, back to a forced calm. "No," he said with certainty. "No, there's no way. You couldn't have planned this. You wouldn't even know how to get out. And there are far too many mercenaries here. It's preposterous. Stop smiling!"

Airen was grinning by then. Mirth contrasting against her bruised face. "I must admit, I didn't expect *you* to be here, but in a way that makes it all the more, what's the word I'm looking for, exciting, maybe."

Chapter Three

"You didn't. You *couldn't*," Commander Jenkins said, though he looked less sure by the second.

A scream of agony echoed down the stairs and into the room. His neck cracked as he looked over his shoulder quickly. Another noise of pain followed. High-pitched screams of terror and pain bounced off the walls, reverberating around them.

"You might want to go check on that," Airen suggested in a stage whisper.

Commander Jenkins bolted out of the chair, sending it crashing into the ground. He sprinted past the door. He regarded her for a moment before tugging the door closed and locking it. She heard his boots pound against the stairs.

Airen waited until they were drowned by the noises of screams before slowly beginning to pull her legs towards her chest. It was slower than she had anticipated. She moaned in frustration. Airen gave several vicious tugs before her right leg came out of the boot. She eyed the wooden hoops around the shin area in her boot that had kept the rope from tightening completely around her actual leg. The mercenaries had made the rope as tight as they could, but to a false measurement.

"Beautiful," she muttered. She worked quickly on her other leg. Throwing glances up at the door every few seconds. She'd been bluffing when she acted so under control. Having Jenkins there was more than a minor inconvenience.

"Come on." Her left leg came out with a little more force. The wood scraped roughly against her leg, skinning it in places. The leg was littered with splinters but she had bigger problems. "It'll be easy, they said. I'll just get to walk out the front door, they said. Typical."

Airen stood up as much as the chair allowed. In her hunched

position, feeling more than slightly ridiculous, she looked around the room. She couldn't help but wonder if she looked like a turtle. Airen allowed herself a smirk before continuing in her escape. She scooted over to be closer to the wall. She pushed the chair legs against the wall, feeling the strength of the chair. It squeaked at the hinges.

"This is going to suck," she muttered. "Alright, Airen, you can do this. On the count of three. One, two, three," she said, as she threw herself backwards to the ground. The wood snapped and broke under her. The wind was knocked out of her.

She groaned as she rolled over in the wreckage of the chair on the ground. She tugged herself out of the ropes and scrambled to the table. Throwing on her sword and daggers. She pulled her boots on in a flurry, threw on her coat. She pulled the lock picks from the collar of her jacket. Put them to the door. She cursed examining the lock. It was massive. It would take her at least two minutes.

Airen heard Commander Jenkins racing back down the stairs. Quickly she tucked away the lock pick and drew her dagger. She stepped into the shadow. All he could see when he looked through the small window was a broken chair and the water jug sitting untouched on the ground. She saw his fingers go through the window as he tried to peer in deeper.

She struck out then, grabbing the collar of his shirt through the barred window, and pressing the tip of her dagger against his throat. He drew in a shocked breath.

"I suggest you open this door," she said, her voice iron.

"And if I don't?" he breathed out.

"Then I'll kill you and pick the lock myself," she said with more force than she felt. He hesitated. "Open the door,

Chapter Three

Jenkins. Open the door!"

He drew one hand out of the window and she heard the jingle of keys. His eyes never left her face. "Your eyes used to be blue. They were beautiful blue."

"Just open the door," she pleaded. The lock clicked. She twisted the blade in his throat in a quick motion. He winced and flinched back.

At the same moment she let go of his shirt collar and kicked the door. It slammed into him, throwing him back. She surged out of the room. Their daggers met in a clang. He stumbled back some more. She threw a punch, he dodged. He tried to push her back. She landed a kick to his knee. Her crumpled. Airen grabbed hold of his wrist and twisted until he let the dagger drop. With one fierce motion, she hurled him into the cell and shut the door. She leaned against it, breathing heavy, as she locked it. He slammed into it moments later, panting.

"What did you do to them?"

"Me?" she asked. "That was all Allie. She's a fan of the poisons. Don't worry, they'll be fine in a day or two. Be in a little pain, but pretty much fine."

Jenkins rested his head against the bars of the door. "Did you ever pick his pocket?"

"Whose?"

"The one you saw at the market. With the silken shirts? From your story."

"Oh, him. No, I never got the pleasure. But I've had a penchant for stealing from silk wearing self-righteous men ever since. Like so," she said, holding up his coin purse and jingled it. His eyes widened. Then flushed with rage. "Sorry, but you always did have taste for the finer things."

His face contorted in rage. He slammed his fists into the

The Kraden Job

door. "Let me out of here," he growled.

"I'd love to stay and chat Jenkins, but I really must go. They're waiting for me."

"I'll get you for this," he yelled after her as she retreated. She could hear him banging against the door. Rattling at the bars. "You hear me. I'll get you for this. Don't you think for one minute I'll stop hunting you down. I'll find you!"

Airen got to the main chamber to see the mercenaries rolling around on the ground. Several of them too weak to move. The black haired woman was groaning loudly. Airen stepped on her rib-cage as she went by payment for the condition of Airen's face. Seven of her crew stood in the room with strong amusement. Jacob was sitting in head chair of the table. His boots thrown up on it. He was swirling around a necklace of pearls on one hand and tossing an apple in the other.

"Nice to see you, Airen," he grinned.

She nodded and looked to Allie, who stood looking far too regal and elegant to be part of a pirate crew. Her blue dress hugged close to her body, brown hair pulled back in a bun, a sharpened stick poking out of it. She raised an eyebrow in salute and swirled a gold goblet of wine.

"We have to get out of here," Airen said abruptly, leaning heavily on the table for support. The exhaustion of the past few days and injuries catching up with her.

"Why?" Jacob asked, biting into the apple. "Thought we might stay a few hours at least. Raid their stores. Tell tales over the moaning. You know, catch up over their rum." The other men laughed.

"Yeah," Airen said, slowly catching Allie's eye, "I just locked Commander Jenkins in a cell downstairs."

Everyone froze and looked at her. Allie's goblet halfway to

Chapter Three

her lips. Jacob dropped his boots to the floor with a loud thud. "What's he doing here?"

Airen shrugged. Allie and she exchanged a meaningful look.

"I don't see why it matters much," one of the other men said. Jacob turned to glare at him.

"Are you out of your mind, man? Commander Jenkins has killed more pirates in the last year than King Dupont has in five. We have to put as much distance between us and him as possible." He turned to Airen, "Will the cell hold?"

Airen nodded. "For a bit. And this lot won't be able to help him out for a few hours at least." She kicked the man with the face scar in the stomach. He didn't even grunt. Jacob scrutinized her. The unasked question was in his eyes, 'Why didn't you kill him?'. But since she hadn't killed Jenkins no one else would. In absence of the captain the first mates voice was law. She looked away not wanting to give an answer.

"Grab the silver and back to the boat," Jacob muttered.

Allie nodded before raising her voice. "Alright, you lot. You have forty-five seconds to loot this room. Anything you want, you'll have to carry."

There was a commotion as the pirates swung into action, grabbing things almost at random. Allie dumped the wine out of the goblet and watched Airen struggle her way across the room. She didn't look back as she left, making her way towards the boat without touching any loot.

Jacob hovered close to Allie. "She doesn't seem to be in as much cheer as usual after a job well done."

Allie gave him a look before smoothing out the fabric of her dress. "Yes, well. It's Commander Jenkins fault."

"He's just a pirate hunter," he said with a smile. Trying to be dismissive despite what he'd said earlier. He thought of Airen as fearless and this was disquieting.

"No," Allie said, "for them it's personal. Airen and I have stolen many things. Before and after we've joined this crew. Lots of planning and consideration goes into our style of heists. Airen has only ever stolen one thing on accident."

"And what was that?"

Allie threw a look towards the stairwell that led down to the basement. She bit her lip, gave Jacob a look and said, "What do you think? Just – don't tell Nick, okay. Otherwise that ships going to get mighty small real fast." She smiled at him, pulled an untouched apple from his hand, bent over to pull a ring off the groaning woman's finger, and headed off to the boat.

Chapter Four

Airen limped back to her quarters, ignoring the looks of the crew. Most smiled at her. A job well done. She would gain a lot of respect from this one, after all, she'd had the most painful role. Success is intoxicating, they say, but as she shuffled into her room, with blood slithering down her shins, she didn't feel any joy. She shucked off her boots, picked up one, and yanked at the wooden structure. It showed no signs of coming out. She frowned at it. Clearly, she'd need to get help with that later. She loved those boots.

Allie came in behind her, her dress ruffling around her when she closed the door. She took a deep breath before turning to look at Airen, who was staring quite fiercely at her boots. Allie cleared her throat a few times before giving up trying to catch Airen's attention.

"These worked out rather well. We'll have to give Arnold something special next time we drop in on him," Airen said in an overly conversational tone, ignoring the tension in the room, indicating the wooden frames in the boot. "Thankfully, Clarissa and company didn't see them. Means we can use them again. I think, it'll be a mighty fine mystery how I slipped out of my cell."

"Airen -"

"Maybe I'll be a legend. The pirate who can slip from chains. Bit long for a tag line I suppose. And technically it was ropes."

"Airen-"

"Though, if I'm going to continue to use these, we might want to make them more comfortable. They chafe horribly. Not to mention the splinters."

"Airen!"

"What?" She snapped, her head jerking up to meet Allison's gaze. The yellow of her eyes glistened. She was pissed.

Allie glared back, but quickly gave it up in favor of a sigh. Her gaze drifted around the room. To all the little knickknacks and blades the two of them had accumulated over the years. The Wanted posters, that were too humorously drawn to pass up, taking one for themselves. The monikers that didn't stick. All symbols of their long friendship and adventures. All seemingly useless, when one name came up: Commander Jenkins. It was something neither of them wanted to discuss, something they both pretended they could forget as the years rolled by. Forget the mistakes and the pain. The confusion and the anger. Allie looked back at her longtime partner.

Airen looked exhausted. Deep rings of black under her eyes, throwing the yellow into harsher contrast. Her lip was puffy, and there was blood caked on the side of her face. Allie could see the bruises blooming above the collar of Airen's shirt. She wondered how far down they went. It was impressive

Chapter Four

that Airen was still standing, even if just barely. Blood was beginning to show on the bottom of her pant legs, and she was covered in a pretty solid layer of filth. But even all that wasn't the worst of it.

"Are you okay?" Allie asked finally, softly.

Airen shrugged, plunking herself down on her bunk. She pulled the braid out of her hair and ran a hand through it, wincing when she caught knots. "Why wouldn't I be?"

"Oh come on, Airen. You can give that to everyone else on this ship, but don't give that to me. Not now."

"I don't know what you mean," Airen said. She didn't even try to make it sound like nothing. Her voice was rigid with agitation.

Allie saw this was going to be like most things involving Airen and emotions; difficult. "I just meant you haven't seen Jenkins since -"

Airen shot her a look. It made Allie pause. "Drop it or get out." If words could cut.

"Airen -"

"I'm serious," she deadpanned. She looked away then, becoming intent on examining the material on her blanket. Her shoulders shook for a second, and she drew in a ragged breath, fighting to keep calm. Allie took a hesitant step forward, put her hand out, then thought better of it, and drew back. She was about to speak, when the door was unceremoniously thrown open.

Captain Nick and the ship medic, Thom, came bustling in. Airen stood at the intrusion, giving them a bored look. Nick had a killer grin on, the sort that made people trust him even though they really shouldn't. Nick was a handsome man, standing somewhere around six feet, with dark brown hair.

The Kraden Job

His brown eyes had that trustworthy quality to them. He'd started as a con man more than a pirate. Robbing people of their hard earned money through flattery, rather than a knife.

That was until he got himself into a rather sizable debt in a game of cards. With his inability to pay the pirates back, and discovering a man he finally could not give the slip, he was given two options: enjoy the knife or pay off his debt the old fashion way, by stealing for them. Nick discovered he liked the pirate's lifestyle. He didn't have to con his way into a place to stay when he wanted to pull a heist. His targets never saw him coming, and he was safe on the sea by the time they noticed their losses. Being a smart trickster meant he was respected, not hunted. And he could brag all he wanted about his conquests. It also gave him something he'd always wanted, the chance to be a leader.

Airen and Allie had run into him rather by accident and, after a small disagreement on territory, had simply decided combining forces was a lot more pleasant than spending the future trying to kill each other. Subsequently, neither woman questioned his authority as captain because, after several failed attempts of their own in the past, they both found the role of captain more a headache than anything else.

"You did wonderfully," Nick said, gathering Airen into a tight hug. She grimaced a bit, but returned the hug nonetheless. Thom frowned at them, tapping his fingers against the tray he was holding. It was laden with food, water, gauze, tweezers, a small vial of a pain relieving potion Allie had whipped up, and a jug of, what Airen hoped was, rum.

"Not that I don't appreciate the enthusiasm, Nick, but I was pushed off a wall," Airen said in a strained voice.

"What?"

Chapter Four

"Sore ribs," she gasped.

"Sorry," Nick said, letting her go so abruptly that she stumbled. He still had that grin on. "I'm just excited. It was great. And you should have seen the stronghold. You would have loved it. Gold everywhere. The whole thing shimmered. Of course, we barely touched it. Don't want them to get too suspicious, now do we?" he said with a smile.

"Too bad you left it all. They're going to know we were there anyways," Airen said, easing herself back onto the bed.

Nick laughed. "Of course they won't. Not like Clarissa and her crew can tell anyone what we were up to. They'd have to explain what they were doing there in the first place. Not likely to tell the authorities, are they?" He faltered at Airen's serious stare. "No one knowing the stronghold was plundered and that we were there was a major part of the plan."

"Plans go wrong."

Thom, who seemed bored by the conversation, came to stand by the bed, placing the tray close to Airen. Airen snatched up a roll and began to rip it into little pieces, avoiding the eyes of everyone in the room.

Nick scrutinized her. "How wrong?"

"There was a slight hitch," she said, between popping bread in her mouth.

Nick seemed to contemplate this for a moment. "What kind of hitch?"

"A *slight* run in with Commander Jenkins," Allie mumbled off to the side, looking at the wall of the cabin, avoiding Airen's glare.

That got Nick's attention. Even Thom tensed at the name. It was a name feared among pirates. Three years ago a pirate only needed to worry about being nabbed by the local muscle

The Kraden Job

during a job, but then, somewhat suddenly, Commander Jenkins appeared on the scene. He had a knack for tracking pirates and was a stickler for punishment. There were rumors he'd even left sailors on sinking ships because they *might* be pirates. Evidently, he hadn't the time or desire to figure it out for sure.

"Commander Jenkins," Nick said slowly, "*the* Commander Jenkins. The Pirate Hunter."

"That's the one," Airen said, taking a drag of water.

"Wow," Nick said. Airen expected the panic to start any second, but when she looked at his face all she could see was a sort of excitement. He smiled. "Adds a little extra, doesn't it? So, he'll report a robbery in the stronghold. Maybe put up some posters. It's not like he got a great look at any of you, right? Just lay low for a few weeks."

"He knows us," Allie said. She tugged at her sleeve. "Rather well," she added after a moment.

"What?" Nick asked Allie. He looked between them with a fierce scowl. They'd been upfront about a lot of their exploits. Airen enjoyed sharing tales of their travels from over the years, but they'd never mentioned the Commander to anyone. That was a tale they had thus far left untold.

Allie cleared her throat. Opened her mouth to speak, failed, and then tried again. "We may have…"

"…ruined his life…" Airen cut in with a hollow voice.

Allie glared at her. "Or near enough to it."

For a moment, Nick struggled with looking somewhere between shocked and impressed. He shook his head, "That is not a slight run in. When did he show up?"

"A few days ago." Airen avoided his eyes, looking everywhere else in the room. He knew her well enough to know

Chapter Four

that that meant something was going horribly wrong.

"What did you do?" he accused.

"Nothing," she blurted. He scrutinized her. "I mean, not nothing nothing. A problem arose and I took care of it." Her shoulders were hunched and tense, the unease evident to see.

"How, exactly, did you take care of it? Did you kill him?" Nick asked, his voice quiet, almost intimate in the crowded room. Allie blushed and looked away, feeling like she was intruding. Thom sat there with a neutral look, not seeming to mind that no one had appeared to remember he was even there.

"No," Airen's voice was cold when she finally spoke, "I didn't."

A dropped pin would echo in the silence that followed. Tension sprang up in the room. Allie eyed Nick warily, taking a deep breath when his hand seemed to wander towards the hilt of his sword. She looked at Airen, who was used to his moods more than Allie was. Airen enjoyed fighting with him, of that Allie was sure. It wasn't uncommon for discussion between the captain and first mate, Airen, to deteriorate into a sword fight to see who ultimately won the argument. She'd smile the whole time their swords smashed together and laugh at times when his anger got the better of him and he'd misplace a step. But not now. Now Airen was looking almost shamefully at the blanket beneath her; refusing to meet his eyes, seeming to back down from this fight before it even started. That did not bode well.

"You didn't? Great choice, Airen. *The* Commander Jenkins is there and you don't kill him. It would have made all of our lives a lot easier, not to mention safer."

Airen snorted. "It's not like he was just going to stand there

The Kraden Job

and let me stab him. I did what I could, okay. You scared of him, Nick?"

"Hardly. That's not the point and you know it." He ran a hand down his face, pinching at the bridge of his nose. "You're aware that a major reason this somewhat shifty plan works is *because* no one is supposed to know what we're up to. And here there is a pirate hunter, who may be out for revenge, in the mix. Whatever possessed you to let him live? And don't give me crap about not getting the chance. If you wanted to, you would have found a way."

"It's complicated," Airen said in a tone meaning: conversation over.

He gritted his teeth. "It's complicated? Airen, you've just pissed off a pirate hunter, who already *knows* you, and will now probably come after us in the middle of the biggest heist of our lives. I'm going to need a lot more than, 'it's complicated'."

"Well, that's highly unfortunate, since it's all you're getting."

Nick glared at her, his hand twitching. Allie wished she was carrying some weapon besides the stick in her hair. There was the possibility of this getting dangerous fast. Airen was certainly not helping the situation, pressing Nick's buttons and refusing to give at all. Nick cast a glance back at Allie, she shrugged. There was no way she was getting in the middle of this one.

"Airen," he said, in an attempt at a calm, but commanding voice, "I'm the captain of this ship, and as such I command your loyalty and the information you have. While I appreciate your self-sacrifice in this mission, I can't overlook the fact that you've allowed a known pirate hunter, who apparently carries grudges, on our trail. How am I supposed to explain this to the crew?"

Chapter Four

Yellow eyes snapped with aggression. He flinched back for the briefest of moments. "I don't know what you should tell them," Airen spit out, enunciating every word. "It's not like they're going to ask about it. We continue as planned. There are plenty of pirates for him to hunt. Let's not waste the plan on the chance that he comes after us."

"Can't you see, you've ruined everything?" Nick accused, his voice growing in volume. "We're planning to blackmail a king. Commander Jenkins will be there waiting for us. He will be looking for a way to colossally screw us. He will-"

"He'll be going there for Airen," Allie cut in. "*If* he comes at all."

"Excuse me?" Nick snapped, not too happy about the interruption of his tirade.

Allie pulled a fly-away hair from her bun, an attempt to appear calm about the situation. Her voice came out confident as she said, "Commander Jenkins is a tunnel vision sort of man. He'll likely come to see the deal, but he probably won't tip them off."

"It's his duty to tell the authorities. He *is* the authorities. How could he possibly not warn the king's guard?" Nick asked, exasperation ruining his much desired victory of the day.

"Because, if he warns them of our plan, then they heighten security. If they heighten security, then we see it and don't do the deal. If we don't do the deal, Airen isn't there. And if Airen isn't there, well, then he can't get his revenge," Allie summarized.

"You think Commander Jenkins will risk his entire reputation for simple revenge. Reputations aren't built overnight, as you well know, but are destroyed in an instant."

The Kraden Job

"He's pretty pissed," Airen said. She was swirling the glass in her hand, but not really gazing at the water but through it, as if she could see memories at the bottom of the cup. Her quiet voice cut through the room. "In any case," she said putting down the glass and running a tentative hand down her shin, "I think you should leave, so I can get myself de-splintered."

Nick studied her for a moment. Her eyes were averted, the emotion they reflected didn't seem to match the shining yellow they'd become. He knew when he'd lost. "This discussion isn't over yet."

Airen didn't look up. "Didn't think it was," she muttered.

He huffed in frustration when it became clear he wouldn't be getting any more from her. He turned to Allie, but she simply straightened the ruffles of her dress. He slammed out of the room, muttering something about a drink and stubborn female pirates.

Allie looked at the closed door, she clicked her tongue, smoothed down her dress some more. Making sure all the little wrinkles flattened out. She tugged at the collar, making it frame the bottom of her chin, and then drew a finger over her necklace. "He won't stop hunting you now, you know."

"Jenkins has got more important things to do," Airen muttered.

"Airen, he won't stop," Allie said in a reprimanding sort of voice.

"Oh, don't be dramatic, Allie."

"Airen, I'm serious. He'll hunt you."

"I know!"

"Fine. You don't need to snap at me."

Airen's shoulders sunk. She buried her head in her hands. "I know, I just…" she sighed. The sound coming out muffled.

Chapter Four

"He was after you."

Allie jerked in shock. Her eyes widening in fear. "What? Why?"

"He's been looking for you. Your lovely father's orders it would seem. And I ... I don't know, Allie. I'm pissed. I know I shouldn't be. It's stupid. But I just..." she threw her hands up, "am."

Allie became tight lipped. "I thought you'd forgiven me for all that."

"I did too, but seeing him again..." Airen bit at her lip, shame and anxiety showing in her eyes, and a twinge of something close to pain.

Allie's face morphed in disgust as she came to a sudden realization. "You didn't kill him so he'd chase you, didn't you? So you'd be his priority." Airen looked away and silence fell. "That's got to be the stupidest thing you've done in a really long time. That's worse than that time in Artigul."

That time in Artigul had often been known as the dumbest thing Airen had ever done. It involved five goats, a mountain of treasure, a cave, a storm and the words 'I have enough time!'. She didn't.

"I know! Don't you think I realize that? I couldn't help it. He was just there... and I just..." But apparently Airen didn't know what 'just' was, and gave up trying to explain it.

"Airen, you practically ruined the man's life."

Airen snarled at her. "I recall that being a combined effort, so don't you dare blame this all on me."

"I didn't... you... Airen, I don't know what you want from me."

"Just get out."

Allie contemplated her friend for a time but moved to leave.

The Kraden Job

She paused at the door. "Airen, if I could take it all back I would, but you're going to have to talk to me about it sooner or later if it's ever going to get better." She shut the door behind her.

There was only silence in the room. Airen ripped into another sweet bun. It was a bit stale. Allie had lead during this scheme, she wouldn't have had time to make a special meal for Airen. Though she knew sweet rolls were Airen's favorite. Airen felt vaguely guilty for her behavior.

It was true, Allie had gotten her into the mess in the first place, but they'd been through a lot since then. Allie had even broken her out of prison once, and that was a deed that deserved much thanks. Airen was yanked from her thoughts when Thom gave her a gentle touch on the shoulder. She near shot out of her skin.

Thom had constantly worried eyes. She faked a smile. Thom didn't seem to care much. He just indicated towards her covered shin. She swung the leg into his lap. Slowly, delicately, he pulled back the fabric to reveal a splinter infested leg. His lip twinged a bit, but she couldn't gather whether it was meant to be a smirk or a frown.

Thom was a veteran on Nick's crew, there long before the two women. However, no one seemed to know much about him. He'd joined with a close friend, one who was long since dead, and so the man remained, for the most part, a mystery. He wasn't a mute or deaf but was often treated as such, allowing him to know more than most were privy to on the ship. What they did know, was that he'd taken a vow of silence for an allotted amount of time, but without his friend around, no one was quite sure for how long the vow was in place or why. Everyone supposed Nick knew, but Thom

Chapter Four

mostly kept to himself, so no one really bothered to ask.

Thom never seemed to give any indication himself that he missed speech or was ever going to start talking again. The most they got out of his opinion was the occasional significant glance. And even those were often reserved and open to interpretation. Needless to say, his silence made him an ideal medic on the ship, whether it was simply the appearance of patience or was real patience, didn't seem to really matter as much.

Nick considered him as nonthreatening as a eunuch. Airen and Allie weren't quite as trusting as all that, but close. He dipped the cloth in water before sweeping it softly down her right shin. She winced. She really hated splinters. The rag came away dark, and he rose a single eyebrow.

"Whatdaya want? I was tied to a chair in a dirty cell!"

Thom picked up a pair of tweezers from the tray and, with great precision, brought them to a little stick protruding from her leg. He tugged at it. She winced, less from pain and more from watching it latch on and slip through her flesh. He gave her a glance before focusing more on the sliver of wood. She sighed, examining him examining her leg.

"It must be odd for you," she said after a time, "hearing all the things you do. You probably know more about everyone on this crew than anyone else."

He gave no indication of having heard her. She leaned back on her elbows. His eyes held steady on task as he hunched over her leg.

"They say you don't read or write. Is that true?"

He gave her a quick glance. Then nodded once.

"Pity in a way. Though I suspect it makes you more trustworthy. Not about to tell anyone our secrets." He dropped a splinter into a small dish. She frowned. "This is going to take a while, isn't it?"

He nodded again. She groaned. He held the small vial out towards her.

She raised one eyebrow. "Painkiller?"

Nod.

"Strong enough to put me to sleep?"

Shake of the head.

"You want me to shut up, don't you?"

He just stared at her. His expression neutral. She snatched the vial from his hand. It didn't taste that awful. There was a residue of honey in it. She sighed, flopping down on the bed, just barely missing the wall. She glared up at it. She could hear the water lapping against the side of the ship.

Airen closed her eyes and felt the swaying of the ocean. A flash of a concerned face came flying through her mind. Her eyes flashed open, and the image of Jenkins was gone. She heaved a deep breath, her heart beating hard in her chest. In part, she could still hear him calling up the stairwell towards her. Not sure whether he was cursing her or promising revenge to himself. Was he angry, desperate, both, or something else entirely?

She stared up at the ceiling, attempting to calm down. Focusing instead on the clip clip clip of the tweezers. She linked her hands behind her head and after a few beats began to speak.

Chapter Five

"I spent most of my childhood pretending to be a boy. So much so, it was a surprise to me if someone noticed I was a girl. It came to be that I believed I really looked more like a boy than a girl. I truly thought that no one would ever see me as a girl, let alone a woman. Even after crews knew I was a girl, they still called me 'boy', and when I got older, I got the tag of affection: 'young lad'. I sort of liked that one. Young lad.

"Sure, I started to grow my hair out when I got older, too lazy to cut it really, but when Allie was picking out nice fabric for dresses or learning new ways to put up her hair, I was getting beaten to the planks of the deck learning sword fighting. My hair was either in a ratty braid or shoved under my hat, sometimes both. I owned one pair of boots, and all my clothes were frayed. I wasn't overly worried about appearance. At the time I thought that was something women worried about, especially ladies, or beauties, like Allie, who would be mistaken for a proper lady. It wasn't for me, since

I didn't feel like any of those things. And who knows how different it would have been if I hadn't been that way.

"I know this sounds like a stupid place to start, but it's important for the rest of the story of Commander Jenkins. Though, at the time, he wasn't a commander yet. He was just a young man who loved fancy parties and the sea. Honestly, I think I ruined that for him a little," she sighed. The was regret in the undercurrent of her words. Thom kept quietly at his work.

Airen closed her eyes. She could see it then; feel the warm breeze on the back of her neck. The soft heat from the summer at night. Staring out at the sunset, watching the colors bleed different shades in the sky. She could feel him there, a foot behind her, watching her, as she watched the ocean. She knew he'd come up behind her, put a gentle hand to the small of her back. Whisper a smile in her ear. Kiss her on the cheek with lingering lips. She could feel the cold stone of the balcony beneath her hand, but when she clenched her fist there was only felt the worn fabric of her sheets in the ship's cabin.

~~~~~X~~~~~

It had started years before. The plan, I mean. Way before I was aware of it, before I was even a part of it. Over the years, Allie and I had been on a few different ships. Some because they offered us better opportunity, and a few crews we simply got thrown off, so we need better prospects. Some thought having us on board was a good idea, but then the superstition of having a woman on board worried them so much, they said Allie had to go. They never quite told me to leave. But we're a package, me and Allie. They forced her off and I went too.

Chapter Five

When we were fifteen we found a real solid crew that we stayed with for several years. We'd found them in a bar, not entirely uncommon. Well, truth be told, Allie found them. I was busy. I'd sunk myself in debt after five hands of cards and several cups of rum. Needless to say, I'd gotten myself into a rather troublesome bar fight. Or so I've been told. I'm a little fuzzy on the details.

We were between crews at the time and I was burning up some of our loose change. Allie was less than amused. She laughed pretty hard the next day though. I came to on a foreign ship. Scared the crap out of me. Had been passed out cold on the floorboards. Allie was lounging above me on the only bed in the room.

She smiled down at me. "Cozy, isn't it?"

I groaned, the headache shooting straight through me. My mouth felt dry. I coughed, it only made it worse. I rubbed the sleep angrily from my eyes. She twirled the bottom of her hair in between her fingers, enjoying my discomfort.

"Where are we?" I rubbed my stomach, feeling more than slightly nauseous.

"On our new ship, of course," she replied cheerfully.

I shot up, regretting the decision. My vision spun. My stomach lurched. I groaned.

"Don't get sick in here; it's our new quarters."

I laid back down. "I thought we agreed to discuss crews before we joined up. Especially after last time. Oh man, throw me a bucket or something."

Allie rolled her eyes. But sat up out of bed anyways, long enough to grab a bucket close by and chuck it at me. It smacked me in the side. I grunted, curling up around it.

"Actually, you did agree," she said casually, getting comfort-

The Kraden Job

able again.

"When?" I asked, my voice coming out muffled from my place inside the bucket.

"Why, last night. I asked if you thought it'd be a good idea to join up with them and you said yes. Maxwell was rather persuasive to you, I think."

"Who's Maxwell?"

"The first mate."

I glared up at her. "You know I don't trust first mates. And I certainly don't find myself persuaded by pirates."

"Well, it was after he helped yank four ruffians off you."

"Is that why my head hurts so much?" I asked miserably.

"No, but I imagine that's why your ribs will hurt when you stand up." I groaned again. She shook her head at me, "You have no one to blame but yourself, you know."

"I know. Doesn't make it feel any better."

"You're lucky, Max was kind enough to give us his room."

"We're in the asshole's room?" I shot back.

"Don't be so ungrateful, Airen," she hissed. "It was very kind of him. He thought a lady shouldn't have to sleep in the regular bunks with the men."

I retched a few times. When the bile stopped I looked up at her. "Are we still playing the brother-sister bit?"

She shrugged. "I dunno, no one asked."

I glanced up at her. She had a bit of that teenage wonder on her face. "You think he's cute?" I accused.

She blushed. "That has nothing…"

I groaned. "It has everything to do with it. Stupid choices," I mumbled. It probably would have sounded more effective, if I hadn't retched directly after saying it.

There wasn't anything particularly *wrong* with Maxwell. As

Chapter Five

far as pirates go, he wasn't that bad. He didn't ask too many questions, never brought up the pesky question of loyalty, gave us his quarters, accepted that we were part of the crew, and didn't treat us worse because we were girls. But I wasn't overly fond of him.

He was charming and warm, and always seemed to have the right thing to say. I didn't trust him. Though I was amused how hard he laughed when he found out I was a woman. He'd tip toed around me and Allie for three months before the discovery. He was under the impression we were pretending to be brother and sister but were actually young lovers. Something Allie didn't find nearly as amusing as I did.

They got on exceptionally well. In fact, she thrived on that crew. It's where she really started to come into her own. I think a lot of it had to do with how many of the men on the ship wanted her attention. They gave her a lot of gifts, not that she encouraged them. Well, maybe she did a little. But why not? She was just sixteen and beautiful.

At fifteen she had begun to fill out and at sixteen she was casually stunning. They bought her fabric and dresses to show off her figure, she stood tall with confidence in herself and her growing skills as a cook and potion maker. She was praised often. Her hair shone in the light and her smile... Well, the way she smiled at them could stop them in their tracks. She was a force to be reckoned with so early.

I, on the other hand, sunk deeper into despair in that area. Compared to her, I was nothing. Not a single man on the crew had showed me any attention, expect from sparring. Which they did quite often. The only thing my apparent lack of suitors did was spur my frustration and anger, making me a more challenging foe. Can't complain, those few years got

The Kraden Job

me to the skill level I'm at now. My bruised ego was a good motivator.

Though, I suppose what you really need to know is that Allie and Maxwell got on exceptionally well. Rather, that is to say, she had a blinding crush on the man, and he used it to his advantage. I think, she held onto hope that he'd kiss her, if she just kept on helping him out. 'Course she tended to turn a blind eye when the first stop he made at port was the whore house. Real charmer, that one. Not that I'm one to talk. People are stupid when it comes to romance.

The trouble really started a few months before Allie's seventeenth birthday. She seemed preoccupied, began spending more time with Maxwell. I could tell that they were plotting something, but she evaded the question whenever I asked. The distance was new for us. It was difficult for me take, she had always been my constant ally. On some crews I had made some close friends among the men, but Allie had been the only one I really trusted. The one that I really could rely on, and now, on this crew, I was suddenly finding myself alone. My anger with Maxwell only grew as time wore on and the whispering continued. Then the day came when their great plan was to be revealed.

I remember I was lounging in our quarters, well, I still called them Maxwell's, out of stubbornness. I had been seething all day, watching Allie flirt with Maxwell, him lapping it up and dragging her along with a touch on the arm, or a sweet smile. I'd come to the room to gain some peace and quiet, which to me meant sharpening a dagger. I was muttering to myself when they burst through the door. He had a barely contained smile, and she was positively overflowing with joy. I straightened up on the bed, rubbing harder at the dagger as

Chapter Five

Maxwell let his hand rest casually on her shoulder.

"We're pulling a heist!" she exclaimed.

I raised an eyebrow, looking between them. "Yes, I hear that we do that on occasion."

Two days earlier, we'd taken all the gold in the Temple of Tolrous. Most of the men were still in the throes of enjoying the score, which meant Allie was too. She was wearing the newest necklace that several of the crew had obtained for her. They'd pooled the money. Even though she had become a pirate, she still refused to wear stolen jewelry. She was still an idealist at sixteen. I was less fussy with my stolen boots that came from some guard captain.

Maxwell laughed. He did that a lot when I spoke. I think, it was an attempt to get on my good side. In almost two years, it hadn't worked. Allie threw me a warning glance. Maxwell's and my rivalry was the one sour note on the ship to her. As far as she was concerned, my attitude was ruining her good fun, and her chances with the man that may very well be the love of her life, or at least that is what she imagined at the time. I remained less than impressed, and was obvious in my distrust of the man.

"This will be a historic heist," Maxwell said, coming around her. "One that could make us legends. A heist that everyone will hear about." He had that glint in his eye, the one that showed up every time he challenged the captain. The power hungry look that got us into tight scrapes, because it led to him going a little too far. But he knew what he was doing.

He was playing to my greatest weakness, the desire to be a renowned pirate. I craved for people to know my name. Legends and myths surrounding my person. I wanted to hang Wanted posters above my bunk, the comical as well as the

The Kraden Job

glorified. I wanted to have monikers and public speculations about who I was. I could feel that itch. The one I had when the sea was calling me out to adventure.

"What did you have in mind?" Asking was foolish, but damn that Maxwell, taking advantage of my desires. I knew it was a bad idea from the way that he was smiling, the glint in his eyes held mischief, and not just the usual sort. He had something devious up his sleeve, and for some reason, I felt that it was going to come down on me, but in that instant, with the word 'legend' floating above me, I couldn't resist.

"We're going after Amelio Kraden," the words fell out of Maxwell's mouth like tantalizing daggers, intriguing, yet so very, very dangerous.

I froze, the smirk falling from my face. "You're kidding, right?" I looked between them, Allie nervous and Maxwell mirthful. They weren't. "You want to go after Amelio Kraden. The wealthiest man on Kamero Islands. He practically owns them."

"Exactly," Maxwell said. "If we pull it off, we'll be legends. No one has robbed Amelio Kraden before."

"And for good reason. If we don't pull it off, we'll be worse than dead." I looked over at Allie. She was giving me that look as though I was betraying her somehow. I scoffed. "You want to steal from your parents? What has Maxwell done to convince you of this one?"

She bristled. "It was my idea in the first place." I rolled my eyes. "It's true. Those people left me in the hands of *pirates*. They didn't pay my ransom even though they had plenty of money. Don't give me that look. It's more for revenge than for the money. We're only going to take the amount I was to be ransomed for. They owe me that at the very least."

Chapter Five

I eyed them warily. "Truly? Only the ransom amount?"

Maxwell smiled. "Of course. Surely you can see it's got, what do they call it, poetic justice. It's not really for the money at all. For Allie, its revenge and for us, well, stealing from Amelio Kraden, no matter the take, we'll be famous." He sat down next to me on the bed. Allie and I were not amused. He lifted a hand to my shoulder, but thought better of it, instead settling for leaning in, but keeping his eyes on Allie.

"Don't you want that?" he asked in a cheerful whisper. "Don't you want to have them know who you are? Be chased out of taverns when they recognize you? Have a secret way into all the undergrounds in the big cities?"

I glared at him. He was sitting too close, fixing me with those scheming eyes. I felt like punching him, but the tempting offer was more than I could bear.

"Tell me the plan. Let's see how far you've come." I was bluffing, as though my opinion was important. Everyone knew I was bad at planning, schemes have never been my strong point. I could figure out a way into small places, scale walls, throw knives, fight, improvise myself out of trouble, and drink half the men under the table, but I couldn't plan a heist to save my life. A fact that I had proven with several narrow escapes and many scars.

Maxwell smirked. "As you may know, the Kraden Estate is essentially impossible to penetrate. Guards everywhere, top security, fortress walls..."

"..Spikes at the top, a little bit of razor wire on the wall. Guards patrolling at random intervals, practically his own private army," I finished the list.

Allie gaped at me. I shrugged. "Figured you want to do something about them eventually. They can't have that much

The Kraden Job

security and people not know about it. I've kept an ear to the ground. The last tavern we were at, I met a few people from a crew that tried to get into the place few years back. Just to say they got into the place. Get in, mind you, not even take anything. There were only three of them left and they didn't look very good for it either. It sounded like a disaster. And they all got caught, spent ten days down in the personal dungeons before getting sent to Ersten Prison, an experience I'd rather not live through, thank you very much."

"That's why we aren't going to try to breach the walls," Maxwell said with a smile. Riddles, I hated riddles. He indicated towards Allie. "It's her idea, really."

Allie blushed under the praise and bit her lip for the briefest of moments. "Well, you helped a lot. I couldn't have done it without your suggestions."

"Don't flatter me, Allie."

It was endlessly tedious to watch them perform this dance. "Right, if you could stop flattering each other and explain what you mean, that'd be nice."

Allie turned bright red, Maxwell threw a wink at her before continuing. "The idea is that we get access from the inside. We put in one of our own, a simple, run of the mill lesser noble, and they won't even think twice. Place a person of interest within the walls and become close to the family. From inside they can observe the patrols and security, pass on the information, and plan the perfect moment to strike. They won't see it coming, and if we do it right, even after, they won't know who the inside man is. We walk away with the money, the legend, and no one to chase us. It's perfect."

"So, your plan so far is getting someone on the inside, stealing their secrets, and then counting on them to let the

Chapter Five

rest of us in to snag the money?"

"Well... yes."

"That does sound simple, and therefore rather questionable," I said, skeptical.

"Oh, Airen," Maxwell said, putting a hand on her knee. Allie glared at me, like it was my fault. I liked it even less than she did. "The hardest part is getting someone inside. After that, it takes minimal advanced planning. Once we have access to the estate we can develop the details as we go. The real trick is getting one of us in there. The rest will fall into place."

I removed his hand, dropping it onto his lap. "And how do you plan to get a guy in?"

"That's the true brilliance behind it," he said. "They'd suspect a man, be cautious of him. And to trying to scrub up a pirate would be quite the mess, I'm sure."

"If you aren't planning on sending a pirate in, whom exactly are you planning on sending?"

"We're sending a pirate, just not a male pirate. They never suspect women," Maxwell smiled. "Most female pirates aren't of note. None have become notorious yet."

"True, but most try so hard to be famous, they'd never blend into society, especially not high society," I said, beginning to think it was the worst plan I've heard in sometime. And that was saying a lot, because I was the master of awful planning. Most female pirate's I'd met were laden with fierce tattoos and earrings. They reeked of strength, ferocity, and were marked so clearly that straying into ever the wealthier parts of the city would likely get them in trouble. There was no way any of the female pirates I had met at that time would pass for a lady. I eyed Allie, true, she still had the regal air of high society about her, but I knew they couldn't possibly think to use her.

The Kraden Job

"Women get overlooked so easily. And this way we don't need the support of the main house to get someone on the estate. A vulnerable lady would be invited in with little to no questions," Maxwell carried on, eager to get me to agree. There was something odd about the way he said it that gave me pause.

"What do you mean?"

He waved a hand, brushing the thought aside, but it was Allie who answered me. Her voice was brimming with enthusiasm as she said, "What we really need is a clever, quick woman who can convince one of the men that she needs protecting. A woman who gets a man to take an interest, and we'll create a little scenario, and when push comes to shove, he'll not take the risk of losing her and invite her to stay in the estate. She'll become privy to all the information they think women find boring. Women are often overlooked in these big households. She gains the confidence of someone important and it allows her time to meander about. A courtship takes quite a time in high society. It's the perfect in."

"Right. That almost sounds plausible. But, correct me if I'm wrong, Allie, but isn't your sister a twin?"

"Yes," Allie said bluntly, as though she didn't see the problem with this.

"How exactly do you plan on getting in there to flatter your way into the high society if you look exactly like the daughter of Amelio Kraden? Because you *are* the other daughter of Amelio Kraden."

Allie rolled her eyes. "Well, Airen darling, we weren't planning on using me. We were planning on using you." As though that was an obvious solution.

"You... you ... WHAT?" I exploded, launching off the bed to

Chapter Five

pace around the cabin.

"It was Max's idea, really. It's a good one. I mean, we know we can trust you, you're our best sneak, and no one knows you from the estate," her voice was fading as my thudding boots echoed throughout the room. "Airen, it's a pretty good plan. You're smart and crafty. You'd be able to get us the information. You could steal plans, get the messages to us. No one knows code quite like you."

The panic was rising rapidly in me. A plan pivoting around me, I had tried that before, the scheme had not ended well. I didn't like being the center of attention, I wanted to hide in the background in my cloak and steal things without anyone noticing. I wanted to be notorious for the sneaking and thievery, not for making a fool out of myself and getting my crew killed.

"If you want to do this, you'll need to find someone else." I glared at Maxwell, I was sure this was all his fault.

"What? Why?" Maxwell asked. "Airen, this is a golden opportunity. And the whole plan would hinge on you. You can't back out on this."

"Find someone else."

Maxwell stood, moving next to Allie, creating a united front against me. "There is no one else. We'd have to be ready in eight weeks. We can't get anyone else ready in eight weeks. It has to be you or we abandon the plan."

Eight weeks, it was impossible. "You want to turn me into a lady in eight weeks? Are you absolutely out of your mind? I couldn't be ready in a year."

Allie sighed. "They drilled us like crazy with proper etiquette lessons at the estate. I knew all the rules by the time I was twelve, and I got some reference texts. I will teach

The Kraden Job

you everything. It'll be hard but manageable."

I looked between them. Allie was fidgeting. Maxwell was battling a frown, trying to look excited. His eyes looked concerned. It hit me then. "Ah, I see. You've already started putting things in motion, haven't you?"

"Well yes…" Allie started.

I fell back onto the bunk. "How could you? Before even asking me. How many other people are working on this? Oh crap, I think I'm going to be sick."

Maxwell lost his patience and threw his hands up. "Airen, there is only one way to introduce someone into that estate without it being suspicious and that's at their annual party. It took weeks to get an invitation. It was pressing that we get it for this year, we didn't have time to debate this with you. We had to act."

Silence fell in the room. I ran my tongue over the edge of my teeth, trying to contain my anger. "Maxwell, there is no need to lie to me. You did it this way so that I *couldn't* say no."

His face fell. "Not exactly…" he began, but the truth was written all over his face. He'd backed me into a corner on purpose.

Allie tensed, noticing the glint in my eye. "Max, I think you should…"

Before she could finish her sentence, I was on my feet, my sword swinging at his chest. He blocked it, barely. Allie shrieked when he staggered back and hit the wall. Using it as leverage, he pushed back on my blade. I pushed back as hard as I could.

"Stop it! Just stop it right now!" Allie looked at us both, pleading. Maxwell was gritting his teeth, trying to keep steady ground at the awkward angle. His blade was moving ever so

Chapter Five

slightly closer to his body. I tilted the sword to a tougher angle and shoved, his blade hovered an inch from his face.

"Airen, control yourself!" she yelled. I hissed, giving one final shove, the momentum smashing his head into the wall, then backed off. "Airen!"

I rolled my eyes as she rushed over to him. Rubbing at the back of his head, I heard him hiss and her coo in a comforting voice. He mumbled a response before getting up and leaving the room, a trail of blood trailing down his neck. I chucked my sword on the bed and turned to face her.

"That was uncalled for," she said, attempting to sound mature, flattening out the ruffles of her dress. I gave her a deadpanned stare. It was probably true, but I was pissed and didn't care.

"You had no right," I said, my voice tight with restraint. "You had no right to sign me up for this."

"Airen," she started in a worn tone. The tone she used when speaking in a mock sympathy to some of the crew, the tone of correcting bad manners.

"Don't! I just can't believe you'd do this to me. I can't really turn it down, can I?"

"Airen, it won't be that bad. I mean… I thought it was something you always wanted to do. You know, pull one over on everyone. You do it every time we come into port anyways."

"Well, yeah," I said exasperated. "I do. I make everyone think that I'm a man. A man Allie, the complete opposite of what we're going for here. How in the world do you think I'm supposed to trick a gentleman into thinking *I'm* a lady?"

"Seduce him."

I scoffed, then saw she was serious. "You've got to be out

The Kraden Job

of your mind. I can't seduce female deprived pirates who've been at sea for months. I hear gentlemen are a bit more picky than this lot."

"I shouldn't have said that. I didn't mean actually seduce seduce him. It wouldn't be proper, anyways. For this to really work you just have to make him want to protect you and see you as a vulnerable girl…" she coughed into her hand.

I gritted my teeth, the pressure in my jaw relieving some of the pain shooting through my head. "I actually want to hit you right now. I can't do this, Allie. I'm not qualified to do this."

She threw up her arms, exasperated. "And why not? You're smart and stealthy. You're an absolute liar."

"But I'm not you!" She stared at me in shock from the outburst. My voice grew quiet as I sat on the bed, pulling the sword into my lap, running my finger across the edges. "I'm not beautiful. I'm not even pretty. I'm a fighter, not a girl. No man is going to want me. They don't even *see* me the way they see you. Even if I wanted to do this, I couldn't. Physically couldn't. You," I motioned towards her, "you got curves, and a pretty face and all that girlish charm stuff. Me, I'm flat chested as a boy and nearly as ugly."

"Oh Airen." She came beside me, rubbing circles between my shoulders. She nudged my knee. I could barely see the points of her boots sticking out from under her dress, the sleek slope to them, the shine of well-kept attire. "You aren't ugly."

"But no one -"

"Airen, we're on a ship of mostly disgusting pirates, most of whom you've given at least one broken nose, and the other half you've upstaged. You may have looked like a boy when

Chapter Five

we were little, but there is more than a little bit of woman showing now. You just cover yourself in dirt, wear those pants, walk like the guys and hide under that hat. Of course, no one knows you're a woman, you spent so much time trying to blend in and slink in the shadows, no one would see through your scam. It just shows how talented you are."

I snorted, but in truth, the flattery did make me feel quite a bit better. She pushed my hair out of my face. "I bet if we got you all dressed up, put on a little make up, and washed this hair of yours, maybe put it in a braid, half the crew wouldn't know what hit them. They'd wonder when such a beauty stumbled on board."

I punched her in the knee. "Fine. I'll admit maybe it's not hopeless, but I doubt anyone would mistake me for a beauty."

"Ouch." She rubbed at the spot. She bonked me in the shoulder. "We'll see. Just stop being so mopey. You don't even know how you'll look when you dress like me."

I laughed. It was true. "Not like you."

"Well no, but still nice I don't doubt. Oh no," she said after a moment. "We have to get you a pair of heels."

Allie went to rummage through her closet. I laid back on the bed, trying to imagine myself beautiful. It wasn't working.

"You really think I'll look nice?"

"I think you're pretty already, and the only reason no one notices is because you scowl something awful all the time. Don't get me wrong, there is going to be a fair amount of work put in. I mean, your walk for one. Not to mention your language," she said digging around.

"What about my language?"

Allie smiled at me over her shoulder. "Let's just say, unless things have changed drastically, courtly men don't like their

The Kraden Job

women to swear like sailors. If any of them find out you're a pirate, they're likely to try to take your head off."

I grinned. Risk taking. I liked that part of the job. Yet, I couldn't help but sigh. "You're our seductive one. Everyone knows that. You get the keys to the castle with a wink and a smile."

"And you manage with just a sleight of the hand," she said, chucking a heel at my head. "And when I'm done with you, you'll be able to walk right up and take it with a smile on your face and a coy look in the other direction."

I held up the shoe. A few inches balanced on a rather thin back. "You're kidding, right?"

Allie raised an eyebrow. She was not kidding. "Just wait until I get you dancing in them."

Chapter Six

The dancing didn't happen for a while. First came walking. During the first few times I fell over and threw one of the shoes out the port window. Allie was not amused. Overall, I was angry and miserable. For the first time in years, I spent most of my time confined to my cabin. I spent it walking and attempting to dance. I got blisters on my feet in places I never had during years of sword fighting practice. I had to relearn how to eat, to sit, to speak. My mannerisms needed a re-education. I had to smile pleasantly, which I found was a mysterious trick. Actually brushing my hair, figuring out how to throw it into a style that didn't scream commoner, which meant no more long braids. Although the hardest part, I must admit, was to fake confidence.

I had to pretend as though all this behavior was the most natural thing in the world. I read dozens of books trying to figure out what gentlemen and ladies liked to talk about.

The Kraden Job

It was my own personal nightmare. How I hated it. Allie gathered a special pleasure from it, I think. For the first time, she wasn't the only woman on board.

I remember the first dress that I put on. It was a light blue, one of Allie's. I had secretly coveted it for half a year. Every time she wore it, I wanted to touch the delicate fabric. I loved the pattern on the sleeves and the heart frame on the top.

I looked at myself in the mirror as she began to pin it. My frame was slighter than hers, mostly due to my modest curves. Though, to my surprise, I actually had curves. The bottom of the dress swished around when I moved, the looseness around my legs bothered me.

"Stop moving. This is tricky," Allie said, her mouth full of needles, as she tucked the fabric into itself. I took a shuddering breath. I didn't feel ready for dress up, but the festival started in three weeks and I needed to be.

There was a knock on the door and Maxwell let himself in without prompting. Much to my displeasure, he'd been around a lot during my training. Making sure his investment was well spent, I suppose. He'd spent tedious hours with us, acting as a stand in gentleman, trying out conversations, and attempting to be a dance partner. He was silent when he spotted me. I looked at him in the reflection of the mirror, frowning. I knew, if I couldn't pass his scrutiny, I would never survive the festival, yet, with him in the room I felt terrified and useless without a blade by my side.

"Not bad," he said after a moment. Allie smiled at him. Her hope that Maxwell and I would bond through this project wasn't working, but every little nudge from him made her beam. He came closer and scrutinized me. "Got to do something about her face, though."

Chapter Six

My face flushed with shame. I tugged at the dress, feeling stupid and ugly again. Allie hissed at him, "She looks great. You have no idea how long it took me to get her into this dress. She's lovely. May need some gloves, though," she said prying my hands off the gentle fabric. She gave him a severe look.

Maxwell nodded, looking me over again. "I'll stop in the next port and buy some. Well, the dress does match her eyes. It'll make a good first impression."

In less than twenty-four hours a pair of white silk gloves, and a pair of dark riding gloves were left at the door. Whether it was an apology for the insult or to keep Allie happy, I doubt I'll ever know.

Allie was intolerable for the next two weeks. She was quite proud of herself for my transformation. I had to hand it to her, I almost looked like a proper lady. Though my mannerisms were a bit off, especially the regal confidence one; I was meant to exude it, instead I simply feigned. On no day did this show more, than the one before we arrived in port.

"So," I said, clearing my throat and fidgeting with my gloves, I could feel my face heat up. A blush was my constant companion when I was in a dress. Allie thought it would help me. Maxwell had called it quaint. Neither comment, though, was a comfort. "I get off the ship and I'm meeting Maxwell's friend."

"Yes," Allie said in a tired voice. "Lord Stevens. He'll be waiting for you. We told him to keep a look out for the ship. It's registered as a light trade and passanger vessel. We've paid the taxes for the ship. Max did think this through, Airen."

"It makes me nervous. All of this hinging on his contact."

She leveled a heavy sigh. "I don't get why you just can't trust Max. He's known Lord Stevens for years. Lord Stevens is our

The Kraden Job

best way in. He's esteemed by the titled Lords in the area, and has been building the story of a large mysterious family for years, waiting for it to become useful. He's a smuggler after all, he has to have some excuse for always sending away big packages and getting dozens of letters. And most importantly, he has the invitations we need to get you into the festivities and a status no one will question."

I grumbled.

"You just don't like him because he's Max's contact. If he was one of yours, you'd be fine. Or if he had been one of Rick's," Allie said in frustration.

I shrugged. She was right, but I didn't want to admit it. I hadn't trusted the plan from the start with Maxwell holding the cards, so being at the mercy of his business partner was less than inspiring.

"For the love of –," Allie started, " Airen, trust Max, won't you? I do."

"I don't trust pirates," I said, straightening my sleeve.

"I'm a pirate."

I rolled my eyes. "That's different. You're Allie."

"How about if this heist goes well, you start trusting Max some?" she asked, coming up behind me. She put a necklace around my neck and fastened it. I fidgeted. She'd been trying to help me with it but closeness still made me uncomfortable. Usually, if someone touched me, they were trying to throw me in jail.

"Fine," I grumbled. "But only if it goes well."

"Don't worry. Max, Shane, Stout, and I will be setting up in the basement of Lord Steven's house shortly after you arrive. You won't be completely alone."

"Not until I get into the Kraden Estate anyways."

Chapter Six

"Well, yes," she said, fixing up my hair. A distant look in her eyes. Through the weeks of planning we'd all been talking about the Kradens as though they were strangers we were robbing. We all ignored the glaring fact that technically Allie was going home. To her credit, she ignored it too.

"Nervous to go back?" I asked biting at my lip.

"Don't do that," she tuttered. "And a little. I haven't been since I was twelve. I wonder how different it looks."

"Are you ready to be back there?"

"I don't know. I guess we'll see when we get there."

I sighed. "This role reversal disturbs me."

"Really? I kind of like it. You'll do fine. Stop biting your lip. And put on your gloves, you have so many callouses."

"I like them," I mumbled, "They make me... well, me."

"Yes," Allie smiled, "I know. I'm rather fond of them myself. But I doubt that Graham Jenkins will be as fond of them. Lords want their women to have soft hands."

The Jenkins were an old family that had risen through the ranks of citizenry with their tradition of being in the city guard for generations. Lord Jenkins, though having his own title, considered it an honor to serve and encouraged his sons to do the same. He was, however, no fool when it came to profit and advancing his family name. After Allie had been kidnapped by pirates as a child, Amelio Kraden decided he wanted a more professional private security and asked his acquaintance Lord Jenkins for advice. Lord Jenkins promptly took over the entire security of the Kraden Estate. He still encouraged his sons to join the city guard but, after they had made a good impression, he allowed them to make choices of their own career. Graham, the oldest son, had decided to follow his father in the business of private security on the

The Kraden Job

Kraden Estate. Rumor had it that he more or less ran the private guard and his father was enjoying a semi-retirement on the estate grounds. This made Graham the perfect target for our scheme.

I frowned, pulling on a pair of gloves. "Why they want useless women, I'll never know."

"They aren't useless. They're just different," Allie corrected in a gentle tone.

"Dumb beauties," I muttered, feeling resentful.

She glared, but didn't respond. I smirked. "You're lucky you're the one who got kidnapped, aren't you? Got you out of living proper, pretty, and boring."

"Yes," she said, looking away from me, "I suppose."

Lord Stevens was not what I was expecting. I had run into a lot of smugglers in my youth, most were rugged, terrifying, and all were aggressive. One had threatened to take off my ear for snarking back at him about a shipment. To my mind mercenaries had pierced ears, tattoos, and anger management issues. They were fit, and half of them threw knives. The others shot at you, but not him. He was a gentleman's mercenary.

Lord Stevens smiled at me when he saw me disembark. He actually smiled. His shirt was pulled taut over his bulging belly. Rings on his fingers, but ears bare of metal. He had short hair that was showing gray, and a pin of local status on his chest. He wore the most impractical shoes I'd ever laid eyes on. They simply slipped onto his feet with no backing, an ornamental buckle lay on the side covered in gems, and high heels tacked on the back. I was vaguely horrified.

"Cassandra," he said, opening up his arms to me. I walked

Chapter Six

into the awkward embrace, feeling my face flame from embarrassment. "It's been too long." He smiled at me. I had to admit, with his twittering about the my voyage to the islands, it did sound as though he was the concerned uncle glad to see his niece for a long awaited visit. It was the first time I thought maybe we could pull this job off.

"The carriage is this way, my dear." The endearment was not welcome, but I figured I would need to get used to it. Allie had warned me the idle rich were fond of endearments.

I felt myself being escorted with a solid hand on the back of my spine. I had to resist the urge to punch him. I resented the causal contact, but people would be touching me more often now that I was a lady.

"You aren't quite used to dresses yet, are you?" he asked me after I'd climbed somewhat awkwardly into the carriage.

I shook my head. He chuckled. "When my old friend Maxwell said he was putting one of his best thieves inside the Kraden Estate, I couldn't help but be skeptical. I half expected a scarred up pirate with missing teeth. But you, well, you could entice Lord Kraden himself, couldn't you?"

I blushed feeling uncomfortable. "I highly doubt that." I slouched into my seat in the carriage. He scrutinized me. "How much did Maxwell tell you?"

Lord Stevens smiled a warm smile. He was a good actor, that one. "Enough. Maxwell is cautious but thorough. He's had his fair share of bad luck with heists."

My interest perked up at that. "Really?"

Lord Stevens looked at me for a moment: his face pleasant, but his eyes calculating. "I take it you haven't been with them long."

There were secrets under that response. I could sense it. I

shrugged. "Long enough."

"I have no doubt you believe that. I've known Maxwell for many years and he's always liked the idea of his own ship, not caring who he climbed over to get it."

I frowned. Captain Maxwell. I didn't like the sound of it. He often acted like the captain of our ship anyways. As the first mate he always seemed to have too much power on board. There were only two ways to move up to Captain and keep the same ship: death of the current captain or mutiny. "He certainly does seem ambitious."

"The smart ones often are," Lord Stevens said in a distant voice, before focusing on me with that smile again. "I trust, they've made you ready for the festivities."

"As much as one can on a ship, I suppose. They found me a dress for the festival."

"A dress?" he asked raising an eyebrow.

"Yes. It's really nice… bits of lace and stuff." I still hadn't mastered the art of speaking about my broadening femininity.

"Oh, my darling girl, one does not wear a dress to the festival. One wears a different dress every evening. And to be really noticed, you simply cannot have a simple one that has been bought and fitted. One made from scratch is the best for our purposes. We are, after all, trying to entice a man of some repute."

"We weren't aware," I said uncomfortably. I'd actually liked the dress that Allie have fitted for me. The prospect of sitting through more fittings and learning how to move and dance in various types of skirts didn't appeal to me.

"No matter. I have a woman," he said flippantly. "She shall see to it that all things are taken care of. After all, you are from the countryside and your customs are different there."

Chapter Six

I smiled. "Am I now?"

"Why, yes," he said with a large smile. He twisted a ring around his finger. "A bit more of a country girl than a city girl. From the upper echelons, of course, but an area a bit more isolated. So one simply cannot fault your lapses in high city manners."

"How convenient," I smirked. It seemed as though Lord Stevens really had thought things through and my trust in him grew slightly.

"Isn't it, though? I'm quite proud of that detail myself. I wasn't sure what to expect from you, so I gave us a bit of leeway with your lapses in manners. Ah, here we are. My home and, for the time being, yours," he said, moving his arm in a grand gesture towards the carriage window.

It was modest for a townhouse. Three stories squished among the other houses on the street rather than a free standing structure. All the windows had shutters and the paint looked new. The stairs were made of stone and a statue guarded the door. Compared to the other houses in the area it was grand, but still in a lower quarter of the city. Though he had money, this section was for middle class traders, not the upper-class. The side of the wall would be easy to scale but with little cover. The roof had spikes on it. High risk. I wouldn't be going for any joy runs on the roof tops here.

"I see your skepticism," he said, misinterpreting the glance. He shook his head when I reached for the doorknob, holding it open for me. I cringed. "It's the location I like. It's deep enough within the inner ring that it gets respect, but is old enough to have some secret entrances to the lower levels of town. It is nice to leave a place unseen every once in a while. I'm sure you're familiar with the concept. And the nobles like that I'm a business man and a house this low in town means I'm not trying to rise above my station. They accept me because while I bought my title I didn't try to encroach on their positions in the city. Though they're aware that I'm one of the wealthiest men in the city. I never do let them forget that. Try not to flaunt your power, my girl, but when you have it over others, don't let them forget it."

I nodded. The man may have been a bit of a cur, but he did hold some good advice. The inside of the building thoroughly surpassed the exterior. The walls were covered with pieces of art, sculptures stood in the halls. My heels clicked on stone floors. I could see what he meant about not letting people forget his wealth. If any of the nobles entered his home, they had no illusions that the man had more than enough money to burn. A woman came out of the kitchen, wiping her hands on her apron. His woman.

She was pretty. I suppose, it's cruel to say I was surprised, but I was. She was lean, and had a soft face. Doe brown eyes and shoulder length dark hair. Her dress fit her pleasantly, but not snug.

Lord Stevens leaned over my shoulder to whisper to me, "Too nice for me, I know. I bought her."

I felt a shiver run through me. Allie and I kept clear of the slave trade. It was not our idea of cargo. I was beginning to wonder what sort of man Maxwell had sent me in with. Perhaps one more like Maxwell himself. It was not a pleasant idea.

"Maxwell and your friends will be in the basement soon. They have to get out of port and reenter after they've changed the name of the vessel. Cassandra can't be linked to their ship in any way. You will not be seeing them much, I fear. Notes

Chapter Six

can be passed most likely once you're in the Kraden Estate, but I'm not entirely sure what you're up to, and I don't want you, any of you, gallivanting around the house the way you would on your ship. You need to get yourself endeared to the men of the Kraden Estate, and laxity at home won't provide the type of behavior we want from you." He smiled at me, a sort of predatory smile. I didn't like it.

I had dealt with sleazy men and mercenaries, thieves and assassins, but he was a new breed of criminal. One I hadn't seen much of. The polished criminal. The kind that had a permanent home and name, and would kill anyone who risked exposing them.

"My woman here will help you with all the arrangements," he said. "The men have brought your chest up to your room; she will help you figure out what is suitable and what we may need to have fixed up. Remember, the festival draws near."

~~~~~X~~~~~

The next few days passed in a blur," Airen said, rolling her shoulders and ignoring the pain. "I don't know what Lord Stevens was up to at the time. I'm sure he went around telling everyone that his niece was in town. His poor little niece, from the lowly countryside on the mainlands, who didn't know much of their superior customs in the glorious city. Stirring up interest was important. His theory was that I needed to be pitied and intriguing to catch the eye of anyone at the Kraden Estate."

Thom worked slowly on her leg. He kept his eyes on his work, which she found comforting. The calmness he exuded soothed her rather frayed nerves. She hoisted herself on her elbows. He looked at her with steady eyes.

"Have you heard this story before?"

He pulled a face.

"Part of it."

He nodded.

"Which version?"

He raised an eyebrow.

Airen smirked. "Never mind. In the end, Maxwell was right. The heist did make us legends, of a sort. There are so many versions of the tale of course. Separating fact from fiction is rarely the interest of most people, so the more fantastical the story the more widely it was told. I think one version has me scaling the wall in broad daylight as Maxwell fights off forty armed guards, and Allie breaks calmly into a vault. A bit more heroic than what really happened. Do you know what happened to Maxwell?"

He shook his head.

"No," she murmured, "I don't suppose many people do."

Thom cocked his head to the side. She ignored the implied question, and he huffed. She flinched, when he poked a little harder than necessary to dig out a splinter.

"Really? You had to do that?" she said, when he smirked. "Just be grateful I'm telling you any of this. I've heard the story a few times, when we were in taverns and people didn't recognize us. The two female pirates that robbed and crossed Amelio Kraden. But I've never told the story. I haven't even told Allie all of it. I'm not entirely sure why. Maybe I'm still a little mad at her. The real problem with this heist was that I wasn't ready for a ruse like that. Neither of us were really. We were used to heists that involved talking to people a few times at most. The emotional side of a heist like this was completely

Chapter Six

unknown to both of us. We hadn't ever dealt much with the target's emotions. That was our biggest mistake. Feelings are murder."

~~~~~X~~~~~

To be frank, I honestly didn't expect being a lady to be so much work. I barely left the house in the first few days. I was used to being stuck on a boat at sea, but you get some activity there. Fencing, running around, and cleaning the decks. There, I was like a caged bird. Lord Stevens had to teach me the newest dances. The ones Allie had taught me had all but died out in the society circles. Then there was how to sit properly, drink tea (a horrible drink if I may say so), how to choose a wine, and butter my bread. Some of the skills seemed more practical than others.

A seamstress came to the house to make my dresses for the festival. I can hang on a wall for over an hour waiting for a solider to leave his post, but standing in one spot and having someone prance around me with pins and lace drove me near mad. I almost smacked the gushing woman upside the head a few times. Before I knew it, his lady was helping me into the over cumbersome dress and shoes, gloves that went up to my elbows. At the time, I had considerably less scars than I do now. One of the perks of being an unknown is spending a lot less time in cells or captured. If they don't know who you are, you can be a messenger. It was certainly safer for me when people thought that Airen of the Marooned Isle was a man.

Before I knew it, the first day of the festival arrived. I was a nervous wreck on the carriage ride to the Kraden Estate. I've never been sea sick but I imagine the feeling being the

The Kraden Job

same. I'd spent the last week dancing around the living room, trying to remember the steps, spending so long in torturous high heels that I staggered in the evening when taking them off. I missed my boots and my knives. Going into a fortress without weapons wasn't sitting well with me. I was convinced that as soon as I left the safety of the carriage that the nobles would notice that I didn't belong, and I'd be shot on the spot.

You know, you hear about the Kraden Estate. Just the sheer size of the thing: big fortress walls, dozens of men standing guard along the perimeter. The fact that the walls are a sheer drop, nothing to grip on the whole thing. The Kradens spent a fortune getting rocks to fit just so, eliminating even the slightest chance of a scaling surface. I thought it had been exaggerated, but when I saw it, I was sure even I couldn't climb it. The idea of Allie and the Maxwell attempting to scale it was not comforting. I either needed to find an alternate way out of the complex after we robbed it or the plan would unravel fast.

As soon as Lord Stevens and I passed into the interior wall of the compound, I knew we'd taken on a bigger task than we could handle. The inside of the estate was a miniature city, with large lawns to walk on, fountains and hedge mazes, even housing for the servants and a gigantic building where the Kraden and Jenkins families lived. The structure was also home to their several ballrooms, parlors, and painting galleries. Allie had sketched out the grounds in a preliminary map weeks before, but her memories and basic sketches didn't match the size and complexity of the grounds in reality.

"Cassandra," Lord Stevens said to me in a serious voice. He never used my real name, even in private, so when he spoke sternly to me I knew he was still speaking to pirate me rather

Chapter Six

than his niece. "I need you to understand something before we go in. I have been in this game for a very long time, but I've never done anything quite like this. We're about to start playing games with some very dangerous people. If this turns sour, leaving the city won't be an option, it will be a necessity. I have worked for years to establish myself here. I do not want to have my prosperity and place in this town threatened because you let your pirate antics show through the feminine facade. I need us to be clear on that. You cannot fail in this."

"Thanks for the pep talk, Uncle," I said in a cold voice. "I do know how to do my job."

I didn't really know how to do it though, and almost lost control of my lady demeanor when the door of the carriage swung open and a servant extended his hand to help me down. I took his hand as gingerly as I could, suppressing the urge to push him aside, and stepped softly out of the carriage. Several heads turned my way. Being a newcomer was bound to get me more attention than I desired, but it was necessary. Attracting interest was one of the main reasons I was making my debut at the festival party thrown by Lord Kraden, rather than me attempting to run into the Jenkins boys in town.

Lord Stevens led me calmly into the main building in which the festivities would take place. Great columns swung up on either side of the stairwell. Tapestries hung from every wall, completely hiding the stone that built them up. Walking into the grand entrance was a spectacle. Below us hundreds of people talked and flitted around the floor in dance. An orchestra played off in the distance. Great tables were laid out with food. The hall was filled with tall windows, but with only two doors, the one we arrived through and a small wooden one in a corner, which I assumed led to a servant

The Kraden Job

hallway. I couldn't help but whistle under my breath.

Lord Stevens leaned close to me, "Enjoy the life of nobility while you can. It won't be long before you're back on that boat."

"I prefer the boat."

It was wonderful and terrifying and intimidating and beautiful. I could feel my heart race with anticipation, excitement, fear and joy all at the same time. I'd robbed rich men before, been into the homes of nobility, and on one memorable occasion made off with a duchess's dowry, but I'd never seen decadence on that scale before. My ankles wobbled on the way down the stairs, though no one seemed to be paying much mind to us. The great hall was so large, that people seldom looked to the entrance for new arrivals.

"Don't look so serious," Lord Stevens said under his breath, a smile of mirth plastered over his face. His tone of voice didn't match it. "You want to fit in here. Be shy, but excited."

"I'm trying," I muttered back. Feeling the incessant need to find a pillar to hide behind.

"Try harder," he hissed before bellowing out, "Deloris."

I dropped his arm as a woman came to greet him with a kiss on his cheek. "It has been too long," she twittered. There was self-importance there, in the way she swiveled her head to cast her gaze over those around her. She spoke a little too loudly, as though she wanted people to notice her in the crowd. Her eyes flickered on me for a moment; then she paused and stared. "And who is this delightful creature?" she asked, bringing the fan to her face and giving it a few waves. She was mimicking demure, though I would have put her age in her early fifties.

Lord Stevens turned to me with a look of pure joy radiating off of him. "This is my niece - Cassandra. She's come to visit

Chapter Six

me for a few months. Poor girl is from out in the countryside. Can you believe she's never seen a festival ball before?"

"I scarcely can," Deloris said, appraising me. Her head was held high, her chin elevated, so that she seemed to be looking down at me constantly even though she was shorter than me. She was trying too hard to copy the other noble ladies in the room, and her neck just seemed strained and tense. "You have a lovely dress, Cassandra."

"Thank you," I chocked over the words, feeling a blush flood my face.

"Why, it's true! She hasn't seen much society, has she? Poor dear." She pushed out her lip in mock pity.

"Don't poke fun, my dear Deloris. It isn't kind," Lord Stevens said, giving her a cheeky grin. It was all rather nauseating. "Cassandra, may I present Lady Deloris Jenkins, wife of Lord Kraden's very noble second in command."

Lord Stevens certainly didn't waste any time. It was a clever stroke I hadn't thought of. Endearing me to the mother, it certainly merited an invitation to meet the sons. I would begrudgingly have to give Maxwell some of that credit Allie believed him due. But for now, I supplied my very best curtsy, which Allie had deemed slightly above passable.

"Oh oh, none of that, my dear. I'm not so great as that," Lady Jenkins said, waving her fan off in embarrassment, but her cheeks were flushed with pleasure, her eyes sparkling with delight. I gave a nod. "Oh, Harold, she is perfectly humble, isn't she? Look at that innocent face, that shy stance. I simply must steal her from you."

I gave him a sharp glance. I didn't like the sound of that. He must have seen the panic in my face because he smiled. He actually smiled, the bastard.

The Kraden Job

"Oh, my dear Deloris," he said, leaning towards her speaking low with his eyes on me, them shining with mischief, "that was exactly my plan."

He was smart and crafty, but not exactly one to share his plans. This did not bode well for the trust between us. I made a mental note to get him back for the desertion later. Perhaps, I thought, I'd have too much wine and get sick in the fountain or make up an embarrassing story about my 'uncle' to share for Lady Jenkins's delight. The possibilities were endless. Lord Stevens touched my shoulder in a gentle, reassuring gesture that pushed me towards Lady Jenkins. Oh, he was good.

"Well then, dear," she smiled and held out a hand toward me, "why don't we leave your boring Uncle Harold and find men of more pleasurable company."

"Ah, Deloris, how you tease me," he said with a charming smile and she laughed, pulling me with her before I had the chance to object.

She guided me across the ballroom, holding my hand into the crock of her elbow, tugging me lightly along. She chose to wander in close to the dancers, bringing us in front of other guests. Eyes followed us as we moved across the room. Lady Jenkins with the new mysterious young woman. I could see their little brains turning over this development. They looked more like vultures than gentlefolk. It felt odd to be on the inside. Usually, I would observe them and the point was being invisible. Now the idea was to gain as much notice as flatteringly possible.

Lady Jenkins pranced me around the floor for a time, indulging in the attention it granted her, before taking me to a more secluded corner of the room. She smiled at me. I could see it behind her eyes, a similar look Allie had when she

Chapter Six

taught me how to walk in a dress. I was to become a project for her ladyship. She was going to make me fit into high society. She wanted to show off her own skills and abilities and what better way to do so than to polish a country girl into a gem of the party. That was a bit more attention than I was hoping to attract, but did mean one thing for certain. I was going to be introduced to her sons. And with some luck, I would somehow trick that first born boy into desiring me. Graham was following his father's footsteps as the head of the private guard on the Kraden Estate and we needed all the help we could get. After all, the security around the estate was more impressive the more I saw of it.

Guards were everywhere, dressed in finery to blend into the party, but you could tell who they were in the way they looked around, in their stance. Dress swords seemed common among much of the nobility. Some were for show; the ones on the old men with their large bellies and white beards, whose arms shook under the glass of wine they carried. Others were considerably more worn around the clasp. They had been drawn, many times, and recently. These men weren't just guards, they were on duty guards. At a party it seemed to be overkill to have more than ten filtering among the guests. Yet after the kidnapping of their daughter all those years ago, it made sense the Kradens got a bit paranoid about the security of their home. I'd imagine after Allie and I finished our business there, they've heightened security again.

Anyways, in our private corner of the ballroom I turned away from Lady Jenkins. I didn't want a lecture on etiquette and those eager eyes seemed a tad intrusive. I'd spent hours with Allie learning how to be proper and less time than I should have on my back story. I thought about inventing a brother or two as I watched the couples dance gracefully across the floor. I didn't know the steps. I was becoming glad that I was off with Lady Jenkins instead of near any young man who might be fool enough to ask me to dance.

The music enveloped me as I stood with Lady Jenkins. She smiled around the room. I felt odd and self-conscious. I'd heard bands play before in bars and taverns, a half drunk man on a banjo, but never a full scale orchestra: the beauty of the violin, the harshness of the drum, the slice of a bell. Like a sword clang in my skull. I stood mesmerized. It was fascinating, unlike anything I had heard before. I loved it.

"Cassandra." I heard vaguely over the swell of the music, choosing to ignore it for the crescendo of the string instruments. "Cassandra!"

"Hmm?" I asked, forcing myself back into the room. I paused seeing two young men standing with her: one stern looking and the other with a pleasant smile.

Lady Jenkins's smile was forced. It seemed I may have let my mind wander longer than I had assumed. Perhaps she'd said something important and I missed it, offending the need I'd already seen in her to appear important.

"Dear, are you quite alright?" she asked.

"Oh, yes," I said, blushing. "I was simply admiring the dance."

Her face brightened instantly. A shrewd look coming into her eyes. Part of me began to panic. Part of me realized it was probably a good thing.

"Do you enjoy dancing?" I caught the glance she cast at the men with her. This dance was something I didn't know. The plan was fragile, all about me fitting in. One second on the dance floor with me floundering and we were done for. Or at least, my ability to attract a suitor would be hindered by the

Chapter Six

sheer embarrassment I'd foist upon them at the undoubtedly mocking from the others.

"I-I am, however-" I started, thinking of some excuse that would be proper.

But Lady Jenkins had seen an opening and spoke to the stern man beside her, talking over me. "Graham, dear, you must honor our dear Miss Cassandra with a dance, as she likes them so."

Graham frowned. His eyebrows creased into a most displeased look. I hadn't seen a look like that since Maxwell stabbed a man who threatened not to pay us. Only in the knee, mind you, but the man was still pretty perturbed.

When Graham spoke, his voice was cold and distant. "I've told you, Mother, I'm working tonight."

It was true, the sword at his side looked quite scratched around the top of the scabbard. His fingers ticking at the handle, callouses covering his fingertips, a scar ran across the back of one hand. The head of Kraden's personal guard was a serious man and, judging by the quality of the metal, good at his job.

Lady Jenkins bristled, "I saw you dance with Miss Kraden. Was that for work too?"

I perked up at the name. A Jenkins boy with the Miss Kraden. That was worth looking into. My eyes scanned the crowd on reflex, I was curious to see just how much she looked like Allie. I'd heard of twins but never seen any before. Professionalism be damned, I wanted to get a comparative sketch.

"Mother," Graham hissed, his voice disapproving. He cast me a glance. "That is not appropriate to speak of in front of a person you barely know, especially one I haven't even been introduced to."

The Kraden Job

Lady Jenkins dismissed her son's rebuff. As though she hadn't heard this complaint for the first half, she only sought to rectify the second. "You're quite right. I've not introduced you yet."

Graham's jaw tightened, the restraint showing in his eyes. This intensity for propriety and his job didn't lend itself well to female manipulations. At least not to a novice in the art, such as myself.

"Miss Cassandra Stevens, these are two of my sons. The eldest, Graham, who heads the private guard for Lord Kraden's Estate." She drew herself up with pride. "My second is off at sea. A navy man. And well, this is Kristoph, my youngest," her tone was a tinge dismissive when she said it. Kristoph was dressed nicer than his brother, his buttons brighter, less creases in his jacket, and no sword hung from his belt.

Graham Jenkins took my hand somewhat begrudgingly and bowed over it. I inclined my head like a real proper lady. I tried to give a coy sort of glance and hoped I was doing it right. If I was doing it wrong, he didn't seem to notice. Didn't really seem to notice me at all. His eyes were scanning the room and something seemed to catch his eye. He gave a curt nod to his mother as he straightened before striding away, muttering a halfhearted excuse about patrolling the room. Kristoph smiled at me when I glanced after his brother. He took my hand without me noticing and gave it a squeeze. My eyes shot back to him.

"Miss Stevens," Kristoph said with a bow. He didn't hover like Graham had. I could feel the press of his lips through my glove. "I apologize for my brother's behavior. He can be rather serious about his work. Makes him rather dull, I'm afraid. I don't have such a problem. Please allow me the honor of a

Chapter Six

dance."

"That really isn't necessary, Mr. Jenkins," I said, wondering how I could possibly get the eye of the rather serious Graham.

"I insist," Kristoph said, not releasing my hand. His mother beamed at him. Clearly she seemed to think he'd done good. He tugged lightly on my hand, coaxing me out toward the ballroom floor. I followed him with a queasy sort of smile. The ladies swished around in their beautiful gowns, the men stood tall guiding them with graceful expertise. All beaming with excitement and joy. Quite a few tipsy smiles.

I knew it was inexplicably rude to refuse a dance from a nobleman. Lord Stevens had warned me about that, realizing that I might otherwise be tempted to bat away the hand of anyone inviting me to dance. He'd impressed upon me the graveness of the offense. I would be shunned by the other ladies, and in high society, if one does not have the company of ladies, one never amounts to much.

Thankfully, this dance I knew. Kristoph's hand came to rest on my waist ever so gently. My face burned. I'd only danced with Allie and reluctantly with Maxwell, who'd spent half the time laughing and only stopped after I punched him in the face. I'd been off balance in my dress and heels, but still broke his nose. He'd bled on my dress the next series of dances, but performed all of the steps without so much as a snicker. This dance, being in the hold of Kristoph Jenkins, was a completely different experience.

Kristoph pulled me through the first round of steps. Everything in me resisted being held by a stranger. I was tense. Too tense. Noticeably tense. In a way a girl shouldn't be when dancing with a handsome young man.

Kristoph's hand tightened for a moment on mine, the fabric

The Kraden Job

of our gloves sliding together felt odd, and I shifted my gaze upwards. He was staring at me. Just staring. Intensely. I lowered my eyes quickly, focusing on his chest. The corner of his shirt collar. Anywhere else.

I felt my cheeks burn hot. Kristoph chuckled, a light and pleasant sound. I could feel it. That proximity was foreign to me. Actually, that's wrong. It wasn't the proximity. I was used to cramped quarters and the closeness of picking a pocket. This was different. I had never been so close to anyone who looked at me like that before. Like I was there. Really there. Like I was a woman.

"You aren't accustomed to grand parties are you, Miss Stevens?" he asked.

"N-no. I'm afraid not," I choked out. Clearing my throat as subtly as possible. "I fear I'm out of my depth in such a grand place as this." I drew my hand down his shoulder, a motion to pull away and rejoin his mother at the edge of the dance floor.

"Nonsense," Kristoph said, his voice warm. His arm keeping me strongly in place. I could break the hold if I wanted to. Even while pretending to be a proper lady, I could break the hold. He was suggesting I stay, not forcing me to. Calm. I told myself. Be calm.

"I fear I'm not a good dance partner," I countered. The first time I'd put on a dress I felt like a fool. The second time, I began to wonder if men would see me as a woman. The third time, I hoped they would. Now that Kristoph was staring at me like men looked at Allie, I wanted to sink into the ground, or at least get a strong drink.

"I think you're doing just fine," his voice soothing, and his hands giving a slight pressure, a suggestion for me to stay there with him. We continued through the steps.

Chapter Six

I looked down at my feet but only for a moment. It was bad form. I could feel my dress frill against my leg as he spun me around the room. Allie had taught me my steps well. Being led was not easy for me.

"My mother seems to have taken a liking to you."

"A very sudden one, sir," I said trying to remain polite and calm. Above all calm. Calm was good.

"That is much her way. She takes a quick liking and hangs on," his arm tightened and a charming smile tinted his face. I wondered if the trait ran in the family. For our plan, I hoped so.

"She must be a very kind woman," I shifted my gaze away from him. Was forced to bring my eyes back. Rude to stare. Rude to look away.

"My mother is many things, kind is not on that list. There are some she doesn't like, but we'll make sure to keep you off that list." Kristoph leaned in and I could smell him. Actually smell him and didn't feel the urge to recoil. I wasn't used to people having such ready access to bathing facilities. Everyone smelled so clean. He was no exception. And when he leaned in, I could see his eyes. I blushed under the gaze. I think he enjoyed that. I began to wonder if this heist would be the one to kill me.

He pulled back into his full height, with something smug about his look. I relaxed. He looked away from me, eyes scanning the crowd. It gave me a moment to observe him. He had a strong jaw and a pleasant countenance. He smiled a lot. I always liked that about him.

"Ah," he said, swinging us back around in a circle, "there's the star of the party: Miss Kraden." He nodded his head off to one side. I followed his movement. I knew her instantly.

The Kraden Job

Allie had told me they were twins, but hearing and seeing are different things.

Seeing the spitting image of Allie standing in the center of a group of men, flirting, when I knew Allie was sitting down in Lord Stevens' basement, probably drinking a nice mug of rum, was odd to say the least. Her hair was blonder than Allie's. A life of luxury giving her the ability to bathe out in the sun. Walk out into the gardens whenever she pleased. Instead of locking herself into dark, dank rooms, cooking food or poison. This Miss Kraden was graceful, regal even, but mine was better.

"Miss Emily Kraden, the young lady of the house," Kristoph said, his voice a conspiratorial whisper. I kept my eyes on her, even though I felt his gaze move to my face.

"She looks lovely," I said. I scrutinized the group. Graham stood behind her, his eyes looking fiercely at the other men around her. Emily laughed and tossed her hair, seemingly blissfully unaware of the moody man behind her. I bet he had a hand on that well worn sword I'd seen earlier.

"She is, I suppose. Would you like an introduction? My family is well ingratiated with the Kradens. Truth be told, I think my brother means to marry her. My mother can't stand her, of course," he said casually.

If I had any doubts about Graham as a target this solidified them. I was not going to fight a Kraden girl for anything, especially not a man. If Emily was anything like Allie, I didn't stand a chance. With the middle son out to sea, it left Kristoph Jenkins as a key figure in our plan. Whom I miraculously had not bored or scared away yet. I lifted my eyes up to him. He smiled. We drifted across the floor. I followed him without question. I studied him with renewed interest.

Chapter Six

Kristoph had dark blue eyes. His lips quirked upward at the edges, a habit so ingrained, a frown would seem unnatural on him. I could feel his strength in his hand that had slid to my back, drawing me closer, and his agility in the movements of his arm under my palm. He knew sword work, of that I was certain. But he wasn't wearing a blade. So, not a member of the guard. His mother hadn't mentioned what he did. A man with no occupation could be dangerous. Idle rich men tended to make their job stealing the hearts of young ladies.

He was several inches taller than me and solid. His buttons were polished bright, his hair combed, but he didn't seem to be worried about it staying perfectly in place. There was a bit of recklessness to him. He seemed the type to fall for our damsel in distress routine. Someone who wanted to view himself as the hero. And he'd be a worthy opponent in a fight.

I guess I had what Allie called my calculating face on because he was scrutinizing me. "You're different, aren't you?"

"Excuse me?" I asked, snapping out of my analysis.

"You're different from the rest of the ladies here," Kristoph elaborated, casting a glance around the room.

Calm. Play it calm. Allie had told me many things about flirting as a distraction, mostly that I was bad at it. She'd told me if I started to flounder to act embarrassed, any self-respecting gentleman would try to save me from devolving into shame.

"Is it that obvious? How much I don't fit here? I know I look too much from the countryside to rival the city ladies." Which was true enough. Even though I'd spent the last few days inside Lord Stevens' house, I hadn't been able to fully get rid of my sun burned skin. I looked a bit rougher than most proper ladies would, even with the makeup outlining

The Kraden Job

my eyes.

Allie was convinced if we played up my eyes no one would notice the minor kicks and scars I'd gotten over the years. Access to mirrors was rather limited on ships, not that I cared much to look at myself anyway. But I've been told they were beautiful. My eyes. They were a pale sort of blue. Kristoph liked them blue. Of course, they aren't blue anymore.

Kristoph was staring at my eyes then, distracted. "No," he said, a little too quickly. "That's not what I meant at all. I just mean, you seem different." But he didn't seem to be able to elaborate on that feeling either.

I smiled. He'd been thrown off balance. I remembered Allie said that was a good thing. To her, throwing a man off balance pretty much guaranteed interest. "Men are as curious as cats and as persistent as puppies," Allie used to say, "Snag their interest and they will pursue you until you tell them to stop and sometimes, after that, they pursue you even more."

"You're beautiful," Kristoph said softly. As if it slipped out, a mistake, an accidental admission.

I stopped. Brain coming to a screeching halt. We were jarred out of the dance. Usually people exited the dance floor with more elegance. Thankfully, we were at the edge of the dance floor, so no one really paid us much heed.

Horrified by the compliment I drew back from him. He let me. Confusion was written all over his face. This was definitely breaking the rules of etiquette. "I'm—"

"I'm sorry," Kristoph said, though it sounded more like a question, unsure as to how exactly he had offended me. I simply nodded and retreated away from him. No one seemed to notice. No one, except Lord Stevens. He circled round me with a smile, but I could tell in his eyes, he wasn't pleased.

Chapter Six

"You left your dance partner," Lord Stevens said, handing me a glass of wine. I sipped it with a nod. "That was very rude." His voice was pleasant but there was an edge in it. A sharp one.

"I'm sorry," I mumbled.

"I've made an excuse for you to Lady Jenkins. She and I were having a pleasant talk whilst the two of you were dancing, which you were doing quite well until your little hiccup. Care to explain."

"Not really," I said, reeling from Kristop's gentle compliment. He'd said it like it was a causal fact, rather than a shocking observation. "So, what's this excuse then?'

"Low energy. You were so nervous before the festivities you didn't eat, nor barely slept," Lord Stevens said. "Your hunger had undoubtedly made you dizzy or fatigued."

"Undoubtedly," I took a sip of the wine, tried not to pull a face. Some of the finer things in life didn't take my fancy.

"You will have to apologize, you know," he said.

I nodded. I could feel my hands shaking. "I'm completely unqualified for this. This entire thing is madness."

Lord Stevens hand came to grasp my elbow. He squeezed hard. "Madness is what will happen if you disappear. This plan has been formed for quite some time. *You* are the key to it. We shall never have this opportunity again. You have been introduced as part of *my* family. If you don't go through with this and disappear then I'll have to answer for it. And I'd rather not," he said, tightening his grip. It hurt.

I spared the hand a glance. "The only reason you can do that is because I'm acting a lady."'

"I know."

"I'm not a lady."

The Kraden Job

"Yes, I'm well aware it's an act, my dear niece."

We glared at each other for a moment. His grip not loosening.

"We will talk about this later," I said, my voice cold.

He released me. We broke eye contact.

"So, that's Emily Kraden," I said to break the tension. Their young Miss Kraden seemed to have gathered a few more admirers. One being bold enough to hand her a flower of some sort, she took it and playfully batted his shoulder. Emily seemed giggly and silly. I wondered if Allie would have turned out that way too if she'd stayed in that world. Somehow I doubted it.

"Does she really look like your girl?" Lord Stevens hadn't seen Allie yet. True to Maxwell's word, we kept largely out of his way while at his home. He had, undoubtedly, dubious business to conduct and it had kept him quite busy.

"Yes. I don't like it."

Graham was still standing with Emily, a general look of disapproval on his face. "Is he her personal guard?"

"I didn't think so. To my understanding, he leads security for the whole estate. Though, he has seemed extra preoccupied with that girl of late. Naturally, as acting leader of the guard, I thought he'd go well for your plan. However," Lord Stevens trailed off.

"However?"

"You seem to have a new target."

Kristoph was talking with his mother. It looked like she was scolding him. Probably thought our abrupt end was somehow his fault. I could live with that. He looked over and our eyes met. He blushed, looking back to his mother, and a hand went to rub the back of his neck as she continued to lecture.

Chapter Six

"New target," I confirmed.

"Maxwell won't like this," he said, "though I think Kristoph isn't a bad target. He certainly is more pleasant than his brother. And much less serious. Though he holds no rank of his own."

I took a sip from my glass, looked around the room; the guards were more relaxed, a few of them had been into the wine themselves. Many of them looked at the women with lustful eyes. Some looked only at the decadently rich ones. Corruptible. Many of these guards were corruptible. That could be helpful. Fooling a man could take more time than it was worth, but buying a man was almost always worth the investment.

"I don't particularly care what Maxwell likes," I said, walking off. Lord Stevens was forced to follow me. I downed my glass and deposited it at a nearby table not breaking my stride.

"What are you doing? You must apologize to Kristoph."

"I'll apologize tomorrow. There is, after all, another dance here tomorrow night."

"Is that wise?"

I shrugged. "Perhaps not. I think he'll keep a day. He did, after all, take the time to mention to me that his brother's affections might be elsewhere. Which even I know is a break in decorum."

"But-"

"I'm tired, Uncle." I said with a smile. "After all, I didn't have anything to eat before the festivities."

Lord Stevens grumbled some, went to fetch the carriage. I examined the layout more on the way out of the festival. Big hallways flowed out before the entrance, there were pillars that stood tall and far apart. It would be difficult to sneak

The Kraden Job

around once inside the premises. I looked up, pretending to examine the murals on the walls, happy to discover that the archways that held the roof were high, but still looked accessible. It would take some tricky moves, but I was confident I could move up there. Before I could figure out a way to scamper up the pillars our carriage arrived and I was pulled away. I tried to smile at the footman, but it may have come off more grimace than joy. On the second time through the estate gates the security seemed even tougher than when we'd come in.

"This is a nightmare," I said pulling my hair pin out, once we were safely out of the complex and on the city roads. The hair fell in my face and I reached for the ribbon I usually kept on my wrist, but it was just a soft glove. I sighed and leaned back in the carriage. "This much security. Even if I get in, I have no idea how everyone else will get in. Never mind getting everyone out again." I rubbed my eyes.

"Don't do that. You'll smudge the makeup. And slouching is not becoming of a young lady."

"Fine," I snapped. I took a deep breath, then reclined into the back of the carriage, crossing my legs. "So, let's talk about what happened tonight."

Lord Stevens nodded; a stern and serious expression on his face. "You made some progress. Lady Jenkins liked you considerably. She seems to think that she can actually polish you up to make you a proper city lady. And you may have made some progress with the youngest Jenkins, that foolish Kristoph boy. However—"

"That's not what I'm talking about. And you know it," I rubbed my elbow through the fabric of my dress reminding him of his grip there earlier. "You've taken advantage of the

Chapter Six

act I'm playing, which has given me more confidence in you really. You truly are a mercenary. And while I appreciate that fact, if you ever try to take advantage of my feigned weakness again, you can be sure you'll regret it."

"Will I?" Lord Stevens had a smile on his face. I twirled the hair pin between my fingers, agitation rising in his belief of control over me. "The way I see it, I'm doing the lot of you a great favor, and if you aren't going to be cooperative with me, I don't see how I'm supposed to keep my end without a particular amount of persuasion. You're aware I could say I was press-ganged into this at any moment and have it be believed. I know many people of note in this city, and several prominent officials I've spent years collecting in my pocket. In fact, I don't think you understand the position you're in."

I smiled. "Lord Stevens, I do believe you're threatening me."

He smiled back, it was sharp and confident. "You misunderstand, my dear. Think of it as a simple pleasant warning of your place."

My smile fell and I was across the carriage in a flash. Pinning down one of his hands, and bringing tip of my hairpin to the soft tissue of his neck.

"I believe," I said, "you're the one that misunderstands."

Lord Stevens gasped when I pushed the pin harder but careful not to break skin. His eyes were wide and I sensed real fear in him for the first time.

"You haven't met *our* Miss Kraden yet, I know. So, let me explain something to you. She is a very curious woman who likes to experiment with poisons. She's also rather protective of me. Doesn't want me to go anywhere unarmed. Allie likes to make sure I leave the ship with something she's cooked up at all times. The one in this hair pin for example, well, it would kill you quite quickly," I paused, letting him sweat for a moment with that little pin so close to breaking skin. "At least that's what I think it does. Or, it's the tortuously painful but leaves you alive batch. I can't quite remember."

Neither was true of course. At that time Allie hadn't quite developed into the poisoner she is today. Not only in the range of skills but also in the fact that she was still restrainedly moral. True, she cooked up some draughts here and there, but most put someone to sleep or gave them a decidedly uncomfortable bowel for a day or so. Allie's youthful projects were more to distract or get someone out of the way quickly, but not to cause actual harm. She'd made a brew once that left one of the crew curled up on the deck rocking in agony, but that had been a terrible mistake on her part. She'd wanted to chuck it over the railing but Maxwell had convinced her to keep it stowed in a back cupboard of the kitchen. Of course, I wasn't about to tell Lord Stevens any of that.

He sputtered, arching his neck as far away from me as my grip would allow. "Get that thing away from me."

I smiled at him. Sweetly. "Do we have an understanding?"

"Yes," Lord Stevens gasped out. "You've made your point."

"Good," I said, flowing back to my side of the carriage. "I won't make it again."

Chapter Seven

Airen could feel her mind sinking. She tried to focus on the thought of Lord Stevens, his repulsive manners. His thick fingers and gaudy rings, but it was too late. In her mind she was already there, with the soft touch of Kristoph's hand running across her cheek, coaxing her to look up at him. A strong, soft hand pushing back her hair when they stood close together, sharing space and air. But now Airen became acutely aware of the rough calloused hands and warm touch on her legs.

She cleared her throat and eyed Thom. He was done with the splinter extraction. He was done with the cleaning. Now he was simply sitting there. Listening. His hands resting lightly on her shin. She looked at his hands and raised an eyebrow.

Thom jerked his hands up and gave a sheepish smile. As though even he hadn't realized they were there. Airen clicked her tongue. She hadn't meant to share that much. She'd actually shared emotions and the thought made her feel vaguely ill. At least Thom wouldn't tell anyone about it.

"You done?" she asked, a bit brusquer than necessary.

He started at the tone, but looked over her shins for a moment before nodding. Swiping up the last bit of blood leaking down the side of her calf. He put the tweezers back on the tray and was reaching for the cloth and ointment, but she swung her feet off him and reached for her boots. Cramming her feet into them she winced. Thom tugged at the sleeve of her shirt, but she needed to get out of this room. Get away from her memories and focus on the present.

"Best go talk to Nick before he starts smashing things. Don't know how many times we need to replace those charts before he cuts it out."

Thom gave her a look.

She paused for a moment, clearing her throat, before shuffling around to get her coat. "Right, well, I'm off, so thanks for the de-splintering. Time to go deal with the good ole captain."

Airen made a bit of a show of putting her coat on and buckling on a sword. It was no secret that Nick often went into his moods because he and Airen were on the outs. Their arguments were hard, their fights vicious. Sometimes she needed to be reminded she was not captain of the ship, on occasion, by the point of a sword. It'd motivated Allie to work on a quick acting range of sleeping draughts, just for some quiet on long journeys out to sea. Airen was known for loving the adventure and the freedom of being at sea, but didn't handle being cooped up that well.

Right now, she had bigger problems. Explaining Jenkins would not be pleasant. She tried to think of what to say as

Chapter Seven

she tramped down the corridor of the ship. She sighed and looked down at her boots. She wouldn't be able to do this alone. Turning she and made her way towards the galley.

Seeing Allie in the kitchen always amused Airen. The young woman would bustle about, especially when on edge. Checking pots and tending to the fire. Picking at her nails and twirling the bit of hair that fell out of the messy bun that was kept in place by a metal stick. All the while wearing an extravagant dress, glittering jewels, and heels that clicked against the wooden planks of the ship.

Allie seemed particularly irritated at this moment, going more in circles than accomplishing a task. Airen leaned against the doorway with a smile. Allie drove her nuts sometimes, but without Allie, Airen wouldn't have been nearly as successful. Or had nearly as much fun.

"Are you making muffins?" Airen asked after a moment.

Allie startled, dropping a spoon to the floor. Allie whirled around on her, slamming the mixing bowl on a counter. "What's the rule, Airen?"

"Don't creep up in the kitchen."

"And where are we?"

"Well, you're in the kitchen. I'm decidedly outside it by a few inches," Airen said with a smug grin.

Allie glared at her. "What do you want?" she snapped.

Airen kicked the doorway with the back of her heel, scanned the room for a moment. The stacks of pots and pans. The glistening glass of the poison cupboard in the far corner. "I'm going to talk to Nick."

"And?" Allie asked, grabbing a cloth and dabbing at the batter specks that had gotten onto her dark blue ruffle of a dress.

"Well I ... you know..." Airen faltered.

Allie looked at her for a moment before going back to the batter. She turned her back to Airen and resolutely started to focus on work at the counter.

"Oh, come on, Allie. Don't make me explain Jenkins by myself."

"If I were you, I'd avoid explaining as much as possible," she said, her voice crisp.

"Come on, Allie," Airen pleaded.

"I'm annoyed with you."

"I can tell..."

"Mmmhmmm." Allie was practically whipping the batter now.

"Come on," Airen bit her lip, anxiously working it between her teeth. She tapped a rattle of notes on the door-frame with her fingers. Allie continued with her mixing. Airen sighed. "You know that I'm not good with the words thing most of the time. I'll probably say something stupid."

"That is rather likely."

"What you want him to do? Shoot me or something?"

Allie snorted, "It'd probably only be in the leg." She turned her back to Airen, and the thief knew she was losing this argument. She watched Allie mix for a moment, consult her books, splash a few drops from a vial. It was time to resort to drastic measures.

"I'll buy you berries. Real fresh berries. Melt in your mouth glorious berries." The mixing stopped.

Allie looked back at her, squinting her eyes to seek deception. Airen held her ground. "You jerk. You know how much I love berries."

"A variety." Airen smiled, braving a step into the kitchen.

Chapter Seven

Allie tapped the spoon on the bowl, thoughtfully. "Three baskets full?"

"Be reasonable Allie, you know fresh fruit isn't cheap. Two smaller baskets."

"Medium sized," Allie countered.

Airen let out a bit of a huff, that was going to cost a fair amount of coin. "Deal. Two medium sized baskets of berries that you can enjoy to your heart's content. Now tell the youngster to mind the food. Nick's mood won't improve if dinner's burnt."

Allie nodded, and Airen wandered off in the hall to try and calm her nerves. The anxious energy balling up in her. Usually, she'd just fight someone to take the edge off, usually that'd be Nick, a bit of sword play would calm her right down. But this wasn't a fighting time. This was a time for talking, and talking wasn't exactly her friend, not when it came to something like this.

Allie eyed her as she came into the hall. "Are you biting your nails?"

"Shut up," she said, digging her hands into her pocket, wincing when it jerked her ribs.

Allie gave her a skeptical look, but dropped it. "If I'm going to help you with this, you're actually going to have to listen to me. Not just jump to your own way of doing things. And so help me, if you take a swing at Nick, we're done. You get that?"

Airen nodded, pulling a face somewhere between a sheepish grin and a grimace. "No hitting the Captain, got it."

Allie almost felt bad for her. "Just don't go mentioning any particulars. There are many ways to ruin someone's life, Nick doesn't need to know how we did it. Let him assume we

The Kraden Job

robbed Jenkins or something."

"Yeah, okay. Makes sense."

"And whatever you do, don't mention anything about the two of you together. It's enough of a mess already, we don't need to go throw in male pride and jealousy."

"Not an idiot, Allie."

"Sometimes I wonder," Allie said in a low voice, but there was affection buried in it. She stopped abruptly in front of the door to Nick's quarters, giving Airen a serious look. "I know this is going to be hard for you, but if he wants to change the plan, just go with it."

"But-"

"No! No arguing. You zip it. You're talking part in this meeting is minimal, you understand?"

Airen smiled after a moment. "All that authority, Allie, reminds me of old times."

"Just remember that you enjoy it during this," she mumbled knocking on Nick's door.

"Come in," his voice rang through the door. It was sharp. They took a deep breath, exchanging a look before heading in. Nick's feet were thrown up on his desk in the center of the room. It made the room seem smaller, but he had placed the workspace in front of the only window in the room. Nick was holding up a map, scrutinizing it. Airen could see the stress in his disheveled hair, sticking up at odd angles from him, pushing it out of his face. He looked at them silently; neither of them did anything to break the silence, so he placed the map on the table. The parchment barely escaping the candle's flame. Allie looked ready to scold him, but his attention was rooted on Airen, displeasure evident on his face. In one of their many unspoken agreements, fights were

Chapter Seven

punctuated with a break period of at least two days before seeking resolution, or, more commonly, simply ignoring the incident had ever happened.

"On your feet, I see," he said, putting a hand on a stack of papers and sliding them into a desk drawer.

"So it would seem," Airen said, "Oddly having the splinters out, doesn't feel much better."

"How are the ribs?"

"You pushed me pretty hard off that wall, but I've had worse."

He nodded, before grabbing a flask off his desk, he kept his eyes intent on her face as he tossed it at her. Airen grunted, but caught it, taking a sip, and plunking down in a chair. Allie repressed the urge to scream. The two of them drove her nuts, despite the massive blow out that was possible, a little verbal pinch, and a wince of pain, and the disagreement was over. It was more convenient than the alternative, but made her want to smack Airen in the back of the head for getting involved with Nick in the first place.

Allie slid into the plusher of the remaining chairs, smoothing out her dress and adjusting the stick in her hair before speaking. "We've come to discuss our plans. Since circumstances suggest we may need to make a change or two."

"You don't say," he replied. Airen tossed him the flask and he drank deep. He sighed. "I've spent half a year planning this. It was a fantastic project. Mostly because it ended in a truly nice pay out that no one would ever come after. And all that planning, gone, in a flash. Because of your little visiting friend."

Airen shifted in her seat, but Allie gave her a warning gesture and Airen held her tongue letting Allie speak. "He's not our friend, Nick, and there was no way to know he was looking

The Kraden Job

for us. You figured the man would let it go. Let's not get petty and deal with the task at hand, shall we?"

"Allie's right. We'll deal with Jenkins in time, but first things first. Are the papers as good as promised?" Airen asked, throwing a look at the documents piled high on the corner of the desk.

Nick smiled. "A piece of luck this. They're better. No wonder the place had more traps than a labyrinth. I think we can double our original asking price. I almost feel sorry for the bastard. Almost want to set fire to these on principal," he said, nudging the tall stack with his foot.

"Good thing you're a man of questionable morals instead of integrity," Airen said.

"Very true."

Allie cut in with a roll of the eyes. "But now we need to make some minor adjustments."

"Right," Nick said, "the Commander Jenkins problem."

"Ah yes, him," Airen said, becoming increasingly interested in the tips of her nails.

"The self-proclaimed pirate hunter that the two of you managed to piss off. The one who prefers the noose to the jail cell."

"That'd be the one," Airen cleared her throat.

"So, now he'll be after us."

"Yes, I suppose so." Allie said calmly.

"Just tell me he doesn't know what we are up to," Nick said, giving Airen a hard stare. Her face was unreadable, which usually meant she was trying very hard to hide something.

"About that. He might have a vague inclination," Airen said.

Nick pinched the bridge of his nose and took a steadying breath. "Airen, I'm starting to feel as though we shouldn't have

Chapter Seven

come back for you."

"Stop being so dramatic, Nick," Allie said. "You must simply look at some of the good aspects of this."

"There are good aspects? Please, Allison, enlighten me," Nick said sarcastically.

"For one, we didn't see another ship at the fortress, which means Commander Jenkins was there without his crew. They're probably set to come back fro him in a few days, which gives us a bit of a head start. Besides, he can't get himself out of that cell Airen locked him into and the mercenaries won't be standing for a least a day, let alone letting him out anytime soon."

"So, the poison was strong then?"

"Very," Airen said, casting a glance at Allie in her proper posture, fine dress and jewels, not a hair out of place. "She tested it on me."

"I *may* have over done it," Allie said, waving a hand dismissively at her friend.

Nick looked between the two. "Right… So we have a head start. That'll be good for all of a few days. The problem is that my entire plan dealt with King Dupont being compliant, which would be easier if he had no idea we're coming. Jenkins is a Commander of Lord Kraden's forces. It is part of his job to warn his Majesty and it's likely we can't beat a messenger with the winds we've been having lately. Even an extra day or two might not be enough to beat a real messenger. If the King knows we're coming then he'll post extra guards and sentries. The castle will be hard to breach and getting close to the King will be near impossible."

Allie reclined in her chair, folding her hands in her lap. "I already told you that Commander Jenkins won't go to the

The Kraden Job

Kng. Not at first anyways."

"And why not? It's his job. Duty and honor, that's what those solider types are always going on about."

"Because he's not a moron, Nick." Allie rolled her eyes.

"I'm afraid I don't follow," he said, through gritted teeth.

"He won't risk a chance at nabbing Airen, even if that means not reporting her plans properly. Mention of blackmail or pirates would send the castle into chaos and he'd lose his chance of getting Airen into a trap. He already knows where she's headed, so it is in his best interest to set a trap for her rather than getting the castle completely blocked off for her entry."

"You must have pissed him off pretty good if Allie thinks he'd risk his reputation for you," Nick said, looking Airen over with a mixture of distrust, envy, and curiosity.

"What can I say? I'm a fucking genius," she muttered darkly.

"Anyways," Allie said, shooting her sulking partner a glare, "instead of building a plan around avoiding Commander Jenkins the best thing to do is to view him as part of the plan. He might even help us avoid King Dupont becoming properly prepared. All the Commander knows is that we're probably going to blackmail the King, but he doesn't know when or where we might strike. If we get him to follow us then we might be able to turn his pursuit into our advantage."

"Yes, because baiting pirate hunters ends so well," Nick said.

"Will you just listen to me, Nick? It's not that complicated. If we lure Jenkins in, make him think he's figured out where we're headed then he'll show up at the King's summer palace. The King will know he is there, someone of the Commander's rank cannot be ignored, and then the King won't feel it necessary to bring more guards into the palace once we

Chapter Seven

show up. After all, why should he be alarmed? He will have Commander Jenkins, the pirate hunter at his disposal. Commander Jenkins thinks he's helping the King by being there, even if he doesn't tell the King of our plan, and the King thinks he has someone who can protect him from pirates, without him having to tell the Commander that we're blackmailing him."

"And why," Nick asked dryly, "would King Dupont not tell Jenkins exactly what we are up to?"

Allie tutted. Annoyed at being interrupted and at what she seemed to find a silly question. Though Airen had been thinking the same thing. "Remember Captain, I know more about upper society politics than you ever shall know. But if you want me to draw it out for you, it's simple really. The King can't risk news of these documents and the break in at the stronghold getting back to Amelio Kraden. No matter how far the Commander may travel he is still in the employ of Amelio Kraden, who many of the nobles have seen as power hungry for decades. King Dupont can't risk being seen as weak nor can he let it be known what is in these papers. If he tells Commander Jenkins he risks the nobility knowing a stronghold can be robbed and what is in the documents. After all, the King won't know that the Commander found us near a stronghold. I'm positive he'll come up with some other reason for why he is visiting the King's summer palace, but he'll have to mention it is on the behest of Lord Kraden, which will keep the King wary to divulge too much."

Nick nodded, thinking over this plan. "Alright, so, we use the snobs paranoid nature to keep them from actually helping each other. But we'll still have to deal with the fact that Jenkins will be in the palace at all. And even if he doesn't tell the King

The Kraden Job

what we're up to he is bound to have his crew with him."

To that Allie waved a hand dismissively. "He won't be able to find a reason to bring his whole crew to the palace. Most of them will be on the ship. Besides, we'll set some bait. Instead of Airen picking up the loot, as we had planned, someone else will speak with King Dupont and Airen will run as a diversion. The Commander and his men will be so busy chasing her that we'll be free to collect from our dear old monarch and disappear."

"It is an appealing plan. Especially in that we don't need to alter much, but how do we lead our new friend?"

"We'll just need a few Airen spottings littered throughout the well known dubious haunts. Pirates gossip. He'll investigate them and figure it out. He's a smart man after all, otherwise he wouldn't have found her in the first place. Though investigating the sightings will slow him down a bit too, which will be a small mercy. We do still need to arrive at the palace first."

"Okay," he said, sliding his feet off his desk. His boots thudding hard onto the planks. "Okay. So that takes care of Jenkins and gives his King an illusion of security. That is possible. But we need a new route into the castle."

"True," Allie agreed. "I think its best changing from the obvious, so walking in through the front doors disguised is no longer an option."

"Airen, how's your climbing?" Nick said, turning to the brooding woman for the first time since Allie began to speak.

She wasn't entirely thrilled where this plan was going, but she'd asked Allie to take charge and, despite Allie's protests, the woman came up with good plans on the quick. Airen sighed and dragged a hand down her face. "Not sure. It's fine

Chapter Seven

I suppose. Though Clarissa spent the better part of a week hitting me with a big stick."

"You saying you can't do it?" Nick asked in a challenging tone.

"No, Nick. I'm saying I won't be sturdy. I didn't plan on climbing a tower in the near future. If I had I wouldn't have let you push me off a bloody wall."

"Airen, are you telling me you can or cannot do it?"

"I'm telling you we'll need rope. And maybe a rig," she said, running a hand over her cheeks, across her chin and back again.

"You would need to climb up unaided to hook up the rope anyways…" Nick said slowly, "And a rig? I've never known you to use a rig."

"I am aware of that, Nicolas. The rope and rig would be for Allie. She's not exactly an expert climber."

"Wait a minute," Allie chuckled, the panic edging into her voice, "since when am I scaling walls?"

"Since we need another person to collect," Airen said, "and because the only thing more intimidating than a female pirate with the sheen climbing up your walls to blackmail you is a noblewoman-looking pirate with an unruffled dress magically appearing in your chambers to blackmail you."

"No," Allie scoffed, "I couldn't possibly."

Nick put his hands together. "Oh, you will. Airen's right. You show up there all graceful and in one of those huge dresses and it'll look like you can reach him anywhere." Allie made to object, but he raised a hand. "It's as good as done. It was, after all, your suggestion that we use Airen as bait. Someone needs to take her place. There's only one thing left that I need to know, Airen. When the time comes do you really think

The Kraden Job

Jenkins will chase you rather than protect the King?"

Airen fixed him with a stare. "Absolutely."

The two stared at each other in a fierce match, before Nick lowered his gaze to the maps on his table. "Fine. I won't argue with you over it. I'll let you play with your little friend. Meanwhile, Allie will work on the ropes we got on board the ship, and Airen, you're confined to the ship until the night of the heist."

"Ah-ha-ha," Airen laughed, until she saw the hard lines on the captain's face. "Nick, I can't stay on a ship for three weeks. I'll go stir crazy."

"Be that as it may, I won't have you putting us in more risk by going into the ports. You, my dear, are always one hand of cards away from the prison."

"It wouldn't hold me long," Airen protested.

"That's not the point. We want to entice Jenkins with rumors, not make you catchable. This is not a discussion. You will do as I say. That goes for both of you," Nick said, voice hard, and looking between the two female pirates. Airen gave Allie a 'I hope you're happy now' sort of look. "Now, Airen, go get yourself patched up. You're bleeding all over my chair."

"Yes, Captain," she said, shoving herself out of the chair and giving him a half-hearted sort of salute. The door slammed behind her.

"You know, keeping her cooped up is likely to cause trouble," Allie said, straightening out the ruffles of her dress skirt as she stood.

Nick turned back to his maps. "Airen is willful, but she'll do as she's told. She respects a strong captain and my orders will be followed."

"Maybe," Allie said, leafing through the papers on his desk,

Chapter Seven

noting how he moved to lean against the drawer where he'd shoved a bundle of pages upon their arrival. "Maybe that sort of authority works on that silly wife of yours, but Airen isn't her. She's a pirate. And *no one* has figured out how to keep her locked up yet."

Nick gave her a cold look. "Is that all, Allie?"

"At the moment, yes," Allie said, refusing to be cowed by his glare. She'd faced off with scarier men than Captain Nick in her time. "Just remember, Captain, you don't control female pirates, you strike deals with them." And with that she swept elegantly out of the room.

By the time Allie caught up with Airen, she was in a heated argument with Thom. Allie shook her head watching her stubborn friend argue with the silent man who only made gestures and was getting extremely miffed by the fact that Airen threw up her hands and smiled, "Sorry Thom. Can't understand you 'til you use words." He glared at Airen. Allie approached them calmly.

"Problems?" she asked kindly. Thom looked at her with exasperated eyes, indicating towards Airen, holding up a basket of bindings and what looked to be rags and water. He then waved his hands around and opened his mouth in a mock silent scream, then indicated the floor.

"Seriously, Allie, that make any sense to you?" Airen said in a baffled tone but she was barely hiding a smirk when Thom glared at her again.

"I'm fairly sure he wants to finish his job and patch you up," Allie said rolling her eyes.

"He already fixed me up. I'm fine."

"Don't be difficult, Airen."

"I'm fine, Allie," Airen said in an agitated tone.

"You have a cut on your collarbone."

"It's minor. I can barely feel it. I hardly need a medic for that."

Allie sighed. "Why are you always so difficult?" she muttered, reaching out and hitting Airen soundly in the ribs. The wind rushed out of her in one solid breath and she fell against the wall, glaring at Allie, who stood there calmly in her elegant gown, as though she hadn't just caused shooting pain to radiate out of Airen.

"Yes," Allie said nicely, "Clearly, you're fine. Thom, drag her back to her quarters if you have to and patch her up. And don't fuss at me, Airen, I'm quite frankly not in the mood for that right now. But I'll come by later, with wine and cards," she said as she watched Thom pull Airen to her feet, none too gently. "Or rum?"

"Rum would be nice," Airen muttered darkly.

Allie smiled. "Wonderful. And I'll expect to see the coin for my berries when I get there," she called, disappearing down the hall.

"And they call her a lady," Airen said, pushing off of Thom and grabbing her side. "Think I taught her to hit too hard. And don't you dare try to drag me anywhere."

Thom held up a hand and backed away.

"Fine. Let's get this done then. Check to see if I broke anything will you? Ribs are giving me a mighty twinge."

He nodded and followed her back into her cabin. She groaned, easing herself back onto the bed. She pulled at the belt that kept her sword on, flinging it across the room, and wincing with the effort. "Don't start," she said, when Thom let out a tutting noise at her action. He pulled a chair next to her as she lay down and held up the water, she shook her

Chapter Seven

head. "Check for broken ribs first. If they aren't broken I can clean the cuts myself. I got beat, I'm not a child."

Thom rose an eyebrow, but reached for her side anyways. She hissed softly when he started to apply pressure, but then suddenly, it stopped. He looked at her expectantly, his hands hovering.

"You're waiting for more of that story, aren't you?"

He nodded.

"Well, tough," she said, closing her eyes. They flew open a second later, blinding pain radiating from her torso. "Curses Thom! What kind of medic are you?"

He gave her a wicked smile, pulling down the top of his shirt to reveal a smooth brand under his collarbone.

"Right. A pirate. Hilarious. Fine, have it your way," she said, sinking back onto her pillow.

Chapter Eight

I got back to my room in Lord Stevens house to a truly unpleasant surprise. Maxwell was reclining on my bed as though he planned to use the room whenever I wasn't there. His boots were still on, leaving dirt on the base of my bed sheets, his arms folded over his chest, and his eyes closed contently, as Allie ran her fingers through his hair, her body curled beside him. I cleared my throat, tossing my gloves as loud as one can onto the vanity. Allie shot up, a blush erupting onto her face. Maxwell opened his eyes slowly, regarded me for a moment before closing them again, and sinking further into my pillow.

"How'd we do?" he asked, shifting his shoulders to become more comfortable.

"We thought you'd be out longer," Allie said, grabbing one of my pillows and hugging it to her chest. I stared at her, and she looked with intense interest out the window. I couldn't tell what she'd been hoping for but alone time with Maxwell

Chapter Eight

seemed high on her priorities. It was nearly impossible to be truly alone on the ship, so the base at Lord Stevens offered the possibility of something beyond stolen moments.

"Right," I said after a moment, plunking myself down in front of the vanity mirror, looking at their reflections on my bed as I spoke. "We did alright, but I'm changing focus to another of the Jenkins boys"

Maxwell cracked open an eye and glared at me, I stared at the reflection with challenge. "Why?" his voice had an edge to it that I distrusted. It was a tone I'd expect from a captain, but he wasn't our captain, and I never appreciated him acting like it.

"Because," I said with irritation, struggling to pull the pins out of my hair, "the eldest Jenkins is taken. And as we're on a bit of tight schedule already. I figure that's more trouble than its worth."

That got him to sit up. "By who? We were told he's unattached."

"Well, I suppose he is officially unattached, but he's deeply interested in someone."

"And you don't think you can compete with the girl to win him over," his voice was smug. Allie gave him a scolding look. I just kept pulling out pins, listening to them ting as they hit the hand mirror.

I kept my voice neutral. "It's Emily Kraden. I think it best not to meddle with that."

Allie dropped the pillow. "Emily is in love with a guard? My Dad isn't going to like that. He'll think he's beneath her... not that it...matters," she trailed off under the face Maxwell was making at her.

"Well, I wouldn't know if it's mutual interest, but Graham's near enough in love with her. Which is enough for me. Especially, when there are easier solutions to our problem than for me to try to take attention from Emily Kraden."

Maxwell flexed his fingers against his forearm. That didn't bode well. It was one of his nervous ticks before he struck a crew member for idiotcy. His voice was barely restrained when he spoke, "Need I remind you that Graham Jenkins is head of the private gaurd in the Kraden Estate?"

"I am aware."

"And as such, would be in the best position to get you a place in that household without a large amount of scrutiny."

"I know."

"And that getting into that estate without invitation is essentially impossible."

"Thank you for the pressure, Maxwell."

"So, please explain to me, how exactly you plan to get a lodging in the estate without him granting you one?"

I could feel a headache coming on. "There are *three* Jenkins sons, and whilst the youngest doesn't hold such an impressive title or the same level of access within the estate, he could get me invited into the estate with little problem. Their mother has already taken a liking to me, she has no daughters of her own, and might decide to protect me like one. Especially, if any of her sons show a romantic interest in me."

They exchanged a glance. Their surprise was rather insulting. I tore at the tangles in my hair, cursing under my breath when I made no progress.

"Well... that's quite good, isn't it?" asked Allie. Maxwell only grumbled. She tittered at him, abandoning him to come behind me tugging my hand away from my hair and picking up the comb. She set to working the knots out lightly. Physical

Chapter Eight

contact was a habit she'd developed when she was set to interrogate me about something.

"Sooo?" she asked in an excited tone.

"What?" I asked, feeling nothing but grumpy. Her face was eager. I knew what she wanted. She stared at me expectantly through the reflection, I shifted my glance to Maxwell who had gone back to reclining on my bed.

"Max, could you give us a bit?" she asked, giving him a winning smile over her shoulder.

He raised an eyebrow. "If it has to do with the plan, I'm sure-"

"That I will tell you pertinent information later," Allie said, cutting him off. "After all, a girl must have her secrets." Her tone was practically dripping with sweetness. They shared a glance that I didn't care to interpret, but he extracted himself from the bed and headed towards the door.

"Oh, before you go," I said, "thought you'd want to know that Lord Stevens was talking on turning. I took the liberty of reminding him of his place. You might want to keep a closer eye on your friend."

A grunt was my only response. Allie could barely contain her impatience, she shifted while waiting for him to close the door behind him. She tugged at my hair restlessly, until his footsteps faded on the stairs. She pulled over my other chair, sat down next to me, and again started working on my hair, but keeping an eye of my face.

"Tell me. Tell me. Did you have fun? Did you dance? Please, tell me you danced. Was it grand? I bet it was grand." Her hands were calm and relaxed, but her voice swayed out in excitement.

I felt bad. This was more her thing. If the circumstances had been different, she'd be telling the whole crew about her great success. How she'd made a grand entrance, causing everyone in the room to stop and notice her. How the two brothers would have stumbled over themselves to gain a moment of her attention. She'd be invited to stay in that house within a day if the circumstances allowed, whereas I was shooting for a month, if I was lucky. But as it stood, the crew had me. A poor substitute, who only wanted to whine to her mentor.

I sighed "I wouldn't call it grand. I don't think it went very well."

"Really?" she frowned, her hands beginning a braid down my neck. "Tell me about it."

"Fine," I groaned, slouching in the chair, the fabric of the dress cutting into my sides. I'm still convinced that proper dresses are impossible to get comfortable in, "but I'm not happy about it."

Allie raised an eyebrow. I knew that I was being difficult, partially because I was still in that stupid dress. I just felt so out of place. I pulled at the necklace, dropping it heavy on the desk, Allie scowled. The earrings followed. Her scowl deepened.

"I don't belong there. And I'm sure they know," I said, having removed the finery.

Allie tensed for a moment. "Why do you think they know?"

"I don't know, Allie. They aren't complete idiots. The Kradens are already paranoid. The security is insanity. And everyone stared at me," I said rubbing at my face, smudging the make up all over the place.

"Don't worry over that. They were staring at you because you're new. And you really do look quite lovely. Mysterious beauty enters the room. Who wouldn't look?" she asked, her

Chapter Eight

voice gentle as her hands that fastened the braid in my hair.

I blushed. "I'm not. You'd have made a grand impression, but me... Wolf in sheep's clothing. I look ridiculous."

"You do not. So stop whining and stop with the self-pity," she snapped. She sat up, tilting her head back in a way to show off her fine features. I marveled at the quick change in presence, there certainly was an air about her. "I thought you were professional enough to not worry about such things."

I opened my mouth to protest, but knew she was right, then struggled not to sulk. She let it go, with a knowing smile. She always used to know when she'd won. She pushed her advantage, gathering up a few clothes and water to help remove my make-up.

"So tell me about your handsome man."

"Kristoph Jenkins? He's hardly mine," I scoffed at the very idea.

"In time," she said calmly, "What's this Kristoph like?"

"Tall."

She laughed. "That's the first thing you think of? Tall? Only you..."

"I wouldn't want to fight him," I said in all seriousness, relaxing into her care. There was no way I could beat Kristoph in a fair fight. Not that I was often inclined to fight fair.

Her hands froze. "You think you'll have to?" Her voice sounded sad. I opened my eyes to see her face had gone serious.

"Maybe," I sighed, picking at my nails. "This goes badly I might have to kill him."

Allie cringed. She knew killing was part of the pirate life, but she had a strong urge to avoid it. That always reminded me that she'd once been a noble. Thrown into our world, not

The Kraden Job

a born pirate. At the time, she was naïve enough to think that a pirate could survive without killing. We had managed to avoid any killing since we were kids, but I held no such optimism that it would last much longer. Blood unnerved her too. At one point, our captain had hoped to make her a healer because she was good with mixing remedies, but the sight of blood made her ill. She'd only patch me up if it was real bad, and no one else was around.

At that moment, she looked serious. Serious and distressed. From the fun of fancy parties and pretty dresses to the reality of dead men at her feet. Because if it went bad and he died from her plan then that soul would be knocking on her door one cold evening. That forlorn face made me feel all kinds of guilty. So I said the first thing I could think of to cheer her up.

"But, uh…he was nice. Really."

"Yeah?" Allie looked a little less queasy.

"Yeah."

"He dance with you?"

I could feel my cheeks heat up. She smiled a wicked smile. I cleared my throat. "Yes, we danced."

"You think he's handsome," she accused.

"I didn't say that. I mean, he's not bad looking. He puts a lot of effort into it. Really leans into that finery and polished buttons look. Stop looking at me like that."

"You think he's handsome." She was practically beaming at me. She just looked at me eagerly. Waiting.

"Fine. He's handsome."

Allie practically cackled as she began removing the rouge from my cheeks. "How was the dance? Was it nice?'

"I guess. I don't know. It was different than dancing on the

Chapter Eight

ship."

"Better?"

I thought of him smiling at me, the look in his eyes as he moved me confidently around the floor. The way his hand held me close but not tightly. I turned to her suddenly. "I don't want to worry you, but I'm so unqualified for this. I'm not ready. I'm really not. I'm not trying to be modest. It's too much for me. I 'bout near had a heart attack when he kissed my hand."

Allie stopped short. "He kissed your hand?"

"Yeah, and it made me feel all… well it made me…"

She put a hand on my shoulder, causing me to look at her. "No, no, but he actually kissed your hand?"

"I already said that," I said, confused by the urgency in her voice.

"Kissed it?"

"Yes."

"Not fake kiss but really-"

"Yes, for fucks sake, he actually kissed my hand. Or my glove, rather, since calluses and nobility are a no-go."

"Huh," she said, sinking into the chair and giving me an appraising look. "You're doing better than I thought," she muttered.

"Thanks for the confidence…. But, uh, what did I do?"

"I'm not sure, but you must have done something. He's not supposed to actually kiss your hand. Rather sort of hover over your knuckles."

I turned thoughtful. "His brother hovered."

"Actually, kissing isn't proper, strictly speaking, unless he knew you much better than a basic introduction. That was rather presumptuous of him."

The Kraden Job

"Did I do something wrong then? By not noticing?" I asked my voice going small.

"No. I mean, I don't think so. If anything, he probably found it encouraging. No reaction is better than a slap in the face."

"That is true." I knew that from very painful firsthand experience.

"Did he do anything else odd?"

"I don't know. I didn't know that was weird. Nobles are strange," I said, exasperated.

She only nodded. "What happened after the kiss?"

"We danced."

"Did you talk?"

"A bit. I wasn't very good at it. The talking thing."

"I'm sure it was fine," she said dismissively. "Then what?"

"I left."

Allie looked dumbstruck. "But why? It sounds as though he was interested in you."

I shifted. The truth was that I had panicked. My first time out in society, and I found the world of proper ladies scarier than the prospect of falling between two buildings in a narrow alley. The truth was that the attention made me sick to my stomach and excited at the same time. The truth was that I wasn't exactly manipulating Kristoph, just being my baffled self, and he found that endearing.

"Oh," I said, feigning calm, "I was just taking your advice to leave myself a mystery."

"Good going," she smiled a secretive smile. "You're learning quite quickly."

I looked away. I wouldn't tell her it was a complete accident. Actually the more I think about it, the more I realize on that aspect, they all gave me way too much credit. I was

Chapter Eight

never a very good seducer. It wasn't my amazing skill at tricking Jenkins that got me into that estate. Maxwell and Allie had planned for months, going over what they thought might be every possible scenario. Turns out, there were a few possibilities they didn't think of.

The thing about embedded heists is that a lot of it comes down to luck. I hadn't entirely realized it at the time. Little heists are all about planning. Get in and then get out. Every detail worked out to avoid getting caught. But the big ones there are too many variables. Most of that comes to luck.

What we're doing now with the King and these papers, I'm not sure Nick knows exactly what he's doing. Not that he can't plan a heist of this level, but rather that I'm not sure he understands what it really means to do what we're doing. The fact that anarchy is a possible outcome doesn't seem to bother him in the slightest. Course pirates aren't known to think on the consequences much. As far as we're concerned, you finish a job and disappear. Off to the sea. Off to freedom. Don't get me wrong, I tend to see it like that in too, but it's a bit different with the Jenkins… disaster. After all, in its own way, it's been stretching on for years. Mostly because he hates me. Not that I blame him.

But, at the time, I was hardly thinking about that. I had more pressing matters, than what might happen in the next few years.

Looking back, the next evening was a turning point for all of us. Me, Allie, Jenkins, even Maxwell and the crew. It had started like most evenings in that we were in Lord Stevens's home. Allie, Maxwell, Lord Stevens and I were having dinner. Allie said she arranged it to make sure I knew how to be a proper dinner guest with the correct table manners, but part

The Kraden Job

of me always thought she did it so that she and Maxwell could have dinner together in a grand setting, as though they too were living in the upper echelons of society for the duration of the job.

"Have you thought on how you shall apologize to Mr. Jenkins and, undoubtedly, Deloris for your rude exit yesterday eve?" Lord Stevens asked.

I shrugged, flipping my knife around idly between bites, "I'll think of something. How hard can it be?"

"Hard," Allie cut in, "you need to make sure they aren't offended without acting as though their opinions are overly important to you. If you end up simpering then, no matter the fact he is third born, Kristoph is likely to lose some interest. And will you stop twirling your knife! Ladies certainly have no desire or knowledge on how to handle a blade in that way."

I rolled my eyes but placed the knife down gently. "Can't I just act all pathetic and as though I was tired from their extravagance?"

Maxwell laughed loudly but both Allie and Lord Stevens fixed me with a look of extreme unamusement. "You know, that might well work," Maxwell said, drinking deeply from his wine. Lord Stevens glared at him in a displeased sort of way. "These nobles like to think they are above the common folk and even if you're from noble stock, you're country born. To them you're barely better than an illiterate farmer."

"And what would you know of such things?" Lord Stevens asked.

"More than you'd think," Maxwell said, motioning forward Shane who was lurking large and imposing in the doorway. Shane was one of the larger men from that crew, unruly with a cruel streak. He came forward into the room and handed

Chapter Eight

Maxwell a sealed envelope, hovering next to his chair until Lord Stevens cleared his throat. Maxwell looked critically at Lord Stevens for a moment before dismissing Shane with a wave of the hand. Shortly after we heard the serving girl let out a small shriek and Shane's loud laughter there was the thunderous steps as he made his way into the basement.

"I don't like that man," Lord Stevens said.

"Not many do," Maxwell replied, not looking up from the letter he was reading.

"I don't want him in my house."

"This again?"

"Yes, Max, this again. I'm taking a great risk allowing you to stay in my home. Helping you with this -"

"Will be highly lucrative."

Allie tried to soothe them by changing the subject, "What news did he bring you, Max?"

"Nothing for you to worry about," Maxwell said, tucking the paper into his inside coat pocket. "The usual concerns from our captain, but I have it all in hand."

Allie frowned. She didn't like to be kept out of the loop ever, but especially not on this heist. However, before she could seek to interrogate him further Lord Stevens brought up the argument about pirates flittering in and out of his house. I left the table as the two men continued to debate the necessities of it all and whether the majority of the crew should be relocated to one of Lord Stevens other properties.

A little later that evening, Allie found me making conversation with my reflection, because as much as I hated to admit it, Lord Stevens was right, I would have to apologize to Kristoph, and, most likely, to his mother.

"What in the world are you doing?" she asked, coming up

The Kraden Job

behind me.

"Getting ready," I muttered, sweeping on some eye shadow.

"I'm just going to help you with that," she said, reaching to take it from my hands. My stubbornness rejected it.

"Allie, stop! I can do it."

She watched me for a second. I tried to cover up the scar near my chin. She tittered, but I continued on. She sighed. I ignored her. She sighed again, louder. I focused.

"Airen, you look liked a paid woman!"

"Or you could help me." I tossed the make-up down and grabbed a towel, wiping viciously at my face.

"Stop that! You're going to rub it raw." She snatched it from my hand and made me face her. "Now, pay attention," she said, smoothing the makeup off. "How are you going to do this without me?'

"I'll have to think of something," I said, closing my eyes, feeling the brush slither across my lids. "Maybe you can write me down some hints."

"I probably should. Being beautiful is not your strong suit," she laughed.

"Thanks."

"No, I just meant ... well, you're much more interested in sneaking around corridors than dresses."

I sighed. "Sorry. I'm just nervous about tonight. I have to apologize for leaving early. You know I'm not great with apologies. What do I even say?"

"You'll be fine. Just elaborate on Lord Stevens excuse. They're proper folk. They won't want to seem like they are prying into affairs that don't concern them. The hard part is getting near to your dear Kristoph in the first place. I know, you'd just like to settle it straight out, but do not approach

Chapter Eight

him. Ladies must be patient and coy."

"I'm patient."

She moved to my neck and collar bone. I'd had a rather unfortunate incident with a stained glass window not five months before. Some of the scars were still shiny white. "Not always. Not when it comes to conversations. You know, it'd be really helpful if you didn't fight with Max every time he tried to go over the plan."

"He annoys me."

Allie let out an exasperated sigh. "I'm glad this plan doesn't require you to get Kristoph to propose to you to get you into that estate."

"He wouldn't… no man would… I mean…. I'm not really the marrying type." I cracked an eye open to see if she was mocking me. She was simply smiling.

"Perhaps. I think this Kristoph might like you very much, if you give him a chance. Remember, you have to be nice. When you announce that Lord Stevens is going away on business in three weeks and would take you with him, we need Kristoph to be desperate to keep you around and find you a spot in that estate."

I snorted. "Desperate."

"You laugh, but don't let people fool you, men can be twice as crazy as women when they are in love, or think they are."

I laughed, mostly because I was uncomfortable. Allie had been pursued by several men by the age of seventeen, some more attractive or pleasing than others. I hadn't even flirted yet. The pressure was almost overbearing. I was sure everyone could see it, or feel it. My lack of knowledge was a large suffocating presence. To my surprise Allie seemed not to notice this blaring flaw at all. She simply continued to

The Kraden Job

help me get ready. She tightened my dress, laced my shoes, and shuffled me down the stairs to a waiting Lord Stevens, who didn't notice my anxiety either. Nor did anyone in the ballroom that night.

Despite my frayed nerves, I couldn't help but notice that not much had changed from the night before. There were the same people, the same music, the same foods, and the same conversations. A world like that seemed horribly boring, and within ten minutes, I wished I could have snuck out with Maxwell, Shane, and Stout, though I normally couldn't stand them. They were all going to the peasant festival in the city. They had spoken of fire breathers and tumblers, fattening treats and fiery drinks. There were masks and cloaks, archery contests and knives for sale. Instead, I was stuck with the twirling butterflies. It was better than Allie's fate of waiting alone at the house, but to me, not by much.

I walked around the room admiring the dancers and trying to think of a way to apologize. Lying was a strong suit of mine, being apologetic was not. I kept an eye out for Kristoph, but didn't spot him. Lord Stevens had gone to talk business with some guards. Despite his complaints of Maxwell's plans interfering in his business, his minor smuggling operations and bribery schemes hadn't seemed to slow down.

I found myself in front of the table lined with cakes and wine. Typical. Pretending to be interested in the flowers, I wondered if it would be unladylike to eat the biggest pastry by myself. Suddenly, I felt someone come up close behind me. Sure that it was Kristoph, I smiled and turned around. However, I was surprised to see a tall young man with blonde hair smiling at me. He was wearing a worn uniform. His boots had also seen many miles. The sword on his belt had

Chapter Eight

been heavily used, but the top of it had a new tassel tied on. So shiny, he had surely put it on that night or the night before. There were no scars on his hands, and he didn't seem much older than myself, which classified him as a dressed up patrol solider, enjoying the festivities, but from his coat being fully buttoned and the sword belt slung above it, he was on duty at the party, rather than attending as a guest.

"Hello," he said, his smile was too large, like he knew he wasn't supposed to talk to me without being introduced, but he was doing it anyways.

"Hi," I returned cautiously.

"You're Lord Stevens's niece from the country."

I smiled. "I am."

"Us country folk don't need all those proper introductions. Ceremony can be so bothersome," he said easily, as though I would find no reason to argue that statement

"Can it?" I asked, mostly because I was unsure what to say. This was not something I had planned for.

"I saw you here yesterday," he grinned cheekily.

"Did you?"

"You were with Lady Jenkins."

"Yes."

"And danced with her son, Kristoph."

"Yes," I eyed him warily. He was up to something, but I wasn't sure what.

"How did you find him?"

"Pardon me?"

"At dancing. I hear, he is quite talented. He's always been a big fan of parties," he said with a knowing look.

"He was a fine dancer. I'm sorry, who are you exactly?"

"Jonathan," Kristoph said from behind me. I hadn't noticed

him approach, which concerned me. The shadow of him had appeared over my shoulder, my heart sped up. I wondered if people I dealt with felt like this when I suddenly dropped in behind them.

If anything, Jonathan's smile widened. "Kristoph. How're you doing this evening, my fine friend?"

"Fairly well. And yourself?"

"Well, I was just making conversation with young Miss—-" he paused.

"Miss Cassandra Stevens," Kristoph said, his voice a pleasant rumble. "The lady had graced me with a dance and then disappeared from sight."

"A crafty one then," Jonathan said, smiling at his friend, "Though she was kind enough to say that you're quite a nice dance partner."

I felt my cheeks heat up. It wouldn't have been proper for me to object.

Kristoph moved to the side of us so he could see my face. He smirked, but turned to his friend. "You're in the Kraden Estate guard rotation again?"

"Only for the ball," Jonathan said, patting his sword, pride in his eyes. "Then it's back to the city with me. You know, this man is the best swordsman that I know," he said to me in a conspiratorial voice. "But for some reason, he isn't in the city guard."

"Not this again," Kristoph groaned. "I'm not that good."

"Ah, he protests. Don't let him fool you, I've never been so clearly bested by a blade," his bare hands bouncing off the hilt of his sword.

"Just because I can beat you, doesn't mean I'm any good."

Jonathan grabbed at his chest. "I'm wounded. Words sharp

Chapter Eight

as your blade, my friend."

"Jonathan, give it up will you? It's a ball. People come to dance, not talk of fighting."

"Some people," Jonathan muttered. He sighed. "I suppose, I should know better. Dear Kristoph, he prefers his parties to sword fights."

"Not one for heroics?" I asked. They fell silent, not sure what to make of that. Jonathan looked uncomfortable. Kristoph gave him a look, it was not a good one.

"I think, he prefers gallantry in fine clothes. But I have no doubt he'd rise to the occasion of heroics," Jonathan chuckled, but the noise was weak.

"Oh, would he now?"

"Certainly," he said, but the assessment was evident in his eyes. He wasn't entirely sure. "Kristoph's a strong fighter. He's often helping us out."

I smiled, amusement leaking into it. Doubt playing in my mind, but I could use this to my advantage. I turned, gave Kristoph an appraising look. "So, I suppose even though you aren't a guard, you must go on patrols all the time?"

Kristoph tugged on his gloves and cleared his throat. "Well I—-"

"Of course he does," Jonathan said, throwing an arm over Kristoph's shoulder. He had one of those lying smiles that I was all too familiar with.

I bit the inside of my lip to keep the smile from creeping onto it. Jonathan looked between us. Clearly, his job to make his friend sound more enticing wasn't working out as planned. Not that I needed any convincing. He was my only option. The fact that he wanted to impress me was a good sign though.

"Well, you know, Kristoph already promised to go on the

The Kraden Job

rounds for the next three weeks with us soldiers," he clamped down on Kristoph's shoulder, who opened his mouth to speak, but closed it, when Jonathan gave a squeeze.

"Of course," he said, after a moment, an uneasy look on his face. "I wouldn't dream of leaving my friend in a lurch. I may not be a guard, but when I can I like to help keep order."

"That's wonderful," I said, a smile on my face. "There is something rather comforting about a guard with a sword."

Jonathan chuckled. "I like her. Miss Cassandra, possibly you can convince him to wear the uniform."

"I can certainly try," I said, my eyes subtly scanning over Kristoph's body.

Kristoph cleared his throat. "Well, I rather think I've had enough of your conspiring. I'd much rather convince the fair lady to a dance." His face lit up as I blushed, taking his extended hand. He led me out onto the floor and I thought I heard Jonathan chuckle behind me.

"Sorry about him. Johnathan has always been a character, but a true friend," Kristoph said, swinging me round to begin the dance.

"He does seem a bit strange."

He smiled at that. I let him carry me through the steps. We glided across the floor in silence. Couples smiling at us as we passed by. Graham was standing behind Miss Kraden in the corner again. Lord Stevens was deep in conversation with a woman much too young for him.

"You disappeared last night."

I turned quickly. The voice had come low and close to my ear. He had that smile again, the mischievous one that he got whenever I blushed.

"Yes, Mr. Jenkins, I did," I said, fighting to keep my tone

Chapter Eight

under control. "I fear the extravagance of the ball rather wore me out. I'm not used to such excitements. I have a rather delicate constitution," I said, with a secret smile lingering under my cheeks at the absurdity of it all.

"Calling me, Kristoph, will be just fine."

"Right," I said.

"Don't they call people by their first name out in the country?"

Good question, I thought. "Yes, they do. I'm not quite accustomed to the finer points of the city. My father always warned me to be on my best behavior in society."

"Stick with my mother, and you'll be tutored before you know it. She wants to have tea with you on Thursday. She told me to mention it, if I saw you before she did. She gets so sad after the festivities are over." He paused, to study my face. I realized a little too late, I should have shown sympathy. "Would you like to join us?"

"I would like that very much ... Kristoph." I said the last bit softly and his smile widened.

"As would I."

"Will that not interfere with your guard shift around the city?"

"I think that I could step away long enough to escort you through Lord Kraden's Estate. It's rather beautiful. I'd love to give you a full tour."

I was torn between smacking him, as I could imagine how forward that was and what it might entail, or giving him a sarcastic remark, so I laughed. Softly mind you, but still. He chuckled with me and a few couples turned to look at us severely.

"I hope you don't find it too forward, Miss Cassandra, but I must say you surprise me."

"How so?"

"You don't react the way I anticipate. Most ladies don't find humor in such statements."

I smiled this time, my heart speeding up. "I suppose most city ladies don't have the same humor as us country girls."

"Perhaps that is it," he agreed, thought he eyed me with a skepticism for a while longer.

"Kristoph," a voice called out. His mother stood near us. Her body swaying slightly. Perhaps Lady Jenkins had been enjoying the wine a little bit too much. "You didn't tell me you'd seen Miss Cassandra," she said as we drew close to her.

He sighed, "I only just found her myself, Mother."

"Hoping to hide her away for yourself, I see," she said sternly, but there was a mirthful glint in her eye. "Dear, go get us something to drink, will you?"

He looked hesitantly between us, before excusing himself. She smiled sweetly. I watched him walk away. Strong shoulders filling out his coat as he moved with an even stride. He had good spacial awareness. I really didn't want to fight him. His mother misinterpreted the glance.

"Yes. Kristoph is quite the handsome young man, isn't he?"

"Yes," I said absentmindedly.

"Oh," she tittered, "a lady in high society does not admit such thoughts. Especially to the mother of the man. Unless they are engaged, of course."

"I apologize, Lady Jenkins, I meant no offense."

"Nor I, dear, just trying to teach you the way of things here. It must have been hard on you. All those years taking care of your little sisters after your mother died," she said, her voice wavering in sympathy.

Chapter Eight

"Yes," I said confused by this new layer of my tale. It seemed Lord Stevens has been working on creating much sympathy behind my back. "That was hard."

"Lord Stevens has told me only some of your troubles. It seems only right that I take you under my wing. A young woman needs a mother in high society."

"That would be very kind of you," I said, each word coming out halted.

She didn't seem to notice. She linked her arm in mine. "Now, tell me, has my son invited you to tea or has he decided to try and hide you off all to himself? He can be a bit persistent, that boy. Tell me if he's showering unwanted attention."

"Oh no. He isn't … that is to say… it isn't… really unwanted…" I trailed off.

Lady Jenkins smiled as though she'd won a victory. I just felt like an idiot.

Chapter Nine

"How are your ribs?" Allie eyed her friend over the hand of cards. Airen ignored her and poured more rum into her cup. "They all say that Thom is a great medic. I haven't been injured enough for a medic in a long time, so I wasn't sure how'd you be. I mean, it's been a few days."

"What is it, Allie?" Airen took a sip of her drink, looking at Allie over the cup. "And the ribs are feeling much better."

"Good, about the ribs. I just want to make sure you aren't angry. You've been really quiet lately."

"There's a lot on my mind."

"Airen, you can talk to me about it," Allie prodded, putting her cards on the table.

"I give up," she tossed down the cards.

"Oh, Airen, what ever is wrong we can-"

"The card game, Allie. I had bad cards," she smiled, throwing her boots up on the bed despite Allie's glare. "And you can

Chapter Nine

stop the fragile concerned thing."

Allie sighed. "Sorry, I thought my execution was getting off beat with such things I'm a bit out of practice."

"Nah," Airen said, filling Allie's glass of wine. "You're still great. So what's bothering you?"

"Well, you do seem a bit distant lately. Spending more time in your room. You haven't once climbed up into the crow's nest, or started a fight with any of the crew. They're worried about you."

Airen laughed, dealing the cards. "Allie, a wall, I got shoved off a fucking wall, and then the mercenaries threw a few good hits in. Why does everyone seem to forget that?"

"Since the last time you got shot you bounced back quicker. Besides, I'm worried about you," Allie said. "Actually worried. Not fake concerned, like when you got pinched for stealing that cloak."

"Yes, the help with that one was fantastic, by the way."

"I charmed the jailer into giving me the key, didn't I?" she asked, pushing back a strand of hair that fell into her face.

"After three days," Airen smirked, her yellow eyes shining.

"How would you learn otherwise? That cloak was hardly worth twenty coins and you tried to steal it," she tittered, laying down her hand of cards. "This is a good set, right?"

"Don't look all innocent. Remember who taught you to play cards."

Allie laughed. It was full and honest. "It's been a while since I played though."

"Liar," Airen said good-naturedly. She fiddled with the edges of her own cards on the table, before pouring Allie some more to drink. "I've been thinking about the Jenkins thing a lot."

The Kraden Job

"What?"

"That's why I've been distant. I've been thinking about the Kraden job and Jenkins a lot. I, uh, started telling Thom about it."

"Why?" Allie asked, confused in the abrupt shift of topic.

Airen took a long drink. "I don't know. Because he can't tell anyone else. And he won't judge me."

"I wouldn't judge…okay, so, maybe I would; stop looking at me like that! But you could have talked to me about it."

"True," Airen said, shuffling the deck.

Allie reclined back in her chair, swirling the wine. "Do you want to talk about it?"

"Stop being so regal, will you?" Airen laughed, flicking a card at her face, but if fluttered harmlessly towards the door. "Our run now just has me thinking about facing him again. This plan is more solid than the one we had then, but somehow, I still don't think it will run smoothly."

"Jenkins is a bit of a wild card. Who would have guessed that he would have risen so high, or turned so brutal?" She stopped when she saw the look in Airen's yellow eyes. Guilt, she wasn't used to seeing that in Airen. "But you know what, I still can't believe you agreed to stay on the ship. The great Airen-Yellow-Eyes brought down by her little captain."

"Shut up," Airen scowled at her. "You got me trapped into that."

"And you have me going up in a rig! You know I hate heights."

"It'll be good for you. And Nick needs a boost to think he's got control every once in a while."

"He must have yelled pretty loud for you to agree in the end to stay aboard the ship."

Chapter Nine

Airen shrugged, a smirk forming on her lips. "There are other methods besides yelling."

Allie rolled her eyes. "You two are the worst couple ever. And I really didn't need to know that."

"We aren't a couple," Airen mumbled.

"Right," Allie said after a moment. "His lovely wife, who doesn't know anything about you I suppose."

"I haven't asked." Airen bit the tip of her nail, it made a sharp click. "I doubt he's going to bring it up now. We're only in port for two days. Besides, she thinks she married a respectable sailor. Not a pirate. "

"So you're both lying to her?"

"Never met her, so wouldn't say I am. Come on Allie, we're pirates, hardly respectable."

Allie stood abruptly, finicking with her dress. "I think I'll go into town. After all, who knows when I can buy supplies again."

"That's very true," Airen said with reluctance to being left behind.

"Do you need anything from town?"

Airen shuffled the abandoned cards. "I'll be fine." She waited until Allie had left, before lifting her shirt to look at her stomach. She swore.

The right side of her hip was covered in deep yellow and purple bruises. She touched it lightly, the flesh jumped when she poked it. She winced. She poked it harder and groaned. The mercenaries had been more brutal than expected. Yet she almost welcomed the distraction. Ever since she'd told Thom about Kristoph Jenkins, she couldn't get the man out of her head. She couldn't stop thinking about that second night at the dance, where he'd held her close and snuck flowers off a

The Kraden Job

table to tuck them into her hair. His sharp blue eyes staring down at her with a look she now knew to be admiration. The expression had been so different from the cold one that looked at her when she locked that cell. The ice in his voice calling after her.

Airen looked at the rum on the table. She sighed, getting up, and made her way to the kitchen in search of some comfort food, and maybe a vial of the pain elixir Allie had been working on. She was surprised to find Thom sitting on one of the counters munching contently on a muffin.

"Allie poisons those on occasion," Airen said. He regarded the muffin for a moment before shrugging. As he tore into his second one, she rifled through Allie's vials as carefully as possible, the woman always knew when something was out of place. "Why Allie can't brew more pain reliever, I'll never know. Half of this is quarter done poisons, and this one is only experimental at best. I rather think she got herself with it a few years ago." She shuddered looking back at Thom. "Nasty stuff. Why'd you stay behind anyways?"

He ducked his head a bit, but pointed. Airen blinked. "Because of me?"

He nodded, then pointed to his ear.

"Head? I didn't get a head injury, Thom. Not that I'm aware of anyways."

Thom shook his head pointed to her, brought his hand to his mouth as he made the motion of words pouring out, then pointed to her and his ear again.

Airen smiled, but felt vaguely bashful. "You want to listen to more of the story." He smiled. "Why not? I can't stop thinking about it anyways. Okay, where was I. Oh, the third night of the festivities. Well, I guess we can skip forward a bit." Thom

Chapter Nine

scowled. "It really wasn't that interesting. I actually skipped the ball the third night, much to Lord Stevens displeasure. I retreated to more familiar ground. Trousers, a deep hood, and a smile. I went to the festival with Allie instead of the high society party at the estate. This was after Maxwell had given us a stern lecture on not doing anything stupid. We'd covered our hair in charcoal, so we wouldn't be recognized. It'd have been bad if the town folk had seen Emily Kraden running around that part of town. With me no less. It would certainly have raised unwanted questions. It was fun to sneak about. We felt like kids again, with the deep hoods and long cloaks that we'd tripped over a few times. Though, oddly, I don't remember much of the festival itself.

~~~~~X~~~~~

I do, however, remember having a vicious hangover the next day. A splitting headache, swollen tongue and dry throat. I was woken by Maxwell, slamming at my bedroom door. He burst in and all I did was groan. I pulled the covers over my head in protest to the intrusion.

"What are you doing?" he demanded. He was seething, I didn't need to crawl out of my oh so comfy bed to see that.

"Recovering," I mumbled from under the sheets.

Anger splintered his tone. "You cannot be resting, Airen. Did you forget? You have an appointment today. A meeting with Lady Jenkins and a chance to run into her 'oh so charming' son."

"Ah, yes," I mumbled. "That."

"Yes, that. And you have half an hour to get ready."

"Give me ten more minutes," I groaned rolling over.

The Kraden Job

"Airen, this is serious, and I have something to discuss with you—"

Allie shot up from beside me. We'd fallen asleep in our festival clothes, and for the first time in years, she looked a mess. Her hair in all directions, soot smudging her face. "Half an hour?" she said, in what felt to be an earsplitting pitch. "That's not enough time to get Airen ready!"

"Thanks," I mumbled.

"Airen, you have charcoal in your hair and smell like a fire pit. Be realistic."

"I told you not to go out yesterday if our plan falls through because Airen wanted to see a fire dancer, we've had months of planning for—"

"We get it, Max. Thank you," Allie said curtly, taking off her cloak and attempting to smooth out her horribly wrinkled dress. It was a dismissal, but he was Maxwell.

"No," he said shortly, "you don't. Get her into the chair."

Allie coaxed me out of my cocoon with some minor threats and a few rather unpleasant remarks to my character. Thankfully, I mostly needed to sit still. She washed the charcoal from my hair. "What is it that you wanted to discuss, Max?"

"We have to accelerate the plan," he said. He was pacing. He never paced.

"Define accelerate," I said, regretting agreeing to tea with Lady Jenkins.

"You have to get an invitation to reside in the estate today."

Allie and I froze. I started to laugh but stopped. "You aren't kidding. Are you out of your mind? I've only met with them twice. Twice! Even Allie couldn't do it that quick."

He pulled at his hair. I'd never seen Maxwell agitated like that before. "Look, I'm not saying it's a good change. I'm just

Chapter Nine

saying it needs to happen."

"But why?" Allie asked.

"Because it does!" he snapped. Maxwell may have never completely given into Allie's advances, but I'd never seen him raise his voice to her either. She was in shock. "Get her ready," he barked at her. "And you," he pointed at me, "you find a way to get yourself into that house. I don't care if you have to throw yourself on him. You get in, or so help me."

He slammed out of the room. We sat in silence for a moment. I could see tears building up behind Allie's eyes. She bit the side of her lip, hard, putting on a weak smile. "Now, hold still. You know the makeup is bad when you move too much."

"Allie, he—"

"He's very stressed and he knows what he's doing. Just sit still."

So I sat. She worked quietly. Painted my lips and eyes. Rinsed the charcoal out of my hair. Piled it high in an intricate bun, then, in a moment tore it down, and pulled it back with a simple pin. Brushed a veil of powder over my cuts and scars, her own face making a concentrated frown.

She sighed. "How did you get so many scars again?"

"Proving myself," I said, my voice was slightly sharp.

"Right," she said, clearing her throat. "Be that as it may, we don't want your suitor to see these now, do we?" she asked in a pleasant tone, bringing her brush across my face some more.

I shrugged and pushed her hand away. "Its fine," I said, tired of dealing with the façade. "Go pick me out something to wear."

She bit her lip, but shuttled off to the closet anyways. She hummed to herself as she went through the outfits. I refrained

The Kraden Job

from rubbing the makeup off my face. It still felt itchy to me, but I didn't want to upset her. "How are the elixirs coming along?" I asked.

"Pretty well," she beamed back at me, but it was a hollow gesture. She was getting good at facial manipulation., but she enjoyed talking about her potion making hobby. "I've almost mastered the art of ransinque, minor aches and pains, but the shivers will pretty much incapacitate whoever takes it. It could prove useful against guards."

She brought a dress to me. It was blue and yellow; the dark blue was meant to make my eyes stand out, create some sort of attention. I sneered at it. I can't tell you how often I wished for the plain whites, browns, and blacks of my common clothes. To wear trousers, and billowing shirts, instead of dresses with tight fitting tops and flowing bottoms.

"He'll like the color of your eyes. They'll look that much brighter when you burst into tears. Crying from the idea of being separated from him so soon."

"I'm not going to cry."

"Well," she said, her voice wavering, "you should try to. How can Kristoph turn you away when you are crying on his shoulder?"

"Shh," I soothed, as best I could, taking the dress from her. "I'll try, okay. Maybe you should go back to the boat today. Just for a night or two."

She shook her head, pushing at her eyes with a hand. "There's a library down in the second sector of the city. I haven't seen it in years. I made a disguise special to visit it. Maybe I can find some plans of the estate. A good way out. The halls and passageways have started to get mixed up in my mind."

Chapter Nine

I groaned. "I really hope this plan doesn't involve sewers. I hate those plans."

"But you always get away," she smiled, tugging out some of my bangs to dance across my forehead.

"Yeah, and yet I seem to be the only one who has to go into them. Right now, I'm more worried about what I'm going to talk to Lady Jenkins about. Not to mention, if I actually get invited to stay in the estate today. How many conversations shall I have to have in that wretched mansion?"

She started tugging on my hair, pulling it up and away from my face, letting the strands go through her fingers, clipping them up the way she wanted. "Lady Jenkins sounds like a chatter box. Honestly, I think if you sit there, listen, and nod your head, she'll be over the moon. You'll be fine. Just don't be yourself, and you'll be fine."

Allie, as it turns out, was right. Lady Jenkins prattled on for hours. Most of it useless nonsense. She was quite the gossip, which was fascinating, because it never seemed to occur to her people would discuss her in such a manner. She had a desire for propriety, but the sort of clumsy personality that made that life goal entirely impossible.

"You know, dear, I was saying the other day to Lady Kraden that she'd get so much out of her daughter if she allowed her to make more visits to me here in the west side of the estate. That girl may be raised to dance and be a charmer, but she has little practical sense when it comes to men. Always going on about her jewels and flirting with every guard that happens to be in her eye line," she sniffed indignantly into her tea. I wasn't sure if she was so upset because young Miss Emily Kraden flirted with her son or because she was unlikely to marry him.

The Kraden Job

"The girl rampages around as though she already owns the place, which we all know, she never will, and if she marries a good man he'll make sure she stops that nonsense, and she's quite distracting, I might add. You're very lucky you've come into my care rather than hers."

While I couldn't disagree with her on that point, I wished she'd shut up about it after the third time she went on a similar rant. The best part about the woman was when she went on a tangent, I didn't need to listen at all. As she went on about some or other nobleman, I mapped out the way we'd gone through the halls in my mind. The Jenkins family resided in a small corner of the Kraden Estate, one that was closer to the front gate than I would have liked. It showed, while they were respected, their primary function was still the job of security rather than noble guest or, as Graham would like to be, family.

There were two options for me. Either I'd be placed close to the Jenkins, as they were the ones who would need to pressure the Kradens to invite me to stay in the Estate. Or I'd be moved further in towards the normal guest rooms, which were closer to the Kradens but farther from Lord Kraden's papers in his study. Though the slight tour Lady Jenkins took me on hardly gave me an idea of where they kept their coin. And Allie's revenge was the whole reason I was in the mess, I knew I'd have to do my fair-share of sneaking about if I got invited to stay.

I was in the middle of calculating whether or not the beams in the hallways that looked to be purely decorative would support my weight when Kristoph and Jonathan came into the room. Jonathan approached me first.

"The lovely Miss Cassandra," he said bowing over my hand. "How lovely to see you. When Kristoph suggested we visit his

Chapter Nine

mother I had no idea you would be here." I gave him a smile and a head bow.

Kristoph took my hand in his and bowed over it, keeping his eyes on me. "Have you been enjoying your tea?"

"Very much. Thank you." I tried to hold his gaze. He had to like me today. He had to really like me.

He turned to his mother. "And have you been behaving yourself?"

Lady Jenkins fanned her neck and looked away. "I don't ever know what you mean, Kristoph, by your accusations. But I can tell you two that if you've come to bother Miss Cassandra and hope to gain her attention, you boys have come too late. Just not a moment ago her Uncle sent up a note announcing he has some urgent business to take care of out of town and will be coming to fetch her within the next hour."

Kristoph turned to me, his face somewhat stern. "But surely you won't be leaving us as well? You've only just arrived."

I gave him my sweetest smile, which I only hoped didn't come out sour. "I fear, I'm at my uncle's disposal whilst I stay with him, Mr. Jenkins. If his business takes him out of town I'm likely to go with him."

"But this will not do at all," Jonathan said, actual distress evident on his face. He was either a good actor or Kristoph had been talking about me. "You cannot leave us when we've just started to know you. Who will Kristoph beg to his beloved dances?" Kristoph glared, but Jonathan continued as though he had not seen. "This must be rectified at once. We shall have a chat with your uncle. Let us escort you and your uncle home. We shall talk him into letting you stay."

"Oh, yes. That would be grand," Lady Jenkins said, a smile creeping into her face. "Maybe we can have you stay here with

The Kraden Job

us. Just until your uncle gets back from his business out of town. It would hardly be proper for you to stay in that large house all by yourself in town." She turned to her son, "I know you fine young lads have been keeping the higher sectors safe, but I hardly think it's a good idea to leave her on her own. We simply must ask the Kradens to allow her to stay during Lord Stevens travels."

"Well..." I started to say. This part was crucial. This part, Allie had told me, I needed them to fall in love with me a little, or create deep sympathy. 'Cry,' she kept urging me, 'don't forget to cry.' Instead, I looked around them to give them the idea that I was thinking about an offer, when my eyes caught Jenkins. He was giving me this intense stare. No one had ever looked at me with such eyes. I felt my face heat up, the burn on my cheeks radiating out of me. I ducked my head away from his gaze, feeling it on my face, even as I looked away. "Such an offer would be most welcome." I felt rather than heard my voice quake. I hated every second of it, but it was real, and, if anything, it endeared me to them.

Jonathan had a big smirk on his face when I looked up again. I wanted to stab him a bit for that. "Then that's all settled. All we need to do now is convince Lord Stevens to allow you to stay, and I'm sure Kristoph and I can manage that. We are, after all, gallant young men. The wise Lady Jenkins certainly can convince the Kradens to allow you to stay for a few weeks. She is quite capable."

"Oh Jonathan, you're too much," Lady Jenkins said, but it was clear she was pleased. "I'll speak with Lady Kraden today. I'm sure she won't say no, dear, but just to be sure I'll speak to her before this evening. That woman does like a few glasses of wine at dinner, and we want to make sure she speaks with

Chapter Nine

her husband before your uncle starts to pack your trunks," Lady Jenkins said, looking with more than a small amount of delight between me and Kristoph. I managed a weak smile and wished Allie had left my bangs down, so I could hide behind them.

Jenkins and Jonathan chattered animatedly as they walked me down to where my "Uncle" was waiting. Jenkins was a lot more cheery back then.

"Who do we have here?" Lord Stevens asked in a jovial tone. He shook both the young men by the hand, not truly surprised to see either or them. He could tell that the tea had gone well. It was a good thing too as Lord Stevens and Maxwell had gotten into a screaming match before I'd left the house to meet with Lady Jenkins. None of us knew exactly what had Maxwell so on edge, but we both wanted today to go well rather than deal with Maxwell's ire for a third time that day. I gave Lord Stevens a smile.

"Kristoph and I would like to do the honor of escorting you and your lovely niece home. And perhaps make a suggestion on the way," Jonathan said, taking charge of the conversation after all pleasantries had been observed.

"By all means," Lord Stevens smiled at them, "I'd be glad of the company. How about you, my dear?" I simply blushed when they all turned to look at me. They seemed to agree amongst themselves that this was a yes. "Sadly, as I shall need my carriage later this evening, I cannot lend it to you to get you back to the estate."

"Don't worry," Jonathan said. "Kristoph and I'll have our horses tethered to the end and we'll simply ride back once we've seen you to your door. Kristoph and I planned to take a tour of the lower district today in any case."

The Kraden Job

The brief moment of surprise on Kristoph's face showed that this had not been a plan, but Jonathan was cunning. If he wanted to ask my uncle to allow me to stay with the Jenkins family then showing Kristoph off as a responsible and upstanding man would have any legitimate business man of means impressed. Though in our case, they really needn't try so hard.

"How splendid of you. What fine men they have in the Kraden Estate. We could use more of you out and about town these days."

"I do not disagree with you, sir," Kristoph said as he gave me a hand into the carriage, "There is far too much violence in the streets. Petty thieves and pickpockets. Thankfully, mostly in the lower quarter for now."

"True, but it has already begun to creep up," Jonathan said. "I know we could use at least one more solid guardsman."

"Oh, stop lobbying for today, Jon. I told you that I'd think about joining the guard officially," Kristoph said, releasing my hand and giving his friend a brief glare.

"Thank you, Mr. Jenkins," I said softly, settling my skirts about me in the bench of the carriage. He mumbled something I didn't hear as Lord Stevens and Jonathan followed me in. And with that the carriage door was shut and I found myself, to my thrill and horror, squished next to Jenkins and across from Lord Stevens, who smiled at me, before turning to Jonathan to discuss his idea of me staying at the Kraden Estate while Lord Stevens was away on business.

"I remember telling you to call me 'Kristoph,'" Jenkins said, leaning over further than was strictly necessary into my space and speaking in a tone that was far too soft for the conversation.

Chapter Nine

The heat burned at my cheeks and my fingers tugged at the edges of my gloves. "Yes, well, it didn't seem quite proper in front of your mother, or my uncle for that matter."

"I don't think either of them would mind horribly, and I would find it pleasing," his breath ghosted down the side of my face. I looked at Lord Stevens, but he and Jonathan seemed to be locked in a deep conversation and a bubble of obliviousness that could only be forced.

I hated upper society. Kristoph thinking he could get away with such closeness because we were among friends, Jonathan ignoring it to help a friend, and Lord Stevens thinking it's best for the plan. What kind of girl did they think I was? Not that I could exactly be outraged on my scope of morality. That would only be comical, but prudence, I could go with that. I wanted to grab Kristoph by the collar of his shirt, pull him real close, before smashing a fist into his face, but instead, I just gave him a sweet smile with a scalding look.

"Rather presumptuous that at this point I want to be pleasing you."

His eyes widened, and I thought I heard a slight chuckle from the other side of the carriage. After a moment, Kristoph looked more amused by the rebuff than anything else. It wasn't the smartest thing to say and Lord Stevens was looking mighty pissed. Thankfully, Kristoph didn't seem offended in the slightest, but the rest of the ride progressed in silence between the two of us.

When he helped me exit the carriage, he bowed low over my hand, pressed his lips to the fabric on my knuckles, and kept his eyes locked on mine the entire time. I suppressed a shiver, but couldn't hide the embarrassment.

"Miss Cassandra," he said, before straightening and walking

The Kraden Job

towards their horses. I kept my eyes on him as Lord Stevens and I walked up the stairs. Jenkins smiled back at me. I huffed as the door opened.

"You did very well today," Lord Stevens said as we walked towards the living room, "Jonathan was most eloquent when trying to convince me of his plans. Not that I would have objected if they had stuttered through some silly excuse..." his voice trailed off when we rounded the corner into the living room. I stopped dead.

There were slashes in the furniture. A shelf of books had been thrown to the ground, the pages strewn across the floor, paintings half hung on walls, glass smashed. In the center of the room kneeled Lord Stevens' servant girl, tears rolling down her cheeks in steady streams, and behind her, gently cradling a knife to her throat stood Maxwell.

"Hello, my friends," he said. The girl just whimpered.

"Maxwell," Lord Stevens said, his voice stunned and quiet, "what are you doing?'

"Have they agreed to let Airen stay in the house?"

"Deloris is going to inquire if Airen may stay at the estate during my absence from town. But, Maxwell, what is this? Let go of my servant."

Maxwell instead pushed the knife closer to her throat, a drop of blood leaking onto the blade. "Have they *agreed* to let her stay?"

I felt my hand twitching for a sword and cursed knowing that mine was locked away in a chest upstairs. The floor boards creaked under the feet of three more men from the crew as they slipped into the living room. To say I had a bad feeling would be an understatement.

"Maxwell, I demand to know what this is about this in-

Chapter Nine

stance," Lord Stevens said, this time in a louder voice, trying to gain control over the situation.

"You see, I figured they might invite our girl to stay with you going out of town. But did you know that our dear Lord Kraden is not inclined to do many favors for the Jenkins out of whimsy. So I figured, a little scare in the home, and they'd have to take her in. After all, she isn't safe out here in the world. It's a dangerous place," as he said the last sentence he squished, the servant girl's cheeks. She let out a muted sob. "So, we must sell the part. If you want to be helpful, Airen, I suggest you scream. We want your Kristoph coming back to rescue you."

I opened my mouth, but no sound came out. This was lunacy.

"So, it's all an act? Just to make sure they let her stay?" Lord Stevens asked, his voice becoming more frantic.

Maxwell's eyes were cold as he gazed at the man. "Has Lord Kraden himself agreed to let her stay?"

I was aware of someone coming up to stand in the doorway behind us. Fear was crawling over my skin. I was acutely aware of my dress and the fact that I had no idea how to run in heels. Beside me, Lord Stevens gasped in breaths, sweat evident on his face.

"No," he said in a voice so small I barely heard it.

Maxwell smiled. "Pity," he said, before dragging the knife across her throat. "We have to sell the part."

I screamed.

Maxwell dropped the girl to the ground and leveled his gun at Lord Stevens. There was a bang and a flash. I screamed again and did the only thing my brain could think to do. I started to run. Or at least tried to, but smashed straight into

The Kraden Job

Shane who grinned down at me.

"You're kinda pretty when you're scared. Almost like a real girl," he said.

I tried to punch him, but he grabbed my wrist and smashed me across the face. It leveled me to my knees and my ears rang. His grip tightened on my wrist while his other hand grabbed me around the waist. Before I could register what was happening, I was thrown over his shoulder and being carried up the stairs. I could hear Maxwell's voice in my head, "We have to sell the part" as the door to my room was kicked in and I was thrown on the bed.

In all my years as a pirate I had feared many things: death at sea, being caught and hung, an infection after a sword wound. I had feared many things being at the mercy of men and the sea, but I had never feared this.

I screamed again. His hands ripped at the top layer of my dress, I heard the fabric give way in a loud rip and I batted at him with hands in little gloves. Soft gloves that hid any sign of imperfection of my battle scarred hands, and also my nails.

"Get off of me!" I tried to scratch at his face. Kick him, but his weight on my dress kept me from being able to move. Panic settled in me in a way it had never before as his hands pawed over my torso. He laughed until I kneed him in the groin.

"Stupid bitch," he said, punching me in the stomach. I coughed and tasted the blood in my mouth.

"I *will* kill you for this," I gasped, the words feeling funny coming out of my swelling mouth. I spit blood up at him as a knee squished one of my wrists into the bed. The other trapped under a strong hand.

Shane leaned in close to me and I twitched trying in vain

Chapter Nine

to get out from under him. His lips were close to my ear and tears sprung to my eyes.

"Want to bet?" he asked, before he grabbed my throat. I kicked my legs uselessly as the grip tightened. A muffed yell tore its way out of my mouth.

"Cassandra?" A voice called out, then the sound of feet pounding up the stairs.

Shane smiled a sinister smile. "Looks like your boy is here. Too bad. I'll be seeing you, 'Cassandra'." His grip tightened for just a second more, before he sprang off me and launched out the open window. I slid off the bed onto the floor, curled up into a ball and sobbed.

~~~~~X~~~~~

There was a silence in the kitchen. Thom stared at Airen wide eyed, his half eaten muffin forgotten in his hand. Airen pointedly ignored his staring. Discomfort radiated from her as she twirled a large kitchen knife in her hand. Thom closed his mouth, letting his eyelids drop to a nonchalance of disinterest. But she still felt the eyes on her when she began picking at the grit under her nails with the knife. The sharp blade raked against the half-moon of her nail, making a small scraping noise that sounded clear and loud in the kitchen.

"How bad are my ribs?" Airen asked, sparing the medic a glance.

Thom put his hand out level, moved it back and forth a little. A frown on his face.

"So-so, huh?" Airen sighed. "Well, there's no helping it. I need a favor."

Thom raised an eyebrow. She cleared her throat under his

The Kraden Job

gaze, wondering what he could be thinking.

"I'm sure you've heard that Nick is none too keen on the idea of my leaving the ship at the moment," Airen said, her controlled voice trying to feign a casual attitude. He nodded, though his eyes were narrowed in suspicion. "There is a high possibility that I might want to wander off as it were. Just for a little bit mind you, and —"

Thom shook his head.

"You don't even know what I was going to say," Airen said, indignant.

Thom gave her a small glare. She paused her work to greet it. In a flick of the wrist Airen began twirling the huge knife, the blade catching the candlelight throwing flashes of yellow slicing across the ceiling and walls. A small frown formed on Thom's lips watching the ease at which she handled the kitchen utensil. For the briefest of moments, his eyes dipped to the dagger tucked into her belt, which was much longer and sharper than a kitchen knife. Though he was sure that she could dismember him with either weapon.

Airen smirked. "As I was saying. I need to get off the ship for a spell in a few days time. There's something I need to collect. You willing to help me? Just a small favor."

Thom shook his head again, more vigorously. His eyes were unsmiling. His mouthed a defined 'no'.

She eyed him with annoyance. Barely resisting the urge to huff. "Were you this stubborn when you talked?"

The ice in his stare made her stop twirling the knife. She met the look full on, squinting her eyes in a way she knew made the yellow shine and shimmer. Thom dropped her gaze and studied the floor. He rested his elbows on his knees and laced his hands together. Shaking his head again, almost sadly.

Chapter Nine

Thom's head shot up at the loud thunk noise of a blade sinking into wood. Airen smiled at him sweetly.

"I just need a small life boat and a few hours of diversion. I'd do it myself, but you said my ribs aren't doing so great. Doubt I could lift down a boat right now."

The knife was embedded in the ceiling. He stared at it. It was in several inches, the handle shaking slightly as the blade vibrated in the wood.

"Come on. Just a tiny favor," she said, attempting an innocent tone. "I'm injured."

He nodded, but he didn't look happy about it.

"Excellent." Airen grinned, swinging herself out of the chair. Rolling her shoulders, they cracked loudly. "I'm going to go sulk in my room so Nick doesn't suspect anything. Let me know when we are close to the Ridged Shore port, will you?"

Aware of Thom watching her, Airen didn't let the smile fall from her lips until she was a few steps down the hall. Subtle manipulation had never been her strong suit. She'd hoped telling him the story would rope Thom in, and telling it did make her feel better, but she'd hoped to make him more compliant. She'd probably have to tell Thom the rest of the story, to keep him interested, but not now. She'd scraped the surface of those memories and Kristoph stood there in her mind slicing through years of running away. Dragging up the pain and uncertainty. A wave of nausea hit her as Shane's phantom hands pawed at her clothing. She gasped in a deep breath, wrapping her arms tight around herself and stalked down the hall. She slammed the door to her cabin, fell on the bed, and let the memories of that day pour over her.

That day, years ago, Kristoph had busted into the room. He had seen her there, curled up, clutching onto the shoulders of her gown in an attempt to keep the torn fabric from exposing her more. For once in her life she didn't try to hide her weakness, as she trembled there on the ground, sobs raking her body so hard she thought she'd never breath proper again. Relief had washed over her when Kristoph knelt down in front of her, brushing hair out of her tear streaked face. She remembered feeling her helplessness as he bundled her up and carried her down the stairs.

Airen could remember the feeling of his arms wrapping around her, the strength in his hands and chest. She had nuzzled against his warmth, tears and snot leaking onto his neck as Jonathan brought the carriage around. Airen clutched at him, when he tried to go back to the house to take care of Lord Stevens.

"No. Don't!" She'd sobbed, grabbing onto him almost frantically. "Please don't… don't leave me." He climbed into the carriage with her, draped his cloak over her, and held her close until they arrived at the Kraden Estate. Jonathan had run ahead when they arrived. To inform Lord Kraden of what had happened, a murder so grim and close to the upper sector of the city. Kristoph had guided her slowly, protective arms around her, leading her down the halls. Airen couldn't remember any of it.

"Don't worry," he kept saying, "It'll all be alright. I'm just going to talk to my dad and Lord Kraden. We'll make sure you're safe."

Lady Jenkins rushed around the corner, Johnathan hot on her heels.

"I told you, she's fine," he half-shouted, jogging to keep up with the older lady.

Lady Jenkins whirled back on him. "Fine?!" she screeched.

Chapter Nine

"How can you say that? I can assure you she is *not* fine!"

He looked like he'd been slapped. Face swimming with guilt. "I didn't mean *fine* fine I just meant ... she hadn't been hurt.... Cassandra is alright... it could have been worse...."

"Of course, it could have been worse, you foolish boy," Lady Jenkins snapped. "Now get out of my sight before I decide to show you how much worse I can make it for you."

She made her way over to Airen and fussed over her, wiping at the tears running down her face and tucking the cloak more securely around Airen's shoulders. "Oh, my dear, dear girl. Let's come away from here. Get you settled into my quarters for the time being. Then we can have a spot of calming tea. How does that sound, dear?"

Airen looked at Kristoph, a pleading look. He nodded at her. "I'll just be a few minute to talk to Lord Kraden and my father. I'll come see you soon."

Lady Jenkins gently took Airen's hand, like she was a little girl, instead of a fierce pirate, and led her down the hallways towards Lady Jenkins rooms. She muttered soothing sentences that Airen blocked out in a sniveling haze. Airen walked like a zombie, following numbly. It took her a few minutes to realize that if the plan was ever to work then she needed to focus on remembering the layout of the estate.

Airen forced herself to focus. Counting hallways, keeping track of the rights and lefts they took until they reached Lady Jenkins's private chambers. She opened the door and guided Airen gently inside. She brought Airen past the drawing room and into the large bedroom beyond.

"I think that I have a dress in your size around here somewhere, Cassandra. I'll send one of the boys to get your things from your uncle's house soon. Always keep a few

The Kraden Job

beautiful dresses from your youth, never know when you might have a daughter… or daughter-in-law in need," Lady Jenkins prattled on. The chatter her own defense mechanism. "Come dear, do you need help with it?"

Airen took the fabric in her hands, feeling the delicate softness of it. It was finer than any of the dresses she'd ever seen. She shook her head, knowing if Lady Jenkins discovered the scars on her hands and arms it would cause problems. The lady smiled at her, patted her cheek and walked quietly out of the room.

Airen changed quickly, tossing the torn dress into a corner and glaring at it. No matter if they stitched it to look like new, Airen knew, she'd never touch it again. She crept back into the drawing room before Lady Jenkins could worry about her. Away from the house and tucked safely away into the Kraden Estate, Airen felt her fear give way to a straight shot of hot anger. She had always understood the importance of herself being ingrained within the estate itself and appearing weak beyond reproach to obtain their trust, but for Maxwell to go to such lengths stirred an anger deep in her soul that she'd never felt before. Airen had never liked Maxwell much, but now she felt a murderous anger take hold that she doubted would ever let go.

There was tea waiting for her, a sympathetic smile, and a tray of cookies. She sat numbly on the sofa, playing with the tips of her gloves and casting glances at the door wanting nothing more than Kristoph to walk through it, and hating herself for wanting that. Lady Jenkins didn't say anything. Just sat there, nudging the cookies closer and closer to Airen every few minutes. After what felt like forever, Kristoph and Johnathan came through the door. Kristoph's face filled with

Chapter Nine

worry and a small hint of annoyance. Johnathan seemed to be avoiding the gaze of Lady Jenkins. Airen and Kristoph stared at each other, she let out a deep breath.

"Well," Lady Jenkins said, looking between them.

"She'll have a room made up on the south side. Near the library," it was Johnathan who answered.

Lady Jenkins nodded, grabbed her shawl off the back of the couch and stood. "Well, it is only fitting that she will be able to sleep in her own clothes tonight. She's gone through enough to feel strange in a strange new place. Johnathan, I think it would be best if you escorted me to her uncle's house. I will pick out what is best." It wasn't a question and, though he seemed reluctant, Johnathan left the room.

Airen was barely aware that she'd started crying again. Kristoph came and sat by her, turning inwards to get a good look at her.

"Are you okay?"

She let out a laugh. A wet, sad, pathetic noise that was still clouded with tears. She sniveled. "Did you just ask me that?"

"Sorry. Wrong thing. I just… I'm not sure what to say after… and you… It just… I felt so helpless, and I'm sorry we left when we did. There were no signs anyone…"

"Stop, and thank you. If you hadn't arrived when you did…" she stopped, choking on the words. She shuddered, thinking of Shane's fingers in the cloth of her dress. The way he looked at her mouth, wanting. Maxwell had made sure she didn't need to fake terror.

Kristoph reached out a hand to her. Quickly and instinctively to soothe her, but fell short. Eyeing her carefully. Seeking permission. Airen smiled, sad and fragile. He wiped a finger across her cheek bone, and pushed chaotic hair behind her ear.

"I won't let anyone hurt you. Not like that. Not ever."

She started to cry. Deep sobs jerking out of her lungs. Her body shaking with a flood of fear, gratitude, anger, and frustration. He pulled her into a deep hug, rubbing circles along her back as he held her and waited for the storm of emotions to pass.

Chapter Ten

Allie sighed, looking over the papers. After the heist, Nick had let her take a quick glance at most of the documents they'd stolen before spiriting them away into his cabin. But there had been one batch, one stack of papers, that he'd kept hidden. Sliding it into a drawer or under maps anytime Allie dropped by into his cabin. Even after the many jobs they had done together, Nick still didn't trust Allie to keep her hands to herself when it came to mysteries and sequestered the documents away from view. Overall, the other papers had been boring treaties, secrets worth paying, killing and even dying for, but nothing that half-interested her. But something that Nick was trying to hide, now that was interesting.

Even before she touched them Allie could sense these papers were somehow different. Most of them were in a thin yellowing parchment that looked older than the others she'd seen. She'd 'borrowed' them when Nick wasn't looking and squirreled them away with a sleight of hand that Airen had spent weeks teaching her years ago. The last four days Allie had spent hours pouring over the documents. Turning, matching, shifting, and scrutinizing. The result was nothing but frustration.

Hours spent sneaking these back and forth between her and Nick's desk, hours she spent over the paperwork and nothing. She sat in her cabin, tucking a stray hair behind her ear and tugged at her earring before shifting through the paperwork again. In annoyance, she shoved the papers across the table, a few skittered to the floor. Most of the writing was in the common tongue and the writing was surprisingly legible, but even after reading it several times, she still had no idea what more than half of it meant. Airen sauntered in just as Allie was leafing through the pages for the fortieth time.

Airen stopped in the doorway. Observing the scattering of papers and her usually composed friend's pained face. "Whoa. Look at you. Rage against the blackmail materials. Careful with those. I hear they're valuable."

"Worth killing over," Allie said looking up and smiling at her. "You coming to apologize?"

Airen shrugged, going over to a bookshelf. She ran her finger across the shelf until coming to a small set of books. She yanked the middle one and they came out in one big chunk. Clicking the little latch on the side, she opened the book shaped box and pulled out a small bottle of amber liquid.

"Oh, Allie, you should know me better than that. Besides," she said, chucking the box to the side and gathering up two small glasses, "since when do we need to apologize to each other?"

Allie glared at Airen's disregard for her personal space and

Chapter Ten

tossed a book at her friend, who ducked. "Never. You've been forgiven already anyway."

Airen smiled, placing the cups on the table and pouring out a small amount of the drink. "So, what's bothering you?"

Allie looked exasperated, pushing at the papers in distaste. "I'm smart, right?"

"I think so. Smarter than me at any rate. Why?"

"This," Allie said, waving her hand over the strewn paperwork. "This is so frustrating. I don't understand what it means. It's covered in these little pictures, and I could swear these are runes in the margins, even though no ones used those for actual writing in about three hundred years. Not to mention the little diagrams. And what in the world is this mark anyways?" she asked, vague hysteria in her voice, whirling around the paper towards the yellow eyed pirate.

Airen handed Allie one of the glasses and picked up the offending page. It was full of curves, jagged lines, swirls, and what looked to be a very bad depiction of hands twisting a particularly thick swirly line. The hands seemed to be reaching into something, or holding something that looked like a box.

Airen shrugged. "I haven't the faintest idea. What are these all about anyways?"

Allie made an annoyed noise, taking a dip from her glass before responding. "That's the odd thing. I mean, we stole information to blackmail King Dupont, and I had assumed it would be a secretive treaty, or a secret document on the line of succession, or something like that. That's not to say that there isn't a very odd treaty in the package, but our information told us to take the dark red leather satchel from the tenth drawer on the seventh desk—"

"Because that isn't confusing," Airen muttered into her drink.

"—and we did. We found it, and everything was all well and good. And we have treaties, *secret* treaties that I'm sure the King will pay us handsomely for, but there was also this big stack of papers. Nick's trying to keep them hidden, even from me. They're so strange and seem unreadable, but they were kept with the most secret of documents, so they're bound to be important. We had to go through five different doors to even get into the room where they were kept, and Nick had to blow up the last door. No one could pick the lock, and to be honest, I'm not sure you could have—"

"Careful."

"—and then I find these. King Dupont must care about them or why would he hide them with the rest? But…" Allie threw up her hands, glaring at the yellow parchment, as if staring long enough would reveal their secrets. "They're just odd. Most of it is in the common tongue but speaks in some bizarre riddle and the rest is illegible jibber jabber. The only real bit I've managed to work out is that it's all about magic—"

Airen bolted up in her chair.

"—which doesn't make any sense because we all know magic isn't real. There's some ramblings about lights and something called 'the surge', whatever that means, and I could swear that part of this is about crafting lanterns, which is beyond ridiculous. Who locks up information about lanterns?" Allie finished her tirade and took a delicate sip of the amber liquid, dragging in a long breath. She let out a soft hum of appreciation, relaxing back into the chair.

"You know, I can see in the dark," Airen said casually, gathering up a few of the pages to examine. The brief sections

Chapter Ten

she skimmed seemed to talk about iron and structure, nothing about magic there. The faintest idea of magic had intrigued her since her childhood. Her father had told her stories of ancient orders and the blood bond, back when its words used to mean something. A time when violating a blood bond ended in a sudden death. A time when you could speak words to move objects. Shower fire from your hands. To most they were just stories based on myths. Strange tales passed in the forgotten countryside or between pirates. But Airen dreamed that perhaps they were real. That some truths lay behind the old legends because of how serious her father had seemed whenever he told her such tales.

Airen looked over the pictures. The runes seemed to hint at a spell, but she wasn't quite sure. If only she could get into the underground of a big city. There might be answers there, down under the houses in the filth of mud and murder. Like in Tecletha. There were schools of mystics down in the underside of Tecletha. They might have an idea of how to understand the script written on the parchments. Not that she'd be willing to return to that city.

"Not in complete darkness," Allie reminded her, pinching the bridge of her nose against the headache that was surfacing. "The sheen isn't magic. It's just weird science."

"Says the person who can freeze a man in place."

Allie huffed. "How many times do I have to tell you? That's from a mixture of very specific chemicals. It has nothing to do with magic. And the sheen is the same. It's chemicals, not mystical."

Airen raised an eyebrow. "How would you know? Or have you been playing with that stuff?"

"No," Allie bit out, her agitation reaching new levels. "I

never did figure that one out. The sheen is a strange mix with some chemicals I've never encountered, and its impossible to find a recipe written down anywhere... but that's not the point. There's nothing magical in it!"

"Well, just don't go testing people to see if you've learned anthing. That stuff is nasty," Airen said. She combed through the documents, trying to find anything that might look familiar. She'd settle for understandable. But Allie was right, there was a lot of gibberish. That was until she noticed a dot sequence on the bottom of one of the parchments.

Airen ran her finger over it, the bumps were slightly elevated from the paper and the lines sunk in just the slightest. She flipped the paper towards Allie. "You look at these?"

Allie regarded them with a vague disinterest. "They're just dots. Probably some mess someone made when copying out the text. Or they were bored."

Shaking her head, Airen inspected the text again. "You might know poisons and people, treasures and cooking, but I know theft and sneaking. This is a code."

Allie perked up, regarding the documents with a new found interest. "What part is code?"

"All of it I'd reckon. These dots are just a part of it. I'd wager that they are some kind of ledger. I'd imagine they could correspond to some of the text."

"So," Allie said with excitement, tugging the paper out of Airen's hands, "if we can figure out what the dots mean then we can figure out the rest of the document? Brilliant."

"Well, no. Not exactly. The dots are just the beginning." Airen sorted through the rest of the documents. Writing spun in circles, moved in little patterns. Sentences ran every which way, creating more of mess than a document. Pictures seemed

Chapter Ten

to be divided in half, intent on keeping the reader confused. "Honestly, I don't think we'll ever be able to read it. It's at least a three part code, but with this kind of disheveled script, I'm likely to say it must be at least five parts before you can actually read it."

Allie deflated. "So, what are the dots for?"

"I'd think they are the first part. You'd need a special key to see how the dots can be read. They likely don't say much, but what they say is important. My guess is that they will give you a clue as to how to decode the rest. Like the name of a book, or the location of a key to the code. That sort of thing. And then you need to find that second key, work out the words into the correct order, not to mention realigning these diagrams. It's a mess. Whatever it is, I'm sure King Dupont has a key to understanding it. Or maybe he's hiding it for someone and he has no idea what it is."

"You think he'd hide documents for someone? He's a king," Allie said skeptically.

"We're about to blackmail him. His power is not absolute."

"Fair point."

They stared at the table strewn with paper in silence for a time. Enjoying the quiet of each others company and the taste of the fine liquor.

"You know," Airen remarked off hand, "Nick would have a fit if he knew you were playing around with these."

"Only if I figured them out before him," she said, taking a deep sip and reclining in her chair.

Airen shook her head. "He's hid them for a reason but he's never cared about these kinds of details. He's more worried about getting his money. Probably he'd be more worried of you dirtying them. This kind of puzzle only bothers you.

The Kraden Job

Patience and an intense interest in detail. That's you all over."

"True. But I can let it go," Allie said, swirling her glass and smoothing down the lines of her dress in an act of calm composure.

"No, you can't," Airen said, amused.

"Yes. I can," Allie said, with a non-too convincing voice.

"It's going to bother you all day," Airen pointed out, a smirk growing.

Allie let out a half groan and slammed her forehead into her table. She whimpered and batted at the paperwork gently with her hands. "It's going to bother me all year!"

Airen laughed. "Knowing you, you'll funnel the frustration into a new line of poisons."

"Probably," came the muffled reply. "Wouldn't be the first time."

Airen feigned disinterest, but her eyes continued to skip over the documents on the table and floor. The likelihood of ever understanding them was slight to nonexistent, but any secret on magic, real magic, piqued her interest.

"So," Airen said casually, "Nick ever mention to you who his source was? He never told me who put us onto that stronghold in the first place."

"Nick wouldn't tell me exactly who it was. He got all agitated when I kept badgering him. But I thought it was a big risk for us, not being clear on who sent us after these papers."

"No hints at all?"

"If you didn't get it out of him not sure how I would."

Airen rolled her eyes. "Because you're better at getting people to talk than I am."

"All I got is someone he trusted and knew well. Annoying really. Must be a source from before we joined the crew.

Chapter Ten

Probably afraid we'd steal them from him."

Airen smirked. "Not entirely unlikely."

There was a knock from the door. Allie lifted her head off of the table, a stray paper sticking to her cheek. She ripped it off, trying too quickly to fix her hair and look dignified. Thom leaned in her doorway, tapping a finger against the door-frame. Allie stopped trying so hard upon seeing him.

"Can we help you?" Allie asked in a pleasant but embarrassed voice.

He nodded at Airen in a large jerk. A frown cemented on his face. Airen smiled at him, stood, and walked towards the door. "Sorry, Allie. I forgot I was going to help Thom with a bit of sparring."

"Since when have you had an interest in fighting?" Allie asked Thom, sweeping up the paperwork into a big messy pile. It was well known on the boat that Thom never fought unless absolutely forced to. And even then he would look for an opening to flee. After a few failed skirmishes Nick had practically banished Thom to the ship. Something that didn't seem to particularly bother the silent medic. Thom shrugged at Allie's question, but threw Airen a glare. But Allie was too distracted to notice. "Thom, are you headed round to see Nick anytime soon?"

He looked between them for the briefest of moments. He cracked his neck but gave a definite nod.

Allie smiled at him. It was warm and flattering. Open and kind. Airen rolled her eyes. It was Allie's 'I want a favor' smile. "Could you run these papers to him for me? I would, but if you're headed to see him anyways, just drop them on his desk. No need to bother him really."

Thom nodded again.

The Kraden Job

"Thanks," she said in an overly relieved voice, as though the favor was a large one rather than simply running papers down a few doors. He took them from her. His face stoic.

Airen headed out and didn't look back until she heard the click of Allie's door closing. She smiled at Thom, but his frown only deepened. "What? Don't be like that. You do *her* favors, why can't you do me one?"

He glared as if to say: 'They really aren't the same thing.'

Airen walked quickly to her room with Thom trailing behind her. She threw open the door in her excitement. She grabbed her jacket from the chair and swung it on, pulling the laces tight. She pulled the daggers out of her sleeves. She wouldn't need them where she was going. She chucked them haphazardly across the room over her bed. They thunked loudly into the wall, slicing a wanted poster in the face. It was of a young woman, two parallels lines running down next to her eye. "Wanted: Dead or Alive," it read, "Airen of the Yellow Eyes."

Thom gave her a 'you done?' look before leading the way onto the deck, moving quickly and quietly. The moon was covered by the clouds that seemed to be saying rain would be coming by soon. She smiled, this would be easier than she thought. She looked back at Thom, he was standing close to the stairs.

"You coming with me?" she asked, challenge in her voice.

Thom shook his head and tossed a bundle of rope at her. She caught it and gritted her teeth. Pain shooting through her side. Thom was right in his assessment that she had not entirely healed yet. Maybe this would not be without its challenges.

"One of these days, you're going to have to get off this boat and have a little fun" She looked up at the stars, felt the wind

Chapter Ten

in her hair. "I'll need at least four hours. Can you give that to me?"

He nodded and watched as she tied the rope around the edge of the ship. Slipped into her gloves and leaped over the side, snagging the rope. She climbed down, landing soundly in the small boat below. She untied the oars, slipped them soundlessly into the water, and headed towards the shore.

The wind was gentle in the evenings this close to the coast. She had missed the way it slithered around her with the smell of the salt, the water coming into the boat in small splashes. She steered the little boat away from the lights of the town, dragging it up on the shore. Airen stared at it for a while. Gave up on dragging it further up the bank, straightened her coat and headed towards the nearest tavern. The darkness of the night not bothering her in the slightest.

Airen headed up the path with ease, lightly stepping around sharp rocks and tree roots. Since the sheen, the darkness was easy for her to navigate. On days when she was truthful with herself she'd say that she preferred the dark. The smallest pebble fell into clear relief in the faint star light for her now. The dead of night showed her a world few else could see.

When she entered the edge of town she kept her head down, shielding her eyes from view. She tugged the collar up on her jacket, pulling her hair down, scanning the streets for the local haunt. A tavern that was frequented by pirates, thieves, smugglers, and forgers. If there was any place in the town where she'd be recognized then it would be there. It didn't take long to locate. The building was close to the harbor and in dire need of repair. The paint was chipped on the outside walls and the sign hung from only one rusted hook. It looked shabby and run down. Definitely the sort of place that

The Kraden Job

attracted the lowlifes of the town. A place where they were happy to spend their ill gotten gains. Airen cracked her neck, rolled her shoulders, and took a deep breath.

Like most taverns Airen went to, this one was nearly as dark inside as outside. The windows were covered up by wooden planks. Maybe during the day a few sunbeams would sneak in, but it was now just sparse candlelight. Those who came to these types of taverns didn't want to be seen. Darkness was their friend and ally. They could only trust others who would step into the shadows with them.

To Airen's eyes the darkness in the bar was brighter than the night outside. In the moments it took the sheen to refocus on the level of brightness, she took in the surroundings. As far as ruffian taverns went it was rather nice. Actual detail work in the wood panels, engraved stools, and an inlaid bar. The proprietor had put a far share of coin into the place, and it seemed it wasn't raided too frequently by the local guard, if the lack of destruction was any indicator. While normal people looking around would likely only see shades of gray and black, Airen could make out the color of people's hair, their clothes, and even the grime and blood under their fingernails.

At this time of night most patrons were busy in their drinks or deals. The musician was just loud enough to hide the details of conversation and offer a slight veil of privacy to the men as they planned their nefarious deals. Taverns like this one were scattered all throughout the kingdoms, safe places to have shady deals usually near the docks or edge of the city, which was a good and a bad thing.

If any official from the city came into the tavern uninvited, the knee jerk reaction was to kill him, dispose of the body and, therefore, the immediate possibility of arrest, but that would

Chapter Ten

often draw too much attention to the bar itself once the man was officially noticed as missing. So there was generally a type of unspoken arrangement between the proprietor and the local guard. The local officers and leaders kept out of this particular tavern, and the thieves kept their plots out of the town itself. The streets were as near violence free as any small city could be with a healthy thieving underground.

When Airen entered the men were caught up in their evening's activities, so the sole female pirate went unnoticed. She walked up to the bar and leaned against it, forgoing the chair. Airen was never a fan of chairs in bars, too easy to get stuck in one during a fight. She preferred standing, her sword knocking at her side, easy to reach. Lifting two fingers signaled the bartender over. He nodded in her direction, but shoved a couple of rowdy men away from the bar before coming to her. Airen studied the two men. They seemed to be in a debate over who was going to pay the bill. The man with red hair was shoving his light haired friend pretty hard. It seemed money had been hard to come by of late. Airen smiled. This would almost be too easy.

"What'll it be?" the bartender asked, trying to uncork a particularly problematic bottle.

"A mug of your finest rum," she said, pushing her hair back in a causal motion that brought attention up to her eyes. She smirked at him as he stared. The bartender's mouth fell open slightly. He dropped the bottle he was holding and it shattered on the floor. His face paled and he made a strangled sound. The red head and his friend looked over at the noise. Slowly, the red head lowered his glass back onto the bar.

"Airen Yellow Eyes," the bartender said, his voice rough, probably a little louder than he meant to. The men behind

The Kraden Job

her stopped playing cards, a silence fell over one side of the bar, a few heads snapped around to take a peek. Some looked skeptical, some wary, several looked rather curious. She could feel the eyes on her back. Her hand slipped under the bar, traced the handle of her blade, just in case, but she stayed focused on the bartender who was looking alarmed at the attention. Anxiety flashed through his eyes following the movement of her hand under the bar.

"I didn't mean to… I shouldn't have… please don't…" his voice squeaked.

Airen tapped her right hand on the counter. "I just came in for a drink, old man. So pour it."

His hands shook as he grabbed a bottle from the top shelf. He poured the mug to overflowing. Quickly he mopped the liquid from the bar before presenting it to her. "No charge for you, of course. Stay as long as you'd like."

"Thanks. I appreciate the drink," she said, the yellow of her eyes shimmering in the candle light. She lifted the mug slowly, drinking from it as some of the spicy liquid sloshed against her fingers and her coat cuff.

"Don't worry," the bartender says. "My place is safe. It's a great place. Very discreet. No one here will say they've seen you."

"Ah, no. Don't worry about that. I'm running a scheme on Commander Jenkins," Airen said with an overtly casual air.

"Commander Jenkins," he stuttered. Panic increasing in his tone.

"I reckon he's been following my ship for some time," she gulped down some rum. "And ya know, he's bound to find this place. First place he'll check are any taverns that have boarded up windows. Don't worry yourself about discretion.

Chapter Ten

Give him a message if you see him. Tell him he's running the wrong way. Or you might want to just close up and avoid him. The Commander doesn't like bad news. Or care much for the agreements between the city leaders and proprietors of a local dive."

The tavern was dead quiet.

"I appreciate the warning. How long?"

"I'd say in about two weeks you might want to close up shop and wander off for a few nights. Others might want to take to talking about deals elsewhere. I know many of your patrons wouldn't like to meet the dear Commander Jenkins."

The bartender gave her a look of wonder. "It's generous of you to tell us. I'd heard many things about you. Those with the sheen aren't known for being particularly ... nice to us more simple folk."

"I know what they say." Airen smirked. "I'm a pirate first. I still live by the code."

A man to her left shifted his arm. The butt of his gun all but invisible in the darkness as he began to pull it from it's holster. Airen swirled in one fast movement, the knife sailing out of her hand before anyone could blink. It sunk into the wood between the man's legs, cutting ever so slightly into his flesh. Surprised, the man pulled the trigger, shooting into the ground.

Airen raised an eyebrow at him. "Just because I live by the code doesn't mean I'm gonna let you shoot me in the back."

The man stood in a rush, anger evident in his eyes. "Yellow eyes aren't welcome here. You people aren't pirates. You're... you're less than human," he spat in her general direction.

The mood grew dangerous. Everyone looked from Airen to the man. She cocked her head to the side, allowing the candles

The Kraden Job

to illuminate in her face and her unnaturally colored eyes. Her eyes flashed in the brightness, and she smiled, running her tongue under her teeth.

Other men at the table grabbed their friend, pulling him back into his chair. They looked at her warily.

"Our friend is very drunk," one said in a rush. "I'm sure he didn't mean that. No one would ever say that you weren't… it couldn't… he doesn't mean… We're going to leave."

"I think that's a good idea," Airen said, rolling her shoulder in agitation as anger bubbled deep in her chest. "Because I can assure you whether I'm human or not, I'm still faster than the lot of you."

The man with red hair at the bar moved. Her eyes shifted towards him, but he put up his hands in mock surrender. "I'll guide him out. I got a deal to talk with him anyways. Might be easier when he's this drunk." He grabbed the trigger happy man and half-guided, half-dragged the man out of the tavern.

"I-I-I'm sorry about that," the bartender stammered. "I can assure you, that you're most welcome here. My tavern certainly doesn't discriminate against… your…. your type of…"

"All pirates are welcome here," boomed one of the men from the round table near the back wall. "Jack, why don't you get a bottle from the back and bring it over. Come, Airen yellow-eyes, play cards with us."

The tension had risen as Airen looked around the room. Men were returning to their drinks but hands were in their coats, likely holding onto pistols or daggers, ready for an eruption of violence at a moments notice.

Airen grabbed her drink off the counter, taking a deep drink. "Yeah, I could play a game of cards." She glided to the table

Chapter Ten

and kicked out a chair. Slumped down into it. The man began to deal out the deck, and noise returned to the tavern, as immediate danger had been avoided.

"Playing for coin or jewels or deeds?" the man asked, chucking out cards around the table. His friends looked more than a little nervous about the newest addition to their group.

Airen smiled, pulling a small bag out of her boot and dropped it on the table. "Coin. Not about to owe you lot any favors. I got places to be."

The men grinned back, getting over their fear at the thought of money flowing easy in their hands.

One hour later the tavern was back to being its usual level of loud and cheery. Airen had lost most of her coin on the table. They were through their fifth bottle, a new one appeared whenever one was emptied as though by magic. The men she played with seemed to be regulars at the tavern, trusted by the proprietor. They were all deep into their cups when movement outside the wooden slats of the window caught Airen's eye. Even in the darkness, she could make out the shine of a silver button on the top of a coat.

"I'm going to step outside for a moment," Airen said, as she stood with a stretch. "Don't you go finishing that game without me?"

The men grumbled, but didn't object. Though curious glances had shifted to her eyes now and then, none of them were dumb enough to ask questions of a sheened person, especially not Airen Yellow-Eyes.

She exited into the moonlight. Alert to the loud noise of a gun being pointed at her head before the tavern door had swung fully closed. Three additional men stepped out from behind a tree, two with swords, and one with a pistol. The

The Kraden Job

one with the pistol, who seemed to be in charge, stopped in front of her.

"The famous pirate Airen Yellow-Eyes. Can't say we expected to see the likes of you around here. Notorious pirates are smart to stay out of Lord Patrick Locke's town," the man said pompously, standing straight, with pride in his local lord. "He'd like a word with you."

"I'll assume that he's not asking," she said calmly.

"You assume correctly," the man said, holding up chains in one hand.

"Lovely."

They were on her in a flash. She was smashed against the tavern wall, pulling her arms roughly behind her back, and tightening the chains around her wrists. They pushed her into a carriage and headed towards the Locke Estate. Airen coughed at the rough treatment, her ribs still twinged, which reminded her that Allie would have said this was a bad idea. Airen sighed. She'd be in for it later, she was sure of that, but for now she'd simply enjoy the carriage ride. She leaned back, closing her eyes as they rumbled on.

The ride was smooth and fast. Once in the compound the men brought her to the top floor, down a long hallway, and into the largest room. Slammed her down in a chair and stood on either side. Their guns pointed directly at her head.

"The great pirate: Airen. There aren't many famous female pirates, you know. It's always a pleasure to catch one," a man said coming into view. He was tall and storm weathered. His face was that of a fighter, his dark hair hanging long around his face to cover up scars on the left hand side.

"Lord Patrick Locke, I presume."

"Correctly," he pulled a chair in front of her and sat. "Ah,

Chapter Ten

the sheen. Very distinct. You should know that it makes you very easy to recognize. How many women have the sheen done, I wonder? Perhaps one in every sixty female pirates."

"Perhaps."

"And how many women have survived the sheen?"

"Three," Airen said, shifting in her chair causing one of the men to shake. The gun rattled in his hand. She glanced at him, then back to Lord Locke. "He looks a mite twitchy."

Lord Locke nodded. "Jefferson, why don't you clear out? I'd rather not have you shooting her in the head. I'd say she's worth rather more alive."

The man nodded and backed off, but he didn't look happy about it. The chains were chaffing her wrists. She felt the skin being rubbed raw. It would take a while to heal. Thom was going to be pissed at her for this.

"So, I'm curious and I hope you'll indulge me, why did you come to my town?"

"I wanted a quiet drink."

Lord Locke looked her in the eye for a moment before throwing his head back in guffaws of laughter. "A quiet drink."

Airen smiled slightly. "Word on the sea is, that some of the taverns are safe in this town. Safe for people like me. Sounds like you have a snitch about in that place."

"I admit, in most cases, I do turn my head the other way to tavern talk. Half the men are drunk and what do I care if people are simply talking. On occasion, I will pay for the information of an asset worth claiming. You should know, Yellow Eyes, that there is no safe place for people like you. Unless you go to the league up in Fairehen City or down the underside of Tecletha. But I rather think you like the waves too much to be land locked or underground."

The Kraden Job

Airen didn't reply, but the pointed silence was answer enough.

"See, a young man came in with a tale that I had a notorious female pirate at a local tavern. He thought this might be worth my time. To catch a woman that was ... how did he describe you? Ah, yes, 'less than human'."

She ground her teeth, giving him a steely glare. "I suppose, I'm a rather large catch for a Lord in a small province."

"Indeed. I've heard Commander Jenkins himself has been looking for you. There's quite a bit of money there. These pirate hunters are so very anxious for their prizes. And while I have plenty of money myself, more never hurts," he smiled at the seething pirate. "He seems to be rather interested in tracking you down. They say you escaped from a locked cell that he was holding you in."

"Yes, well, they only tied me to a chair."

Lord Locke smiled. He stood and leaned down close to her face, scanning her strange yellow eyes. "I won't be making that mistake," he stood quickly and looked at his men. "Put her in a cellar room. One that can see the ocean. I want her to be able to look at it. She'll never be able to touch it again. And chain her to the wall. Make sure her feet don't touch the ground."

The men grabbed her and panic started to set in.

"Locke. Locke! I can pay you! Just don't give me to Jenkins. Locke!!" she screamed as they dragged her down the hall, pulling and pushing at her arms and back. Jefferson gave her a heavy blow to the ribs and she stopped screaming, the pain radiated up the side.

Down in the dungeons the men slammed her down on her knees to remove the chains. Replacing them with proper cuffs.

Chapter Ten

They dragged her into a corner room, yanked her up onto a chair, raised her hands above her head and threaded a chain around her cuffs. She heard the loud, dismal click above her. Arms raised above her head, she'd been chained to the wall. The guards climbed down from the chairs and grinned at her. Her eyes widened as one kicked the chair out from under her. Airen's body slammed downwards, the chains biting against her wrists. She hung there. Her feet dangling against the wall, far above the stone floor. The men glanced back at her before locking the door and then they were gone. She looked down at the ground below her, then up at her chained wrists. Airen sighed.

For a long time, she looked out of the window. Listened to the waves lapping against the cliffs off north. It was a beautiful sound. How sad it would be to stay in this cell and never touch the water again. Never again sail on the ship. Never again get into and out of trouble with Allie. And then after she felt it had been long enough, she kicked her feet against the wall.

"Time to get to work then," she muttered. She grabbed onto the chain attached to her wrists on either side, placed her boots firmly against the wall behind her and pulled up. Several strong pulls later, she was eye level with the lock. She hummed at it. It looked simple enough. She bit her jacket collar, pulling it up once more to a standing position. Took a long hard look at it, before delicately nipping at the middle seam. Out of the coat collar came a very small lock pick. She held it between her teeth and set to work on the first lock.

By the time she heard the telltale click, her lips were bleeding and her arms had started to cramp. With her free hand, she tightened her grip on the looped chain to steady herself against the wall. With a fierce determination, she tugged

The Kraden Job

herself level with the thick metal cuff and started to unlock the other wrist. The lock pick dug deeper into her bottom lip when she bit down but it gave her the edge she needed to finish the final turn.

Airen hung there for a moment, satisfied at a job well done, before dropping to the ground. Twirling the bloody lock pick between her fingers, she walked to the door. There were no torches in the hall, which meant no guards. She fiddled quickly with the door's lock. Swung it open quietly, and snuck into the hall, heading for the stairs.

Ducking behind statues and columns she made her way to the top floor again. Trying the handle of the corner room she found it was open. She crept inside. Lord Patrick Locke sat writing at his desk. He didn't look up, just scratched away at his papers. His brow was knit in concern over his work, unaware of the dangerous pirate that had slunk into his quarters. Airen leaned against the tall frame of his bed.

"It's been a long time," she said. He jumped, splashing ink everywhere. Lord Locke glared at her over his shoulder, mopping at the mess on his desk. She smiled, looking around his room. "Nice place. I like it better than the last one. This one has a good view."

"Airen," he said standing, "you know I hate it when you pop out of nowhere like that. This is why no one likes you."

"It's one of my few skills," she shrugged, taking in the full set up of his master suite. "Nobility suits you. You seem happier."

Lord Locke smiled. "I never did care much for ships. Giving up piracy was the best choice of my life. Seems to suit you rather well though, I must say. You broke out of that cell quite slower than I expected."

"Broke a few ribs recently."

Chapter Ten

"Clumsy," Locke said with a playful smile. "So, how'd you manage it? Lock pick in the coat collar?"

"That was one of the best ideas you ever gave me."

He smirked and Airen could see the shadow of a pirate there. "You really are better than the rumors."

"A woman's got a reputation to protect. You know me, want to be a legend and all that. It's hard work. Keep any of the old equipment around?"

"If you're asking about *your* rig then it's behind the tapestry," he nodded his head towards the opposite wall. Neither of them made a move to go take it. They stared at each other for a long while trying to read each others faces. "I was starting to think you weren't coming back for it."

"Wasn't sure you wanted to see me."

Patrick Locke pushed a hand through his hair revealing his scarred face. He nodded. "True. But I wasn't hard to find. I've been running this area for years now. You could have snuck in and stolen it."

"Last time I angered you it didn't end well. Angering you is bad for my health."

"That seems to be an exaggeration."

"You shot me, Petra."

He frowned. "If you want to get in my favor you should stop calling me 'Petra'."

"It's your name."

"My name is Patrick." He glared.

"Your nobility name is Patrick. Your pirate name was Pete, but your real name is Petra."

"I never did care for you much."

"Oh shut up. I was your favorite."

'Petra' Patrick Locke laughed and walked towards her. Airen

slunk off the bed frame and walked into an easy hug. "You certainly haven't changed. Which, as I take it, is a good thing. Always the interesting one."

"And you were always the sentimental one. How've you been? Running your own province I hear."

"Turns out I have a knack for running estates. The other nobles can't seem to gather how I could be so charming and efficient."

"Pirate," she said, flicking him in the forehead. With the new calm between them, she found it easy to tug the tapestry off the wall. Her rig hung on the stone wall behind it. The cords and ropes gleamed, the metal positively shining. "You've kept this in good condition."

"It's a nice piece," he said, coming to stand beside her. "I know how much you like your rigs. Couldn't bring myself to get rid of it, but couldn't have it lying around for anyone to find."

"Ah, yes, that might be hard to explain," she said, checking the buckles and bolts. "You got married yet?"

"No, not yet. Though I do have a lovely group of men who are trying to set me up with their daughters. It's a rather nice change from being chased out of bedrooms at sword point."

Airen laughed. "Amazing the power a piece of paper has. A simple change to your name, and viola, instant nobility. Perks can be nice."

"You keeping to your thieving, I see."

"Well, not many options when you got eyes like mine," she said, running her fingers over the edge of the rig and looking away from him. "As you so nicely pointed out earlier. No safe place for my kind."

He cleared his throat. "Sorry about that. I like my post.

Chapter Ten

Didn't want to lose it."

"No worries. I wouldn't have come to see you if I didn't think you could do your part. I expected some rough treatment."

"You were quite impressive, if I may say so myself. Nice screaming, by the way. Very dramatic."

Airen shrugged. "Didn't want people to doubt that I believed you were turning me in. Besides, I need Jenkins to know I've been running this way. So your guards overhearing is good for me. After they hear of my escape, I'm sure they will be willing to sell the information to every pirates' favorite Commander."

Locke rolled his eyes. "You certainly get yourself into a fine patch of trouble. Ever thought about going straight if you could? Get yourself some documents and change that name of yours, Airen?"

"Leaving the life?" she asked, yanking the rig off the wall and throwing it over her back. "Did it once. Didn't end well for me. Thanks for hanging onto this for me. I'll keep my eye out for enemies of yours. Send a letter if I hear anything."

"I'd appreciate it. Doing something crazy again?" he called to her when she reached the window.

"When do I do anything different?" she asked with a smile.

He went to the table, picked up a small bag and handed it to her. She opened it to find several large coins of pure gold. "For the papers. It's been years, but I think you got yourself into a mite bit of trouble getting them for me. Airen, hey, Airen, look at me. You're an artist at what you do. They'll call you an escape artist after this one but, listen, if you keep going on like this, you're going to get yourself killed."

She tucked away the money and put a hand on his shoulder. "Look, Petra, I wouldn't be alive if I was afraid to die."

The Kraden Job

He let out an exasperated noise. "Just be careful."

She nodded and hoisted herself onto the sill.

"And Airen, the reason I shot you back then was because I thought you'd come to kill me."

They stared at each other. Him in his finery, polished silver, clean coat, she covered in mud, blood and those bright, bright eyes.

"It happens," she said, and she was gone.

Chapter Eleven

By the time the lights of the town had faded to small pinpricks of light, Airen's arms were killing her. She tugged the oars back into the little boat and dropped her head in her hands. The waves pushed against the edges in a soft rhythm. She let out a shaky breath and rubbed at her arms, massaging the tense and swollen muscles. They shivered in protest, making her groan, as the pain blossomed up her arm.

Leaning back, she gazed up at the night sky. Smells of the ocean came in around her as she breathed deeply. The salty spray, the coolness of the night, and the water. There was a gentleness to the waves this evening. This was her favorite part of living on the ship. The world at night. The large separation from the land. Feeling like she was floating outside of space, in a place of freedom. Away from people who looked at her strangely or barked orders. Away from pressure, or gold, or voices. The one problem with being way from those

The Kraden Job

things was that the mind could wander to places she didn't want it to go. So as the current lapped against the sides of her boat, memories resurfaced from where she had meant to leave them buried.

When Airen had first arrived at the Kraden Estate, playing the much more delicate Cassandra, it was hard to sleep without the calming noises of the waves. Airen was used to smelling the wind and hearing the quiet of the open sea, not the confines of an estate where, even at the dead of night, men patrolled the halls. Their armor clicking and swords clacking as they walked past her chamber. In the first few weeks at the Kraden Estate, she'd spent most of her time on the battlement perimeter, looking out at the ocean that seemed so far away. She'd watch ships disappear on the horizon and miss the comfort of knowing she'd wake up somewhere different than where she fell asleep.

Early on, Kristoph took to joining her on the walks around the grounds. They'd talk as they passed through the gardens, down the halls, by the pond, but when they reached the tall walls and Airen stared out at the sea, they would fall silent. Standing there, she'd place gloved hands on the battlements, and just enjoyed the silence. Kristoph didn't seem to understand these moods, but he humored her, which gave the silence more meaning to her.

Strong salt wind didn't reach the height of the Kraden Estate on the hill. But sometimes a soft breeze would bring up the ghost of salt water scent. Then she'd close her eyes and just inhale the familiar smell. Her mind would go blissfully blank and quiet. Sometimes Kristoph would catch strands of her hair that flew in the breeze and tuck them gently behind her ear. Often chasing the edge of the hair down her neck and

Chapter Eleven

running a finger along her collar bone until the hair slipped from his fingers. In these gentle, soft, quiet moments, Airen would give into the intimacy of it all. Curl her cheek closer to his hand, open her eyes to meet his. Staring deep into Kristoph's blue eyes, she'd regard her own reflection, the small version of herself in there. She always thought that little Airen looked so content up there with him.

Back in the present, Airen sighed and looked out at the dark ocean. It was black in the moonlight, only the tips of the waves catching the reflection of the moon. Far below she could see fish moving in the water. Circling and swirling around her little boat. Leaning further over the edge of the boat she squinted, taking a deeper look into the ocean. In the depths a shark was circling, hunting for food. Beyond him was a squid, leisurely stroking itself through the water. Slow pumps propelled the creature. It was slow and cathartic. Airen watched it move. It calmed her. It passed, and there, resting on the thorny reef, was a ship.

The wooden sides were splintered and shattered. It looked as though it had seen cannon fire. Coral was growing up the mast. A mermaid sang from the bow. Her mouth open in a silent, drowning song. A Jolly Roger was caught about her neck, rippling softly in the undercurrent far below the waves.

Airen blinked, and only saw the reflection of her face, and the shimmering gold of her eyes in the water. She eyed herself with distaste. She slammed the oar back into the water, disturbing its flow and the reflection it held. With definite sturdy pulls, and ignoring the growing pain in her arms, she rowed herself back to the ship.

When Airen threw herself over the railing of the ship, she knew Thom had not been successful in distracting Nick. Nick

The Kraden Job

and Allie stood talking at the bow of the ship, his hands were flailing around him, as they did when he was particularly agitated. Allie was wringing something between her hands. It could either be Allie feigning worry to try and diffuse Nick's anger, or possibly true worry. Airen sighed. Sometimes you just couldn't win.

She walked over to the pair, adjusting the rig on her back. She thought perhaps by the time she came up to the pair that she'd have something smart to say, but she didn't. The darkness was hiding her pretty well and the two seemed unaware of her presence. Lost in their little argument. They were standing real close to be able to see each other in the darkness. Airen could make out every detail, despite its various problems, the sheen did come with some perks.

"Hey," Airen said, for a lack of anything better. They both jumped. Nick whirled around on her, Allie settled for a cocked head and a glare. Perhaps Allie hadn't been worried, simply annoyed.

"Hey?!?" Nick half screeched. "Hey! You disappear, steal a boat, wander to who knows where after I expressly tell you not to leave the boat, and all you have is 'hey'?"

Airen played with the strap of the rig. "Couldn't think of anything else. Thought it would be a pretty standard greeting."

Nick's face colored, rage flinted across his features but faded quickly. When he spoke again his voice was cold. "You deliberately went against my orders."

"You didn't leave me much choice. Your orders were unreasonable, and I needed to get something that was not on the ship."

"I'm the captain of this ship!"

"I don't need reminding," she said, rolling her eyes. Then

Chapter Eleven

realizing, that was probably a bad idea since he could see the yellow in the darkness.

"Evidently you do," he said, his hand moving towards the blade on his side. Allie stepped between them quickly. Putting her hand on Nick's shoulder, throwing a look at Airen that she knew the stubborn pirate would see.

"Come now," Allie said in a soothing voice. "Let us not get carried away. We were worried Airen had jumped ship. But she's back now, however rude she has decided to be. You know her ways, she just acts without thinking. If you were to punish her for every time she rebelled we'd have to make her live in the hold."

Nick was not to be soothed completely but he took his hand off the blade. "Insubordination on my ship is unacceptable. If I can't keep control on my ship, this mission is never going to work. I know you've been a captain before, but I will *not* allow you to have my crew! This is my ship, not yours. I have no interest in fighting you for power. When this is done, I want you off my ship."

Airen bit her lip in annoyance. "After I get my cut, you won't have to worry about seeing me around. I'm off. I'll be gone."

"Good."

"Fine."

They glared at each other for a moment, before Nick went below deck, muttering angrily to himself about the idiocy of sheened pirates. Allie walked to the edge of the ship, resting her hands gently on the railing. She stared up at the sky. Airen watched her for a moment before heading over to stand next to her. Airen dropped her rig down on the deck and leaned her elbows on the rail, looking not up but down at the sea.

Allie spoke first. "You didn't have to do that you know. Nick

The Kraden Job

would have calmed down eventually."

"I don't feel like waiting for eventually. Besides, we have a lot of work to do. I don't need him running around fuming, or worse, sulking. Better to just blow out now. Why's he so upset anyways?"

Allie cleared her throat, trying to cover up a laugh. "I'm guessing, you asked Thom for help."

"I asked him to buy me a few hours. Figured he'd start up a card game or something."

Allie laughed. "You should have been more specific. Thom evidently is not one for subtlety. He tied Nick to a chair in his quarters. I only found Nick because I wanted to talk to him about the castle."

"He tied Nick to a chair," Airen deadpanned.

"Thom seems a little odd."

Airen smirked. "I like him. He doesn't judge me. Or if he does, he keeps quiet about it." She chuckled. "Tied Nick to a chair. Classic."

"Nick didn't seem to think so. Actually, I think he's more angry because you got Thom to do dirty work for you. He expects me to help you out, but not other crew members. You're not exactly the most friendly person here. Nick'll get over it. Maybe we can still talk him into letting us stay," Allie said.

"We don't need to worry about convincing him that *we* can stay," Airen said, tapping her fingers on the wood. "He never threw you off."

Allie looked up at the stars. Refusing to look at her longtime friend, she stood very still. Too still. After a moment she spoke, low and quiet, a sigh of sadness in her voice, "You're planning on leaving again, aren't you?"

Chapter Eleven

"It will be a lot safer for you with a solid crew, if we manage to pull this off. The king might be willing to pay us without raising an alarm, but you can bet, once he has those documents back, he'll sound a search, and you're always safer with a crew than on your own."

"Remember the last time we split up. It didn't exactly end very well. You got yourself in Ersten prison," Allie said, her tone cold and harsh.

Airen sighed. "I remember. But I also remember that *you* did fine. You can manage without me."

"That isn't the point, and you know it. I don't like the idea of you being on your own after this one. Not with something that has to do with Jenkins. I'm worried about how you'll feel if you have to... I mean, we don't know if you're going to ..."

"Kill him?"

Allie nodded, but looked away.

"If I kill him or not, I'm going to need a few months underground anyways. Don't worry about me, Allie. You'll have your own problems after this. You don't need me to drag you down with this."

"This isn't about my safety, so stop using it as an excuse. This isn't about me, and you know it."

"I know," Airen snapped. "It's about me and it's my choice."

Allie looked at her. Winced at the bright yellow that met her and bit her lip. "You know sometimes I can't help but hate myself a little each time I see those eyes."

Airen looked down quickly. She picked at the wood on the railing. Pulling up fragmented splinters. She tossed them overboard into the ocean far below. "It wasn't your fault."

"It was a little my fault."

"Allie, it was my decision to have the sheen done. Mine and

The Kraden Job

mine alone. Just like this. When we finish this job. I'll try to get some things done on my own. It'll be best for everyone."

"You're always so stubborn. You can't do everything all on your own."

"Fine, I'll think about it. Now, if you'll excuse me, I have to check on this rig. I want it fixed up before we're too close to the castle. Anything goes wrong with it, and that'll be one long drop."

Allie paled. "Do I really have to climb a wall with that thing? It looks a little worse for wear. Can you be sure that thing is even safe? And you know I don't really like heights."

Airen threw back her head and laughed. "Don't worry. You won't be using this one. I've got something different in mind for you. After all, I have to compensate for the fact that you'll be wearing a dress."

"You're plans are insane," Allie sighed.

"They always are. That's why you don't let me make them anymore."

"Going to tell me where you went tonight or are you keeping more secrets from me?" Allie asked, her voice a little crisp.

"Met up with an old friend, who was holding onto this for me," Airen said, giving the rig a small kick.

"I don't remember you lending out any of your gear."

"Was a long time ago. When we weren't working together."

"Must have been a strange time," Allie said. Airen could see the small smile Allie got when she said it. They didn't talk much about the time they had spent apart. Brief little stories to uncover or correct rumors, but never had Airen told Allie how chaotic her life had gotten without her oldest friend to help her reign it in.

"Indeed it was."

Chapter Eleven

"Which 'friend' was it? One you stole from or one you stole for?"

"The one that shot me."

Allie raised an eyebrow. Giving Airen a skeptical look. "Pete? I thought you said he was dead."

Airen shook her head. "No, just relocated. Dead pirate. Alive official. Left the sea life. Got himself half a province these days."

"Only half?"

"Well, you can only do so much when you stop breaking the law," Airen said, leaving the railing and heading across the deck. Allie followed her, bumping into Airen's side.

"Promise me, we never will."

"Deal."

They walked slowly across the deck. The wind was soft and they enjoyed it tickling along their necks. Allie looked up, watching the stars move slowly across the sky. She moved in a graceful flow towards the door that led downstairs. The few men that were still above deck watched her move. Some with longing, others simply with interest. Allie smiled softly, aware of the effect she had on the crew.

Airen, in contrast, kept her head down, running her hands up and down the strap that held the rig onto her back. Her eyebrows were furrowed. While she hadn't expected things to run perfectly smoothly this was not what she'd had in mind. She stole a glance at Allie, who was swishing her long dress back and forth, enjoying its slight shimmer in the moonlight. Allie seemed so at peace, so comfortable, but Airen knew, it was a front. Allie was worried. While they would figure out a way to handle Commander Jenkins, there was no way that it would run smoothly.

The Kraden Job

They separated at the door. Allie went off to the kitchens, to see to her poisons, and Airen headed back to her room. The rig felt solid, and Pete had taken decent care of it, but she needed to be sure it would function properly. She opened the door to her chamber to find Thom sitting on her bed. Airen stopped and stared at him. She regarded him for a moment, before coming into the room and casting the rig off to the side.

"What do you want?"

Thom held up a little box. It held an ointment for scratches and bruises and some cloth wraps. He smiled a little guiltily, laying the contents out on the bed.

"You want more of the story, don't you? Coming here to act nice and hear more," she said, yanking up the rig and placing it on her table, scattering books onto the floor. She yanked at the leather that kept the rig tied close together. It unraveled into a mess of ropes and hooks.

She started to tug and untangle, and gave a bit of a start when a hand stopped hers. She looked at it. Thom pulled her hand off the equipment, turned her hand over and slowly tugged back her sleeve, revealing the bruises and cuts from the shackles. He ran a thumb over the discolored flesh.

"Fine," Airen said, tugging back her wrist. "You can tend to my stupid bruises, but I'm not telling you any more of that story." She slumped over to her bed and sat down abruptly, glowering at Thom as he sat calmly across from her. Airen tugged back the sleeves of her coat harshly, annoyed at the gentleness in which he took her wrists and started to rub the ointment on. The silence stretched in the room as he softly wrapped up one wrist, tugging her sleeve a little higher up to inspect the cuts. He was always so calm and quiet. Airen let

Chapter Eleven

out a loud breath.

"Fine. I see how it is," she said. Thom didn't react. She cursed lowly. "I'll tell you more of the story."

He kept quiet, but for the briefest of moments, his lip twitched up into a small smile.

Chapter Twelve

"Living in the Estate was strange. Days blended into weeks, which blended into months. There was a routine there. Every morning started promptly at eight, when there was breakfast, followed by tea with the ladies, tours of the grounds, and dress fittings. To be honest, some part of me forgot it was a heist. I was just there, for weeks, spending time with him. Having long walks in the gardens, visiting his mother, feeding the birds and picking flowers. It was easy to forget in some ways, living comfortable and happy up in that Estate. Maxwell and his cruelty so far away. Everything was gentle and light and soft, and people treated me like I was those things too. After a while, I started to half believe it, as though I had stumbled into another life. A better, more peaceful one. I spent weeks doing nothing but enjoying the sunshine and the company of my new suitor.

Things started to change after I had been there for three

Chapter Twelve

weeks. I remember walking around in the garden, looking at all the new flowers, their bright colors and smells, so different from a life at sea. Kristoph came up behind me; he held a bunch of flowers. He smiled handing them to me.

"Thanks," I said, taking it and playing with the petals. He plucked one from the bouquet and tucked it behind my ear.

"Notice anything new?" He stood proud and straight. The deep red of his coat bright, buttons clear, and newly shined.

I smiled. "You joined the guard."

Kristoph puffed out his chest and played with the ends of his coat sleeves. "I did."

"Jonathan must be very happy," I laughed. He took my hand and started to lead me into a walk around the garden.

"He is. I'm sure he'll come to thank you. He thinks this is all your doing. Of course, he isn't entirely wrong. After what happened, I realized there is more to life than parties and living well. My mother will also thank you, I'm sure. She believes you're a good influence on me."

"I'm glad something good came out of … that. Does your father have you attending all the meetings now for estate security as well?" I asked. Those first few weeks had been spent flitting around the Estate, I'd marked out exits and entrances, looked at the guard schedule, but had found nothing particularly helpful for breaking through the walls.

"Not yet. I'm just on the city guard rotation. I have to start normal, like everyone else. We're doing a lot of patrols in the upper ring of the city. There used to be more guards in the lower sections, but now that those animals have snuck into the higher level of the city we cannot ignore that."

"Ah. The guard. You've assimilated rather quickly." I nudged at his shoulder playfully, as he turned us down a path into a small hedge maze. He looked around before tugging me around to face him. He caught a loose strand of my hair and twirled it between his fingers.

"What can I say? When I find something that is worth my time, I invest in it," he smiled down at me. He leaned in, sweeping his thumb across my jaw bone. I blushed and looked away, trying to find a way to distract him.

"That's new," I said, pointing at a silver dagger in his belt. He leaned away from me with a disappointed sigh, but pulled out the dagger. He held it up. The engravings on the blade shimmered in the sunlight.

"A gift from my father. To show me how proud he is to have another guard in the family." He handed the blade to me carefully. I tested the balance. It was a beautiful dagger. "He says if I work hard, and with his influence, I'm bound to be a captain in two years' time."

I ran my gloved fingers down the length of the blade, wishing I could take off the infernal things and touch it with my bare hands. I loved it. "Nice dagger for a guard." I muttered and could feel his silence looking at me. "Not that I know anything about weapons," I said quickly, handing the blade back to him. If I kept playing with it, I knew I'd end up scrutinizing it more than any lady should.

Kristoph put it back in his belt, but gave me a bit of a weird look. I played with the flowers he'd given me, hoping it would look ladylike and make him forget about my interest in weapons.

"It's more of a show piece," he said slowly, "I don't expect I'll ever use it."

"Personally, I hope you never have to use any weapons," I said, taking him by the arm to begin our walk again. "I'd much

Chapter Twelve

rather you get involved in very little fighting. Selfish, I know."

Kristoph laughed, deep and pleasing. "You always say something to surprise me. I came to see you with a purpose and you have distracted me."

"Have I?"

"Yes. My mother is a little worried about you. In three weeks you've barely left the Kraden Estate. Actually, you haven't left it at all. Jonathan and I are headed to the market. Would you be so kind as to join us?"

I smiled. "I would love to. Having two guards all to myself. How flattering."

By the time we met up with Jonathan, I was sporting a rather vicious blush and Kristoph a huge grin. Jonathan looked between us with amusement, but simply held the door open for me. We took a carriage down to the market. There were more guards than I had ever seen in any upper city circle before. They patrolled the streets in even intervals. I looked at the men curiously.

"Sir Kraden has decided it would be best to have extra patrols. There is a lot of fear around the upper ring right now. To be honest, people may not have loved your uncle, but no one can believe what happened."

I counted, spotting five guards between three streets as we exited the upper gate and headed to the midlevel of the city, where the market was held. "Does this mean there are less guards down here?"

Jonathan shrugged. "They would rather protect the upper class, I suppose. Perhaps Sir Kraden is worried about King Dupont saying he can't control his city. If an important person dies it might get back to the King, if a merchant dies, maybe he'll hear about it, maybe not. But if a person from the low district dies, well, let's just say the King couldn't care less about thieves and farmers."

Kristoph hit his friend hard in the shoulder. He shot Jonathan a look, and then looked tentatively at me. I decided not to react to that one. I was too busy wondering if this was a strange part of Maxwell's plan. By killing my 'Uncle' in the upper quarter, it guaranteed a stronger presence. Which would give him and the crew a lot of reign over the lower and middle quadrants. However, this made getting them into the upper level and the Kraden Estate more difficult. Jonathan and Kristoph seemed to be in a silent nudging and glaring match, so my distraction went unnoticed.

Ever since Allie told me about the festival market, I had wanted to go. However, I was much too distracted to fully enjoy it. I simply held onto Kristoph's elbow and let the men guide me around. Kristoph wanted me to try a special bread, and they left me by a scarf cart. I ran my gloved hands over the fabrics, wishing I could touch them, but taking off my gloves to reveal scarred hands was not a good idea.

"I suggest the light blue one. It'll compliment your eyes."

I jumped at the closeness of the voice, turning quickly to see Maxwell wearing a low hat and finer clothes than I had ever seen him in.

"Where's Allie?" I asked, keeping my eyes focused on the scarf cart in case Kristoph looked my way.

"Does it matter?" Maxwell asked, stepping in close beside me.

"Don't make me stab you," I said, feeling my hand itch.

"You'd ruin the heist." I could hear the smile and amusement in his voice.

"True," I sighed, "but I'm sure I'd get out of here without

Chapter Twelve

being apprehended. It'd be a bigger problem for you."

"She's safe. In a house in midtown."

I fingered a particularly red scarf. "Does she know what you did?"

"No."

"That why she's not with you?"

Maxwell turned to look at me. "Couldn't have you telling her, could I? I need her to trust me."

"And you can use her to control me," I finished for him.

"Something like that," he admitted with a casual shrug.

"You're a bastard. She actually *likes* you."

"I can be charming when I want to be," he said, throwing me a dashing smile.

"You disgust me," I muttered.

"I know," he said, reaching a hand to touch mine, knowing I couldn't flinch away without drawing attention. "But now we have an understanding, you and I, and you know what lengths I'll go to for what I want."

The comment brought an image of Shane's leer back. I nodded, feeling for the first time afraid of Maxwell.

"What kind of information do you have for me?" Maxwell asked.

"Nothing good. Guard rotations. A bit about the architecture."

"A way in?"

"Not yet."

Maxwell groaned. "Airen, you've been in there for several weeks. I need more, and you know it. I need prints, or a route."

"It's not a museum. I can't just wander around."

He pulled a black scarf off of the stand and wound it around

The Kraden Job

my wrist. "Get sneaky."

I blushed in rage at his casual touches. "I'll get more."

"You think you can convince your guards to let you come down here often?"

"If I like it, I'm sure Kristoph would be willing to take me here."

He nodded. "Good. You have four weeks. Then I want to meet you back here. And you better have something better for me."

"I want to see Allie," I said before he could step away. He paused, thinking it over.

"Fine, but I'll be close by. You tell her anything I don't want her to know, and it won't end well. And keep an eye on your soldier. Many women like a man in a red coat."

"See you in four weeks," I said, lacing the black scarf through my fingers. Maxwell disappeared off in the crowd. I glanced back but in a moment he was gone. My eyes focused on the red coats.

Kristoph and Jonathan were talking happily, heading back my way. They strode next to each other, turning the heads of many ladies who walked by. I have to admit, they were handsome. Kristoph was taller than Jonathan, and he had an ease. The ease that is born to privilege. Jonathan was more guarded in his walk, and his eyes occasionally scanned the crowd. It was obvious, he had been a guard longer, but this nervous behavior made him less attractive to the women, who stared more adamantly at Kristoph, with his strong frame and dark hair.

"What are you looking at?" Kristoph asked, sliding up beside me.

I blushed, the man was ruining my subtlety.

Chapter Twelve

"Just admiring the view, I think," Jonathan grinned, puffing out his chest dramatically.

I looked away. Kristoph seemed to take pity on me. "What's this?" He tugged at the scarf I was holding.

"Oh, nothing. Just something I was looking at."

Kristoph gently took it from my hands and went searching for the vendor. Jonathan smiled at me.

"Well, look at you. You've gotten my friend rather smitten. Kristoph may like fancy parties and dancing with beautiful ladies, but he is rarely willing to part with his money. And here he goes, buying the fair lady a gift."

I gave him a soft glare. "You stop."

Jonathan scrutinized me seriously. "You *do* care for him?"

My face was on fire.

He grinned at me. "Just checking. I think you make a fine pair. His mother already cares about you. Worried about the little girl who…" he trailed off. Cleared his throat. "Sorry. Sometimes I don't know when to shut up."

I was saved from replying as Kristoph came towards us, taking a dramatic bow before handing the scarf to me. I took it coyly, before wrapping it around my neck. "Thank you."

He held out his arm, and I took it without hesitation. We chatted idly, meandering through the market, but I couldn't help but wonder if Maxwell was up on some wall, watching us.

The next day I was in a panic, I needed to find something, anything that could suggest a way into the estate. The longer I stalled the greater risk I was of being discovered, I knew that, but also if I didn't have information by the time I had to meet Maxwell again, I knew that Allie's safety could not be guaranteed. I took to going to the Kraden's library early

The Kraden Job

every day and combing through the stacks. Households like that always have a section on its own personal history and glory. If one is ever-so lucky there is also detailed pictures on how the building itself was constructed. My biggest problem was finding the stuff.

These great houses, they have their own libraries, and their own librarians, but to ask about such things, well, it might look suspicious. Especially when a theft would take place after I had looked at them. So I was unable to ask for assistance in locating such documents. Instead making it out as though I was just someone who was using the library as a diversion. Picking up books at random to bring them to a table in the back. The only thing I did ask the librarian about was its classical romantic legends, allowing them to think that this was my true interest. It also had the benefit of being collected in a far back room of the library, where few of the guards or men of the house went, giving me ample time to pursue my finds. However, in a drive to hide my purpose from the librarian, for every one book I pulled that related to the history or building of the estate, I pulled three romantic story collections or poems. I mixed them all up together in untidy stacks on my table, easier to hide my true purpose.

It was then that I made the discovery of the gate. Not a large one, or a friendly one, but one that seemed mostly to be abandoned and shuffled off as unnecessary. The notes of the parchments weren't very clear, and I knew I'd need to check the physical location of it, to make sure it wasn't blocked off, but the local history of the city spoke of some underground passageways that I dreamed to explore. I was completely wrapped into the drawings when I heard a voice, loud in the otherwise silent back room of the library.

Chapter Twelve

"Who are you?" a feminine voice asked. I jerked with surprise, shifting the books on the table, the stack of novels I'd collected falling onto the papers showing the passageway.

I looked up to see a young woman in a bright red elegant dress standing before me, a large book of knightly plays held under one arm. There stood Miss Emily Kraden. I was again struck by how hauntingly odd it was to look at someone who looked almost exactly like Allie, but was nothing like her. For a second, when she stood there staring at me with a bit of a scowl, I almost forgot it wasn't Allie about to berate me for the slight mistreatment of books. Thankfully, before I could say anything stupid or grin at her like she was an old friend, she moved away to look at some books on the shelf.

Emily Kraden moved nothing like her sister. Allie had an elegance when she moved, a purposefulness. True, at times she was still clumsy and not in full control, but her presence demanded you take note. Her sister, Emily, in contrast moved with entitlement. She moved as though you should bow to her, head slightly tilted back and face slightly pinched. They were both beauties, but Emily had the personality of someone who was born in privilege. Someone who expected to be catered to. I struggled not to grimace at her.

"I apologize. You startled me, Miss Kraden," I said, standing to deliver her a slight curtsy. She was the type of girl who would revel in that. It was clear after a few moments of silence and the look on her face that she had no understanding of who I was. I shifted uncomfortably, nudging the books of romantic legends further over that of the structural plans of the estate. "I'm a guest of the Lady Jenkins."

"Oh," she said, "you're that girl. The one whose house was burgled or some such thing and then Father decided you could

The Kraden Job

stay here."

The flippancy stunned me. "My uncle died and I-" but I trailed off, not wanting to relive it, especially not to her.

"Oh yes," Emily said, looking around at the shelves in a bored manner. "And now that your uncles death has darkened our doors Father won't allow me to host a birthday party in the city gardens. It really isn't fair. He promised me I could have something really special this year. Now its all ruined and I'll just have a few of the ladies around for tea."

"Can't you just have an extravagant party here?" I asked before I could think better of it.

She looked down her nose at me, quite a feat as she was shorter than I. "It's really not the same thing. Though I suppose it might be for someone like you. But a true birthday extravaganza requires games and performances in a style that makes one forget we're in the city."

I bristled but even I could sense the opportunity here, if only I could get her to bite at the tantalizing suggestion I was about to make, which meant a bit of simpering on my part.

"Of course, you're right, Miss Kraden. Being from the countryside myself, I've only been to one festival in town."

She smiled condescendingly towards me, shifting the grip of the book, and the sight of the maze and masked lovers on the cover gave me a new idea. Throwing another party at the estate would help our plans. If I was in the estate itself and there was a large party, I might find a way to get the others to the gate inside and help them open it so they could come while it was busy. A large birthday party was a great excuse. After all, Amelio Kraden would be kept out of the way with his darling daughter, so moving about the place would be easier. And if Emily enjoyed plays, well, that would make things even

Chapter Twelve

more convenient for sneaking around.

"It does seem terribly unfair that you're unable to celebrate properly," I said, slowly. Emily sniffed a little huff. "Surely your father is a reasonable man and would make sure to please you on such a special day."

"Well, yes," she said, "Father would give me the best celebration possible but, as you may know, this little estate is so limiting."

I tried not to cringe, that was certainly not a way anyone would think to describe the massive estate. "Miss Kraden," I said softly, demurely, "if I may, unsuitable as it may be, make a suggestion to solve this terrible problem?"

"I suppose it couldn't hurt," she said, looking me over. Likely she thought I was trying to grovel and get into her good graces, given she was more or less the lady of the house. All the rumors I'd heard stated that Amelio Kraden bent to Emily's whims more than his wife's.

"Well, the first ever real festival I came to was here and when I entered I was amazed at seeing the grandeur of the place. But really, that courtyard, it is so stunning. And large. Its only grass now, but I could image large flower bushes there or a hedge maze. It seems like it wouldn't be too much work on the part of your father to bring in some glorious trees from the city gardens to use for your party."

"Go on," she said when I paused, checking her reaction to the idea. "What other thoughts did you have?"

"And don't you just think that the entrance way, with those great awnings, would be the perfect place to stage a play? Surely you can have elegant invitations made, and no one who doesn't possess such a card would be admitted into the halls. That might quell some of your father's fears. How could

The Kraden Job

he object to that?"

Emily scrutinized me, thinking about what I was saying. Her dreams of a large party weren't dead after all. The real question was, how much would she be willing to argue with her father. How far could she push him.

"It doesn't sound entirely unreasonable," she said, though she looked as though she was trying to hide how pleased she was with the idea. Condescending, superior sort of woman, that Emily Kraden was.

I went in for the final push. "It seems silly to let some scare in town effect your life in here. After all, is not this estate the safest place in the city? You cannot be expected to give into the pressures of those thugs. Then it would be as though they have won. Throwing a celebration, well, I think it'd rather comfort everyone wouldn't it? And, of course, give you the proper birthday that you deserve. It'd be like something out of a storybook. People would talk about it for years."

And that was it. That was what sold her. The idea that her ball, her birthday, would be remembered and talked about. That her popularity and prestige would rise. I could see it in her eyes. She wanted the glory.

"I suppose it is worth a try," she conceded, but there was a fire in her eyes that said she'd be heading straight back to her father to make demands soon. "You're more interesting than I would have thought. Though I don't expect we'll see much of each other during your stay," she said, reminding me of my place. That I was a country girl, barely above a commoner. She turned to leave, and I gave an aborted half-curtsy to her retreating form. It didn't really matter if she thought I was dirt. I'd given her a solution to her problems and she, unwittingly, was going to give me a solution to mine.

Chapter Twelve

Three nights later I emptied the trunk Mrs. Jenkins brought me from my "Uncle's" townhouse. I dumped all the dresses haphazardly onto the ground, tearing past the ribbons and delicate fabric. I got all the way to the bottom. Knocked happily on the false bottom. Tore off my gloves and dug my nail into the side of the box, pulling out the little wooden key I used to gain leverage, and lifted out the wooden plank to reveal the secret compartment underneath.

I pulled it out, being careful not to rip my dress. I tugged out the piles of black clothes hidden on the bottom. Finding my black stealth pants, a black undershirt, a flowing black over shirt, my black gloves and my lock picking kit. I swore, seeing the notches made to hold my knives and sword were empty. Maxwell left me with enough equipment to get around, but not to get myself into any trouble, or defend myself if I got caught. I really hated that man.

I carefully placed all the dresses back into the trunk and slipped into my sneak gear, and tied my hair back into a braid. I waited by the window until I saw the lanterns go out in the gardens. They kept it minimally lit at night. Amelio Kraden decided to let many of his personal guards go patrol the city, not concerned with thieves getting into this home. The reputation of his fortress-like estate kept all sane thieves away. If not, rumors of what he did to those he caught, did. I watched the lights start to go up on the perimeter of the wall. Waited until they were all done. There would be few to no guards in the halls that evening, and the ones there weren't likely to be that on alert. The hallway patrol was the safest job in town, the risk of running across a thief breaking in was minuscule.

I slipped into the hall. There weren't that many places to

The Kraden Job

hide in a hallway like that, it was built with only a few columns, no sculptures. But thankfully, Amelio Kraden had invested in beautiful architecture. There were lots of arches, and large arches meant great support systems. I wrapped the black scarf Kristoph had bought me around my braid and tied it up. I pulled my small black mask over my face. Grabbing onto the door frame, I hoisted myself up, placing one foot on a column to give me a jump up, and then I was in the system of arches. And in the darkness with only a few candles lit, I was near invisible.

I crawled across the beams, slinking along in the darkness. In their desire to maintain polite protocol, I was far from the Jenkins rooms, especially the sons' rooms. Which inevitably put me closer to the Kradens and Amelio Kradens' office. I cleared the few hallways without incident. The door to the office was cracked open, but a candle burned inside. I lowered myself softly to listen at the door.

There were the low grumbling voices of men in an argument. I could make out the voice of Graham, heard him address a second voice as Lord Kraden, and the third voice I assumed to be the dear Father Jenkins, who I had yet to meet.

"Look," the fatherly voice was saying, "I couldn't really care less *why* Kristoph joined the guard. I'm just happy he's doing something worthwhile."

"But Father, this girl, this Cassandra, we don't know anything about her. And she starts staying here because her Uncle was murdered, a man of questionable reputation, if I may add—"

"Which were concerns you voiced before we allowed her to stay," the voice of Amelio Kraden said.

"But not before my mother had all but promised her a place

Chapter Twelve

to stay, with complete disregard for propriety," Graham fumed. "Kristoph may be making a good choice for the first time in his life, but I don't like her influence over him. And I don't trust the influence she may have over Miss Emily Kraden. A fine lady such as your daughter should not be associating with girls from the country and, with all due respect, kin to a man with such dubious morals as Lord Stevens."

I heard a deep chuckle from Amelio Kraden. "Relax, Graham. Your brother is turning into a fine guard. He's taking steps in the right direction, no matter his reasoning. He's in love, Graham. As for this girl, Cassandra, I'm sure after a while he'll forget about her too. But I refuse to turn a young helpless woman out into the streets. I understand you're my head of security, and I thank you for your concern. Especially about my daughter, though I hope you focus instead on actual security rather than fanciful thoughts on young ladies."

The image of Graham standing rigid at the insult flashed across my mind. I had seen him walking quite often around the complex. He was often close to Miss Emily Kraden, glaring at any young man who came too close, and suspicious of any lady who approached her. His interest seemed welcomed by her, however, that didn't mean her father thought about it the same way.

"The redistribution of guards has been going well," Graham voice bristled. "In the past two weeks there have been no thefts in the upper quarter. The middle sector also seems to be much safer. However, few guards have wandered down into the lowest sections of town, and I hear, that there has been a little bit of trouble around the docks."

"Can the estate be efficiently guarded?"

"I have no doubt that there are enough men to guard the

estate, provided we stay more on the perimeter," Graham said.

"Perhaps you can authorize more single guard posts instead of them remaining in the conventional pairs. Forgo the yearlong training period before they're allowed to be on their own. It would allow you to spread out more," said Mr. Jenkins reasonably.

I shifted more towards the middle of the hall, so I could look down into the room. Graham had stood stalk still, his eyes blazing fiercely at his father.

"There is a reason for a two man patrol," he said, irritated at the suggestion. "It is safer for them. Besides, I don't want untrained men wandering around the halls with the authority to use blades."

Amelio Kraden waved a hand, getting both men's attention instantly. "As always, you're thorough, Graham, but your father makes a fair point. I want you to distribute the guards into one man patrols, even the new ones. Then we'll have at least one man combing the estates halls. Besides yourself, of course." Graham seemed to flinch at that. "At least until after the festivities are over. I told Emily holding her birthday so close to the ball was foolish, but she's a strong willed girl. I had forbidden her to hold her celebration at the gardens and so, clever girl, she found a way to make a party just as grand here. The extravagance of it is perhaps excessive, but I can hardly refuse her anything. We'll need to keep looking at the estates plans to find the best place to hold the maze games of hide and seek. I think we'll need to buy all the hedges they've grown at the university's gardens." He chuckled. "That girl is fanciful. Don't even get me started on the costuming she has demanded. And, Graham, you shall need to remind me that I need you to do a thorough check on the group of players

Chapter Twelve

for the drama she wants to put on. But that is all for now gentlemen, I'm tired and need a good nights sleep."

I darted back to the darkest recess of the ceiling and watched as Graham Jenkins and his father exited the room and wandered down the hall, apparently still in some argument or another. Amelio Kraden was shifting around documents on his desk. Moving some to cabinets and others to the trash. I rested my head gently against the wall, closed my eyes and waited. The way he was huffing gave the impression he'd be in there for a spell. Eventually, he left. Locked his study door, with two locks, and headed tiredly down the hall to his chambers. He took the closest lantern with him and I watched until the room was enveloped with darkness and not the faintest noise of footsteps could be heard.

I twisted in a flip down to the floor. Plucked my lock pick kit out from my belt and set to work. I tinkered with the locks for a time. They were frustratingly difficult, but eventually gave the clicks I was hoping for.

The office was beautiful. Covered wall to wall with shelves of books. Shiny wooden furniture. Glass orbs and statues decorated the many table tops. I whistled low. Taking only two things from that room would more than cover the amount Allie wanted to take. I closed the door quietly behind me, lit a match and found a candle. I drew the curtains fast, keeping the room with the impression of emptiness. I idly pulled open drawers, looking for anything of interest. Men like Amelio always keep a large sum of money in their office. Even if they are noble, half of them bribe off merchants for better goods, better trafficking.

He seemed smart, so I was betting on finding a box rather than a pile or bag of coins hanging around. I was rifling

The Kraden Job

through his desk when I pulled out a large folder with Emily's name on top of it. Placing the candle gently on the floor, I plunked down on the ground and emptied the contents.

Sketches of tents, cakes, wall-hangings, and costumes tumbled out. I spread them out along the ground. Emily Kraden had certainly run with the ideas I had given her and more. She was having a birthday extravaganza to end all birthdays. There would be a maze planted in the courtyard. A dance in the ballroom, great amounts of food, and a play on the platform at the top of the stairs, just where I had suggested it go. I smiled, turning over the choice of plays.

Emily could not have picked one better for my purposes if I had looked to choose one myself. It was the legend of 'The Princess of Ever-Changing Eyes and the Five Men who Loved Her', known for its deep hooded characters and masked women. She'd turned the whole affair into a masked ball. Getting the crew in would no longer be a problem. I rifled through the costume sketches until I found one that looked like Allie's physique. I cut the cloth swatch in half, placing the sketch aside for copying. I grinned. There was a copy of the official invitation as well, with some of its special paper card stock stuffed in behind it. I hummed to myself, grabbing a bottle of ink from the desk and began my forgery.

Chapter Thirteen

Allie stood, waiting patiently, by King Dupont's desk in the anti-chamber to his bedroom. It had been decided that the appearance of Allie in a completely unruffled ball gown inside a locked room was much more impressive than her looking as though she had actually scaled a wall. Or had help scaling the wall to be more accurate. So she stood still and waited, somewhat impatiently for the King to finish his nightly stroll after dinner and to return to his quarters. The scheme seemed worth it for the look on his face when King Dupont opened the door to his chambers, features morphing from shock into fear. He shut the door quietly behind himself, taking slow and apprehensive steps into the room.

"Majesty," Allie said with a curtsy. She may be a pirate, but she still liked to hold onto proper decorum as often as possible. "I've been waiting for you."

"Who are you? What do you want? How did you get

in here?" he asked in quick succession, sputtering slightly. His eyes darted back to the door he had just closed. The opportunity to call for help was there, but if he admitted that someone had come into his palace without him knowing and without alerting any of his guards, then who could say who was safe in the kingdom at all.

Allie chose to ignore those questions. Instead, she leafed through some of the paperwork on his desk. Treaties unsigned, waivers for prisoners, and other scandalous documents. "My my, you have such interesting things laying about here for anyone to find."

The King regarded her for a moment. "You can read," he said slowly. As if it were a skeptical question, something he highly doubted.

"Yes," Allie said, pushing a few of the papers to the floor. "I can read. And while all these are very interesting, I'm sure you'd agree with me that these papers I have here are of considerably more value." She held up the package. He looked at it. Eyes adjusting to the light. They widened, as he seemed to realize exactly what it was that she was holding.

"Where did you get that?" he eyed the thick package as if it would explode at any moment.

"Where do you think?"

"No!" he gasped out, shaking his head. "That's impossible. I have guards. There are ships. It's… it's … no one could get into that stronghold."

"All problems can be overcome with some creative thinking. But I'm flattered you think so highly of your security. It means I was just oh so smart to get a hold of this."

He sat down on a large chair abruptly, in shock. "If people see that, I could be ruined."

Chapter Thirteen

"That is highly possible, yes. Secret treaties with slave traders to keep them from firing on your personal merchant ships. Tut, tut, Majesty."

"Half the Kingdom could fall. These are not things to be tossed around lightly. They were locked away for a reason."

"True. Lots of these I didn't entirely understand. But what I did, well, is pretty terrifying."

He looked at Allie. Really looked at her. Taking in the coiffed hair, fine jewels, and silk trim on a delicate dress. "Who are you?"

Allie looked slightly put off by the question. She bristled. "Well, if you don't know who I am, I think I'd rather not tell you, Majesty."

"You think highly of yourself then? In your profession, I mean."

Allie arched an eyebrow at him. "Your Highness, I do consider myself one of the very best at what I do. That being said, I could make neither heads nor tails of these and, given that I have your very rapt attention, I was wondering if you would be so kind as to educate a silly pirate on their meaning," Allie said, as she pulled out the parchments that had been haunting her dreams with all their runes and mysterious script.

He paled. "You don't understand what you're playing with."

"Don't condescend to me, Majesty," Allie said, "I do know my business quite well."

King Dupont fixed a hard gaze at her, real fear showing in his eyes. "Those, you don't understand, and it is best well you do not. They would kill me in my sleep if they found out you had those."

Allie frowned at him. "Who are they? And why? It just

The Kraden Job

seems some gibberish about magic. Fairystories and the like is what it seems. I must admit my curiosity has gotten rather the best of me and I need to know more."

"Magic a myth?," King Dupont scoffed. "I suppose simple folk must think it so. You're not granted the histories of our kingdoms the way us royals are. Just because you know not what powers there were before, and what is hidden within those pages, does not mean magic does not exist. That pile of parchment you brandish around so casually has been fought and killed over for hundreds of years. That is until it came into my keeping, until I locked it away, far from prying eyes and fools of fortune. Of all the things in that place, I don't know how you came to find those papers, but it would have been best for yourself if you had let them be."

"Threatening now?"

"No," the King laughed hollowly. "I would leave that to them. There are those in the dark, who move in the night, that have terrible secrets. Terrible secrets that curious men, and women in your case, try to pry into never to be seen again, or if they are seen they are slightly less whole. Those pages can open a world of myths to you, show them to be true, but such things come at a cost, a great cost. It is better for you that their secrets remain unknown."

Allie smiled sweetly at him, folding the pages back into the package. "Now it seems as though you're trying to scare me off with your own fairy-story."

"Oh, what I would not give for that to be true," King Dupont said softly, before turning a hardened glare at Allie now that he'd regained his composure. "What do you want?"

Allie scoffed. "What do you think I want? Money. What else do pirates want?"

Chapter Thirteen

"And you plan to fly out of here with it, do you?" The King asked, sounding amused for the first time that evening.

"Oh, don't be absurd... your Highness. I'm not collecting it now. No, no, no. I'm going to hang onto this," she said tucking the bundle of documents into the folds of her dress. "And when you give me what I want I'll let you have it back. This is just the negotiation. You deliver your side later."

"And what makes you think I'd let you leave this room holding those. That I won't just kill you here and now?"

"Please, Majesty. Don't be ridiculous. I managed to get in and out of your stronghold without being detected. You haven't even gotten word of a break in there. Not to mention getting into your personal quarters here. You really think I came by myself?"

He ran a hand down his face, defeat coming off him in waves. "What do I have to do to get those back?"

Allie smiled, grabbing a pen off his desk and some paper. She dipped the pen into ink, making sure to keep an eye on King Dupont. "It's simple really. Our price is mostly gold, nothing imprinted of course, and a few *minor* papers. You know, a leave notice here, a summons there, some blank pages with your royal seal stamped on them. Nothing too terrible. We'll give you four days to gather these. You personally, and you alone, will meet me and my men at the base of the secret passage way that leads to the docks. Yes, we know about that. Don't look so surprised."

Kind Dupont shook his head. "Sometimes I wonder if I should employ some pirates myself. You're better than half my spies."

"You flatter me," she said with an easy smile. Folding up the paper and laying it on top of the rest of his paperwork. "Now,

The Kraden Job

I don't think I need to tell you that if you ask anyone for help out of your little predicament, it will end badly. We're playing nice at the moment. You don't want to try me. I'm not nearly as proper as I appear."

"It may be my imagination, but I tend not to think of pirates giving warnings to those they blackmail."

"Yes, well, we have reason to believe that you might be getting a visit in a little while. I'm not the only pirate on the ship, and evidently not as famous as I had thought. I'm just making sure you're aware if you let this visitor know that you're having pirate problems, the papers will only be the beginning of your troubles. We may be pirates, but sometimes, we just want to act like businessmen."

"Mercenaries, you mean."

Allie shrugged. "Mercenaries tend to be more violent. We care more for gold than for blood."

Suddenly, there was a sound like a knock on the door. Neither made any move towards it. The noise sounded again. The king looked at Allie, who looked quite content to stand next to the window, gazing down at the desk.

"Aren't you going to get that?" Allie asked after the fourth time a noise sounded behind the closed door. "It appears someone is trying to get your attention."

"I figured that wouldn't be my best option," he said, raising an eyebrow, "Given my present company."

Allie waved a hand towards the door. "By all means, your Highness. This is, after all, your home."

Allie took a step closer to the window as he moved towards the door. He gave her one last look before taking a hold of the door handle and yanking it open. He opened it to an empty hallway. He stepped into the hall, and as the door hid him from

Chapter Thirteen

view Allie hopped onto the window sill. She grabbed onto the rope that had been hidden behind her back and looked down.

It was a long way down. The wall melted down into darkness before a long drop, and she could see little dots of lanterns. She swung her legs over the sill and looked back into the room. The King had wandered out of the room to look further down the hallway, following the noise of what sounded like distant footsteps.

"Allie," Airen hissed. She was perched on the side of the wall. Holding partially onto a spike to which the ropes were tied. "Allie, get out the window."

Allie shook her head, letting out a small whimper.

"Allie! Get out here right now. The hard part was getting up here. Just slide out the window. If the King sees you hanging out the window all the planning is for nothing."

Allie kept shaking her head.

"Allie, he's going to be back any second," Airen hissed before taking a small object out of her pocket and pitching it through a nearby window that led to passageway further down the king's hall. "He's only going to follow the sounds of these for a few more seconds before he doubles back to see if you're still there. At some point he'll realize its a ploy of sorts. You can't be there."

"Airen, I'm scared."

"I know, but you can do it."

Allie's hands gripped the windowsill, her knuckles turning white. "I can't. I can't do it."

"Allie, if you don't drop in the next ten seconds I'm going to pull you out," Airen said.

"You wouldn't dare!" Allie hissed, glaring at her friend.

Airen spun the rope around her hand, giving it a small tug

The Kraden Job

that Allie could feel through the harness she was wearing.

"Try me. One," Airen counted, "Two. Three."

"I hate you," Allie squeaked, pushing herself off the frame. Her body jolted down for a split second before swinging towards Airen. Airen gave a smooth tug on the rope, steadying Allie from swinging too much. The soft fabric of her dress made a soft swooshing sound against the rough stone.

"See," Airen said quietly, "not so bad."

"I think I bit my lip so hard it's bleeding."

"At least you didn't scream. Now hang onto the secondary rope, and be careful on the way down. If we don't keep in the dark spots, we might ruin the whole illusion."

"Need me to help?" Allie asked, but even her voice was shaking.

"Most certainly not. If you grab onto anything your more like to let yourself drop. Just hang on."

Allie did as instructed and held onto the ropes that had been sewn into her dress to allow her to climb the wall and give the illusion of magically appearing inside a locked room. Airen fiddled with a strange clasp that was attached to her harness, one hand on the spike, the other squeezing the clasp gently. Airen watched intently, as Allie floated in a gentle slither towards the castle ground. A face looked up at her. She could see the worry on Allie's face, even at this distance. She watched it fade as Allie dropped further and further down, until she felt four short and two long tugs on the rope. Allie had reached the ground and unclipped the ropes.

"Now for the hard part," Airen sighed. She let go of the clasp. Looked up at the spike. It would be unprofessional to leave it. But her ribs were still a little fragile, and she didn't want to go agitating them by yanking on the cursed thing. The King

Chapter Thirteen

could keep the souvenir. She grabbed onto the rough rocks of the wall with one hand, and with the other took the rope off the spike. She watched the rope slither through the open clasp and rush down towards the ground. She saw a figure far below jump to the side. "I told you not to stand where you landed," she muttered looking down at Allie. She took a deep breath, found another hand hold, looked down and started her descent.

Airen enjoyed the climb. Mainly for the reason that the precarious climb didn't allow her to think about anything else. There was no way around it. She couldn't get distracted. Pain still lingered in her body, a helpful reminder that she was still human. Still able to die. Not as inhuman as people said. The danger of it made her focus all the more. And in the focused trance, she quickly found herself standing at the bottom of the tower wall with Allie.

"You dropped the rope," Allie said.

"Yeah. I usually climb down without one."

"It almost hit me." Allie kicked the pile.

"Then you shouldn't have been standing there, hmmm?"

"I hate you right now."

"Oh, come on, it wasn't that bad." Airen said, gathering up the ropes and shoving them into a bag.

"Yes, it was," Allie said, tossing a black cloak around her shoulders. "I just can't wait to be back on the ship. Stupid climbing."

"Now you see what I have to deal with."

"Yes, well, at least you can see things. To me, it's just all dark and blotchy."

Airen chuckled. "That does help. Come on. Let's get out of here before the next round of guards circle by on patrol."

The Kraden Job

They slinked against the walls, heading towards the secret tunnels. They dropped into them and Allie started to fuss with her dress.

"This is going to be ruined after this," Allie sighed.

"You can take money out of my cut to buy yourself a new one."

"Really?" she asked, her voice perking up as she took Airen's extended hand and followed her through the pitch darkness.

"Why not? I know half the men would cry if they had to go through this tunnel, minus a lamp, no less. And I'm making you go through it twice."

"Nick did seem a little apprehensive when he looked at it."

"Yeah, well," Airen sighed, "that's because he knows what's in here."

"What's in here?" Allie asked, alarmed, stopping suddenly.

"Just keep close to me, and be glad you can't see anything," Airen muttered back, gently tugging Allie's hand. "And whatever you feel, don't start screaming."

Nick met them at the tunnels entrance, which was a grand cave, with a high ceiling where enormous stalactites pointed downward ominously, as if they could fall on wary travelers at any time. He looked at them for a moment in the darkness, seeming to be deep in thought. Airen tossed the bag with ropes at him. He caught it and headed back towards the small boat that would take them back to the ship.

"We got a deal?"

"Of course we do. And, may I say, Allie did a good job of selling it.'

"No problems then?"

"Not a one. Why?" Airen said, her eyes narrowing at him.

He raised an eyebrow. "No reason in particular. Just

Chapter Thirteen

wanted to make sure. Allie, do you think the King will ask Commander Jenkins for help?"

"I don't think so. He got pretty scared when he realized we had those documents. Seems to think they are worth a lot more than we do," Allie said. Curiosity in her voice, trying to pry some more information about the mysterious documents, but Nick didn't give anything away.

"We'll be making a good trade for them. How many days did you give him?" Nick asked.

"I gave him four. We need at least two for Jenkins and his crew to catch up with us. I figure, if we lay low in this cave with a few crew members to bring the loot into the boats, we shouldn't have any problems. Right, Airen?"

"Hmm?" Airen asked, she was staring off into the darkness of the night. Nick gave her a hard look. "Sorry. Was somewhere else. But yeah, I think we'll be fine with a skeleton crew in the caves. We need to keep the ship far enough out that Jenkins won't notice it."

"Still not so sure—"

"I've got it handled, Nick. Don't worry about it. He'll be distracted," Airen said, yanking at the ties of her harness. She fiddled with the knots and frowned when she noticed blood on her fingers. "Shit. Lost a nail."

Allie grabbed her hand. "Really? How did you manage that?" She turned the hand over and over. Looking at the finger. Airen and Nick exchanged a glance over her head. They both knew, this was not going to be as easy as everyone hoped.

"All I can do is wrap it, I think that I have some pain soother in my bag in the boat. Let me go get it." Allie bustled over to the boat, tugging at her dress, when it got caught on stray rocks she was walking over.

"Allie seems to think this will be easy for you. Getting Commander Jenkins attention," Nick said. When Airen didn't respond he added. "Why is that?"

"Perhaps because I'm good at my job."

"Don't try to pull one on me, Airen. I know you. You are one heck of a sneak, but you aren't the best deceiver in the world. What could you possible say to Commander Jenkins that he'll forget he should be keeping an eye on the King?"

Airen shrugged. "Not entirely sure. I thought I might open with 'wanna kill me?' and see if he chases."

Nick groaned. "I can't believe you two talked me into this being a good idea."

"It's our only chance."

"You know, before I took you and Allie on my ship things ran a lot smoother."

"True, but you also didn't make a fraction of what you make with me and Allie around."

"That is true. You do pay for your keep. You know, Airen, if you want to stay after the job is done, you can stay on the crew. You're a good pirate. Drive me crazy, but a good pirate all the same."

"I appreciate it, but I think its best if I keep away from the crew after this one. I'm going to be literally dangling myself in front of Jenkins. If I don't get him killed in this... Well, it'd be easier for everyone if I just disappeared for a little while after that."

"Does Allie know you're thinking about this?"

"I mentioned it to her," Airen said, ripping off a small piece of her shirt and wrapping it around her finger tip.

"She think you might change your mind?"

Chapter Thirteen

Airen nodded, while biting onto the fabric, tying the fabric around her finger, tight.

Nick smiled down at her. "What you gonna give me to keep me quiet about what I know?" he said with humor flowing out of his voice. Clearly joking.

"You can take a part of my cut of the coin."

"Really? Generally, you don't like to share," he said, his voice cautious.

"We all need to learn sometime," she said.

Chapter Fourteen

Airen played with the bottles in Thom's quarters. Being the medic, he was allowed to have one of five private rooms on the entire ship, though his spare cot was often occupied by an invalid. He was bustling around, gathering up cloths and lotions, placing them in a bag for the few days they would spend hiding out at the base of the cliffs under the palace. They were using a cave entrance they were sure even the kings of the land had forgotten about generations ago. Airen wasn't sure how Nick had heard of it, but it seemed, while King Dupont and his guards were aware of the tunnels, that this cave itself had escaped notice. She was clinking the bottles together when they were jerked out of her hands. Thom glared at her, before turning back to his work.

Airen cleared her throat. "Sorry."

She milled about the room, fingers wandering over the chemicals and books. The crude drawings of relocated

Chapter Fourteen

shoulder blades and stitching. She prodded at needles and spun the fine thread around her fingers. Back and forth. Back and forth. Abruptly, Thom grabbed her by the shoulders, directed her to his only chair, pushed her into it, and held out a hand, as if to say 'stay'. Airen glared, but relaxed back into the chair, watching the silent medic run around the office and stuff supplies into his bag. He went through some of the vials, sniffing at them.

"Nick come down on you hard for helping me out?"

Thom had been avoiding her for a few days, and it was the only reason she could think of. He looked at her with a lack of amusement. Then he jerked his head towards the door.

"Oh, come on. Don't kick me out," she said, "I'm bored."

He glared at her before returning to his supplies. She regarded his back. Airen had never paid much attention to Thom before this job. He was silent, kept to himself, and she wasn't much on getting patched up. He rarely left the ship. Kept to himself. Rarely played cards with the other crew members. Never sparred with anyone. He just did his job. Being silent didn't exactly make it easy for him to make friends. She trailed her eyes down his back, as he folded some more bandages and tucked them deep into his supplies. The muscles rippled under his shirt. He was stronger than she would have guessed.

"Can I stay if I tell more of the story?"

Thom paused, but didn't turn around. His hand hovered over a small stack of bottles. Then he gave an abrupt nod of the head and started packing again.

~~~~~X~~~~~

"I spent the next few weeks gathering as much information as possible. Every night sneaking out into the halls. Crawling around in the scaffolding, overhearing conversations about the preparations for Emily's party. In keeping with her word, I saw Emily around the estate at a distance but she didn't deign to speak with me again. I did my real work deep in the night, returning to Amelio Kradens office, taking parchment that had been thrown away and making copies of everything I thought might be important or useful. I hid them in the false bottom of my clothing chest.

By the time I was scheduled to meet Maxwell again in the market, I had a hefty stack. I stared at the pile on my bed, wondering how I was going to get it down to the market without Kristoph knowing. I glared down the stack, hoping that somehow it would magically shrink and work with me.

Grabbing a sash, I rolled up the paperwork and tied it tight. Now it was a smaller cylinder. Twirling it around in my hands, I glanced around. My eyes rested on one of my cloaks and I smiled. In the end, I tied the sash covered paperwork to my forearm, making sure my cloak would cover it, so long as I didn't wave my arms around too much no one would know it was there.

Kristoph and I headed down to the market. It was busier than the weeks before, people bustling around. Ready for another spectacle at the Kraden Estate. We wove our way around, he kept close to me the entire time. He spoke constantly, chattering on about his training or something. I tuned most of it out and kept my eyes open for anyone from the crew.

"Mr. Jenkins," I said, trying to gain his attention, but he kept rambling on. "Mr. Jenkins." I squeezed his arm gently.

Chapter Fourteen

"Kristoph."

Kristoph stopped abruptly and looked down at me. I smiled. He muttered a sorry, but his eyes held mine. Probably just happy I had used his name.

"I know you promised your mother not to let me out of your sight, but I was wondering if I could have a little while to browse on my own."

He looked around uneasily. "I don't know. There are a lot of people about. What if those people that went after your uncle are here?"

I smiled reassuringly. "I think I can manage to stay hidden in this crowd. Besides, I was thinking of maybe finding something for you." I bit at my lip and it seemed to distract him.

"Okay. Just as long as you promise me one thing."

"And what's that?"

His smile turned into a grin. "Keep calling me Kristoph."

"You have a deal, Kristoph," I said, pulling softly away from him. He gave a small bow and walked off. I waited a few minutes, circling the area around the scarf cart slowly. A woman walked up to it, wearing a deep hooded cloak, a man standing a few feet behind her. I smirked.

"Lovely scarves," I said, sliding up beside Allie. She turned to look at me. Her fair hair had gotten a coal treatment, making it dark, near black. It wasn't the best disguise, but it made her look like she might be Emily Kraden's cousin but not her twin. "Nice hair."

"Really?" she asked with a smile, twirling a bit between her fingers. Remnants of the coal coming off on her hands. "I'm not fond of it. How are you?" Her voice was laced with concern.

The Kraden Job

I could feel Maxwell watching me. "I'm fine. And you?"

Allie let out a low sigh. "The house we're hiding in isn't exactly wonderful, but it's a little nicer than the ship's quarters."

It was just as Maxwell wanted it. She was truly and wholly ignorant to what he had done, and why they'd left Lord Stevens's home. Part of me was tempted to grab her, run as fast as we could, and try to get away from the whole mess. But I knew Maxwell would have someone watching from somewhere, probably with an arrow notched, just in case I tried to run. I also wasn't sure if Allie would blindly follow me. Maxwell had pulled the wool deep and snug over her eyes.

"So, how's the information gathering going? Max mentioned you've had a hard time getting information." She sounded worried.

"Not so much. I just had to get adjusted to the buildings and grounds. It's all rather larger than anticipated. I was a little shaken up when I got there," I muttered.

"Why?" she asked, cocking her head to the side. A throat cleared from behind us.

"Oh, you know," I played with one of the scarves in front of us, "it's just so different there. And Kristoph is a bit strange to get used to. I simply needed to make sure I fit in before I went snooping about the place."

"Find anything interesting yet?"

"A way in," I snaked my hand into my cloak. Pulled out the wrapped up papers, handed them over. She tucked it away inside her own cloak without a question. "Emily is throwing a party."

"Is she?" Allie's voice went a little too high.

Chapter Fourteen

"Yeah. How'd you and Maxwell like to attend?"

Her eyes snapped up to me. "Is that even possible?'

"They're putting on a production of 'The Princess of the Ever Changing Eyes' at the party."

"Which one is that again?" Allie asked, giving me a curious look.

I sighed. We didn't have time for her questioning. I scanned the crowd quickly, worried that Kristoph would come back at any moment. "Don't be an idiot. You know the one. About that beautiful princess and all those men who followed her around and died tragically for love or something like that. That's not the point. They've turned it into a themed costume party. There will be lots of masks and cloaks. The package has some swatches of the fabrics you'll need to copy a costume and from the drawings. You know I can't draw clothes, but it's as good as I could make them. Got yourselves two beautiful invitations too, and some sketches I did of the grounds surrounding the estate. If you arrive half an hour after the doors open, it will be flooded, and they'll just glance at your invitation. Trust me. Then you can meet me on the third floor. I marked it with an X. Found a gate we can use to get out, after we've gathered the gold. We could maybe head back out through the party, but it would be pretty risky. But we need at least three people to open it. Some strange security door thing. No doubt Graham's idea. The man is annoying, but smart."

"You're kidding? You already found us a way in and a way out? That's amazing. Before you know it, we'll all be back on the ship. With a sack of my father's money," she said smugly.

I ran a hand through my hair. "I haven't actually been able to find his money stash yet. Been a bit distracted with copying

The Kraden Job

all this stuff. It's a job well done, if I may say so myself."

"But we need to be able to get to the money."

I rolled my eyes. "I haven't forgotten that, Allie. But I'll have time. The extravaganza isn't for another month."

Allie turned to gape at me. "Month? We're stuck here another month? We've been in this city for so long already."

"Allie, really? Why the surprise? It is on your birthday, you're twins."

Allie looked at me for a long time, seeming to process that in her mind. "You know we haven't celebrated birthdays in years. I'm not even sure when yours is and I had quite forgotten my own. Does this mean we are going to rob my father on my birthday?"

I nodded. "I suppose."

Allie frowned. "Isn't there another way? An earlier time, another point to sneak in? I don't want to.. It seems rude to.. Thieving on my birthday wasn't something I ever hoped to do."

"Think of it as a very belated present to yourself. They're throwing her a party, the least they can do for you is pay a six year old ransom demand," I said.

She still looked upset. Mulling it over in her mind. "I just don't like it."

"Trust me, Allie. That place is locked tight. There is no way in there unless we go in through the front gate. This is the only way I can find. Maybe I could find another way in, but it'd take a few months to do that, too. This place is basically a fortress more than a home. I know the wait is gonna anger Maxwell, but that's not my problem right now."

Allie huffed, but consented. "You keep safe, Airen."

"Yeah," I said, as she turned, disappearing into the crowd.

Chapter Fourteen

"You too."

A moment later Maxwell came to fill the void. "A month?" he commented, his voice neutral.

"I can't plan the party Maxwell," I clipped out.

"Fine, but find that gold."

"I will."

Maxwell raised an eyebrow. "You're angry with me."

"You took my weapons."

"A lady with weapons is hard to explain."

"Bullshit. You just don't want me armed when you get in there. Afraid I might do something?" I challenged.

Maxwell snorted out a laugh. "You've never killed anyone and I doubt you'll start now. Believe it or not, I did it for your own protection. I know you. If you had them, you'd want to wear them when you sneak around, and that's too risky."

"You know nothing about me," I snipped out. His face only held amusement.

"I know a lot more than you think. I'll keep someone watching the Estate. When we get in, you take us around, the sooner we get out, the safer you'll feel. I'm sure of that."

"Allie's coming on the heist."

Maxwell nodded. "I thought she'd want to. Being as most of it was her idea anyways, and it being her father. But you made sure of that, didn't you? Telling her about her sister having a birthday party. Sneaky, Airen. Real sneaky."

I shrugged. "It's my job to keep her safe."

"Then do your *other* job and find that money. I'll be seeing you." He leaned in real close and I could feel his breath against my ear. "Even if you can't see me."

And with that, he disappeared. I returned with Kristoph to the estate. Watched as the preparations continued for the

The Kraden Job

party. I searched harder for the gold. The weeks passed in peace. I ate cakes at noon, drank tea. Chatted with Kristoph's mother. Watched him turn into a real guard. He was proud of his job and trying to make a difference. His hands grew some callouses while mine softened. So I lived and waited."

~~~~~X~~~~~

A knock at the door startled Airen out of her story. Airen and Thom looked towards the door. Nick was leaning in it, scowling at them.

"Who's Kristoph?" he asked. Thom quickly began shuffling around, double checking his equipment.

Airen shrugged. "An old lover. Rich civilian type. Got himself killed a few years back," she lied casually. "What do you want?'

Nick didn't look convinced but he dropped it. "We're dropping anchor soon. Found a good spot that should hide us from Commander Jenkins ship when he comes in. I want the two of you out on the deck. I'm rounding up those of the crew that are coming to the caves. We leave for the caves in ten minutes. We'll camp out there til dark sets in, then make our move. You all packed?" he asked, turning to look at Thom. The silent man nodded, grabbing a coat, and hoisting his bag over his shoulder. Thom pushed past Nick, not waiting for any other kind of response.

Airen scratched at the wood on the chair, very much aware of Nick watching her. She pushed up sharply to stand. "Suppose I should grab my things."

Nick put a hand on her shoulder when she tried to move past him. "I don't want you on the same boat as Thom to

Chapter Fourteen

shore."

Airen eyed him. Wondering if that was jealously or concern in his eyes. "Why not?"

"Because I don't like it. You two have never been close before. What's changed now?"

Airen pushed past him. "He listens."

"You could find others to listen. Allie, for example. Thom's more dangerous then he appears. You don't know what him and his buddy did to get on this boat."

Airen laughed. "Nick, I don't think anyone on this ship is more dangerous than me. But you want me to get some space. Fine. I'll go in a different boat. Need to catch up with Allie anyway."

Chapter Fifteen

In her dream the memory surfaced with a clarity she could escape in waking life. Kristoph was laid out on the green grass in a far corner of the maze, the one built for Emily's birthday. Together, Airen and Kristoph, had spent hours running through the maze, discovering secret paths, and the areas no one else wandered too. That afternoon they had escaped after tea with the Lady Jenkins and snuck off into the greenery.

The suns heat blazed down on them and, not for the first time, Airen found the dress of 'proper' ladies too hot and complicated. But Kristoph was laid out on the grass, staring up at her with adoring eyes and laughter on the edge of his tongue. He sat up with a playful smile on his face. She guessed what he was thinking before he moved.

"Don't you dare," she said, but there was no anger in her voice.

Chapter Fifteen

It was too late. Kristoph made a grab at her. She let out a peal of laughter as he tugged her swiftly to the ground. She batted at his shoulder in mock protest but settled down into the soft ground with him, tucked against his chest. The golden blonde of her hair shimmered in the sunlight against his coat.

"What will the ladies think if you dishevel my hair? I'll look an awful mess," she said.

Kristoph readjusted his arm, cradling her in close to him. He cast his eyes over her before saying, "I like your hair messy. I like the way you look different from the other ladies. And your eyes, no, I love your eyes," he said, kissing her nose. "That clear blue could stop my heart."

"I hope not," Airen said lightly. "Then I supposed I'd have to spend my free time with Jonathan."

"Don't you even think it. Not even my ghost would allow it," Kristoph said, poking her nose softly.

Airen ran a hand down the front of his coat, playing with the buttons. "You're different than I thought you'd be."

"What did you think I'd be?" He asked, raising an eyebrow.

"Oh, I don't know," she said dismissively, "people said you only cared about parties and dancing. Rumors had it that you weren't all that serious. Or ambitious."

"I'm serious about things that matter, Cassandra," he said in a definite tone that was new to her. For a moment they lay there, in the silent sun. Enjoying the warmth of the day, the seclusion of the maze. She knew it couldn't last.

Airen smiled sadly at him. "I might have to leave soon. You know I'm only staying here until I receive word from my family in the country. I'm sure after my uncle's death they'll want me home soon. I expect I'll receive a letter from them any day now."

The Kraden Job

"Here," he said, sitting up abruptly. Giving no indication he had heard her. "I have something for you."

"Do you?" Airen asked, scanning his strong shoulders from her spot on the grass. "I'm pretty sure it is almost Miss Emily Kraden's birthday. Not mine."

Kristoph flashed her a bright smile. "It isn't exactly a birthday sort of present."

"No?" she asked, watching him dig in his pocket, "What sort of present is it? One to remember you by?"

"Not exactly."

"Something to show me your undying love," she said, nearly laughing at the absurdity of it.

"Something like that," he said in a nervous voice. He placed the small box in front of her in the grass. The black velvet of the box stood out starkly. Airen couldn't take her eyes off of it, sucking in a breath when he flipped open the lid with a small click.

Inside lay a simple gold ring. It was plain, without engraving or a stone. It sat there, full of promise. She didn't move to take it. Just lay there, with the box barely a foot from her face. Airen was scared to touch it. Scared to breathe. Afraid that any movement would ruin the illusion of him, her, and the box. Her eyes were glued to the small gold band, barely registering what Kristoph was saying above her.

"It's more of a promise than a real ring. I mean, I haven't talked to my father about it yet. Not that I really care what he has to say on it. After I become a captain I'll buy you a real engagement ring. One with a set stone, any kind you want. I just wanted to buy it with my money, not my father's, so it might take a little while. And it makes more sense to wait until I have a better position," he rambled. "I know it isn't

Chapter Fifteen

much—"

"I love it."

"Try it on," he nudged her.

"No!" she said, a little too sharp. A little too fast. The fear of him seeing her hands, her scarred and calloused hands, shot her back to reality. Kristoph looked at her startled, doubt sinking into his eyes. Airen forced a smile and laugh. "If I try it on I'll never want to take it off again. It's a secret engagement. I can't just be running around with a ring on."

"It isn't an engagement."

"Why not?" she asked, cradling the box closer to her body. Her blue eyes narrowing, daring him to try and take it away.

Kristoph smiled at her. "You need to say 'yes' first."

"Well, Mr. Jenkins, I do believe you still need to ask."

"Gods, I love you."

Airen gave him a smile that didn't quite reach her eyes, and said softly, "As you should."

~~~~~X~~~~~

Airen awoke to the sharpness of a rock carving into her back. She wiped the sleep out of her eyes, calmed her breathing, and looked around the cave. Like her, many of the men had decided to take in a small nap before the big night. Some of the men were playing cards, drinking, that sort of thing. It was a nice release for them to be off the ship, of course, being stuck in a cave might potentially drive people just as stir crazy.

Airen stood and stretched, knowing a return to sleep was impossible now. That memory was one she'd buried deep after the escape from the Kraden Estate. Down in a secret place of her mind, she'd never mentioned that day to anyone, not even Allie. Suddenly, Airen was swept with a wave of nausea.

She moved to a rock at the edge of the cave and stared out. Yellow eyes scanned the sea and sky, before turning off left, toward the castle. It was built close to the edge of a cliff base that had jagged edges and after a long, long fall went into the ocean. Airen could hear the laughter behind her. They could be as loud as they wanted. The rush of wind took their voices and gargled them with the waves. No one would hear them down there.

Thom came to stand by her. He followed her eyes.

"Do you know about the old mad king's prison?"

She chose to take his ever present silence as a no.

"Something my dad told me about as a kid. 'Be a good pirate, or they'll throw you into the ol' mad king's prison,' he'd say. When they built that castle, over two hundred years ago, the old king built a prison that has a door that opens onto the ocean. Well, to be more specific, it opens to the cliffs. They say the King had a fear of blood. Maybe he just liked to hear people scream. Those who were sentenced to death were just thrown out that door. People hit the rocks or just drowned in the water. Water gets pretty cold up here, and if the shock doesn't get to you, you have maybe a few seconds before you're smashed into those rocks."

They listened to the water lap onto the shore line. Just staring out at the castle.

"That tower looks over the door. I mean, its higher up than the door, but from its window they say you can see the door. They say, the old mad king would just stand up there and watch as they threw men to their deaths. They say the tower still has seats in it. Wonder if they still use it or not."

Chapter Fifteen

Thom nodded, face grim.

Airen tugged at her sleeves. "Nick tells me you're dangerous."

Thom nodded again. He ran a hand through his hair. He looked away from Airen, turned his body more towards the ocean.

"Anyways," Airen started again, pulling her eyes away from the uncomfortable and secretive medic, "if Commander Jenkins catches me, I'm pretty sure I'm going out that door. Not that he's really a particularly bad guy. He just kinda hates me now. And I can't exactly blame him. I hate me sometimes for what I did. You see…"

~~~~~X~~~~~

In the days leading up to the festivities, I'd begun feigning sickness. Staying late in bed in the mornings, having mild to moderate coughing fits. I would be regretfully too ill to truly enjoy Emily Kraden's party. So I got to sit it out. Kristoph was upset, so he decided to work instead of enjoy the party himself. He told me that if we couldn't enjoy it together then there wasn't really any point in it for him. His mother told me it was the first time Kristoph had turned down a party. She sounded so proud of him, putting work before pleasure.

I waited until the festivities was in full swing before heading out of my room in my pants and dark shirt. The few things I cared about were tucked into the folds of my clothing. If all went perfectly, I would stay a few more days in the Kraden Estate to try and seem innocent. If things went well, we would have a few hours to clear out, but I'd have to leave. And if things went badly, I had a feeling there would be some running and ducking bullets.

I slunk through the estate, waiting in a hallway that had a clear view of the maze that had been erected on the lawn. People were laughing and enjoying themselves. Dancing in the moonlight with masks. I knew somewhere down there were Allie and Maxwell. I could imagine Allie dragging him into at least one dance. Enjoying the mask and anonymity of it all. She has always loved a good masked ball.

To my surprise I found them already waiting for me in the upper hallway. They got in faster than I had expected. Maxwell tore off his mask and half chucked it down the hall. Allie looked happy in an ornate black mask and dark dress.

"Watch this," she said in excitement. She tugged at the side of her skirt. It made a small ripping noise before she twirled the bottom half off to reveal a pair of dark pants. She spun the dress part of her gown around her shoulders and it became a cloak. "Ta dah!"

"Very nice," I smiled at her.

"Can we get moving now?" Maxwell said. He was grumpy, which was odd because so far everything was going perfectly to plan.

We moved around in the darkness of the halls, just the three of us indulging in the quiet of the estate after dark, as the noises of the party faded behind us. The torch lights had been doused, because there was no one to keep an eye on them. Not with the show going on in the courtyard. We had hours. Hours! I'd never been on a heist with so much available time.

We scurried quickly and silently through the halls. Arriving at the door to Lord Kraden's study, I pulled the top lock's key out of my pants pocket, slipped it into the lock, and got out the lock picks for the smaller bottom key hole. When

Chapter Fifteen

it clicked, we smiled at each other. I had to admit, I hadn't expected things to run that smoothly. For all our panic at the beginning, it was nice to be so close to the prize. At all that wealth, I couldn't help but feel proud.

"Right," Allie said, rubbing her hands together, her eyes glittering with the promise of money, "so where's the gold?"

I smiled. "Took me a few tries to find it, but here." I walked around the desk, crouching near to the floor to get at the bottom drawer and a secret compartment within it. "This stuff's not been minted. Right place and we can sell it for more than its worth. You could put anyone's face on these." I pulled out a box of coins. Tossed one up to Allie.

She caught it and inspected it in the light. She let out a low whistle. "Happy birthday to me. That's about as pure as it gets. But remember, to not increase dear father's wrath, we said only take the old ransom amount. Nothing more."

"How much was that you reckon?" I asked.

She glanced down towards the box. Shrugged. "Better make it half, I suppose."

I felt a grin creep across my face as I tossed an empty bag at her. She started to fill the bag with the boxes contents. For a while, I was distracted with the happy clinking of golden coins. That was until she reached for another handful and in that brief moment, I heard the deep mouth breathing. My eyes shot up.

I stared at him for a time. Shane: the man who'd attacked me. He stood near the door, dumbly looking between the gold running between Allie's fingers and Maxwell. I rose slowly out of my crouch, apprehension tingling at the tips of my fingers and running across my skin. Maxwell had his eyes fixed upon a small box high on a bookcase, seeming oblivious

The Kraden Job

to me, Shane, or the loot I had searched for so hard.

"Why's he here?" I asked with a slowness. A false calm.

Maxwell shrugged, but his eyes were hungry as he pulled round a chair and stepped on it to get the box down. "Never hurts to have an extra fighter about. In case there's trouble." His hands closed around the box. "Now, what do you think is in here?" He'd brought the box down with him. His greedy eyes seemed to suggest he knew, or at least he could guess, exactly what was in the box. He dropped it on the table with a loud bang. "Let's have a look inside."

"We said we'd only take the ransom amount," Allie complained.

"Not going to add it to the haul, just want to have a look inside," Maxwell said in an appeasing tone. But his eyes held the same cold they had right before he pulled the blade across the servant's throat.

"Open it!" Maxwell demanded, turning the box round to face me. I stared down at it for a moment, pulled the picks out of my pocket.

The silence felt heavy, as we listened for the little clicks and ticks of the lock. My eyes flicked quickly to Shane.

"Are we expecting a fight?" I asked Maxwell.

"No one's ever expecting it, but strong fighters come in handy."

The lock clicked, and I turned the box back towards Maxwell reluctantly. Still closed.

"Yeah, but why did you have to bring *him?*"

Maxwell held the box to the light, playing with the latch before throwing the lid off.

"Because he has no morals," he said quietly, looking greedily inside the box. Inside was a small lantern. It could maybe fit

Chapter Fifteen

into the palm of my hand. Had a small metal frame, bronze in the light. The glass was a purplish sort of color. There were strange marks on it. I had never seen anything like it before. It looked useless to me, but Maxwell was staring at it with a reverence that worried me.

"Right," Maxwell said, snapping the lid shut. He dropped the box into a bag and slung it over his shoulder, looking at Shane. "You take care of this and I'll see you in a bit."

Shane gave a large grin, lecherous and gross. Allie stared after Maxwell incredulously. I was surprised at exactly how it was playing out, but not at the betrayal.

"So, what? This was all just a trick? You trying to help me, was just a ruse to get to that box? It didn't mean anything?" Tears were starting to fill her eyes and tickle down her cheeks, though from anger, embarrassment, or betrayal, I wasn't exactly sure. Possibly a mixture of the three.

Maxwell turned. He smiled at her, sweet and loving. "Of course it meant something. It got me my box." He turned to Shane. "Kill her fast if you can." He stopped for a moment in the door, throwing a look at me. "Do what you want with Airen. But if you aren't by the ship by sun up, we're leaving you."

Maxwell left the room. The sound of his feet trailing down the hall seemed to echo. I was painfully aware of our situation. I had a set of lock picks, but no blade. Allie had a small knife tucked into a sash hanging low around her hips. From the handle, I could tell it had never been removed from its sheath. And there he stood, Shane. The great ass, sword at the hip, knife in his belt, gun now balanced almost casually in his hand.

Shane stood between us and the door. Allie still had a hand half clasped around discs of gold. I could see her in

The Kraden Job

my periphery, almost feel the shock radiating off her. I didn't dare look at her fully. Shane already had the upper hand, giving him more, seemed more than moderately stupid.

He had this grin on his face. A deep sort of satisfied grin. It made me feel sick to my stomach. I wish I could tell you that I had some clever plan. Wish I could tell you that I was the master of the moment. Wish I could tell you that, because Allie was frozen with fear, I knew I had to buck up and handle the situation. But I couldn't, because I was frozen too.

The panic rose inside me with acidic bubbles. Fear jolted so hard, there were spots in my vision. My ears throbbed and my ribs felt the slamming panic of my fear. Adrenaline coursed through me, but I couldn't use it, so it sat in my veins burning. All I could do, was remember his hands on me, my ears rang with the noise of him tearing the fabric off my dress. My nostrils felt like they were being flooded with the pungent smell of his breath. I could feel his hands and body on top of me, even though I was staring at him across the room. His grin widened, as if he knew.

Move. I willed myself. Just move. But I was as frozen as Allie, with her hand half in the box. He raised the gun and pointed it straight at Allie. He'd always been a fair shot and, at that distance, he was sure to hit the mark.

"Max wouldn't know if I don't follow orders, but one quick death and one much more ... enjoyable, seems fair." He kept his eyes locked on mine as he said it. His finger inched towards the trigger and we just stared. And then it happened.

A loud noise broke into the night, shattering the quiet. The alarm bell. It clanged in a deafening tone. Maxwell had been spotted. Shane whipped his head around to look towards the noise for a split second. The clang jolted me. Allie jumped a

Chapter Fifteen

bit, the gold falling to the floor. I kicked her, hard, in the hip. She stumbled and fell into the desk, scattering the gold coins before falling behind it. Shane whirled around, pulling the trigger as he did. Shooting at the recently Allie vacated space. I hurtled myself at him, chucking gold coins at his head. I sailed through the air. He dodged, and the gold went out into the hall, but the distraction worked. I was able to reach him, before he could get out his sword

I had spent years fighting on ships, being trained to duck and dive, dispatch an adversary. Subdue them quickly and move around. I was good at it, coordinated, graceful even, but this was none of that. I was like a frenzied animal. No control. Just blind fear and rage. I had jumped on top of him: swatting, scratching, baring teeth and screaming. Hitting any spot I could reach. Discipline gone in a flash. Weaponless and frightened, I was like a raging kitten against a bear.

Shane grabbed me around the waist with one arm and threw me. Simple as that. He threw me like a ragdoll. I sailed back across the room, smashing and sliding across the table top. I narrowly missed landing on top of Allie as she ducked. By the time we peeked over the table, he had drawn his sword and was advancing towards us.

The alarm bell was clanging away. Voices were shouting and a figure ran past the door. There was a flash of a coat. A very distinct red color I knew too well. My eyes widened. I wanted the thundering feet to keep going. To run away, but they didn't

"No," I muttered. Allie spared me a confused glance before it happened. Kristoph appeared in the doorway. His eyes wide as he regarded Allie and I hiding behind the desk.

"Cassandra!! Emily!" he called. Mistaking Allie for her

sister and me for someone worth his protection. Shane turned around, pointing his sword at the new enemy. Kristoph pulled his sword out quickly, darting glances between us and Shane.

I had seen Kristoph fight a few times, mostly training with the other guards or sparring with Jonathan. He didn't lack in skill. Kristoph was fast, agile, smart, and brave. All the combinations of a great dueler. However, a horrible skill set for fighting a pirate who relies on force, strength, and cheating. Shane wasn't exactly concerned about the honor of a fight, he just wanted to win. Shane's base brute force alone would crush Kristoph, of that I was sure.

"Kristoph, run!" I called, wanting him gone.

He set his jaw in determination. He moved to square off with Shane. "I won't leave you. Or Emily."

Stupid, brave pride. I imagine, to him it looked like two helpless maidens stuck behind a desk with a crazed pirate towering over them, which is more accurate than I care to admit really, but it wasn't exactly the whole story.

Shane just smiled. This was a fight worthy of his time. He pulled the dagger out of his belt, flipped it back into a defensive grip and began to circle Kristoph. I swore under my breath as Kristoph went for the bait, moving in a half circle with Shane. That cursed pirate was used to fighting in any type of surrounding, ready to drop a body at a moment's notice. Kristoph was used to great halls or training grounds. Shane was twisting him around, close to a bookshelf. When his back was to it, Shane lunged.

Kristoph met the blow well into its arch, but bucked under the strength of it. His eyes widened and he let out a small shout, when Shane's foot smashed into him, throwing Kristoph back into the bookcase. Ever the gentleman in his

Chapter Fifteen

youth, he hadn't expected even a pirate to fight dirty. He slid down the bookcase, blocking blows from Shane with a fierce determination. He swung Shane's blade wide and rolled out into the center of the room, getting to his feet quickly.

But it wasn't enough. Shane was quick too. He tossed his dagger blindly. Kristoph managed to smash it away with a clang of his sword. He was not so lucky with the books Shane launched in quick succession. Kristoph was stumbling to dodge out of the way and avoid the clutter building on the floor. He was barely able to keep his balance and ward off Shane's advancing attack.

I moved to get up, making a grab for the dagger at Allie's waist.

She stopped my hand. "Don't. You'll give away our cover."

"Screw our cover," I said, shoving her arm away and grabbing the small blade.

"He's protecting you, like he's supposed to. I'm impressed. You did a good job with him."

I looked over the desk. Kristoph's chest was moving in heaves to gain breath. Shane looked amused, but barely affected by the fight. I groaned. "But if he keeps protecting us, who's going to protect him?"

Allie looked at me startled. Then recognition snuck into her eyes.

"Oh, Airen," she said sadly.

"Shut up. You can lecture me later," I muttered, tugging at the blade. It wouldn't budge. "Allie, is this melded together?"

"So?" she asked, throwing up her hands defensively. "I never expected to use it. And you shouldn't use it now." She yanked it out of my hands as there was a particularly loud thud from beyond the table.

The Kraden Job

Kristoph had been thrown to the floor again. He was a disheveled, sweaty, bleeding mess. His face exhausted. All attempts to keep Shane's blade from piercing his body were weak and hesitant at best.

"I can't just let him die for me."

"Well, what are you going to do? You don't even have a sword." Allie said, watching the fight with a mixture of frustration and sadness. She tugged at her hair, shifting her bun downwards, and I noticed it, that hair pin she loved so much. The ones she liked to play with and hollow out, fill with potions and wear around like she was a magnificent, beautiful, poisonous butterfly.

I snatched it out of her hair. "I have an idea, well half of one anyways. Gather all the gold that bag can hold. Screw only taking the ransom amount. We should have known better from the beginning. We're pirates, not debt collectors."

"What are you going to do?" she asked, pulling her hair back into a sharp ponytail. Kristoph screamed out, as Shane's sword cut his torso.

"Something stupid." I pulled the pin out of my own hair and held them tight in my fist. "What's in these?"

Allie stared at them. "Nothing deadly. It'll make him sick, in about half an hour. But I don't really think that'll help us out much here."

"You have to work on some faster poisons," I said standing. "Wish me luck."

She grabbed at my pant leg. "Don't do this."

I set my jaw, pulled myself away from her and took a running leap across the room. My momentum carried me hard into Shane's back. I used the power of it to drive the hair pins hard into his side, felt them resist, before their sharp tips

Chapter Fifteen

sunk in. He grunted and twisted, throwing me to the ground. He looked angry, until he saw what I had stabbed him with. Slowly pulling out the pins, his eyes morphed into horror. Everyone on the ship knew Allie poisoned her pins, but no one knew with what. Fear flashed through his eyes, before he turned on me in pure rage. Kristoph lifted his sword, but Shane easily kicked his elbow, sending the sword across the room. I scrabbled back on my hands and knees. An enraged Shane advanced towards me.

"You're going to regret that." He lifted his sword. I closed my eyes, stupidly throwing my arm in front of my face to shield myself. The blow didn't come. I opened my eyes to see Kristoph stagger and fall down next to me, a deep cut ripped into his side. He hit the ground hard.

"No! no, no, no, nonononon," I babbled over and over, crouching by his side. Tears filled my eyes, and I put my hands over the cut, trying to slow the bleeding. The blood simply leaked through my fingers. "Focus, Kristoph," I said, looking into his eyes, but his focus was waning. I pushed back his hair, smudging blood across his forehead.

Shane laughed from behind me. "So, now here's the truth of it. You fell for him. Maxwell was right. You *are* too weak for this." He let out a laugh, a deep full laugh. His head was thrown back, his sword held casually in his hand.

I fumbled at Kristoph's belt, pulling out his silver dagger. In a fluid motion I stood and dug the blade deep into Shane's throat. He fell to his knees. I pushed his body back with a foot and pulled the dagger back out, tucking it quickly into my belt before turning back to Kristoph.

I was aware of Shane's twitchy body as I ripped the buttons of Kristoph's coat, pushing it to the side to get a better look at

The Kraden Job

the cut. It was jagged and deep. I swore. He let out whimpers. His eyes fluttering open and closed. Allie walked over the still corpse of Shane and crouched beside me, putting a hand on my shoulder.

"Airen," she said quiet, "we have to go."

I was crying, and I didn't care. "We can't. If we leave him. .. No one knows he's here… what if he… It's a bad cut and he has another in his arm… I just can't…" I wiped at my nose, covering my face with his blood. "Give me your sash."

"Airen, we don't have time for this. I'm sorry. But we really have to go."

"Allie, just give me the dumb sash, and I promise, I will get us out of here."

She untied it and handed it over. I slipped it around Kristoph's middrift, murmuring apologies when he groaned and cried out when I cinched the sash closed. It wasn't great as bandaging goes, but it was better than nothing. I hoped it would staunch the bleeding at least until the next patrol came by.

"You're going to be okay," I told him, low and soft. He whimpered. I kissed him. Just once. On the forehead. Then stood up, cast one last glance at Shane, the blood in a puddle around his head, and walked out the door.

Allie had to jog to catch up to me. I was scrubbing my face, wiping off the tears, and taking deep sniffing breaths to calm down. Allie was silent for a while, politely ignoring my tears. She seemed to be operating off adrenaline and shock. When we headed down a staircase, she paused.

"Where are we going?" she asked, puzzled.

"Out of here. And we should probably hurry. That bells been going for a while." It was still clanging loud and annoying.

Chapter Fifteen

There were distant voices screaming, and I heard a gun go off somewhere outside. She nodded and followed me down the stairs.

"But I thought you said we'd need three people to get the gate open. But this isn't even the way towards the gate."

"I lied."

"You lied?"

"Never been exactly fond of Maxwell. There is no gate the way he went. I figured, if he did what promised, we could all leave together. If he got greedy, well, that's his problem. He'll have to fight his way out."

"So, you lied to all of us?"

I shrugged, leading her down a hall that looked as though it had been deserted for years. "If he played fair, nothing bad would happen. I didn't trust him. Seems I was right."

"Fine. So where are we going?"

"Down and out. There's a hatch that leads to tunnels under the complex."

"Tunnels?" she asked, her voice doubtful.

I coughed. "They might be sewers. Good thing you aren't wearing one of your nice dresses."

"Oh, no," she stopped. "They're all still on the ship."

"Priorities, Allie. We'll get you some more. Let's just get out of here alive first. If that's even possible." I grumbled. We took the sewers, and she only complained a few times, which surprised and impressed me. But we'd had a strange day. You know, they might still be down there unguarded. Maxwell and the half dozen men he'd brought in had to fight their way out. Think a few of them died. I've heard a few stories about the two women who were involved with the Kraden heist, and in most of them, the women seem to disappear into thin air. Rather flattering, I must say.

Chapter Sixteen

"You ready?" Nick asked.

Airen looked up from tightening a band around her thigh, securing a dagger. She grabbed a pair of gloves off the rock next to her. "As ready as I'll ever be. Let's get going."

"Remember, you draw Commander Jenkins and his men away from the tunnel entrance."

"I know how to do my job, Nick. I'll get them up the northern tower if I can. It'll keep them long and clear from the meeting spot with the King. Don't worry. They won't have any idea of what you're doing. Jenkins isn't stupid. He'll keep men on his ship and, of course, he'll have some with him. His family does run security after all. He'll have at most five men with him. It won't be a problem."

Nick pulled his sword partially out of its sheath, caught the moonlight in it, and dropped it back in again. "You know, if you want me to send a man or two with you, I have no

The Kraden Job

problem-"

"I don't need to be babysat," Airen said, giving him a stern look.

"That's not what I meant. It could be a lot to handle and-"

"I'll get it figured. Don't worry. You'll get the money."

Nick frowned. "That's not what I meant. I know we have our disagreements, but I don't want to send you into a death trap either."

"Don't worry about that. I can handle the bunch Jenkins will have with him. He'll want to be to best me himself, and I can beat him in a fight. So, if I were you, I'd just worry about dealing with the King."

"Look, Airen, I just think that-"

"Not a suggestion, Nick," Airen said, rubbing at the edge of one of her blades that she slipped into the side of her coat. He stood there for a moment, watching her gather her things, but after a time, he sighed and walked off.

Allie walked straight up to her with a look of determination. "You aren't going to do anything stupid, are you?"

"Like what?"

"Starting a fair fight."

Airen sighed. She looked at her oldest friend, who was practically pouting under her glower. "No, Allie. I'm not going to start any fair fights. I'm not a big fan of those, 'specially when it comes to Jenkins."

"Right. Just wanted to make sure. I was prepared to threaten you, if you were thinking about it."

"Threaten me with what?" Airen asked, amused by her serene looking friend.

"Been meaning to try out my newest poison. Not entirely sure if my dosage is correct." She gave Airen a sidelong glance.

Chapter Sixteen

Airen smiled, and they both started to laugh, low and quiet.

"While I appreciate the concern, Allie, I'm going to be fine. It's just a job like any other."

"Yes, but you usually don't play bait. Whenever you do… things tend to go wrong."

Airen stared out at the ol' mad king's prison door. She played with the buttons of her coat. "Don't worry, Allie. Nothing's going to go wrong this time."

"It better not," Allie muttered. She cracked her back. "I'm going to head out. We have more ground to cover than you." She smiled, and was shocked, when Airen pulled her in for a tight hug.

"Be careful."

Allie laughed, low and pleasant. "Of course. But I'm only dealing with the King. Nothing too dangerous there." She smiled, before floating off to gather up the band of men that would accompany her to intimidate and carry the heavy boxes. Instead of being put out, the men all gave Allie a revering look, as if she were a muse.

Airen rolled her eyes. "Don't know how she manages it," she commented idly. Thom jumped, even though he'd been the one trying to sneak up on her. She turned and gave him a ghost of a smile. "Whatever I may tell her, make sure you have medical supplies ready on the boat. This might get rough."

He gave a sharp nod.

"Don't tell anyone," she joked, "but I'm actually nervous about this. I know this Kristoph thing is stupid. It's dangerous. Just can't seem to let it go," she trailed off, adjusting a small pouch on her belt. She checked, then double, and triple checked the knot on it. She let out a low sigh, running a hand over her braided hair, and covering up her eyes. "Guess

The Kraden Job

I'm off."

Airen had barely made two steps forward, when she felt a heavy hand land on her shoulder. She looked back at Thom, his eyes serious in the moonlight. "You know he doesn't see you, right? Doesn't matter if you are doused in blood, and your eyes are yellow. He just sees some fragile, lost girl that still needs saving."

"Did you just-" Airen started in surprise.

"Look, I don't care if you need to work out this vendetta, or closure, or whatever you're doing with Jenkins, but don't do anything stupid. And if you do, I don't care if you get cut up and shot. You get back to the boat. Okay? You drag yourself if you have to. Just get yourself back to the boat."

Thom stormed off before she could reply, leaving her in a state of shock. The sound of his gruff voice from lack of use echoing in her ears. She wasn't sure, if his out of character behavior made her feel comforted, or more nervous. She contemplated running off to a corner to vomit, but instead, yanked hard on the strap of her sword and headed off into the caves. Yellow eyes blazing with anticipation.

Moving through the tunnels was easier the second time. Though she fidgeted at the movement of rats scampering by. She nearly jumped when she heard a bang from deep within the walls. Her yellow eyes glowed as her head snapped around, but there was nothing there. The wind whistled through the pathways, and she felt it deep in her bones, slipping through the fabric of her coat, chilling her. It filled her with anticipation. There were stories among thieves about the things that slunk around in tunnels under castles and cities. The things that lurked there didn't want to be seen. Airen

Chapter Sixteen

smirked a little. She supposed, as a sheened pirate, she was one of those things tonight.

Airen crept along until she reached a wall drain near the roof of the passage. She peeked outside. Sure enough, Commander Jenkins was prowling the courtyard with four of his men. They were trying to look casual, like they were just going for an the evening, but his eyes darted around, and the men had their hands floating above the handle of their swords.

Airen rolled her eyes. This was going to be too easy. At least until they caught up with her. She waited until they passed, before pulling herself up and out of the tunnel, slipping through the bars like a determined cat. She slinked along the wall, careful to keep into the shadows.

She trailed behind them. They appeared oblivious. She followed them until they entered a courtyard with many doors and stairwells. From here, she knew she could drag them away without gaining any attention from the King's guards. Now all she needed was a way to attract their attention. She tapped her fingernails against the hilt of her sword.

Airen moved to climb to a window, surely this would garner their attention. But the men kept walking away as she reached the top of the wall. She glared down at them. Sneaking badly was difficult.

Scampering back down, she pulled out a knife and hit it hard against the stone wall. She heard a shout of 'over there' and suddenly found the group of five men staring at her. Airen feigned surprise, dropped to the ground and bolted. The men followed her, Kristoph in the lead. Airen ran through a doorway leading down a stone hallway. In a quick movement, she grabbed a statue and flipped herself to stand on the large stone door frame. The old castle had thick walls and thicker doors. The top of the door frame was almost a ledge. She lurched forward, but managed to catch her balance. Stopping her movements as the sound of five men running echoed off the stone walls. Kristoph and his guards bounded into the hallway and kept running for a moment, before Kristoph, in the front, skidded to a stop. The other men slowed.

"Where'd she go?" they asked, looking around the empty hall. Kristoph was turning around slowly, eyes darting around for some sort of clue. This was not his first pirate hunt, and not the first with a skilled thief. However, it was his first time against someone with the sheen.

On top of the door frame, Airen slowly slid her sword out of its sheath. Once it was drawn, she tugged a small throwing knife out of the lining of her boot. She twirled it between her fingers, got a good look at the torches, closed her eyes, and with a swift flick of her wrist threw it. The torches snapped off, one after the other.

Airen opened her eyes to the cries of dismay from the men. They were looking around themselves in shock, pulling out their blades. The four men had jerky, uncomfortable movements in the dark. Their eyes would adjust in a minute, she knew, but not very well. It was too dark for *their* kind. Kristoph was moving calmly, his eyes scanning the darkened hall. He registered two little spots of yellow light soaring through the air before one of his men screamed and slammed to the ground.

"Get a light," he yelled, at any of his men. Pulling out his sword, his eyes adjusted enough that he saw a movement. The fast form tripped one of his men, throwing him casually to the ground, before turning on the others.

Airen smirked, stepping in close to one of the guards. The

Chapter Sixteen

man threw his sword up, aiming for the yellow eyes, and outline of a nose, the only things on her face he could see, but she easily blocked him. They danced for a brief moment, before she kicked him hard in the ribs, twisted her sword, and threw his across the hall. She stunned another with a blow to the head with the flat side of her sword, careful not to hit too hard, and pitched the other, one-armed into the wall. They were all groaning and grumbling in heaps.

Kristoph alone was left standing. She stepped over one of his men, making sure to step on his rib cage and earned a low grunt. Airen twirled her blade casually in her hand, letting it catch beams of moonlight from the outside, as she advanced on the Commander.

"Not too smart. That lets me know where you are," Kristoph said, trying to keep his voice steady.

"I know," Airen said before lunging.

Their swords met in a loud clang. She winced at the impact. She'd forgotten how strong he was. The blades flashed through the air, meeting in loud crashes of metal. Airen managed to rotate them throughout the fight, keeping an eye on the other men in the hall, who were struggling to their feet. One of the men was groping around in his pockets, but before she could see what for, she was ducking a rather well aimed blind swing. Airen dodged fast and spun out, landing a solid kick to Kristoph's knee. It buckled, and he kneeled on the ground. His eyes looked up at her, somewhat accusing, somewhat curious.

For a brief moment, time stilled. She stared down into the familiar blue eyes. Dropping her sword to her side, her free hand drifted to Kristoph's face. She ran a thumb under his eyes, down his cheekbone, and under his jawbone. Tilting his

The Kraden Job

face back. Kristoph went with the movement. The stubble along his jaw tickled her hand. They gazed at each other. For a brief moment, she could see the younger man of all those years ago in his face. The man who was excited about a simple guard post. Commander was a large step up, and it had taken a toll on his face. Lines danced around his eyes, his face had wrinkles from deep sunburn, and there was a thin scar on his cheekbone. She touched it, and a ghost of a smile crept onto Kristoph's face.

"Miss me?" he asked, a gruffness in his voice.

In her periphery, Airen saw a torch bloom into light. The men were gathering themselves off the ground, shaking off their disorientation and setting up a formation. They'd never throw knives at her, guards often lacked such precision, and she knew, though they had guns, it was unlikely they'd shoot. Given how close she was to Kristoph. But she only had a few more seconds to indulge.

"Did your father buy your promotion?" she asked, with an acid tone. Trying to ruin any lingering feeling of longing she held for the kneeling man.

Anger flashed in the dark blue eyes, and honor be damned. Airen was shocked, when he burst off his knees in a shot of energy and lunged at her. She'd never seen a guard, never mind a Commander, act in such a way. Airen let out a grunt as her back smashed hard into the rock wall, her blade shot out her hand and spun down the hall towards the group of men who were regarding their commander in surprise. Kristoph was seething, and Airen almost flinched. She'd never seen this level of rage coming off of him.

"I worked for what I got." Kristoph ground out, then grabbed a hold of her jacket near the collar, bunching it up

Chapter Sixteen

and slamming her higher into the wall. "After that incident, I had a stain on my record, because of you. I had to work harder than anyone else to prove I didn't sympathize with pirates, because of you. I was practically banished from the estate, because of you."

Airen grabbed hold of his wrist, pulling herself up slightly. "Things didn't work out that great for me either."

Yanking hard on his arm with one hand, and grabbing the back of his head with the other, she pulled hard and slammed one knee into his ribs. He flipped sideways, his blade swigging up and cutting her in the arm. They fell onto the floor, but she shot up first and ducked instantly as her yellow eyes picked up one of the men hoisting up his gun. Airen barely dodged the bullet, before taking off back down the hall, the sounds of shots echoing behind her. One blasted into the stone right behind her when she turned a corner.

Airen cursed and stumbled, careening into the wall. Grabbing her arm, she started running down the hallway again. Blood came back on her hand. She picked up the pace. Leading the men further into the deserted halls. She darted up a staircase, aware that they were catching up with her. She stopped on the landing, and yanked a painting off the wall, tossing it down the stairs at the advancing men. One guard managed to dodge but it, hit another in the knees, and he fell down the stairwell. She tossed a knife from her forearm sheath, knocking a loaded gun out of the hands of another guard. The gun went off and stone rained from the ceiling. As the three remaining guards and Kristoph made the landing, she drew her daggers.

The first man held his sword, and advanced, as though they were about to duel. She waited for him to take a swing,

The Kraden Job

blocking the blade with her daggers and using his momentum to drop out and throw him into the floor. There were clanging blades, grunts of pain, and the flash of yellow eyes as they all got into the fray. She dodged and ducked, letting the men nick each other more often than they came into contact with her.

Everyone was panting, their arms aching from the fight. Blood was seeping through the sleeve of her shirt. She shook her arm, trying to shake off the pain that was growing there. She'd be weaker soon, and she knew it. But the other men needed a break too. She backed up, finding the base of the next stairwell with the back of her foot. She slowly took one step at a time.

Kristoph stepped forward, covered in sweat and panting. "You know, I talked to King Dupont."

She took another step. "Did you now?"

One of the guards was doubled over, dragging in deep breaths. The man who'd been hit by the painting on the stairs hadn't gotten back up. Kristoph advanced on her slowly, two of the other guards keeping pace with him, but remaining a few steps behind. "He didn't tell me what you were up to. Didn't even let on that you were here."

"You already know what I'm up to. I told you," she said, lofting a dagger at the trio. It was a throw with her now injured arm and went a little wide. Airen frowned.

Kristoph smiled at the sign of weakness. "Blackmail. I remember. You're a fool if you think you can get past me and my men to get to King Dupont. Your plot is ruined. So I can promise you, while I'm here, you aren't getting anywhere near the King, or even his side of the castle tonight."

"Well," she sighed, adjusting her grip on her sword, "that

Chapter Sixteen

works for me."

"What do you mean?" Kristoph paused, as did the men behind him, sensing a shift in the air.

"Really? You thought it'd be that easy to stop us? Oh Commander, no, I'm simply the distraction."

"Then, who…" he trailed off. "Right," he said, "Allison."

"Allison." She smirked. She shifted a dagger in her hand and sighed, remembering that her sword now lay a few floors down in an abandoned hallway. "You have the obnoxious habit of being a better sword fighter than me."

"Years of training," he said, falling into a crouching stance. Anger blazing from his eyes.

"Course, I got years of training too." Her hand shifted to the bag on her belt. She tugged gently on the string, loosening it.

"In what?"

"Evasion." As Airen lifted the pouch, it fell open, revealing a pile of grey powder. She blew on it hard and it poofed out, sailing through the air. Kristoph ducked, shielding his face with his hand, but started coughing as the dust flew over him and the men. One of the guards fell down screaming, wiping at his face. Airen took no time to admire her work, and turned to run up the stairs.

It was a tall spiral staircase. She ran and ran, losing count of the steps, and attempting to focus on her labored breathing. She dropped her dagger, allowing it to clatter down the stairs. She used her now free hand to make an attempt at staunching the bleeding of her wound, as she continued upwards. She came out in a room with lots of benches and a stained glass window. She skidded to a stop. The window was beautiful, and was placed directly over the King's old prison. She was in the viewing chambers. Dead end.

The Kraden Job

Airen stopped and listened. The men were still far down the stairs, given the sounds of the echoes. She yanked a dagger out of her boot, quickly went to one of the drapes and cut a big strip out of it. Wrapped it around her arm and tied it tight. It would help with the bleeding for now. She fiddled with the tip of her rig under her coat, shifted her blade, then turned to the door and waited. When the sound of the footsteps came nearer, she pulled the gun out of the holster at her thigh and looked at it with distaste. She stood to shield it from view.

It was no surprise to her when Kristoph came through the door first. He stalled, shocked to find her standing dead in the center of the room, facing the door in an amazing display of calm. His eyes darted around the room. Looking for some kind of trap, some secret way out. He didn't find anything suspicious. All Kristoph saw was a young woman, her hair frazzled and falling around her face from the fight. Her cheeks were red and flush from running.

"There's nowhere to go. Maybe you could get past one of us and down those stairs, but not two, and I know the rest are coming up here. Throw down your weapons now, before they get here, and maybe I can help you."

Airen looked at him dumbly for a moment. "You really believe that, don't you? That you can *help* me. What do you think I am, some lost little puppy they'll let you keep if you promise to lock me up at night?"

A battle was waging across his face. He looked at her there, and she just seemed so small and fragile. "You're confused and you've been in the wrong place for a while. You've gone the wrong way, but we can fix this, if you surrender right now, and help us get the others. You're just lost. You need help."

"You're delusional. I'm not a broken thing, Kristoph," she

Chapter Sixteen

bit out, tightening her grip on her dagger. "This *is* who I am."

"No, it isn't, Cassandra."

The gun drooped in her hand behind her back, her arm suddenly struggling under the weight. She could feel the blood seeping through the strip of fabric she'd tied there. Airen regarded the man in disbelief. "That's still who you see, isn't it? Some stupid twitty girl who thinks flowers make great gifts, and can't tell if a blade's well balanced. Well, wake up Kristoph! She was never real!"

"You can try to bury that girl if you want, but it's still who you are!"

Airen's yellow eyes hardened, as a guard burst up through the door behind Kristoph. She turned to face the door fully. "You're an idiot."

Airen leveled the gun. There was a blast. Kristoph flinched, and the guard next to him fell to the ground. Kristoph stared down at the body in horror. He looked back to Airen, as she casually tossed the spent gun to the side.

"What have you done?"

"What do you want from me? I'm a pirate. I've been one since I was a kid. That mysterious otherness you always liked about me, this was it. This was the secret the whole time. You fell in love with an image, and that's just not me."

Commander Jenkins looked at her in a way he never had before. She couldn't make out the emotion. She took a few slow steps back, as he looked between the body of his fallen guard and her. The footsteps echoed up the stairs, there would be more soon.

"What were you thinking?" he whispered out. "I could have helped you, but this…"

Airen let out a long sigh. "I'm tired. I'm tired of running

The Kraden Job

from you, and this thing we have." She unbuckled her sword belt, tossing it off to the side, her daggers followed. "Gods, I'm tired of being on a crew and listening to orders. I'm even getting tired of the ocean." She tugged at her necklace, breaking the chain. Airen ran it through her fingers before letting it drop to the ground by her feet.

Kristoph looked at her with a new fear edging into his voice. "What are you doing?"

She met his gaze. Airen gave him a sad sort of smile. "Ending this."

She opened her arms out wide, took a deep breath, and jumped back. Smashing through the window behind her and plummeted out of sight.

"No!"

There was a faint splash.

Kristoph scrambled across the room, disregarding the glass shards that cut into his knees. The ripples shimmered in the moonlight against the dark water. They slunk out, larger and larger in the ocean, until the waves swallowed them up. He waited, watching the broken water of the splash melt into the calm of the waves and vanish. He waited for the water to break, to see her resurface. He waited to see movement. The waves fell into a steady rhythm as they swept against the side of the cliff. The sound was gentle and the night was still.

He sat there, until the other men came, checking their dead comrade. His second in command put a hand on his shoulder. "Where's the girl?"

Kristoph was silent, looked up at his friend and down to the ocean below.

The man nodded. "I prefer to see them on the gallows, but there is nothing wrong with pirates having a death by sea."

Chapter Sixteen

He kicked the gun. "You shove her or shoot her?"

"She jumped."

"What?"

"She jumped. I didn't…do anything…"

The guard shrugged. "Either way, that ends it. Doesn't matter what those fool pirates call her. No one can survive that drop. If the impact didn't kill her, the cold will… or she'll hit the rocks. It's over, Kristoph."

"Right. It's over." Kristoph reached out and picked up the broken necklace, slipping the simple engagement band off of the chain. Closed his fist around it and moved to put it in his pocket. He changed his mind, and looked at it in his palm. So small. A promise from long ago, when he was a young fool, and the girl he loved wasn't a figment. A lie to trick him into caring. He ran his thumb around the edges of the band. Let out a shuddering breath, and flicked it out into the sea. He watched it shimmer in the moonlight, until it was swallowed by the darkness of the night, and eventually the ocean. He stood, adjusting the sword on his belt, and left the room.

Chapter Seventeen

Allie laughed when they exited the caves and were back on the rock covered shore. The men behind her carried big bags of unmarked gold, and she was toting a bag that contained papers that could get them past any check point with King Dupont's seal marking them boldly across the top. She looked back at Nick.

"Always great to see a plan so well executed. And did you see the king's face when Jacob dropped down behind him?" She laughed. Her eyes shining with excitement.

Nick chuckled. "I was there."

"Wait til I tell Airen about this," Allie said, looking around, but didn't see her grumpy yellow eyed friend anywhere. "I'm going to go find her."

Nick just gave a nod. Jacob came up behind Nick. They watched the curvy blonde walk away. "We might have a problem," Jacob said to Nick in a low whisper.

"What is it?" Nick said, turning his head to watch Allie bend

Chapter Seventeen

over to sort out the boats.

"Some of the guys saw a person go out of the ol' mad king's prison window."

The smile fell off of Nick's face in an instant. "Take me to them!"

"Don't need to," Jacob said, dragging forward a crew member by the scruff of the shirt. He looked nervous.

"So," Nick said, impatient, "did anyone see who it was? Please, tell me it was a man."

"We were too far out. Something just fell…." The man refused to make eye contact with Nick.

"Something, or someone?" Nick didn't like this. He knew that Airen had been planning on drawing the men that direction, towards the old King's prison. It was as far from the drop spot as they could get. But there were rumors the tower was haunted and that it only had one exit. Not counting the window.

The man looked uncomfortable. Jacob pushed him away. He stumbled, but wasn't able to come up with a better reaction than, "Uhhhh".

Nick looked at Jacob. "Where's the scout? I need to know what he saw. Now!"

Jacob shifted. "I'll find him."

"Hurry," Nick said, eyeing Allie who was animatedly talking to a few of the others. No doubt reliving her conquest over the King of a realm, to those who'd been left behind to guard the boats.

Jacob came back with a recent addition to the crew. Someone, Airen had actually picked off the streets a few months before. He was scrawny and young. A thief that had barely been making it before he tried to pick Airen's pocket, much to her amusement. She'd slammed him against a carriage, breaking one of his ribs, and then begged Nick to take the boy on the ship. Turn a proper thief and pirate out of him. Nick thought his name was Roy.

"What do you have for me?"

Roy looked nervously between the three men who towered over him. He gulped. "Commanders Jenkins is mighty angry. I saw him crossing one of them big courtyards to meet with the King. He was yelling something awful about missing some of his men."

Nick let out a sigh of relief. "So it could have been one of his guards."

Roy shook his head, there were the beginnings of tears in his eyes. "I know you'd told us not to get so close, but I -I didn't wanta let you down. I mean, Airen saved my life, so I followed them a bit... They may have lost some guards, but only one of them was dead... Airen shot him. But ... the person... the one who went through the window... that one hadn't been shot."

"So, it was Airen," Jacob said, brows furrowing. The man raked a hand through his hair, looking out towards the King's door. The waves crashed against the rocks. He'd seen Airen bust out of cells, houses, and jails, but nothing close to flying.

"Shit. We need to get back to the ship," Nick said, looking around at the men who were packing up. "Tell them to hurry up. And no one, I repeat, no one tells Allison a thing. I don't want her hearing about this until we pull up anchor. Or else she's bound to do something stupid or dangerous."

"Allie won't like not being told, Captain," Jacob said, watching their elegant lady flirt one of the newer crew members into carrying her loot.

Nick grimaced. "You let me deal with Allison's temper. Just

Chapter Seventeen

get everyone on the ship."

Jacob nodded, and went to round everyone up. Nick headed straight for Allie, gathering her up into a boat with smiles and flattery. He pushed out first, watching the castle get smaller and smaller as they headed towards the ship.

Only after he felt the lurch of the anchor come up, did he breathe a sigh of relief. There was no way for Allie to get them into trouble now. That's what he thought, until he turned around to see a panicked and angry looking woman storm up to him.

"What are you doing? We can't go anywhere. Airen isn't back yet," Allie said.

"No," he said slowly, "she isn't."

"So then, what are you doing? I know she said she was off the ship after this job, but I think she meant after she got her cut," Allie said in a condescending voice.

"Allie," Nick said, trying to imagine how she might take this. "The men saw someone go out the watch post of King's Prison. They're pretty sure it was Airen. Allison, she's dead."

Allie froze. A bunch of emotions fleeted across her face but settled on rage. "You didn't tell me."

Nick took a step back. He'd seen Airen really angry before, but never Allie. He'd expected her to cry. To fall down. To scream but not this cold rage facing him. "I was concerned for the entire crew. I have a whole ship to think of, and the loot. I can't spend too much thought on the loss of one pirate. I knew you'd run off and we couldn't –"

"You were *concerned*," her voice was cold. "Don't you dare try to excuse your own cowardice behind what was best for the crew. That isn't the point. Airen is my oldest friend. You had no right to keep this from me." In a quick flick of her wrist

The Kraden Job

she took out her hair pin and stabbed him in the shoulder.

Nick screamed in pain, but his eyes morphed fast to anger. He gripped onto the hair pin embedded deep in his arm. "Of all the things, Allison –"

She looked at him with cold eyes. "What did you expect? It's not going to kill you, don't worry. But it's going to hurt. A lot."

They glared at each other. Nick pulled the hair pin out and tossed it to the deck. Allie kicked it away with a casual air. She was about to turn away, when Jacob jogged up.

"Hey," Jacob said, looking between them curiously. He noticed Nick clutching at his shoulder, blood seeping through his fingertips. "That can't be good. Especially now."

"What now, Jacob?" Nick bit out, clawing at the little puncture wound that had suddenly began to itch quite fiercely. "We're in the middle of something."

"Just thought you might want to know that, well, Thom's missing. Never got on one of the small boats. We all assumed he got on a boat with someone else. Nothing was left on the shore. And about half of the medical supplies are gone from his cabin."

The pair stared at Jacob in shock for a moment. Then Allie burst out laughing.

"You're telling me Airen is gone and I've lost my medic with half my supplies in the same night?"

The man cleared his throat. "It looks that way, Captain. And from the way things are cleaned out, it looks like Thom didn't expect to be coming back."

Nick cursed, low and furious, before storming off under the deck to check on Thom's cabin.

"Nicely played, Airen. Nicely played," Allie said to herself.

Chapter Seventeen

Staring up at the stars, she just laughed and laughed.

Chapter Eighteen

It had been worse than Airen expected. The look on Kristoph's face, when she tore off the ring. Tossed it to the ground, as if it were nothing, meant nothing. There was a glimmer of recognition in his eyes when it had bounced against the hard ground. Then a deep sadness. Then anger. And, finally, despair.

Or maybe, she imagined it all. What she did know for a fact, was that the falling part of the plan was not as easy as she'd thought it would be. The bullet in the gun had been meant for the glass, not to prove some blood drenched point to an old lover.

The pretty, stained glass window had resisted her. When it shattered, she could feel it tearing at her skin. Little rips in the soft fabric of her clothes. She went straight back, willed herself to keep her eyes open. Jenkins, no Kristoph's, eyes widened in terror. His mouth falling open in a scream. Perhaps, she thought, his hand went up as if to catch her, if

Chapter Eighteen

only he were fast enough. And then time sped up, like she knew it would, and she was out of the window.

In a flash, she had tugged the anchor gun of the rig out from behind her back, where it was hooked into her coat. Pointing it to the biggest rocks she could see on the cliff face, she fired. The grapple dug into the stone, making a shrill shrieking noise she hoped was drowned out by the waves. The thin rope slithered quickly through her right hand as she plunged further downwards. With her left hand, she threw out the other grappling hook to steady herself.

Airen wanted to use the two grappling hooks as a pendulum and swing herself out of the line of sight of the window. In her black clothing, if she kept her head down and resisted the urge to look up, she'd blend into the night soaked rocks. Commander Jenkins and his men would look down and not see her. A few hours later, she would lower herself further down to a small hamlet Thom had noticed near the base. The tiniest of places, where a small two person boat could dock briefly. And it would look as though Airen vanished into thin air. Her greatest feat. They would talk about this escape for years. That had been her plan.

When the second grappling hook caught on the rock, and she stared her swing away from the window, a smile crept onto her face. She'd done it. She was safely headed towards the cover of rocks, when she felt the sharp jolt. Her eyes flashed up.

The first rock she hooked onto was unsteady. It ripped out of the cliff face and careened down the side of the slope, falling with a heavy splash into the water below. Airen continued her swing. Her momentum much faster than she'd anticipated. The safety of the rocks she'd seen lurched away. Without the two hooks stabilizing her, she swung out of control. Her remaining rope caught on a jagged rock far above. Her body whipped fast back at the cliff face. Fear gripped her at the sight of the rocks approaching her. Unable to stop. Unable to slow down or move of her own free will. Then there was pain and darkness.

Airen groaned, attempting to sit up. A hand pushed firmly against her shoulder, pushing her back onto a bed. She whimpered.

"Take it easy," said an old, soft voice of a man. "Your friend said you took quite the fall."

Airen felt a little sick, opening her eyes. Her mouth felt cottony. "Something like that."

The man beside her bed was old. He was bent over and had a bald head. A dark robe hid most of his features. He was dipping bandages into a water basin. She noticed a neatly folded pile of clothes on a small night stand next to the bed. There was a small candle burning. The room was sparsely furnished. Only the bed, bedside table, and a wooden chair. A window was on the far end of the room, but it had been bolted shut with great wooden planks across it. She eyed it suspiciously, but the old men kept at his work, wringing out the bandages. The water came out pink with blood. Hers.

"Don't be modest," the old man said. "You took quite the tumble. I'm guessing you did not mean to be unconscious for the past three days. He mentioned you hit your head."

"Three days?" She lurched up, gasped in pain and fell back.

"Yes."

"Where's Thom?"

The old man paused and regarded her. "Thom?" he asked,

Chapter Eighteen

confusion flitting through his face. "Oh. I suppose you mean the man who brought you to me. He went out to gather some supplies. We're running low on food since I've been looking after you. I'm not used to feeding two people here, not to mention a third, now that you are awake. Does him some good to be out of the house. He was becoming quite worried that you weren't waking up."

"He was?" she questioned doubtfully.

The old man smiled. "Yes. Very concerned. He told me you caught on a rock. Had a vicious swing and smashed into a cliff rather than landing on it."

The door opened and Thom was there. His eyes flooded with relief, when he saw Airen with her eyes open. The old man looked between them, picked up his water basin and headed out of the room. Thom held a package under his arm and sat in the chair by the bed. He handed Airen a vial of pain relief potion.

Airen sipped it before meeting his eyes. "I take it that we aren't in the city anymore."

"I thought it would be prudent to leave," his voice was quiet and scratchy from remaining unused for years. He cleared his throat and looked away, self-conscious about its cracking.

"How'd you get me out here?"

A smile curled up his lip. "In a coffin."

Airen stared at him, dumbfounded. It was a safe way to smuggle out a body, but completely surprising that he thought of it.

"In a coffin," she repeated softly. Then it occurred to her. "I saw a rock fall. At least I think I did. It's all a bit fuzzy."

Thom nodded.

"So, I didn't make a silent escape then?"

The Kraden Job

He frowned and shook his head.

Airen heaved a great sigh. Then winced. "They all think I'm dead, don't they?"

Thom gave a non-committal shrug, but his fingers were working on tugging his nails out of his hands. She took that for a yes.

The fall was hard to remember. She didn't know where it had all gone wrong. The rig had worked perfectly for her in the past. Of course, in the past she'd used both hooks at the same time, instead of staggering them into a swing. For certain, when she'd hit her head, she wasn't anywhere near the base of the cliff. Suddenly, she realized Thom must have climbed up a great height to cut her down. That was not an easy climb. It was a huge risk. A risk like that could have killed him. And he did it for her. Her yellow eyes surveyed the man critically. A great risk indeed.

"Your rig's wrecked," Thom said after a moment, looking away from their staring contest. He shifted the package on his lap, pulling out some of the papers.

Airen let out a small smile. "That's alright, I suppose. Guess I won't be needing it right now, since people think I'm dead. Unfortunate, really. There I was trying to make a wondrous escape, and now it looks like I killed myself trying to make an escape. Actually, that's rather embarrassing. Best I lay low for a while then. Might want to find a cabin of my own, though. Not sure I want one that comes with a little old man," she said, much happier than she felt. Thom didn't flicker a fraction of her faked happiness back at her.

Instead, Thom held up the packet of papers. He dropped it on her blanket covered legs. The pages fell out in an array. It revealed meticulous copies of the pages they had stolen from

Chapter Eighteen

the stronghold. The ones that Nick had kept hidden from them all. The ones that Allie had been puzzled and frazzled over. With all of the strange diagrams and charts she'd seen weeks ago on Allie's desk, but on the top of the stack there was a new one. A page, she hadn't seen before.

It was the drawing of a small lantern, with a curvy frame. It only took a moment for her to recognize where she'd seen it before. An image of Maxwell's greedy eyes in Lord Kraden's office. The small box he'd coveted above even the stash of unmarked gold.

Thom's voice broke into her thinking. "I believe you owe me a favor."

Acknowledgments

Back in 2015, I put a very under-edited version of this story onto Amazon as an ebook. It wasn't ready for print. The story had several plot holes, a plethora of excessive commas, and felt stilted at points. Why, do you ask, did I put it online then? Simply put, I put it online because I felt like I needed to. I was in a place where I felt to not put the story up was a failing.

Turns out, trying to force something onto the market before it is ready is a rather poor choice. Needless to say, I removed it few months after putting it online. After that, I more or less ignored the story for years. I wandered off (still wanting to be an author but placing it in the back of my mind) and did other things. I moved to several different continents, changed career paths, went back to university, fell in love, and moved again. Finally, it seemed time to return to this tale.

This version is a labor of love, as well as a lot of hard work to fix it up for public consumption. This would not have been possible without the love and support of my family, especially my little mumsie, who has read every copy of the story over the years. It would be remise to also not mention Renee, who asked me to tell her a story of pirates back in our university days.

There is also the support of my friends, who encouraged me to keep going, even when I was feeling my doubts, Jess, Andrea M, Sean and Melissa Hackett, to name a few. And finally, this edition would never have seen the light of day if it wasn't for my supportive partner, Andy, who kept me going when I thought it was by far easier to give up.

About the Author

S.L. Francisco grew up in the mountains of New England, looking at the mountains and wondering what was on the other side. Since then, there has been much travel, exploring, and creating. S.L. Francisco is always on the search for stories, adventures, and the absurd. The absurd is often found, though the other two remain more elusive.

The Kraden Job is the first of hopefully many fantasy novels in years to come.

Printed in Great Britain
by Amazon